Praise for *Love Is a Four-Legged Word*

"Charming, pacey, funny, and heartwarming, Ms. Shepherd's romantic and doggy debut is pure delight."

—Marion Lennox, RITA Award–winning author

"A delicious, fast-paced read."

—Julie James, author of *Something About You*

"A humorous and fun story. The so-ugly-he's-cute dog is a great character."

—*Romantic Times*

Bee Cave Public Library
Bee Cave, Texas

Sensation titles by Kandy Shepherd

LOVE IS A FOUR–LEGGED WORD
HOME IS WHERE THE BARK IS

Home is
WHERE THE BARK
IS

· KANDY SHEPHERD ·

BERKLEY SENSATION, NEW YORK

THE BERKLEY PUBLISHING GROUP
Published by the Penguin Group
Penguin Group (USA) Inc.
375 Hudson Street, New York, New York 10014, USA
Penguin Group (Canada), 90 Eglinton Avenue East, Suite 700, Toronto, Ontario M4P 2Y3, Canada
(a division of Pearson Penguin Canada Inc.)
Penguin Books Ltd., 80 Strand, London WC2R 0RL, England
Penguin Group Ireland, 25 St. Stephen's Green, Dublin 2, Ireland (a division of Penguin Books Ltd.)
Penguin Group (Australia), 250 Camberwell Road, Camberwell, Victoria 3124, Australia
(a division of Pearson Australia Group Pty. Ltd.)
Penguin Books India Pvt. Ltd., 11 Community Centre, Panchsheel Park, New Delhi—110 017, India
Penguin Group (NZ), 67 Apollo Drive, Rosedale, North Shore 0632, New Zealand
(a division of Pearson New Zealand Ltd.)
Penguin Books (South Africa) (Pty.) Ltd., 24 Sturdee Avenue, Rosebank, Johannesburg 2196,
South Africa

Penguin Books Ltd., Registered Offices: 80 Strand, London WC2R 0RL, England

This book is an original publication of The Berkley Publishing Group.

This is a work of fiction. Names, characters, places, and incidents either are the product of the author's imagination or are used fictitiously, and any resemblance to actual persons, living or dead, business establishments, events, or locales is entirely coincidental. The publisher does not have any control over and does not assume any responsibility for author or third-party websites or their content.

Copyright © 2010 by Kandy Shepherd.
Cover illustration by Kimberly Schamber.
Cover design by Rita Frangie.

All rights reserved.
No part of this book may be reproduced, scanned, or distributed in any printed or electronic form without permission. Please do not participate in or encourage piracy of copyrighted materials in violation of the author's rights. Purchase only authorized editions.
BERKLEY® SENSATION and the "B" design are trademarks of Penguin Group (USA) Inc.

PRINTING HISTORY
Berkley Sensation trade paperback edition / July 2010

Library of Congress Cataloging-in-Publication Data

Shepherd, Kandy.
    Home is where the bark is/Kandy Shepherd.—Berkley Sensation trade pbk. ed.
        p. cm.
    ISBN 978-0-425-23429-7
1. Dogs—Fiction.   2. San Francisco (Calif.)—Fiction   I. Title.
PR9619.4.S543H66   2010
823'.92—dc22   2010008471

PRINTED IN THE UNITED STATES OF AMERICA

10 9 8 7 6 5 4 3 2 1

To the furry friends who are the heart of my home.

Acknowledgments

To my wonderful editor, Kate Seaver, cover artist Kimberly Schamber, cover designer Rita Frangie, and the rest of the team at The Berkley Publishing Group—thank you. Thanks also to my agent, Miriam Kriss.

Thank you to my writing friends, in particular Elizabeth Lhuede—there for me at the most ungodly hours—Cathleen Ross, Christine Stinson, Isolde Martyn, and Anna Campbell. Also to Vanessa Barneveld, Janette Hankinson, Simone Camilleri, and my other critique group members. My thanks also to Kim Castillo, truly an author's friend. And to Amanda Englebrecht, who helped me with that most precious commodity—time to write.

My appreciation to Amanda Raine at Dogs@Play for the time I spent with her and her canine clients, and also to Fog City Dogs.

Thank you to Melinda and Luke Booker and to Mate, that big black mutt who was my inspiration for the character of Mack.

Hugs to my husband, James, and daughter, Lucy, for your unstinting love, support, inspiration—and for putting up with me when I exercise the right to have an artistic temperament!

A special thank-you to the readers of my first book, *Love Is a Four-Legged Word*. For those of you who asked for Serena's story, here it is . . .

· One ·

Nick Whalen was not a Yorki-poo kind of guy. Serena Oakley saw that right away. Alerted by the door chime—a dog barking to the tune of "Who Let the Dogs Out?"—she looked up from the check-in counter of her upscale doggy spa and day-care center.

She tried not to stare at the tall, powerfully muscled man who shouldered his way in through the glass doors from the sidewalk. Then quickly covered her mouth with her hand to hide her amusement. She pretended to cough.

In the six months since she'd opened Paws-A-While, Serena often played a game of matching owner to dog. The new client and the struggling, squirming little Yorkshire terrier–poodle cross he held tight to his impressively broad chest made perhaps the most entertaining mismatch she'd seen.

Just a few of the man's long strides into the compact reception area and the little dog started to yap a cranky "put me down now." At the owner's embarrassed scowl Serena fought to keep her polite smile from breaking into laughter. She needed to be professional here and help him out. She put on her best meet-and-greet smile.

"Hi! I'm Serena Oakley. Good morning and welcome to Paws-A-While." She stepped around the counter. "This little cutie must be Bessie."

The Yorki-poo immediately stopped yapping, stilled, and looked up at Serena, feathery ears alert.

"And I'm Nick Whalen," said the client. "My dog is here to be, uh, assessed for day care."

Serena recognized the deep, gravel-rough voice from the man's initial phone call. It had intrigued her then and it impressed her now. The voice matched the face with its strong, taut angles. And the tough, hard body that strained against businesslike jacket and pants.

"Of course, Mr. Whalen. We were expecting you. I've been looking forward to meeting Bessie. She looks just as sweet as I thought she'd be."

And Bessie's owner?

He was younger than she'd expected, only a few years older than her—around thirty-two, she guessed. Definitely a big-dog type. A man more at ease with, say, a boxer as chiseled and tough-looking as himself. Yes, she could see him with a boxer.

And the adorable pint-sized pooch with the yellow bow tied in her forelock looked as if she'd be much happier tucked into a nice older lady's purse with just her nose peeking out.

But Serena didn't share her thoughts. Dog care was a competitive industry in the canine-crazy Marina District of San Francisco. She could not risk even a hint she might be seen as poking fun at the pampered pooches that brought in the much-needed dollars and cents. She had a year to make her business succeed before she ran out of funds. That meant keeping her private whimsies locked safely away while she built her client base.

Besides, it was no hardship to lavish attention on her canine customers. There was hardly a dog born that she didn't like.

"Hi, Bessie," she crooned to the Yorki-poo. "Are you going to come play with us?"

Serena held out her hand for the little dog to sniff; then, once introduced, she scratched her under the chin. In response, Bessie enthusiastically licked Serena's fingers.

Serena laughed and pulled her hand back. She wiped it with an anti-bacterial tissue from the box on the wall—following her own strict hygiene rule. Cross infection was a disaster any doggy day-care proprietor dreaded.

"I think we're going to get on just fine, sweetie." She smiled at Bessie. Then looked up to the owner and realized patting Bessie had brought her rather too close. Close enough to notice that his skin was tan and smooth and his eyes were a pale, piercing shade of blue.

Suddenly breathless, she took a hasty step back. "And I hope we'll all get along with you, too, Mr. Whalen."

"So I'm here for assessment as well?" He raised his brow, and she wasn't sure if he were serious or not. "Are you going to put me through my paces? What's it to be? Catch? Fetch? Roll over on command?"

Serena reacted with a quick intake of breath, too taken aback to answer. Every day, gorgeous dogs came through the doors of Paws-A-While—but never a human as attractive as this man.

Handsome wasn't the right word to describe him. His jaw was too strong, his nose too crooked, his dark blond hair cropped too short for merely "handsome." But the irregular features added up to something undeniably appealing. Something that made rash, un-bidden fantasies flash through her mind of just the kind of paces she'd like to put him through.

Stunned at her own reaction, she managed to choke out a reply. "Of course not. We only have a formal assessment procedure for dogs, not people." She was aiming for professional but feared that came out just plain pompous.

Flustered, she made the mistake of looking directly up to her new client's face. Even in flats Serena hit five-ten, and although he was tall, she immediately connected with his eyes. Cool, quizzical blue eyes that seemed to enjoy her discomfiture and held her gaze for just a second too long.

She strained to remember the spiel she recited word perfect many times a day. "As we discussed, we cannot accept an animal for a regular day-care booking until we see proof of current vaccinations and, in animals over six months old, of ... uh ... spaying or cas ... castration."

Ohmigod. Why did she have to stumble over *that* word? She *never* stumbled on that word.

"Ouch," he said.

Serena flushed so hot her ears burned. This was beyond embarrassing. Why did *that* word make her think testosterone? Levels of which this client seemed to have in abundance. The muscles. The voice. The ...

Think no further, Serena.

She forced her eyes to stay at the level of his face. Her voice revved up so that she started to gabble. "Then we need to see how your dog socializes with our other guests. The other dogs, I mean. And with the staff, too, of course."

His mouth twisted. It was a sexy mouth, the top lip narrower than the bottom. Did he find her amusing? Dammit. Above all, Serena wanted to be taken seriously. To prove to both friends and critics that she could be a successful businesswoman.

"I see," he said. "So there's no formal procedure for checking out the owners. How do we best impress you?"

Roll over on my command.

No! She would not let her thoughts stray in that direction.

What was it about this Yorki-poo owner that made her forget she was taking a sabbatical from sex?

She cleared her throat. "Pay your bill in advance and never be late for pickup time? Always impresses."

"Want the credit card now?"

"Sounds good to me," she said. "You're a point ahead already."

"Good to know I'm in the race." A glint of humor warmed his eyes. Humor and a fleeting glimpse of something else.

Did he recognize her?

She swallowed hard against a flash of panic. The shapeless clothes, the way she wore her hair didn't fool everyone. Some people—inevitably men—identified her immediately.

But here she didn't see the dawning recognition that quickly warmed to admiration tinged with varying degrees of lust.

No. What she'd seen in Nick Whalen's eyes was something unsettling that she couldn't put a name to. Something that skated around the corners of her mind without letting her catch it. She frowned. "Mr. Whalen, I . . . ?"

"Nick," he said.

She paused. "Nick, I . . ."

For a long moment she held his gaze. Crazy really, for a client she had only just met, she had an unsettling sense of questions unasked and unanswered between them. It was as if a sudden stillness had fallen. She was aware of the tick-tick-ticking of the big beagle-shaped clock that hung above the counter, of the muted barks and yelps coming from the playroom, the too-loud sound of her own breathing. And of his.

Then Bessie whimpered at the lack of attention. She twisted in her owner's arms. She yapped a series of sharp, piercing demands.

Serena blinked. She shook her head to clear her thoughts. "Bessie. Of course. Poor little pet." She couldn't remember what she'd been about to ask Nick Whalen but grabbed the opportunity to switch the conversation back to his dog. "You can put Bessie down now. She seems much calmer."

Bessie's owner was unperturbed. "Bessie sure as hell doesn't like to be carried, that's for sure."

He bent down and carefully placed the Yorki-poo on the polished concrete floor, right on top of the trail of stenciled, outsized black paw prints that led to the counter.

Serena couldn't help but watch his every move. She found it endearing the way such a strong, masculine man was so gentle with the little animal, his big hands cradling her. How would it feel for a woman to be on the receiving end of that touch? A tremor of anticipated pleasure vibrated through her at the thought.

She forced herself to look away. She hadn't reacted like this to a man for a long time. If ever. This was crazy.

"And she hates riding in the car," he added, as he stood back up. "That's why she was making such a fuss."

"That's understandable." Serena made herself stop thinking about Bessie's master and watched Bessie as she cautiously sniffed around the base of the check-in counter, pausing to investigate the interesting doggy smells. "Don't worry. We won't hold her fussing against her. Lots of dog-kids are nervous their first time at day care."

Nick Whalen was silent for a long, stunned moment. He stared at Serena with such an expression of incredulity that she had to bite her lip not to laugh.

"Did you say 'dog-kid'?"

"Yes?" Her voice rose to a question mark.

He scowled. "This animal is a dog, not a child."

"Of course she is. But it's not an uncommon expression, believe me. They say there are more canines than children in San Francisco."

"But a dog is a dog."

"Except when it's a child substitute."

Serena followed his gaze to where Bessie was now sniffing the custom-made doggy toy box with great interest. It was hand carved and painted and Serena was very proud of it. The toy box was also the dumbest thing she could have put there, as it had become a magnet for unsupervised boy dogs to cock their legs on.

"Bessie is not a dog-kid." A shudder of distaste ran through his big frame. "Never call her that."

"Fur baby?" Serena offered.

"Especially not that," he growled.

"I agree," she said, in an attempt to placate him. "More of a cat term, I feel."

"'Dog' will do," he said, again with a growl his pint-sized pooch had no hope of emulating.

Serena frowned at his vehemence. Why would a man who tied a bow on his dog's forehead—the exact same shade of amber as the streaks in her dark fur—object so strongly to such an everyday word as "dog-kid"? An everyday word in the Marina District, that was.

But she aimed to make Paws-A-While the best in this dog-eat-dog business. To prove that at twenty-eight, with a string of abandoned career attempts behind her, she could stick with it long enough to succeed. And that meant pandering to human clients as much as to their pooches.

"Got it," she said in her most professional tone. "Bessie Whalen is only to be referred as a"—she spelled out the word—"D-O-G. I'll mark that on her file as urgent for the staff's attention." She willed any note of sarcasm out of her voice.

"Bessie Whalen?" he said. "You call her Bessie Whalen like she's my—?"

"Kid. Yes. It's shorthand to identify your animal. Very common. First name of dog, last name of owner."

Why didn't he know that was how his dog would be registered in any dog-care facility? Her brow furrowed further. "What do you use on Bessie's Facebook page?"

"Facebook page? For my dog?"

"No Facebook page? What about MySpace?"

His inarticulate splutter gave her his answer.

"Maybe she blogs under her Bessie Whalen name?" she suggested, unable to resist teasing this big, tough-looking man who seemed remarkably uninformed about everyday events in dog world.

"A dog blog? You're not serious?"

His bemused reaction made it more and more difficult for Serena to keep a straight face. "You think I'm kidding you, don't you?"

"Are you?"

"Maybe exaggerating a little," she admitted, giving in to a twitch of a smile. She widened her eyes. "But, Mr. Whalen, uh, Nick, thousands—maybe millions—of dogs have their own blogs. Trust me."

He had trouble sorting his words. "Bessie will never have a blog. Uh . . . that is, I will never write a blog for her. That is . . ."

"Yes?"

His jaw set in a stubborn line. "The dog is a dog. I am her master, not her father."

Serena put her index finger to her mouth. "Shh. Don't say that too loudly. Mustn't risk offending people who find it unacceptable to claim ownership of a species of companion animals."

Nick Whalen paused. "You lost me at the dog blog." He crossed his arms on his substantial chest. "I get it." He nodded slowly. "You do have a test for owners. And I'm being set up to fail."

Serena shook her head and smiled, properly this time. "There is no test." She had to quit teasing him, irresistible as it was when he reacted so marvelously. It wasn't worth the risk he might take offense and walk out. She needed every dollar of every day-care fee. And she loved running Paws-A-While even more than she had imagined. Finally she had found the right career. "Lots of our guests have Facebook pages and blogs. We link to them on our website if you're interested."

He put up his hand in a halt sign. "Thank you. I'll pass."

"But you're okay to have your dog registered with us as Bessie Whalen?"

"If you must." He followed his words with a heavy sigh of resignation.

Again Serena was puzzled. Surely Bessie's vet used a similar filing system. "Nick, is Bessie your wife's dog?"

"No wife."

"Girlfriend?"

"No girlfriend."

No girlfriend. Her pulse gave a disconcerting little flutter. "Oo-kaay. Do you have a shared custody agreement with an ex?"

"No." He frowned. "Is this line of questioning necessary?"

"I'm sorry if that seemed a little personal. But joint custody can get tricky so it's best we're forewarned."

"I have full, uh, custody of Bessie," he said, tight-lipped.

"I'm glad to hear that. It's just I wondered . . ."

He seemed so dog clueless. Why would a guy like this book into an establishment like hers that specialized in luxury beauty treatments for dogs? She suspected he didn't know the difference between a flea treatment and a fur extension.

His frown deepened. "Have you got a problem with a big guy and a little dog? Is that it?"

"Not at all. I'm sorry if I gave that impression."

This big-guy-and-little-dog combo didn't seem right. Her other client, the shaven-head, muscle-bound leather man and his miniature Chihuahua in matching studded harness were perfect together. But a Yorki-poo and this man?

She didn't have time to waste puzzling about the discrepancy. She schooled her face to look very serious. "We're inclusive here at Paws-A-While. Dogs of all sizes are welcome, so long as they're suited to day care."

"Right," he said.

"Personally, I adore little dogs. In fact, meeting my Maltese, Snowball, will be the first stage of Bessie's temperament test. Then if we accept her as a guest, he'll be her first puppy pal and help her settle in."

"That's reassuring." The word was edged with irony but Serena refused to bite.

"The first day of school can be scary for a kid if she doesn't know anyone," she said. "I figure it's the same for a dog."

The word "dog-kid" hung unspoken in the air. She knew it. Nick Whalen knew she knew it. But neither of them was going to utter it.

"So Snowball is your canine customer-relations contact?" he asked, a hint of levity lifting the corners of that so-sexy mouth.

Again, she couldn't be sure if he were serious or not. You never knew with dog people. Not that he seemed like a fully fledged dog person.

She nodded. "Exactly. That's what it says on his job description. His treat supply is linked to his performance. Unhappy client dog, no dog biscuit."

At her words, Nick Whalen grinned. A slow, reluctant grin that nevertheless melted the ice from his pale blue eyes. He was even more attractive when he smiled, less carved-out-of-granite, more hot-blooded male.

She found it irresistible not to smile back, then felt heartened by his widened grin in response.

"I'll go get Snowball," she said, turning toward the door that led into the adjoining playroom. She felt warmed and just a little bit excited by the exchange of smiles with Bessie's owner.

At one time she and her best friend, Maddy, would rate the men they met. Nick Whalen was an undisputed ten out of ten.

He was hot.

With no wife or girlfriend.

Not that a professionally focused woman should be noticing. Hitting on clients was a Business Skills 101 no-no. But she sure hoped Bessie passed her temperament test and became a regular. Owner check-in and checkout times would suddenly become a whole lot more interesting.

Her mouth still curved in a smile, she turned back to ask him to make sure Bessie didn't follow her into the playroom just yet. To find him with eyes narrowed and all humor faded from his face as he rapidly scanned the room—from the blow-up photographs of dogs on the walls, to the shelves of doggy goodies for sale, to the computer on the desk. That look was back in his eyes. But before he masked it again she recognized it instantly.

Suspicion.

Nick silently cursed his premature morph from doting dog owner to private investigator. He grit his teeth. He should have waited a moment longer until Serena Oakley had closed the door behind her.

Damn but this dog business was a bad idea. Yet how else could he legitimately get into Paws-A-While to scope out what kind of shady stuff could be going on in this place? He would never willingly have come here otherwise, that was for sure.

Doggy day care. Beauty parlors for pups. In his book, dogs lived outside in all but the coldest weather and got hosed down if they got muddy. And they were proper dogs. Big dogs. Not cats in disguise like Bessie.

The Paws-A-While director paused with her hand on the door that led to the next room. Her face, so warm and vibrant with laughter just seconds before, had cooled like a sudden frost in September. "Is there a problem?" she asked.

Years of training alerted him to go straight into damage control. He smiled, an engaging, suspicion-deflecting smile. "No problem. But this doggy day-care thing is new to me. I'm fascinated by your setup."

She had eyes the color of dark, liquid honey. Unusual eyes. Lovely eyes. He had noticed that in the disconcerting, long moment he spent gazing into them before Bessie's whining had brought him to his senses. Now her eyes were wary. Her dark brows drew together. "You're not some kind of health inspector?"

"No."

"An undercover reporter?"

That was closer to the mark. She was perceptive. Thankfully he could truthfully answer in the negative. He shook his head. "I'm not a reporter."

Her eyes didn't warm, but he noticed a visible relaxing of her shoulders. "You're sure of that? You're not planning an exposé? You know, the lowdown on the high life of San Francisco's pampered pooches? The extravagance, the waste of money, and so on?"

He put up both hands. "Whoa, there. I'm just looking for a place to park Bessie while I'm at work."

Having to lie was the one part of his job he never got used to. His FBI training had rid him of his childhood habit of crossing his fingers behind his back when he fibbed. And helped him school his expression to hide his real feelings and reactions. But he still felt uncomfortable when he misrepresented the truth.

In his few minutes of conversation with Serena Oakley he had already done that. Bessie didn't belong to a wife or a girlfriend, but then, she wasn't his, either. And he was here for his job, not on his way to his job.

"Okay, then," she said, not seeming totally convinced. "It's just that . . ." Her voice trailed away.

Stay alert, Whalen. She was too smart. Too observant. In only a matter of seconds she had caught him sussing out the room. Hell, he hoped she hadn't noticed him sussing out *her.*

He didn't know what he'd expected the proprietor of a doggy day-care center to be like. But it certainly wasn't this tall, graceful woman with the snarky sense of humor and the sexy curves that loose-fitting jeans and her baggy shirt with the Paws-A-While logo on the pocket did nothing to disguise.

"It's just what?" he prompted.

She shook her head as if to clear her thoughts. "Nothing. This is a new business and I have to be very careful of our reputation." She took a deep breath. "People trust me with their pets. The last thing I need is some damaging press article."

"I am not a journalist."

Finally she smiled again. Strange how relieved he felt to see that smile back and shining at him.

"Sorry," she said. "I'm being paranoid. Of course you're curious about how things work. You're welcome to a tour of the premises. I'll answer any questions you have as best I can."

"I'd like that," he said. The more he found out about this place without having to sneak around, the better.

"Fine," she said. "Now I'm going to get Snowball. Could you hold Bessie, please? She's too close to the door. I don't want her following me into the playroom where the other animals are until we're ready for her."

"Sure," he said, taking the few quick steps necessary to bring him closer to the dog. And to Serena Oakley.

Only to be stunned when she backed away from him so fast she nearly stumbled. Panic flashed across her face so quickly he could have imagined it. For just a second too long, she braced herself against the door.

The hint of fear in those remarkable eyes put him on instant alert.

What was she hiding?

He was an expert on false identities. And something was not right here.

The doggy day-care director was a good-looking woman. But it was obvious she did everything to hide that. Her dark hair was pulled back severely from her face. She wore no makeup. Her clothes were chosen to shroud rather than enhance.

It was as if she wanted to look as dowdy as possible. But she would need surgery and extensive use of prostheses to disguise her beauty. Who did she think she was kidding?

He took a step back and noted the sigh of relief she was unable to disguise. He squatted down next to Bessie and looked back up to Serena, careful to keep his expression neutral. "I'll hold her, you go through the door," he said.

She took a deep breath in an obvious effort to regain her composure. It was not the detached investigator part of Nick that appreciated the resulting swell of her breasts. She caught his gaze, flushed, and clutched the fabric of her shirt across her chest. She cleared her throat. "As soon as Bessie is aware of the other dogs, she'll want to follow me. You . . . you could get a toy from the toy box to distract her."

"Good idea," he said.

Why the hell was she so nervous?

This investigation was getting more interesting by the minute.

He forced himself to open the cutesy toy box. It made a "ruff-ruff" sound as the lid sat back on its hinges. He suppressed a groan. Was there no end of dog paraphernalia in this room?

The box was packed with an assortment of luridly colored balls, plastic bones, and chew ropes. But the first toy he put his hand on was a small, red, heart-shaped rubber cushion bearing the words Puppy Love in elaborate white script.

"No! Not that one. That's not meant to be there—" said Serena, too late, as Bessie, eager to play, snatched it from Nick's hand.

"Get it back from her. Please." Her voice was underscored with urgency.

Nick grabbed the toy and tried to pull it from Bessie's jaws, but the little dog saw that as a game. She growled playfully, shook it from side to side, then bit down hard.

"I love you. I love you," the toy squeaked.

"What the—?" said Nick.

"Oh no," groaned Serena.

Bessie chewed on the love heart again. "I love you," the toy squeaked again in that grating, synthetic tone.

Nick laughed. He looked up to Serena, to the toy, and back up to Serena. He expected her to laugh, too. But her face was flushed and her eyes glinted. She bit down on her lower lip.

"Drop it, Bessie!" she ordered, an edge to her voice.

Reluctantly, Bessie dropped the squeak toy on the polished concrete floor.

"Good girl," said Serena. She lunged forward and bent down to pick up the love heart at the same time Nick reached for it, so his hand closed over hers.

The movement nearly made them collide, brought her face just inches away from his. So close he was kissing distance from her lush, generous mouth. So close he inhaled her scent—something flowery—no, vanilla—no, both. Whatever, it was rich and sensual and totally unexpected in someone who dressed the way she did.

Her face was flushed pink high on her elegant cheekbones, and her eyes were huge. He felt too mesmerized by her mouth, too intoxicated by her scent to do anything but stare at her.

"Sorry," she said, but she made no move to stand up, her eyes locked to his.

He tried to say something in reply but choked on his words.

"The . . . the toy?" she stuttered, finally looking downward.

"Wh-what about the toy?"

He tore his gaze from her face and followed her line of vision down to the love heart. To see his hand had imprisoned hers on top of the red rubber cushion and pushed it down to the floor. She was immobile. Not because she was struck still by the same out-of-nowhere attraction that had hit her like a heat-seeking missile but because he had, effectively, trapped her.

Reflexively his hand tightened on hers. "I love you," squeaked the toy.

Nick snatched his hand away. He cursed.

Serena stood up, still holding the toy. She squashed it in her jeans pocket where it gave a strangled squeak. Her gaze was fixed on the wall somewhere behind his head. A strand of dark hair had escaped from the tight plait behind her head and curled around her cheek. She pushed it back with slender, graceful fingers that must still be warm from his body heat. "Dumb thing. I . . . I should throw it out."

"Yeah," he said, not knowing why he was agreeing, just not certain what else he could say to her. He grit his teeth.

She was lovely. Funny. Sexy. Alluring in spite of her total lack of artifice. Intriguing because of it.

But he could not be beguiled by her.

He'd left the FBI to partner with a former co-worker in a private investigation business that specialized in identity fraud. It was the fastest-growing crime in the United States and there were serious dollars to be made for those who could crack it. His partner and he were working on a major case involving wealthy victims from the Bay Area and Marin County. He'd suspected it was just coincidence that, of the twenty cases of identity theft he was pursuing, twelve of the victims kept their dogs at Paws-A-While.

But there was something about Serena Oakley's demeanor that made him decide not to be hasty in dismissing that coincidence.

He would have to distance himself from her.

Deny that sudden attraction.

Because she was now his prime suspect.

· Two ·

When she returned from the playroom accompanied by Snowball, Serena still felt so awash with humiliation she could not bring herself to look directly at Nick Whalen where he stood beside the toy box. She took a step back, careful to keep at least four sets of stenciled paw prints between them. How could she endure to meet that disconcerting, see-right-through-to-your-secrets gaze?

Instead, she watched with exaggerated interest as Snowball and Bessie cavorted around each other and, with great enthusiasm, participated in the doggy butt-sniff introduction ritual. She forced herself to take deep, calming breaths.

She had long gotten over feeling embarrassed about the things dogs did in full public view. With each other, with peoples' legs, and with a variety of inanimate objects. No. The reason her cheeks still flamed and her pride smarted was that darn love-heart dog toy.

When it started its cheesy declarations of love with that grating, mechanical inflexion, she'd wanted to climb into the toy box, pull down the lid on top of her head, and stay scrunched up and hidden there until Nick Whalen went away.

No way could he know she'd bought the love heart for Valentine's Day seven months ago. Not for Snowball but for herself.

She had never confessed to anyone that, alone in her bedroom, she had encouraged her little dog to chew on the toy over and over just so she could hear someone say the words "I love you." It was pathetic. Embarrassing. But, at the time, oddly comforting. Especially followed by a binge on Peanut Butter Cups.

"Thank God humans have moved on from this . . . uh . . . basic level of communication," Nick Whalen said as the dogs continued to sniff each other along the length of their furry bodies.

"Uh, yes, very primitive," she agreed, fighting the flush that still burned her cheeks.

She screwed up her eyes in an effort to resist sneaking a look at Bessie's owner's rear view. Bet he had a great butt. Tight. Muscular. And long, strong legs. Bet he had—

Don't go there, Serena.

It was her thoughts that were getting primitive. Primeval even. Hot and sweaty and—

She shook her head to clear her wild imaginings. What if he guessed hormones she'd thought long extinct had flared into such throbbing, pulsing life?

This hot guy with the cool blue eyes that didn't give a thing away had her totally off balance. And not just because her body was reacting to him in such a disconcerting way. For some reason she could not fathom, he was suspicious of her.

Was he—in spite of his denials—an undercover animal welfare officer? If so, she had absolutely nothing to hide. Health and safety regulations were followed to the letter. He could search for fault, but he wouldn't find it. She adored her doggy guests and treated every one as if it were her own.

But she could not shrug off the fact that Nick Whalen made

her feel edgy. It was as if he were assessing her and not liking much what he saw. Could he detect the fear and hurt she was trying so hard to conceal from the world?

Not far from the top of the list of those hurts was the fact that she—the woman who not so long ago had been voted the gal American men most wanted to lick all over—had been dumped by email on Valentine's Day.

The humiliating episode was something she'd rather the beyond-handsome Yorki-poo owner did not pick up on. Darn that dumb love-heart toy.

She cleared her throat. "So far, so good," she said as she continued to watch the dogs.

Had he noticed the mortifying way she'd cringed when he'd stepped too close, too quickly? Surely after all that counseling she should be over that kind of reaction by now?

She stole a sideward glance at the tall, muscular hunk. He caught her gaze, and she forced herself to meet it. Even to pull her lips back in a smile. He was a potential client, and she had to act as professionally as possible.

"So far, so good," he agreed, indicating the dogs with a nod. "No need to worry about these two."

Bessie rolled over on her back in a total pose of submission to Snowball, whose flag of a white tail was wagging furiously as he trotted around her. Serena could swear he was grinning and her forced smile widened to something heartfelt. She reached down to pat her beloved pet.

"Good boy," she murmured. The little Maltese had earned his treats for the day. With bonus.

Delighted by the animals' behavior, Serena dared a full-on gaze into Nick Whalen's chiseled face. "If Snowball could talk, I think he'd beg Bessie to stay. I guess you could call it love at first sight. That is, if they weren't both, uh . . . altered."

Ohmigod, there she was stumbling over that word again.

"That is, if you attributed human emotion to dogs," he said.

Was that a challenge? If so, she chose not to meet it.

The love-heart incident might already have him thinking she was a teensy bit weird. He balked at the term "dog-kid." If she argued too fiercely in defense of the concept of dogs falling in love, she could lose herself a new client.

"Which of course you do not," she conceded with a slight shrug of her shoulders. "And I . . . I respect your belief."

Though she certainly didn't agree with it.

Imagine him not realizing that dogs had real feelings and formed lasting bonds with other dogs—not to mention humans? To her that was incomprehensible. She knew from experience that dogs loved and grieved with real emotion.

"Their behavior looks like plain old instinct to me," he said, "neutered or not."

She bit down on a defensive reply. "Instinct? I guess you could call it that."

This guy was definitely a stranger in a strange land when it came to dog world. *Except for that fussy bow on the Yorki-poo's forelock.* That still did not add up.

She took a deep breath. "Whatever your opinion might be on doggy emotion," she said in her best dog-professional voice, "Bessie has proved herself to be one well-socialized little animal. I'm with Snowball on that."

"So she's passed her temperament test?"

"So far with flying colors. Now all I need to see is how she copes with the playroom and meeting the other dogs. Want to bring her through?"

Serena stepped past the powerfully built man, careful to keep a more-than-shoulder-brushing distance away.

But it was only as she escaped into the adjoining room that the realization struck her: in that long moment when her hand had been trapped by his much bigger, stronger one, she hadn't panicked.

No. In such intimate proximity to the Yorki-poo owner, her heart had been racing and her breathing tight for an altogether different reason.

Immediately after Nick stepped into the playroom he was assailed by the smell of dog. Not dirty dog. Or dog mess. Just dog. You either liked it or you didn't. And the good, clean smell of dog had only happy connotations for him.

But to him dogs were animals that earned their keep. They guarded property. Worked on farms. Used their superior senses to sniff out contraband.

Yappy little lapdogs were pure indulgence.

Hold your fire there, Whalen.

He was in real danger of forgetting he was undercover in the persona of an indulgent lapdog owner. He had to go along with whatever nonsense was thrown his way. Mask his real reactions. Curb smart comments about animal emotions to the lovely doggy day-care director. Smile more.

He grit his teeth. It took real application of his skills to act like the kind of guy who would own a Yorki-poo.

Yorki-poo! He found it difficult to get his tongue around the name of the designer hybrid breed without laughing. Let alone go all mushy over her.

Bessie was the last dog he would ever choose to own. But his great-aunt Alice adored her. When he'd agreed to house-sit Alice's place in Sausalito while his aunt was out of town, Bessie came as part of the deal.

She was a harmless little creature, sweet in her own imitation-cat-like way. Importantly, she gave him legitimate access to Paws-

A-While. He had to make certain Bessie got accepted for day care so he had an excuse to spend time here. The contract with the insurance company was a lucrative one. Crack the identity-theft scam and the future of his and Adam's new business would be right on track.

The subtle presence of Serena's scent—identifiable even over the aroma of dog—reminded him that the too-perceptive proprietor stood next to him. Ill-timed references to his true opinion of her business might lose him his opportunity to infiltrate her organization.

"This place is really something," he said as he looked around him.

Serena's smile showed she took his comment as a compliment.

Her smile. It lit up those honey-colored eyes. Warmed the hint of anxiety from her expression. He liked the feeling it gave him to know he could make her smile. But he had to remind himself that the most villainous of perps could have the most charming of smiles.

The doggy day-care director could well be the mastermind behind a criminal scam that was defrauding decent people. Stealing their savings. Trashing their homes. Jeopardizing their futures.

If Serena Oakley was in any way involved, it was his job to bring her to justice.

No way could he let slip even a hint of his attraction to her.

He forced himself to turn his attention away from the allure of her smile to the Paws-A-While playroom.

Never had he seen so many dogs together in the one place, maybe fifty of them, he guesstimated. The large, open room was fenced off with dog-escape-proof pool fencing and accessed by gates at either end. A number of staff watched over their charges.

The owners of these dogs were paying exorbitant dollars to keep their animals here. It would take a lot of guard-dog wages to recover a week's fees. But then, the owners weren't worried about counting their change—they were big earners. Which made them vulnerable to identity theft and fraud.

The more he saw of the setup at Paws-A-While, the more convinced he was that there was something here worth investigating.

A blond girl wearing a Paws-A-While T-shirt came to the nearest gate where he stood with Serena, Bessie, and Snowball.

The girl smiled at him and then pointed to Bessie. "Is this little cutie the newbie?" she asked Serena.

Serena nodded. "Name's Bessie Whalen."

The girl nodded to Nick. "And you're the proud dad?"

Before he could formulate a rejoinder, Serena swiftly cut in. "He's Bessie's owner, yes." She turned to Nick. "Okay if Kylie takes her in?"

Again Nick grit his teeth and endured. *Proud dad to a dog.* Now he'd heard it all.

But—like it or not—he had to remember his undercover persona. A schmuck who thought nothing of wasting hundreds of dollars on pampering a mutt that would be happier playing catch with a stick and eating table scraps.

He smiled a doting dog-daddy smile to Kylie. "Sure," he said.

At the sight of a new animal and a new human, a number of day-care dogs had rushed to the gate. They pressed their noses through the gaps between the metal palings, tails wagging, eyes bright with curiosity.

Nick noted that although most of them were small- to medium-sized, there were a number of big dogs, too. Big dogs for whom Bessie would be but a tasty morsel.

"She's rooming with those guys?" He couldn't mask the concern from his voice.

Serena looked up at him, her expression iridescent with sympathy. Her eyes were the color of dark honey and her voice had the same soothing quality. "I know it can be hard for you to leave your . . . your pet for the first time but—"

In the nick of time she had stopped herself from saying "dog-kid." He just knew it.

"I'm not worried about me—it's them," he said. He pointed to a pair of large Weimaraners and a thickset English bulldog. All three dogs had stopped what they were doing and were looking through the bars at Bessie with great interest.

Serena looked in their direction and laughed. "Those boys? They're cream puffs. We don't accept aggressive dogs for day care. And I limit the number of big animals. Though don't be fooled as to size. Little dogs can be far more argumentative, believe me. They can hold their own."

He looked from shrimp-sized Bessie to the outsized Weimaraner. "You're sure about that?"

"Sure I'm sure. Dogs are pack animals. We work with the dynamics of the pack. Our policy is to only introduce two new dogs a day, max. From what I've seen of her, Bessie won't be asking for trouble. She'll quickly find her place. Watch and see."

Kylie held the day-care dogs back while Serena opened the gate. Snowball trotted through first, followed closely by a more cautious Bessie. Serena ushered the dogs through and closed the gate behind her.

In the big room, Bessie looked tiny and vulnerable.

Fists clenched by his sides, Nick scoped out the animals in the immediate vicinity to the little Yorki-poo.

An enormous black beast lay resting nearby with its wolflike head on its plate-sized paws. It had lopsided ears: one cocked and the other flopped down. But though its tawny eyes were watchful, it looked peaceful enough. Mellow even.

Not like that thickset German shepherd with a metallic studded collar. Or that bulldog with its drooling jowls and powerful jaw. Potential troublemakers, both of them.

Muscles tensed, Nick primed himself to vault over the fence at the slightest sign of aggression. He narrowed his eyes, gauging the time it would take for him to get between Bessie and a possible assailant. To scoop her in his arms to safety.

But the Yorki-poo didn't seem bothered by the canine attention she was generating. She stayed still, ears alert and tail wagging as she let the other dogs sniff over her at their leisure.

Nick was gratified to see that, in fact, tails were wagging all around. Even that bulldog's stumpy butt was in motion. He ratcheted his alertness level down a notch.

Then a Doberman bounded toward Bessie with a tad too much enthusiasm. Nick reacted instantly. Went into overdrive. Sprang toward the fence. Prepared to hurdle over.

"Stay." Serena snapped the order with the power of a cracking whip.

Nick froze, one foot in midair.

Took seconds to realize her order was for the Doberman.

Slowly, Nick lowered his foot, as if he were testing the sole of his size-thirteen oxford. The dog skidded to a halt. Sat panting at Serena's feet.

Nick shoved his hands deep in his pockets. He rocked back on his heels and looked anywhere but in Serena's direction. If he could get away with it, he would have whistled to underscore his nonchalance. He sure as hell hoped she hadn't noticed how he'd jumped to the command of her soft but authoritative voice.

How long until he sat panting at her feet?

From nowhere came an image of what she would be like taking charge in bed. Riding him. Her dark hair tumbling around her face, her cheeks flushed—

He fought his body's instant arousal, angry with himself.

This was insanity.

He could not let this woman guess how she affected him.

But Serena's attention was focused entirely on the dogs, her energies on ensuring Bessie was safe. Nick Whalen, Yorki-poo parent, was not even on her radar.

She was in charge. A boss lady. Controlling the dogs with confidence and authority. If a situation developed, a mere former fed would not be needed to intervene.

He wasn't sure he liked that feeling. It was second nature for him to be the one taking charge, acting the role of protector.

Then, as if at a signal visible only to canines, Bessie shook herself and scampered off after Snowball without a backward glance.

Serena turned toward Nick. "See? No need to worry."

He shrugged. Like he'd been worried?

"Sure," he muttered.

"But we'll still keep a close eye on her," she said. She turned back to say something to Kylie.

Good.

He didn't want attention focused on him. Or his attention focused on her. He was here to do a job. And Serena Oakley was proving a distraction he had not counted on.

But he couldn't stop his gaze straying to where she stood with the dogs. She was laughing at something Kylie said. He stared, transfixed by the animation of her face, the bell-like peal of her laugh. Strained to hear the sound of her voice above the doggy babel. For one extraordinary moment he felt he knew her from somewhere else. Surely he had to have met her before to feel so strongly, so quickly?

She leaned down to pat the Doberman, now slobbering slavishly by her side, desperate for the attention of her touch. As she fondled behind the dog's pointed ears in exactly the right spot, it grinned a doggy grin of bliss.

Lucky dog. Nick would be grinning, too, if she were stroking him like that. How would it feel if she—

He wrenched his gaze away from her. Right now, he was Nick

Whalen the investigator. Not Nick Whalen the man, stirred by the laughter of a beautiful stranger.

This insanity was a first for him. He lived by the motto *He who travels fastest, travels alone.* That meant respectful, mutually pleasurable relationships that ended at the first sign of possessiveness. Not this feeling of something already out of his control.

He switched to doting-doggy-daddy mode and observed the other end of the playroom. But even then, out of the corner of his eye, he was way too aware of Serena Oakley.

Three girls were supervising different groups of animals. One group was chasing after balls that they retrieved and dropped back at the feet of the attendant. Another group was jumping over hurdles, leaping through hoops, and crawling through a long flexible tunnel.

Quantico had nothing on this. It was combat training canine style, and the recruits were having a ball.

Whatever scam might be going on here it wasn't to the detriment of the dogs. The enthusiastic yipping and barking that echoed around the room testified to that. Paws-A-While advertised premium pet care; from what he'd seen so far that was just what they gave.

Serena Oakley, as proprietor, was his prime suspect in the identity theft scam. But there were staff to consider, too. Any one of them could be involved. And then there were the dog owners— around forty of them if he didn't include the identity fraud victims.

Bessie was in for a quite a spell of day care.

He looked across to see the Yorki-poo, now scampering about with a group of other small dogs. She didn't look like she had any objection at all to her induction to Paws-A-While. In fact he couldn't help but feel a tad affronted at how quickly she'd trotted away from him.

As he watched, Serena made her way through the gates toward him with her graceful, long-legged stride. He couldn't help a feeling of anticipation. Although there were four other women in the room, he had no idea what they looked like. She eclipsed every other female.

She closed the gate securely behind her. Hit him with that smile again. He suppressed an inner groan. Didn't she realize that dowdy clothes and downplayed looks did nothing to disguise her seductive beauty? The woman was hot.

And he had to throw cold water on his attraction to her.

He cleared his throat. "So Bessie is in?"

Serena nodded. "I'd be happy to welcome her to day care."

"She seems to like it."

She smiled again. "Dogs are sociable animals. Not designed to stay at home alone while their owners are out."

Her shirt had loosened at the top, revealing a hint of cleavage, a tantalizing swell of breast. That strand of hair had fallen across her face again. He had to stop himself from reaching out and tucking it behind her ear.

"These guys are here all day, every day?" he said, nodding to indicate the playroom.

"Some of the apartment dwellers. But most of our clients come just a few days a week. The basset hound is here while her owner is in hospital. Others visit for the day spa side of things. They spend most of their time in the treatment rooms."

"Treatment rooms?"

She indicated with a wave of her hand a door at the end of the room. "I'll go through the treatments we offer once we get Bessie completely settled."

Nick had already checked out the menu on the Paws-A-While website. Had reeled back from the screen in disbelief. Pawdicure. Fur Coloring. Clay Body Wrap. And other total-waste-of-money indulgences. But if he wanted to see how that side of the operation worked, he'd have to sign Bessie up for something. He'd check out his cheapest option.

He sure as hell hoped his business partner wouldn't query his expense account.

"Yeah. That sounds good." He had to force his voice to sound genuinely interested. Delete any note of skepticism.

"What about Doga or Pawlates?"

This time he couldn't mask his reaction quickly enough and his expression must have given her the answer.

"Uh, I take it that's a 'no'?" she said.

"I . . . uh . . . might consider Pawlates at a later stage." Whatever the hell Pawlates was.

Serena rewarded his in-character-as-doting-dog-owner reply with a disbelieving lift of her dark brows.

A small group of dogs had followed Serena to the gate. Now they poked their noses through the bars. She leaned down to pet the closest. "I know I shouldn't have favorites," she whispered, "but I'm so fond of this particular little gang."

Nick had to lean forward to hear her. So close he felt intoxicated by her subtle, sensual scent.

But she only had eyes for the dogs. Among the throng, he identified a low-slung basset hound with mournful eyes, Snowball, and a number of fluffy lapdogs of various sizes, colors, and markings. Bessie stuck close to Snowball.

One of the smaller dogs was quite possibly the ugliest he'd ever seen, a short, squat animal with brindle fur, turned-out legs, and a pugnacious face with a jutting underjaw.

Serena's face glowed with affection as she looked at the dogs. "Aren't they just gorgeous?"

Nick pointed to the ugly one. "Except for him. Hell, what kind of breed is that?"

"You mean Brutus? He's a Heinz type of dog. You know, fifty-seven varieties. Don't you recognize him?"

"Should I?"

"He's famous. His owner died and left him millions. There was a court case. It was all over the media."

"So what's he doing here?" A millionaire mutt? What a prize that would be for a scammer.

"Brutus is a major investor in Paws-A-While."

Was the woman loony? His doubt must have shown on his face. She laughed.

"Brutus belongs to my friend Maddy. She inherited him. I had the idea to start this place when she needed somewhere safe to leave him and his wife for the days Maddy works away from home."

"His wife. The millionaire mutt has a wife." His own words echoed in his head.

Serena's eyebrows arched. "Coco. The little black poodle next to him. The one in the pink sweatshirt. Isn't she adorable? They had the cutest wedding ceremony on the same day Maddy married her husband, Tom."

Nick cleared his throat. This was surreal. He had dealt with some oddballs both in his time at the FBI and after he'd left. But this took the cake.

"I know all kinds of marriage ceremonies are legal in California. But refresh my memory as to when canine commitment became one of them?"

She smiled that alluring smile. Only this time the curve of her lips made him suspect she was—once again—making fun of him. "It was just for a laugh. Maddy works in magazines and it made a great feature story. Besides, she wanted to make an honest dog of Coco as she'd already had five of Brutus's puppies."

She pointed to a little Brutus look-alike, only marginally more attractive. "That's their daughter Tinkerbelle. Maddy kept her, found homes for the others."

Nick could not suppress a groan. "Don't tell me. All the puppies had christening ceremonies."

"Of course not. But they were blessed at the animal blessing service that's held at the shrine of Saint Francis of Assisi in North Beach."

Nick shook his head to clear his thoughts. "Tell me I'm hearing things."

"Welcome to dog world, Nick," Serena said. Her eyes narrowed. "I guess you must be new to it?"

It was a question, not a statement. Dammit. Why wasn't Bessie more of a doglike dog? She should have been the perfect cover. Maybe he should have waited to find a bigger, more believable animal for him to own.

But solving the identity frauds was too urgent to wait around while he searched for the right canine cover.

He shrugged. "I haven't been in San Francisco long."

Her dark brows lifted. "And you haven't had Bessie for long, either, am I right?"

Whoa! He was the one who should be asking the questions around here.

"Long enough to want to make sure she's looked after properly," he said.

Serena's chin tilted upward. "She won't get better care anywhere else in the Bay Area. My clients are my best advertisement."

"I can see that."

He didn't have to fake his answer. Except for the huge black dog that still lay quietly by itself, the dogs looked healthy and happy. If dogs could feel the actual emotion of happiness, that was.

"You can go to work without worrying about Bessie," Serena said in her brisk, professional tone. "And if you still have doubts, there's the doggy day cam."

She pointed to the wall-mounted camera lens that swung around the room in a slow arc. "I'll give you the password and you can log in to our website and check on Bessie at any time."

As if.

He could imagine what his tough, former special agent partner would think of him goofing off to check in on his pooch's playtime.

Hold on, Whalen.

A camera.

The place was under surveillance. Somehow he had to gain access to that footage.

"That's a great idea," he said. "Make sure you get Bessie to wave to me when she's on camera."

"Of course," said Serena. "I pay Kylie extra just to waggle paws at the lens. All part of the service."

Was she serious? In an establishment that dyed dog fur bright pink and painted claws to match and where furballs had Facebook pages, he couldn't be certain.

"Uh, sure," was all he was able to choke out in response.

"That's settled, then," she said, making to turn on her heel. "Rest assured, Bessie couldn't be in better hands."

He was being dismissed as surely as she might command a puppy to "drop it."

"No tour of the facilities?"

She twisted back to face him. "There's not much more to see."

"I need to see it all."

Dammit. He'd let his voice slip from doggy-daddy mode to interrogation mode.

She frowned. "There's really only the television room and the yard . . . I'm guessing you don't want to inspect the potty area."

"Uh. Maybe not. But the treatment rooms sound . . . Well, they sound fascinating."

She checked her watch. "It's time to get the dogs ready for their mid-morning walk. Can it wait until you come back for Bessie this evening?"

Nick swallowed an impatient retort. "Sure," he said.

He had to gain access to that footage. And any other information that might be of use to his investigation. Legally if she showed him; otherwise if she didn't.

Serena Oakley was hiding something. He intended to uncover her secret. He wouldn't let any inconvenient, unplanned-for attraction to her stand in his way.

He'll be back tonight. Serena gave a little shiver of excitement that she disguised by tugging down the edges of her shirt.

Truth was, she had plenty of time to sort the dogs for their walk. She could easily finish Nick Whalen's tour right now. In fact, she was proud of the state-of-the-art dog-potty facility. Would be happy to show it off.

But she needed an excuse to spend more time with the hunky Yorki-poo owner when he returned to collect Bessie in the evening. She wanted to give him a detailed report of his little dog's first day. Chat to him about Bessie's likes and dislikes; discuss treatment options. Ask him to retie that amber-colored ribbon just to prove he could do it.

Liar.

It wasn't about any of that stuff—except maybe the ribbon. It was about that buzz of awareness she'd thought she'd never feel again. The heady rush of hormones.

She found this guy so attractive.

Not that she planned on doing anything more than admiring him from a distance. Not with a client. Not with a guy whose inscrutable pale eyes didn't show even a hint of any returned interest. Not when her sabbatical from sex made her feel so in control, so at peace with herself that she'd considered shipping her libido to Florida for permanent retirement.

But what harm did it do to look?

She did just that. Felt flustered when he caught her look and smiled. Managed a smile in return. "Get here by six and I'll finish the tour," she said.

"I'll look forward to that," he said.

So would she. All day she'd be looking forward to it. In fact she had already set a mental timer on countdown.

She bent down to scratch behind the basset hound's floppy ears in case any hint of interest in Nick showed on her face.

At that moment when he'd trapped her hand beneath his, she'd felt protected, not panicked; reassured rather than ready to run. She'd thought she would never feel that way around a man again. Not after the Valentine's Day dumping and the unpleasant incidents that had preceded it.

But he still made her feel edgy. She still felt he wasn't a Yorki-poo kind of guy—and that there was something not quite right about the mismatch. There was no way this guy had a valid passport for dog world.

Of course she would make darn sure she was around when he dropped off and picked up his dog. Even if she had to fight the other girls for the privilege. But that was as far as it would go.

Because when it came to Nick Whalen her instincts were on red alert. There was too much unexplained about him for her to trust him.

· Three ·

"She's hot, man, is she hot," Nick groaned to his buddy and business partner, Adam Shore. He rocked back in his chair, feet propped on his desk. "She tries to look like some frumpy schoolma'am, but man, she's so not that. She. Is. Hot."

As he drove from Paws-A-While in the Marina District to the South Beach office of S&W Investigations, Nick had spent way too much time thinking about Serena Oakley. And his instant, unprecedented attraction to her.

Adam looked up from his desk. "That's three times you've used the word 'hot' about this possible perp," he said. "I suggest you stay more detached."

At age thirty-four, with his already-thinning-at-the-temples dark hair and frameless glasses, Adam looked more like a bank executive than the powerhouse FBI special agent he'd been when Nick and he became friends. When Adam had suggested Nick leave the agency and go into partnership with him, Nick hadn't hesitated.

Nick had had a gutful of bureaucracy. And an incompetent manager who'd blocked his promotion and made it very clear he was going nowhere soon. There'd been the money, too. A special agent's salary beat the minimum wage but not by a hell of a lot. He hadn't left a comfortable life in his hometown in far northern California to live in debt.

Nick swung his legs back onto the floor and got up. He paced the wooden floor of the small but smart office in a remodeled bond warehouse on Delancey. Right now S&W Investigations comprised just him and Adam and a part-time bookkeeper. But this was only the start.

"Detached. Focused. Maintain suspicion. I know all that." He cracked his knuckles, a habit he had never been able to get out of. "But you should see her, she's—"

"Hot. Yeah, I get it."

"I was going to say funny and warm and charming. Despite her back-off tactics." He cracked his knuckles again, in spite of— or perhaps because of—Adam's shudder. "The damndest thing, the more I think about her, the more I have this feeling I've seen her somewhere before."

"On *America's Most Wanted*?"

Nick glared at Adam. "No."

"It's possible," Adam replied. "Better check up on this crazy dog woman."

"Don't call her that." Nick surprised himself at the vehemence of the tone he used to his partner.

"Isn't that what you called her yourself?"

Nick stopped his pacing and stood in front of Adam's desk. "Guilty as charged. But that was before I met her."

Adam took off his glasses and narrowed his eyes. "Watch out, Nick. This is a big job for us. The insurance company wants quick results."

Nick ran his hand through his hair. "I know that. And I also know the most corrupt criminals can appear charming and funny, etcetera, etcetera. It's part of their stock-in-trade. It's just she . . . I dunno."

No way would he admit to his partner the feelings the doggy day-care director aroused in him. How far his imaginings had gotten to him. That, in spite of her height and businesslike manner, she had an air of vulnerability that appealed to every protective instinct he had.

"Better check her out ASAP, then," said Adam, putting on his glasses and returning to his screen.

Nick settled back at his desk. Investigating a suspect wasn't as easy as it was when he'd had access to the vast FBI network. And the San Francisco Police Department wasn't known for its happy sharing of information with private investigators.

But it was amazing what could be found by good old-fashioned investigation and surveillance. And then there was the Internet. Sometimes Googling brought him just what he needed.

He'd scrolled through the website of Paws-A-While before he'd called to inquire about Bessie. But at that stage he had been anticipating just a routine check and a quick "all clear."

Now he Googled the name "Serena Oakley." Nothing came up except references to the operations of Paws-A-While. That in itself was unusual. There were no pictures of her on the site or elsewhere. That again rang alarm bells. There must have been publicity surrounding the opening of Paws-A-While. Especially with the connection to the millionaire mutt.

He Googled "Brutus." Was staggered by the thousands of references to the millionaire mutt and his inheritance.

He Googled Brutus's owner, "Maddy Cartwright," to find a cute redhead who was a celebrity chef and magazine food editor. She also had her own show on lifestyle television promoting her

healthy recipes for feeding dogs. Forget the cans and the kibble, her
recipes were canine gourmet. Just another aspect of that whacky
alternate dog world Nick found himself thrust into.

There was an item on Maddy Cartwright's wedding to attorney Tom O'Brien on the website of *Annie*, the magazine where
she was food editor. Even more on the weirdo double wedding
with Brutus and Coco.

Then pay dirt.

Most of the pictures were of the dogs. Unbelievably, Brutus in
a blue bandanna and Coco in a tiny white veil and glittery collar.
But standing behind Cartwright in one small picture of the wedding party was a tall, beautiful, dark-haired bridesmaid.

He zoomed in on the image as tight as he could. It was Serena
all right. Smiling that knockout smile. Her hair caught up behind
her face but tumbling around her shoulders. Her lips painted a
luscious red.

And she was . . . Well, she was hot. More than hot. Sensational.
So lovely that just looking at her made his body react instantly. In
a striking, figure-hugging long dress, she fulfilled all the promise
of the beauty he had perceived behind her disguise. To his eyes,
she outshone the bride.

"Gotcha," he said.

Adam got up from his desk. "What have you found?"

Nick took a step aside from his desk so his partner could see his
computer. Adam peered at the screen. "*That's* the crazy dog woman?
You're sure?"

"Yes. Or it's her double."

Adam turned to face him. Nick was disconcerted to see the
gleam in his eyes. "What did you say her name was?"

"Serena Oakley."

Adam shook his head. "That's not Serena Oakley. That's Serena
St. James. No wonder you thought you recognized her. For God's
sake, man, Serena St. James."

Nick stared at him. "I don't know what the hell you're talking about."

"Where have you been? On another planet?" Adam paused. "Oh yeah. Of course you were. Sort of."

"You know I was in Australia for two years."

His last posting had been to the Australian capital city, Canberra. His cover—legal attaché to the U.S. Embassy. When he got back to DC it had been to the post with the promotion-blocking manager. Not long after, he had resigned.

Adam rolled his eyes in a manner Nick found disconcerting. "Serena St. James. In the time you were away she must have been on every billboard in the country."

Adam grabbed Nick's computer mouse. Googled again.

"This, my friend, is Serena St. James," Adam announced.

Within seconds another image filled the screen. A breathtakingly beautiful, dark-haired woman lay seemingly naked in an old-fashioned claw-foot bathtub of liquid chocolate. Her shoulders were slightly raised as if she were about to get out of the tub. The dark chocolate streamed off her shapely, olive-skinned shoulders and molded her perfect breasts. The peaks of her nipples were visible through the layer of chocolate. Her face wore a slow, seductive smile Nick recognized instantly, and one chocolate-coated finger rested on the full lower lip of her lush mouth. Eyes the color of dark honey were lit with a multitude of sensual promises.

Nick felt like he had been kicked in the gut.

Unless she had an identical twin, this chocolate-coated goddess was Serena Oakley.

He stared so long at the screen the image went fuzzy.

Somewhere he must have seen this picture; that was why he thought he'd met her before. Though how he could have forgotten it . . .

With fingers that felt suddenly thick and clumsy, he clicked and scrolled through some of the multiplicity of websites devoted to "girl in bath of chocolate" and other salacious tags that involved the words "lick" and "eat."

He learned how she was a part-time model who had been photographed in the bath of chocolate for Maddy Cartwright's "The Ultimate Chocolate Fix" food feature for *Annie* magazine. The chocolate company had loved the pictures so much it had bought some of the images for their national advertising campaign. Then the photographer had sold the rest of the series for a Chocolate Girl calendar that had sold squillions.

Serena St. James was a fantasy figure to countless men. But liked by women, too, for her funny takes on chocolate and how hard she had to work to keep in shape. She'd been featured on the covers of magazines. Been interviewed on television. Appeared on *Oprah*.

He'd been on the other side of the world in Australia and missed it all.

But there could be no doubt she was the alter ego of Serena Oakley, doggy day-care director. What was her game, burying herself in disguise as a geeky animal nut?

Nick shut down the websites. Muttered to Adam he was going outside for some fresh air. In the green patch of park outside the office he slouched on a bench and stared ahead across the Embarcadero to the masts of the yachts and the span of the Bay Bridge.

He felt empty. Drained. Like he'd woken up from a dream to find he was living in a nightmare.

Serena Oakley. Serena St. James. Whatever she cared to call herself, she was famous. A modern-day pinup. A celebrity.

What hope would a regular guy from a small town have with a woman like her? Would she even look in his direction? Of course, if she was a crook, did it matter?

He cracked his knuckles so loudly the woman at the other end of the park bench glared at him and moved pointedly away.

* * *

Checkout time from five to seven was the busiest time of the day at Paws-A-While. Serena waved good-bye to the English bulldog's mom and the Weimaraners' dads. She looked at her watch. Twenty after six.

She started to tidy the designer dog collars in the reception area product display. Noted that the more expensive the collar, the more she sold. She was right out of the crystal-studded style that gave no change from a one-hundred-dollar bill.

She looked at her watch again. Shook her wrist as the hands hadn't moved at all.

She started to sort the doggy beauty bar. Who would have dreamed she would sell so many luxury fur care goodies? The mega-dollar products were doing so well she needed to find more space for the display. And the new line of organic dog treats supplied by her friend Jenna was walking off the shelves. The doughnut shapes with carob frosting were runaway bestsellers.

She tried to concentrate on calculating her profit for the month, told herself she could *not* check her watch again. Then she heard the "Who Let the Dogs Out?" door chime as the door to the street opened.

She didn't have to turn around to know it was Nick Whalen. She recognized the sound of his footfall, seemed somehow aware of the amount of air his tall, powerful body displaced in the small room. Despite all efforts to act cool, her heartbeat tripped into double time and a flush burned high on her cheeks.

All afternoon she'd been practicing what she'd say to him. With a friendly yet not-too-friendly greeting on her lips, she turned. But the carefully memorized words dissipated like a puff of vapor.

He knew.

She could see it in the way Nick forced himself to keep his gaze above her neck. That was what the nice guys did. Tried not to think about her chocolate-coated breasts. Even when it was all they could think about.

The more righteous men couldn't hide their outright disapproval.

Dave the Valentine's Day dumper hadn't seen it that way. "Every man you meet imagines you naked and covered in chocolate," he'd stormed. "They can't help fantasizing about what they want to do to you."

She'd protested and protested and protested that not every man who saw her posters wanted to undress her. But Dave could not, would not, believe her. And it had proved true: she had attracted unwanted attention. Scary attention.

But not from men like Nick Whalen.

It was obvious her new client was determined to act the gentleman. He looked above her head with inordinate attention at the beagle clock.

She cleared her throat. "Bessie had a good day."

He cleared his throat. "That's great."

"Made lots of friends."

"Glad to hear it." He picked up a bottle from the counter and put it down again without seeming to register that it was labeled Sexy Beast, fragrance for dogs.

Sexy Beast. She could think of someone else worthy of that label.

She cleared her throat again. "Do you . . . uh . . . still want to finish your tour of the facilities?"

He nodded.

Talk about an elephant-sized bathtub of chocolate in the room.

"Well, uh, follow me out back," she said, stepping toward the door to the playroom.

Would he still treat her the same way now he had recognized her? Or follow the track of so many other guys she'd encountered? Even a hint of innuendo from him and his tour would be terminated.

As she approached the door, Kylie came whirling through it.

Serena halted. She could sense Nick pull up to stop himself from colliding with her back. She braced herself, aware that his chest must be mere fractions of an inch from her spine. If she stood still enough, she would feel his breath on her hair. If she took just half a step back, she would rest against the hard strength of his body. *Just half a step.*

She took a deep breath to steady herself. And keep her Birkenstock-clad feet planted firmly on the paw-printed floor.

Kylie greeted Nick. "Hi, Bessie's dad. She's all tuckered out and waiting for you."

Serena swore she felt Nick cringe at the words "Bessie's dad." She frowned a warning at Kylie—she had briefed her about the new client's aversion to the use of everyday dog-world words. But Kylie gave her the slightest and slyest of grins and a discreet thumbs-up. Serena felt the flush on her cheeks intensify. Was her interest in the new client so obvious to everyone?

Nick found himself kissing distance away from the nape of Serena's slender neck. Her thick plait was coming unraveled and wisps of dark hair waved away from its constraint. Her head was bowed. In what? Guilt? Shame? Or just a feminine flurry at his proximity?

He hoped it was the latter.

When she'd stopped so suddenly, he'd put on the brakes, then braced himself so that he didn't make contact. He didn't want her to freak like she had this morning. But she kept still. So still he knew she must be as aware of their closeness as he was.

So what was that cringe thing this morning about? Him? Men in general? Or perhaps a bad experience with a man? Maybe a coconspirator?

Was that why supermodel Serena St. James was hanging out here in disguise as mild-mannered dog nut Serena Oakley?

Nick prided himself on his ability to interrogate the most difficult of suspects. To broach the most controversial of topics. Dammit. Why didn't he just come straight out and ask her? Tell her he knew her true identity. Present himself as a confidante. Trick her into tripping herself up over details.

Deep down he knew the answer. Adam had nailed it. He was in serious danger of losing impartiality on this case.

Trouble was, the doggy day-care director aroused more than his suspicion.

Right now he badly wanted to press his mouth to the lovely hollow behind her ear. To breathe in the scent of her—warmer, richer, and even more intoxicating than this morning. To reach around her waist and pull her to him so her back nestled against his chest.

But not only was she a possible perpetrator of a serious crime; she was also Serena St. James, chocolate goddess, who could have any man she wanted eating from her . . . well, lapping from her . . .

Whatever.

Do not think about chocolate-coated anything.

He called upon all his FBI training to mask his feelings.

He took two steps back from her.

And made sure he stayed a good distance away as he followed her into the playroom.

After hours, the big room seemed very different. Play equipment sat idle. Just the occasional yip and yelp echoed around the walls. But the doggy cam on the wall still slowly scanned the room, its red light blinking.

Of the few dogs that remained to be picked up by their owners, most were subdued. Bessie was actually asleep, snuggling with Snowball on one of the raised dog beds that punctuated the floor space.

But the huge black dog was in virtually the same position as Nick had last seen him. He still lay on the floor, the massive head with the lopsided ears resting on his front paws. His wrinkled brow gave him a worried expression.

Nick stopped and nodded toward him. "Is there something wrong with this guy?"

"You mean Mack?" said Serena. Her voice was a downward slope of sadness. "He's not having a good day."

At the sound of his name, the big animal raised his head and gave a slow thump of his heavy, white-tipped tail. He had one of those appealing dog mouths that curved upward to give the impression of a smile. It seemed at odds with the depressed look in his eyes.

"I don't get it. Is he sick?"

"His knee is injured. I guess it's like humans; some days he feels it worse than others."

"You mean he's in pain?"

Serena nodded. "He's on medication, but I don't know that it helps much. The vet says he's torn his anterior cruciate ligament."

"Ouch." Nick automatically flexed his right knee as he remembered the agony of his own injury. "I tore mine playing football."

Serena screwed her face up in sympathy. "Poor you."

"Yeah. It hurt." He looked again at the big dog, this time seeing him in a new light. Wanted to pet him. Share some kind of knee-injury-veteran camaraderie. But printed notices around Paws-A-While specifically asked owners not to touch dogs other than their own.

"The vet says Mack probably did it by running and stopping too suddenly. Apparently it's not uncommon in dogs this size."

Or big athletic men like himself. "I had surgery and got my injury fixed. Nearly as good as new."

Serena nodded. "Mack needs surgery on his knee. As soon as possible."

"So why doesn't his owner do something about it?" Nick didn't like to think of anyone—or any animal—enduring the pain he'd endured with his knee. He scanned the room. "Shouldn't they be here by now?"

"Mack doesn't have an owner. Or at least he did, but he never came back for him."

"Some guy just abandoned his dog here?"

"Paid the first week in advance. Cash. Picked Mack up the first day. Picked him up the second. Then I never saw the owner again."

So the pain in the dog's eyes wasn't just about his knee. Nick might not believe in ascribing human emotion to dogs. But he knew dogs got genuinely attached to humans.

For the first time in a long time he thought about his childhood dog. A working dog first and foremost but also a family pet that got taken to the vet when it needed it. Nick came from a line of unsentimental farmers. But not one of them would let an animal suffer unnecessarily. "How could someone be so irresponsible?"

Serena's lush mouth set in a grim line. "Ask the people who run the animal shelters that question. The answer isn't pretty."

The big dog hauled himself upright. Nick noticed he put scarcely any weight on his back right leg. The same knee as his own injury. He winced in sympathy.

"What kind of dog is he?"

"Maybe a mix of black German shepherd, mastiff, and Labrador? It's anyone's guess."

"Why'd they call him Mack? Because he's the size of a Mack truck?"

Serena smiled. "That, too, I guess. But he's got a serious fast-food habit."

Nick wasn't sure he'd heard right. "Tell me that again?"

"Fast food. Burgers and fries. The more mayo and ketchup, the better. His owner told me Mack was a rescue dog. The shelter people were concerned because he was so skinny yet wouldn't eat.

Then a volunteer brought in a burger for lunch and Mack nearly snatched it from her hand."

"You're kidding me?"

Nick looked down at the big dog. Felt again a sense of kinship. He had pigged out on fast food when he'd first left home to go to college. He'd reveled in every bite of every burger. But he'd gone to college on a football scholarship. Optimum performance meant eating well. He had learned how to cook. Now he prided himself on his culinary skills.

"No. His owner told me he gave up feeding him the good stuff because all he wanted was burgers and fries. No onions of course; they're bad for dogs."

"Burgers and fries are on the menu here?"

Serena shrugged. "Not for the other dogs but . . ."

"You seriously feed this dog fast food?" He didn't mean to sound disapproving, but Serena seemed to take it that way. She went immediately on the defensive.

"I've tried with the other stuff, believe me. My friend Maddy has even made him organic burgers in an oat-bran bun. He eats them. And the kibble that's shaped like fries. But he's really only happy with the real deal. He's not overweight, just big." Her voice went to mush. "And he's such a sad sack of a boy, he needs treats sometimes."

Chocolate was Nick's favorite treat . . .

Mack lurched toward Serena, limping heavily.

Immediately Serena's eyes welled with compassion. "Poor baby wants a hug," she crooned.

Baby? The beast must weigh in at 180 pounds.

Serena sat down on a dog bed, tucking her long legs beneath her. "Watch this," she said. "He thinks he's still a puppy and can climb into my lap."

Nick found it difficult to reconcile the image of the alluring siren in the bath with the woman looking so at home on a scruffy dog bed in baggy jeans, a shapeless shirt, and the ugliest shoes he'd ever seen on a woman. But the face was the same. And even the frumpy clothes couldn't completely disguise her curves.

She was beautiful just the way she was.

The dog plonked one enormous paw and then the other onto Serena's lap as he scrabbled for purchase against the fabric of her jeans. Then, still favoring his injured knee, he attempted to launch his outsized frame onto her lap. He got only as far as his forelegs before he ran out of room. Serena laughed, put her arms around his neck, and hugged the big dog.

Nick masked his envy with a grin. "What a wuss."

"He must have been owned by a woman when he was a pup. He never tries it with a man." Serena bent backward to avoid an overenthusiastic licking. "Isn't he adorable?"

"I don't know about *adorable*," said Nick before he remembered his doting-doggy-daddy persona. "But the guy certainly seems like a . . . like a big cutie pie." He nearly choked on the last two words.

"What did you say?" asked Serena, not looking at him, her attention on not getting squashed flat by the 180-pound pup.

Nick started to repeat the cutie pie thing.

But she didn't wait for his answer. "No, no, no," she spluttered, laughing, as she twisted away from Mack's slobbery attentions.

Her face was flushed and those remarkable eyes were lit with affection and pleasure. Nick realized he had not seen her so relaxed.

So that was her story: she felt more comfortable with dogs than with people.

What would it take for her to look like that at a guy?

"Silly boy," she admonished the dog, with another peal of laughter.

Lucky boy, thought Nick.

Serena crooned to the outsized mutt as she scratched behind his ears and patted his neck and chest. The dog drooled in ecstasy.

As you would.

"He's a gentle giant. A really nice dog." She sighed. "I don't know what I'm going to do with him."

Nick frowned. "What do you mean?"

"I've had him for four weeks," she said. "I kept thinking the owner would come back, that he had gotten caught up in something."

"But no show?"

She shook her head. That strand of hair had fallen across her cheek again. Nick clenched his hands into fists to stop himself from reaching out and brushing it away.

"Nada. No answer on his landline and the cell phone number he gave me was disconnected. It's a real mystery. He seemed so fond of Mack."

A dog abandoned. An owner disappeared. Could Mack's owner be involved in the identity fraud? Even if only on the periphery? It was a long shot, but somehow he had to get the guy's name.

Serena gave Mack a final, vigorous pat-down and pushed him gently but firmly away. "That's enough, Mack."

The dog obeyed immediately. He sat meekly back down on the floor, though his woebegone eyes didn't leave Serena.

"He's well trained," said Nick.

"At his size he has to be."

She stood up and brushed herself down. Nick restrained himself from offering to help brush the dog hairs off her chest. Refused to let himself think about how that chest had looked covered in chocolate . . .

He cleared his throat. Kept his gaze concentrated above her neck. "So what's next for Mack?"

"I can't bear to send him back to the shelter. It would be like adopting a kid and then returning it to an orphanage. But I'm not having any luck finding him a home." She sighed again. "He's so big. And the surgery he needs costs thousands."

Finally she pushed the strand of hair back off her face. The gesture was a weary one and he noticed there were bruise-like shadows under her eyes. "Thousands I don't have right now. But I'm working on it."

By skimming clients' details from their credit cards and doing a number on their bank accounts?

This woman was crazy about dogs. Would getting the money for an essential operation be motivation enough to steal? He got a pain in his gut at the thought she could be capable of it. But Serena was still his prime suspect.

"Mack seems like a nice fella." He paused. "Fella. That was the name of the dog I had as a kid. He had another name but that's all we ever called him. He was big like this guy but not this big."

Serena tilted her head to one side. She frowned. "You like big dogs, but you end up with a purse-sized pooch like Bessie?"

She was smart. He'd nearly let his guard down then. Not a good idea to talk about his personal life to a possible perp.

He shrugged. "Different times of life have different needs. We lived on a farm. My family still does. There's plenty of room for big dogs. We always have them."

"Lucky you," she said. "I wasn't allowed to have a dog when I was little. My parents were vegans. No carnivores permitted in their household."

"That was tough."

"Yeah, especially to a kid who loved steak and hamburger." She pulled a face that made Nick smile. "We moved around a lot, too, which they gave as an additional excuse not to have a dog. Or cat for that matter."

"You moved around a lot?" Itinerant parents. A background common to many criminals.

"I lost count of how many schools I went to."

Oakley or St. James? He'd have to check out those dubious-sounding parents.

"I guilted them into a pet eventually," Serena continued. "I was an only child and I played the lonely card. But they never felt comfortable around my dogs."

"What do they make of all this?" Nick gestured around him.

She smiled. "Shall I say they're philosophically opposed to it? But they're cool about anything I do. Even at the time when I wa—"

She stopped mid-word. Met his scrutiny with wide eyes. The air seemed heavy with her unspoken words.

He held her gaze for a long moment. Then finally he uttered the question he had been burning to ask her.

"Why?"

He found he was holding his breath for her answer.

Serena tilted her chin upward. "Why what?" she asked. "Why did I pose naked in a bath of chocolate for the whole of America to see?"

Nick started to growl a response, but she put up her hand to stop him.

"Not naked, by the way. It just looked that way. I was wearing panties." She hated the defensiveness that always weakened her voice when she spoke about it. "Or do you want to know why I look like this now?" She swept her hands down the sides of her shapeless shirt.

"All of that." He folded his arms across his chest and rocked back on his heels.

So far, no sleaze. Just interest. Above-the-neck-type interest.

Serena knew she had good instincts when it came to animals— that was why she understood dogs so well. But she wasn't so attuned to men. She was wary of making yet another mistake.

She didn't have to tell him. He had no right to ask. But there was something about this man that made her want to answer his question.

With the shorthand version, that was.

He was attractive. She liked his concern for Mack. She liked the way he hadn't turned into a number one sleazebag when he'd discovered her past. But she still felt on edge around him.

She noticed a soft plastic ball that had rolled under the dog bed. To gain a few seconds, she bent down to pick it up. When she straightened she realized Nick hadn't taken his eyes off of her for a second. In a moment of pure female contrariness, she wished she were wearing something more attractive than the Paws-A-While uniform she had designed specifically to deflect male interest.

"Posing for Maddy's chocolate feature was fun," she began. "*Annie* is my favorite magazine and Maddy is my best friend. The pose wasn't any more revealing than a swimsuit." Despite her best efforts, she faltered. "I . . . I never dreamed what it would lead to."

"Yes?" Nick nodded in encouragement.

"For one thing, as soon as the campaign started, no one took me seriously anymore. It was like they thought my brain had been smothered by chocolate. I realized pretty soon that I would never live it down."

"You became famous."

"Infamous, you mean." Fight it as she did, she couldn't keep the betraying tremor from her voice. She tossed the ball from hand to hand.

He leaned closer. "What do you mean?"

She took a deep, steadying breath. Struggled to sound unaffected, unconcerned. "I attracted some weirdos. One in particular . . ."

Her voice cracked. She wasn't as disengaged from what had happened as she'd hoped. Her back ached from a long day bending over the grooming tables, and she longed to sink back down on the dog bed. But she had to keep the advantage of her height.

"A stalker. You attracted a stalker?"

She gripped tight on the ball. One part of her was tired of

holding it all in. Talking to no one but her therapist. That part of her wanted to let it all out. Cry on his so-substantial shoulder. Trust him.

She nodded.

He stepped forward. Too fast. Too close. She took a step back. Her throat constricted. *Deep breath. Deep breath.*

In an effort to sound as though it didn't matter, she began to babble. "It wasn't the billboard pictures. It was the other ones. But I wanted to leave modeling anyway. I don't stick at things. Never finish them. Not good at commitment. I—"

She gripped so hard on the ball it broke in a whoosh of expelled air.

Nick cursed.

She started. Looked around to see where the noise had come from. Then, dazed, looked down at the deflated plastic in her hand. The ball was Tinkerbelle's favorite. Maddy would not be happy.

"Serena. Tell me about the stalker."

The abrupt urgency of Nick Whalen's voice broke through the haze. She looked up. That narrow-eyed, suspicious look was back in full force on his face.

"Tell me now," he said. The edge of impatience to his voice flung her back to a time when she'd been interrogated as if what had happened had been her own fault.

Unable to croak out an answer, she stared at Nick Whalen. Now she knew what had bothered her about him from the get-go, what made her feel uncomfortable and edgy around him.

He was a cop.

As sure as dogs turned around three times before they went to sleep, he was a cop.

A wave of disappointment threatened to drown her. Why did the first man in a long time to arouse her interest have to be a cop?

Her unconventional family had brought her up to distrust figures of authority. Cops. Members of the military. Particularly cops.

Her personal experience of men in uniform had only rein-
forced her family prejudice. Dave the Valentine's Day dumper was
a lieutenant in the navy. And there'd been that hard-eyed police
officer who had implied that women who bared their bodies for
the camera got what they deserved.

Nick Whalen was not a Yorki-poo kind of guy. But he wasn't a
boxer type, either. A boxer, despite its tough face and powerful body,
was not a dog often chosen for a life in law enforcement.

No. Nick Whalen was more a Rottweiler type of guy.

And out of all the breeds of dogs, a Rottweiler was the only
one she didn't like or trust. Or want anywhere near Paws-A-While.

· Four ·

Serena stared at Nick with a new awareness. How could she have missed it? That chiseled jaw. The cropped hair. The tightly coiled energy in the broad shoulders and powerful, muscled body.

She could just see him in uniform. A dark shirt and pants. A gun belt slung around his hips. A big shiny badge on his chest. Tough. Authoritarian. A real Rottweiler kind of a guy.

That he would look hot, hot, hot in that cop uniform was a thought she forced herself to suppress.

"Did you know your stalker? Or was he a stranger?" he asked, still with that edge of interrogation that made her bristle.

"Why so many questions?" She fought the tremor in her voice. *Not* a good idea to show weakness in front of Rottweilers.

"Knowing how the obsession started might help you."

She grit her teeth. "So what makes you such an expert on stalkers?"

A muscle in his jaw tensed. "Did I say I was an expert on stalkers?"

She folded her arms in front of her chest, did nothing to hide the note of challenge in her voice. "You know something? You never actually told me what your job is."

He had filled in the online application form for Paws-A-While with the word "Consultant" under the section for "dog owner's occupation." She hadn't thought anything of it at the time.

He shrugged those broad, law-enforcement-type shoulders. "I work for an insurance company."

"You sell insurance?"

"No," he said.

"You're an insurance assessor?"

"In a way, yes," he said.

She frowned. "You don't look like you spend your day behind a desk."

If he did, he spent the rest of his life at the gym. Or Ironman training. Or some other rugged, Rottweiler/cop type workout.

He cracked his knuckles, a sound that made her wince. Her father used to do that, and she hated it. At her glare, Nick fisted his hands by his sides.

"Trust me, I avoid my desk wherever possible," he said.

Trust me.

One of the things she loved about dogs was that they never played games of evasion. It bugged her when people did. "If someone were to ask me, I'd say you seemed more like . . . like a cop."

She looked intently at his face, determined to catch him out. Not by the merest flinching did he react.

"A cop? So that's why you think I'm an expert on stalkers."

No way would she let him twist the conversation away in another direction. She was like a dog with its jaws clamped around a bone now, determined not to let go until she got a direct answer.

"Are you? A cop, I mean?"

Deep down she knew it was unfair to visit her dislike of law enforcement officers on Nick Whalen. And if he were anything other than a hot, gorgeous guy who had dragged her hormones out of hibernation, maybe she wouldn't. If he was middle-aged, balding, and had a paunch, would she care about anything other than he had a nice dog and paid his account on time?

Nick stretched his arms, then brought them together behind his back—a relaxed movement that belied the tension in his jaw. "I'm not a cop."

Like he wasn't a journalist or a health inspector.

But if he was not a cop, how did that explain her gut-level distrust of him? "So why the interest in stalkers?"

"You've got it wrong. I have no interest in stalkers in general."

He took a step toward her. She stepped back, so quickly she nearly stumbled. Gulped a sharp intake of breath that left her feeling giddy. *Damn! When would she stop reacting like this?*

"I'm interested in *your* stalker. In finding out why you cringe every time I get within arm's reach of you."

"I . . . I don't cringe," she said, desperately wanting to take another step backward. Knowing the backs of her calves were already pressing painfully against the edge of the dog bed. That her chest was hurting from the effort to breathe normally, speak normally.

He took another sudden, quick step forward. It wasn't threatening. By no means was it threatening. But she reacted instinctively by stepping back so fast she pushed the dog bed away from her so it scraped across the polished concrete of the playroom floor.

Mack gave a surprised yelp and hauled himself up from the floor. Hindered by his injured leg, he lurched toward Nick. Serena tensed. Did Mack think she needed protecting? He'd shown no signs of aggression thus far.

But no. The dog settled his bulk near Nick's feet. He looked up at Nick as if for reassurance and then toward her. Two pairs of eyes, one human and one canine, observed her. Nick raised an eyebrow. Mack tilted his head to one side, one ear up, the other down. Wordlessly, both man and dog waited for her reaction.

She cleared her throat. "That . . . that wasn't a cringe," she stuttered. "It was a . . . well . . . I was backing off from a client asking questions he has no right to ask."

Nick shrugged his shoulders with great exaggeration. "My mistake. When you told me about the weirdo you attracted, I thought you wanted to talk about it."

"Well, I don't. He's my stalker and . . ." She sought for words. "And I . . . I'm not sharing."

Damn. In a day of dumb utterances, that took the prize for the dumbest.

Nick quirked his mouth in a valiant but unsuccessful effort to squash a grin. Mack tilted his head to the other side. His forehead wrinkled in a frown.

Mortified, Serena glared at both man and dog. But with the sound of her own silly utterance seeming to echo around the room, she found, in spite of herself, she was unable to stop a shaky, answering smile. "Dammit, I think you know what I mean."

Nick gave full leash to his grin. "That's a first. I've never heard of anyone bragging about their own personal stalker." He sobered. "But seriously, it might help to share. To talk about what happened."

He was too darn perceptive. Already, just hours after first meeting him, she was aware of the different nuances reflected in his pale blue eyes. Suspicion. Humor. Wariness. Now they were lit by a glow of something that made her bite her bottom lip to stop it from trembling.

Compassion.

The temptation to confide in him was almost unbearable.

Of course she would feel better if she talked some more about what had happened with her crazy fan. She'd always talked to

Maddy when something bothered her. But now her best friend was married to Tom, and Serena tried not to intrude on their time together. There was Jenna, of course. She'd known Jenna briefly at one of the numerous high schools she'd attended. They'd only reconnected a few years ago. But while Jenna was nice—really nice—she wasn't yet in the top rank of friends.

Whereas she and Maddy had clicked the moment they'd met over a plated entrée of Atlantic salmon with artichoke and almonds and a dangerously dribbly brown butter sauce. She'd been a new waitress almost paralytic with nervousness that she wouldn't remember people's orders; Maddy the sous chef desperate to take over the number one place in the kitchen. They'd talked ambition. They'd talked men. They'd talked more men.

But now Maddy was part of a couple and Serena was aware that although Maddy would always occupy that space in her heart labeled "best girlfriend," her buddy had moved on to a different stage of life.

It would be so easy to cry on Nick Whalen's rock-solid shoulder about the incident that still sometimes made her wake bolt upright in her bed as she relived the scariness—and stupidity—of it.

But, sincere as he sounded, she still sensed that Nick had a different agenda that somehow involved her and the fledgling business she was so determined to make succeed. That feeling niggled at her. She could not risk getting too friendly with him. Not when she'd worked so hard to establish both her business and her emotional equilibrium. She had only enough money left from the fee for the girl-in-the-bath-of-chocolate shoot to keep her afloat for another six months. It hadn't been as much as people thought—the photographer had gotten way more than she had—but enough to set up the business and give her a safety net until she got established.

She made a big show of checking her watch. "No time for stalker sharing tonight. Not if you want to inspect that potty facility. You did say you were interested in seeing how it worked?" she said, knowing full well he had not.

His grin dimmed into something that fought not to be a grimace. "Right. I . . . uh . . . of course I want to know that. Fascinated, in fact."

Serena would have no problem keeping a real Rottweiler out of Paws-A-While. She would simply tell the owner she had reached her quota of big dogs. But Nick Whalen was a different story. She suspected he would be as tough and tenacious as the breed of dog he so suited.

"C'mon," she said. "If we're in luck, you might get to see Mack demonstrating how the potty works," she said. She couldn't resist a sly, sideways glance at him.

Did Nick Whalen's face go a pale tint of green under his tan?

Nick cursed long and hard without uttering a word of it out loud. He'd lost her. Slipped out of doggy-daddy mode for just a second too long. Pushed her too soon, too hard.

He didn't know what made him most angry with himself—that he'd taken a step back from finding out more for his investigation, or that he'd found himself too keen to want to know more about her, to understand the anxiety that shadowed her eyes. Maybe even to want to make excuses for her. Damn but it was hard to keep his interest from becoming personal.

And now he had to go feign interest in a canine latrine.

But just as he made to follow her out back, the door from the reception area opened through into the playroom.

"Serena? Okay to come in? Kylie said you were in here." The unfamiliar male voice echoed through the playroom.

Serena turned. A smile of genuine pleasure lit her face. "Joe! Hi! Come on through."

Her smile was unforced, luminous. Nick had only seen her look like that at a dog. He was curious to see who had elicited it.

A middle-aged man with gray hair and a closely clipped salt and pepper beard let himself in through the pool gate. "Sorry to be so late," he said.

"No problem," said Serena, her face still lit with that smile. "It's great to see you. Rosemary has been doing the pickups lately. I haven't had the chance to catch up for ages."

Serena turned back to Nick. "Joe and Rosemary and their darling golden Lab, Freya, were my very first clients. Joe, this is Nick Whalen; his Yorki-poo, Bessie, had her tryout day today."

The man nodded cordially and offered his hand. Nick was so stunned he hesitated for a fraction of a second before taking it.

He recognized this man.

But he could not in any way let on. He called on all his training to school his face into a mask of polite interest.

Joe's hand felt damp in his hand and, this close, Nick noticed that his skin had a tinge that matched his hair. But the older man rustled up a smile for Nick. "Your dog will be very happy here, if our experience is anything to go by."

There was an almost imperceptible catch to his voice on the last words that Serena didn't seem to register. Or did Nick notice because he knew so much more about Serena's other client?

"So far so good," Nick said. "Bessie seems to be fitting in real well."

And he had to keep up the act so Bessie would be here long enough for him to get the dirt on whatever was going on at Paws-A-While.

The other man hardly seemed to hear Nick's words. It was if he were operating on autopilot on the surface while something altogether different was churning underneath. But Serena appeared oblivious to any hidden tensions in her client.

"Freya's watching a movie in the television room," she said to Joe. "We put the *101 Dalmatians* DVD on for her and she's been parked in front of it all afternoon."

Joe smiled, in what Nick thought was a weary imitation of a doting-doggy-daddy smile. "That movie is her favorite."

Nick forced himself to swallow a smart, decidedly non-doting remark. During his thirty-two years he'd seen quite a bit of life. But nothing had prepared him for the excesses he had encountered at this place.

Was there no end to the pampering of these pooches? Favorite DVDs, for heaven's sake. What next? Was that the way he'd have to infiltrate here? Walking through the dog-dedicated TV room offering popcorn and snacks to the lazy, indulged animals reclining in their armchairs?

Serena's face softened in that indulgent way it did, he was learning, when she was talking about a favorite dog. "I'm not so sure about how much of the cartoon Freya sees," she said to Joe, "but it keeps her happy for an hour or so."

Sure it did. Did the mutt have its personal soda fountain, too? Soft-serve ice cream on call? Twizzlers, anyone?

Joe nodded. "You know, I'm not sure that it's about the actual movie. I think she just likes to hear the human voices. They comfort her."

Serena turned to Nick. "Freya's very old, past sixteen. She's going blind and she's a bit deaf but she's the sweetest thing you ever met." She turned back to her other client. Her voice gentled. "Freya's had a good day, Joe. As good as can be expected."

Her client's Adam's apple jerked convulsively. "One of her last days here, I'm afraid, Serena."

Serena's face crumpled; she snatched her hand to her mouth as she stared at Joe. "Oh no. Not that. The vet hasn't said to euthanize—?"

Nick immediately felt like a prize jerk. The poor animal was being pampered because she was on her last legs. If he'd sounded forth about the popcorn and the soda fountain, right now he'd be wrenching his size-thirteen foot out of his mouth.

But Joe made a waving-away motion with his hands. "No. Thank God. We've been spared that. With everything else at least we've been spared that."

Serena's brow furrowed. "Then I don't understand. Why would this be one of Freya's last days here?"

"I'm sorry, Serena. I'm giving you the week's notice I know you require," said Joe, obviously having difficulty with the words. "We have to . . . to take Freya out of Paws-A-While."

Emotions rippled across Serena's face. Shock. Hurt. A flash of panic. "But, Joe, I thought you and Rosemary were happy with the way we look after Freya?"

Joe groaned. "I'm not doing this very well, am I? We couldn't be happier with Paws-A-While. Freya will miss coming here and so . . . so will we. I know I also speak for Rosemary on that."

"So why—?"

"To be blunt, we can't afford to keep Freya with you any longer. We're broke, Serena. Lost everything." Her client's mouth set in a grim line.

Serena didn't do a good job of hiding her bewilderment. She was either an excellent actor—as the best con merchants were— or she was genuinely distressed.

"But, Joe, you're a doctor . . . So's Rosemary. You have your own business. How do doctors lose . . . ?"

"Identity theft, Serena." He spat out the words as if they were some bitter substance he had inadvertently swallowed. "That's how people like us, who have worked so hard to get everything we have, can lose it all."

"Identity theft," she said, as if she was only barely aware of the term. "Isn't that when someone steals your credit cards, then uses your name?"

Joe nodded, obviously too shattered by the event to say much more.

Oh yes, Nick recognized Joseph Godfrey, all right. His file was in the third drawer down in the secure filing cabinet in the S&W Investigations office in South Beach.

Drs. Joseph and Rosemary Godfrey, San Anselmo, Marin County. The bearded doctor's photo was scanned into the report from the insurance company. Along with the details of the massive fraud perpetrated on him and his wife. Credit cards run up to the max. Bank accounts cleaned out. Debts all over the state. A massive mortgage taken out using their properties as collateral. All orchestrated by a scammer who had assumed the identities of this eminent pediatrician and his psychiatrist wife.

Serena was reeling, obviously having trouble taking in what her client had told her. "Joe, this is terrible. I . . . I can't say how sorry I am."

Joe shook his head. "It's a mess like you wouldn't believe, Serena. And now our poor, innocent dog will suffer, too."

"But . . . she's so frail. Who will look after her when you and Rosemary are at work?"

"We'll have to leave her at home by herself." His mouth twisted. "That is, if we get to keep our home. Not that we feel the same about it since it was burgled."

Serena's lovely, full mouth was trembling. "But Freya hates being by herself. She's too old. She . . ." She bit down on her bottom lip. Nick had the irrational urge to take her in his arms and comfort her.

Comfort her in the distress she feels at having to face up to the effects of her crimes?

She twisted her hands together and Nick got the impression she was fighting tears but was determined not to fall to pieces in front of her clients. "I'll . . . I'll go get Freya," she said, turning on her heel.

An awkward silence fell between the two men.

Nick cleared his throat. "Sorry to hear what's happened to you," Nick said to Joe Godfrey. "It's a bad business."

He would have liked to say, *Don't worry, we're on the case*. But his company's involvement in the investigation had to stay confidential. And he had to remember he was working for the insurance company, not the victims.

"We had no idea what was going on until our credit cards were refused," said the older man. "Then the notices started coming from the bank, from companies we'd never heard of, debt collectors . . . It's a nightmare."

Nick made gruff, sympathetic, man-to-man-type noises that he knew were totally meaningless. But he could not just ignore Joe Godfrey's pain. Anger at the type of scum who would do this damage to innocent people churned in his gut.

This decent, caring man was the human face of the victim—the reality behind the cold, hard facts of his briefing. And Nick could not discount for one second that Serena Oakley—alias St. James—could be the beautiful face of the perpetrator.

When she came back, leading an ancient yellow Labrador, her eyes were red; maybe she'd scrunched her hands into fists to wipe away tears. But she had a decisive air about her, as if she'd spent her time in the doggy TV room thinking.

She had to guide the old dog with its leash as, on unsteady legs, it had trouble walking in a straight line and veered off the path of painted paw prints. The Lab's muzzle was silver and her eyes milky. But Nick could see the joyous expression in those tired old eyes when she realized her master was there. She tottered up to Joe Godfrey and simply laid her head against his leg.

Nick could hardly bear to look. The emotion between dog and man was palpable. He remembered how wobbly Fella had gotten toward the end. But how he had refused to slow down. Funny, he hadn't thought of that for a long time. How upset he'd been when he'd come home from college for the summer to find Fella gone.

His parents had not thought to tell him his dog had died. Not that they were harsh or cruel. An old dog's death was just a fact of farm life. They'd soon gotten another puppy. The pup grew up into a nice dog. But it wasn't his dog. And there'd been no opportunity since in his life to have one.

Until now. If things went well with S&W Investigations, he might settle down in San Francisco. Not settle down in the get-married-and-have-kids-type meaning of the term "settle down." No way. *He who travels fastest travels alone.* And he had a new career to establish. But that didn't mean he couldn't commit to a dog of his own.

Yeah. A dog might be good. Maybe someday sooner rather than later.

Joe squatted down to the level of the ancient Labrador. "Hi there, old girl," he said, with obvious affection. He patted and stroked her head. She licked his hand, her tail wagging as slowly as the rest of her. "So you've been watching your favorite movie? And I bet Kylie gave you some special time, too."

Serena watched them, her hands shoved into the pockets of her baggy jeans. "Kylie loves Freya. So do I. You can't take her away from here," she said. "It wouldn't be right." Her voice wasn't quite steady.

Her client got up but kept his hand on his dog's head. "We have no choice, Serena."

"Yes, you do," she said.

What was her game? Nick could not figure out where she was going.

"Serena, I don't think you understand," said Joe, looking distinctly uncomfortable. "We can't afford to pay you any longer."

"I don't want payment. Freya can stay here as . . . as my guest."

Joe shook his head. "That's so sweet of you, Serena. But I can't let you—"

"I insist. Please let me do this for you, Joe. For you and for Freya. You were my very first clients. You referred so many people to me. Keep Freya at Paws-A-While."

"But, Serena . . ."

Serena refused to hear his protest. "Freya is too old to change. She has her routines here, her doggy friends. Us to keep an eye on her. Imagine if she was home by herself all day and had another stroke. I would never forgive myself. Please let me keep her here." Her eyes were urgent with appeal.

"Serena, heaven knows how long it will take for us to prove that someone else took out the loans in our names, ran up the debts. I don't know when we could pay you back. Months. Years. Maybe never." Joe Godfrey's mouth twisted in a bitter line.

"Joe. Listen to me. You won't be running up a tab. Freya will be my guest. For free. Gratis. No charge."

Joe swallowed hard. "Serena, this is incredibly generous of you. I know leaving Freya here is the best thing for her. But why should you suffer financially because of our misfortune? If we leave her here, rest assured, we'll pay her fees as soon as humanly possible."

"We'll see about that at the time," she said, a stubborn set to her mouth. "Just promise me that you or Rosemary will still drop Freya off to me as always."

Nick could not help admiring Serena's generous response and the passionate way she presented her argument. It was difficult not to believe that she was genuinely shocked by the position her clients had found themselves in. But was she able to afford to make such a gesture because of the proceeds of her crimes?

He wanted to believe in her. But in his years at the FBI, Nick had come across ruthless characters who were so convincing in their assumed personas that no one had seen the king hit coming, least of all their victims. No. He had learned how cunning criminals could be in making themselves appear the most kind, generous, and altruistic people to the marks they were aiming to scam. Just like Serena right now appeared to be the most appealing of guardian angels to Joe Godfrey.

Dr. Godfrey reluctantly accepted her offer. "I promise. But only until we can make other arrangements. Maybe Rosemary's sister can help out. And the meter will be ticking, whether you like it or not."

Serena leaned down to pet Freya. "That's settled, then," she said. Then she hugged Joe. "We'll look after Freya for as long as you need us."

It was only for a moment that Serena stood there with her arms around another man in a hug that was nothing more than an act of friendship. But Nick was shocked at the jolt of jealousy that seared him. A fierce surge of possessiveness made him want to shove this nice, distressed man away and warn him never to lay his hands on Serena again.

He forced himself to mentally chant the mantra of his business. *Stay detached. Remain focused. Maintain suspicion.* Serena was being benevolent to her client and his dog. But it could all be part of a calculated act to divert attention from herself.

Back off, Whalen.

At least until there was proof Serena had nothing to do with this fraud. Soon he would meet with Joe Godfrey and his wife on a professional basis to interview them. But not right now in the initial stages of the investigation. Not when he was working undercover at Paws-A-While.

After Serena said good-bye to Dr. Godfrey and watched him and his dog go through the door to the exit, she turned to Nick. Her face was drained of all color and her mouth was trembling.

She slammed one fist into another with a force that made Nick wince. "Talk about bad things happening to good people."

Nick opened his mouth to try for a soothing kind of response, but she didn't give him a chance to utter it.

She started to pace the floor, unconsciously following the trail of painted paw prints. "The Godfreys are *such* good people."

She spun to face him. "Those two run a clinic for emotionally disturbed kids. They've devoted their lives to helping young people. And the tragedy of it is they couldn't have children of their own. Now they can't afford to look after the dog who is—for all intents and purposes—their baby. And who—by the way—also used to work with those kids as a therapy dog before she got too feeble. Why has this happened?"

Her cheeks were flushed and her eyes sparked with emotion.

"I don't have any answer to that," was all he could say.

He felt an overwhelming urge to pull her into his arms and soothe her. To praise her for her generosity of spirit. To reassure her that, if he had anything to do with it, the bad guys would be caught and punished. But he could not. Not when there was still a very real chance that she herself was one of the bad guys.

"What about you?" he asked.

"Me?"

"Don't you need the revenue? Can you afford to keep Freya here for free?"

If she wasn't so upset, he was sure she would tell him to mind his own business. "Of course I can't," she said. "I have a limit to the dogs I'm allowed to have here. This is a new setup, in an area where there are a number of similar centers. But Joe and Rosemary need my help. Wouldn't you do the same?"

Nick wasn't quite sure how to answer her. But he decided he had done enough lying for the day.

"I have to be honest and say I don't know," he replied. "I guess if my business was in jeopardy, I might have to weigh up what the right decision was at the time. Short-term loss that led to long-term gain. Or vice versa."

Had she made that decision and decided to go for huge gain counted in the hundreds of thousands against the risk of getting caught and spending the rest of her youth behind bars?

"And what about Joe and Rosemary?" she said. "Not to mention Freya?"

"If they were my friends, I guess I would be doing everything I could to help them," he said.

And from his point of view that meant tracking down the scum who were responsible for the crime that had these good people forced to accept charity.

Serena knew Nick was right. Extending the offer of free day care for Freya was a bad business decision. But, the way she saw it, she'd had no other choice. Letting Freya stay for free wouldn't cost her much in actual dollar terms. The poor old girl ate special home-cooked meals provided by Rosemary. And the staff numbers stayed the same, give or take a dog. It was the loss of the fees she could charge the dog that could take Freya's place that would hurt. A dog such as Nick Whalen's Yorki-poo.

One thing was for sure: she couldn't afford to knock back a paying customer just because some vague, unsubstantiated feeling made her distrust him. No. Rottweiler or not, Nick Whalen and his little pooch must be made to feel very welcome at Paws-A-While.

Though she herself would try to stay well out of his way.

Because she knew it was more than a suspicion he might be a cop that made her edgy around him. She couldn't kid herself any longer. Deep down she knew she feared the tumult her attraction to him could arouse. The possible disruption to her safe, insulated-from-emotional-drama life.

Despite her model looks, she'd never had a lot of success with men. A tall, gawky, teenager with a mouthful of orthodontic hardware, always the new girl at school, she hadn't exactly been top of the high school boy's dating wish list. When at age eighteen her curves suddenly blossomed, she'd been unprepared for the attention it brought with them.

She made mistakes. Then retreated. Dated the same, sweet, unthreatening boyfriend for years, until he left when she refused his engagement ring. Realized she was attracted to the broad-shouldered, take-command type of guy like Nick Whalen. Learned that take-command type of guys sooner or later wanted to take command of her. And she didn't respond well to being brought to heel.

Like the thing with Dave. The horrible Valentine's Day still haunted her. That, on top of the stalker episode, had sent her fleeing into celibacy. She'd vowed to take a sabbatical from sex and all the complications it brought with it. So far that resolve had kept her calm, in control, and able to concentrate on establishing her business. She'd like to keep it that way.

Getting too interested in a guy like Nick Whalen could only mean unrest and disruption. Paws-A-While meant everything to her, and she needed to concentrate 100 percent on making it a financial success. She'd do that best by leaving her libido in limbo.

She'd known Nick for just a day. If she kept clear of him, she'd soon forget the unwanted effect he had on her, that frightening rush of attraction. To make sure of that, she would make darn sure she was nowhere near when he dropped off or picked up Bessie.

She made herself smile up at him. "There's still that potty inspection. I'll be surprised if you've ever seen anything like it. It flushes, you know." She clicked her fingers. "C'mon, Mack, be a good boy and demonstrate for Nick how it works."

· Five ·

It was three days since Nick had seen anything much of Serena, and now, by Friday morning, he was getting edgy. He could not let his investigation fall behind. Adam had already been on his back regarding progress reports—his partner was not as convinced as Nick was that there was something suspicious going down at the doggy day-care center. It was vital Nick build up more of a relationship with the Paws-A-While director so he could question her. Gaining access to the doggy cam tapes was also high on the list. Not to mention a look at the center's computer files.

Trouble was, he got the distinct impression Serena was avoiding him.

Again, she was not manning the check-in counter at Paws-A-While. The girl who appeared to be her deputy, Kylie Seymour, was booking in the dogs instead. Nick stood in line, holding a restless Bessie, while a jowl-faced middle-aged woman signed in her chubby pug named Barry.

Bessie was straining to get out of his arms. The little dog voted with her paws when it came to day care. It was obvious she could hardly wait to scamper through the door into the playroom to hook up with her new puppy pals.

Kylie took the pug through the playroom door. She turned to mouth to Nick, "I'll be with you in a moment."

On her way out, Barry's owner stopped to pet Bessie. Nick was too distracted to do more than nod to her. It barely registered when the woman called Bessie an adorable pookie wookie.

Nick was too busy trying—without seeming obvious about it—to look over Kylie's head as she opened the door that led through to the playroom to see if he could catch a glimpse of Serena.

No luck.

Damn.

Yesterday he'd seen her tall, graceful figure from the distance. The day before he hadn't seen her at all. Though he suspected she had known he was there and made sure she wouldn't be seen.

How could he do his job when his prime suspect was being so uncooperative?

He felt frustrated. Impatient. Disappointed. He'd thought he was getting on well with Serena, maybe had even bonded some over the Joe Godfrey episode.

Hell, on what feasible pretext could he get in there to meet with her?

Kylie returned to take Bessie from him. "Your little girl has settled in so well," she said, "she's part of the gang."

His little girl. He gritted his teeth. He forced his doting-doggy-daddy smile. "I'm so glad to hear that."

"She's really adorable," Kylie said. "C'mon here, sweet pea."

Bessie responded by trying to lick Kylie's face. Kylie laughed as she snaked her head back to avoid Bessie's overenthusiastic pink tongue.

Kylie was a short, curvy blond with a pretty, dimple-punctuated face and a tendency to gossip that Nick did everything to encourage.

While Serena had been incommunicado, Nick had made it his business to subtly milk Kylie for any information he could about the staff at Paws-A-While. Full names. Backgrounds. Length of employment. Any possible clues as to their likelihood to commit fraud.

He already knew, for instance, that she herself was a single mom of an eight-year-old boy named Finn and a budgie named Tweety. Ironically, for the doggiest dog nut he had ever encountered, she lived in an apartment with a strict no-dog rule. Kylie made no secret of the fact she worked extra shifts to try save enough to move somewhere with a yard.

She also made no secret of the fact that she was fiercely loyal to her boss. Fiercely protective, too, even though she was only a couple years older. From the start, Kylie seemed to pride herself on picking up that he had more than a dog-kid's parent interest in Serena, had slyly teased him without stepping over the line. But her interest in gossip didn't extend as far as Serena's private life. All Nick had been able to ascertain was that Serena had split from a long-term boyfriend and wasn't dating anyone else.

He cleared his throat. "Uh, is Serena available?"

"Regarding?" she asked. Her knowing look made him cringe right down to the tip of his black polished oxfords.

Damn. He was here to work. Not to have to put up with this. He thought he'd left that kind of female game behind him in Booker River Valley where he'd grown up. There, every woman from the ladies at church to his own mom saw a single person as a challenge. An opportunity for potential coupledom. In fact, of his two brothers and one sister, he was the only one to have escaped from the valley matchmaker's clutches. The last remaining Whalen sibling free to do what he wanted, go where he wanted, without the encumbrance of matrimony.

He had every intention of staying that way.

Out of a list of three valid excuses to see Serena he tried to think of the most plausible. This lying business didn't get any easier. Even after years of training.

"Do you have concerns with the care we're giving Bessie?" Kylie prompted.

"No. That's all good. Bessie, the, uh, little cutie pie, couldn't be happier. I just want to see Serena because . . ."

Because he damn well wanted to see if she really was as disturbingly attractive as he remembered. Because he wanted to see what it was about the woman that made her his first and last waking thought of the day. Because he had to see her to ascertain whether or not she was a ruthless criminal capable of ruining the lives of—among others—her first-ever doggy day-care clients.

And to bring her down if she was.

Kylie's knowing brown eyes did not let up their intent focus.

"Because I want to talk to her about Mack." It was as good an excuse as any.

Kylie's expression showed both surprise and a sympathetic warming. "Mack. We all love Mack. I'd take him home like a shot if I could. Poor munchkin."

Nick tried not to flinch at the thought of the massive animal being called a munchkin. The dog, with his reported capacity to chow down on copious quantities of junk, seemed more cyborg than munchkin. But then there was the animal's knee. The injury made it only too apparent he was made of frail flesh, blood, and fur.

While Serena had been top of his mind in the days since he'd first checked in to Paws-A-While, he hadn't been able to stop thinking about Mack, either.

The expression in those doggy eyes haunted him. He knew only too well what it felt like to be a prime specimen in good health felled by a sudden, agonizing knee injury. He bet his eyes, too, had looked miserable when he'd been waiting for his operation. Not that he'd wanted sympathy. No way. He was a guy. And guys got on with it. They toughed it out and they took the right meds and they did the physical therapy and they put weight on their knees too soon. Because they were guys.

He had no idea what a dog would think. But he knew pain when he saw it in those soulful eyes.

"Yes," he said. "I want to talk to Serena about Mack."

Kylie smiled. "Well, in that case, I'm sure she'll change her mind about not wanting to see you." She flushed as soon as the words were out of her mouth and she realized what she'd said.

So Serena *had* been avoiding him.

Because she thought he was a cop?

That spelled G-U-I-L-T whichever way you looked at it.

He brought to bear all his skills and training to keep his face from showing any reaction. "Where is Serena?"

"In the day spa. I'll go tell her—"

Nick took a decisive step forward. "I know where the treatment rooms are. Why don't I just take Bessie through to the playroom and find Serena for myself?"

"But—" Kylie started to protest, then subsided. "Okay. Why not?" A knowing smile danced around her lips. "I'm sure she'll be delighted to see you."

Did he imagine that Kylie then whispered under her breath, *"Whether she knows it or not"*?

He brushed off his irritation at the not-so-subtle machination but was conscious of her speculative gaze following him as he headed through the door to the playroom.

He knew from his tour on Tuesday that the spa side of the Paws-A-While business was accessed through an open doorway right at the back of the playroom. When he got to the top gate to the playroom he handed Bessie over to Adele (dance student and dog lover saving up for a trip to Europe). He watched his aunt's little pooch scamper off to a group of small dogs without a backward glance.

Then he walked down the side of the fence that separated the playroom and through into the back rooms of Paws-A-While. To the right was Serena's small office with the all-important computer that held the company's files. Then to the left was a spacious area with a row of three treatment cubicles, each with a stainless-steel sink and countertop.

He saw Serena almost straight away. She sat at a high stool in the middle cubicle, holding a small black poodle. Her head leaned toward the animal while she did something to its front paws. As she worked, she crooned a litany of sweet-sounding words in her seductively mellow voice. Something along the lines of what a good little angel the poodle was, etcetera, etcetera.

He stopped in his tracks, greedy to grab the chance to observe her unawares.

Oh yeah.

She was every bit as appealing as he remembered.

She wore the shapeless Paws-A-While uniform that covered so much all it did was make him wonder what lay beneath.

He couldn't be sure, but it looked like she had two buttons of her shirt undone. Just enough to reveal a tantalizing hint of what he couldn't stop himself from thinking about. Curves not coated in chocolate but bare and warm and soft to the touch.

Her hair was bunched right up on the top of her head, revealing the lovely lines of her neck. He noticed she had small, perfectly formed ears. He resisted the thought of how much he would like to trace their delicate curves with his fingers, then follow that with—

Serena looked up, her eyes widened, and she flushed. She must have sensed his presence, the heat of his thoughts. A flicker of something moved across her eyes and was gone before he could analyze what it was. Surprise? Guilt?

He couldn't kid himself for even a second that it might be pleasure.

★   ★   ★

COCO realized someone was there before Serena did, letting the human know with a shiver of awareness and a pricking up of her ears. Serena turned to follow the miniature poodle's gaze. Then felt her own shiver of awareness as she saw Nick Whalen standing there, quietly assessing her with those compelling blue eyes.

Their gazes connected. For a long, still moment it was as if all the noises of the adjoining playroom receded, the whimpers, the whines, the sharp, yipping demands, the deep, growly barks, the voices of her staff rising and falling with commands and conversations and the odd burst of laughter.

It was just him and her.

That hotter-than-hot Rottweiler guy.

She could feel the throb-throb-throb of the knowledge of her attraction to him as it pulsed through her veins, taking a flush high to her cheeks. She'd thought of him way too often in the days since she'd forbidden herself contact with him.

How long had he been standing there? Surely he hadn't heard her debating out loud with Coco the merits of red as opposed to pink claw polish?

The little doggy diva loved to be spoken to, uttered soft, throaty noises in reply. Serena knew Coco was just responding to the attention she craved in her needy, poodle way. But Serena found it fun to pretend they were having a genuine conversation.

She suspected Nick Whalen would think it eccentric at the very least.

She cleared her throat. Channeled cool, detached professional. Someone totally unaffected by the six-foot-three hunk who towered over her. "Nick. Hi. Is everything okay with Bessie?"

"Yes, perfectly okay," he replied. If testosterone had a sound, it would surely be his voice.

"You sound surprised," she said, carefully putting down the claw polish when she realized her hand was trembling. Damn! Her brain and her libido seemed to be at war when it came to this guy. She slid her hands into Coco's fur, and scratched her behind the ears, much to the poodle's butt-wiggling delight.

"Surprised? Maybe. To be honest I didn't think a dog would like being left all day with a load of strangers."

"That she'd prefer being locked in a yard by herself? Remember, dogs are pack animals. It's natural for them to enjoy the company of other dogs. And people, too. We're part of their pack world."

"So it seems. Kylie fixed me up with the password for the doggy day cam, too, so I can check on Bessie during the day if I need to."

"Glad to hear Kylie is looking after you."

Like she hadn't heard every last detail of Nick's visits from Kylie. The new client had caused quite a stir among the all-female staff.

"The day cam is a great idea. When I log on, Bessie looks like she's really living it up. Is it possible to get a copy of the tape?"

She shook her head. "That would be an invasion of privacy of the other clients. Sorry."

He shrugged. "Just an idea."

"We have to be careful who we even give a password. The footage can be used as evidence in a canine custody battle."

Doubt creased his forehead. "How so?"

"Putting the dog in day care can be cited as a sign of neglect of care by the partner suing for custody."

His unsuccessful attempt at masking his "I can't believe I'm hearing this" expression amused her more than it bugged her. He had a lot to learn about the canine subculture of San Francisco.

But she didn't feel inclined to be his tutor.

Now, if he wants tutoring on how to please her, she would be delighted to oblige.

Ohmigod, where did that thought come from? And the tremor

of anticipated pleasure that shivered through her? She gripped the fur on Coco's neck so hard the little dog yipped.

She had spent the last three days trying to tamp down the temptation to fantasize about her sexy new client. Which was just the kind of disruption she'd been trying to avoid.

She'd done daily battle with herself to stay away from the check-in desk when she knew he was due to drop off or pick up Bessie. And now she had to admit to herself that she was losing the battle. She was so glad he had hunted her down she just wanted to sit and feast her eyes on his face.

"How's Freya doing?" he asked with what sounded like real interest.

"She's comfortable and happy. She watched *Lady and the Tramp* today."

Serena saw he struggled with himself not to make a smart remark about the movie. "That's, uh . . . nice," he said. "What about her owner?"

She welcomed the chance to talk to someone about what had happened with Joe Godfrey. She had not told anyone else at the center about the new arrangement with Freya's owners. Her staff would just tell her she was too much of a soft touch. She lowered her voice. Couldn't help but notice when Nick lowered his head to hear her.

She took a quick, deep breath at his closeness. He smelled of leather and sandalwood and—was that pepper? Whatever it was, he smelled good. "You know, it's awkward with Joe and me now? I guess he feels bad about not being able to pay, even though I've reassured him that I just want Freya to be okay."

"That's to be expected. Accepting charity would sit heavily on a guy like that."

"I guess. It makes me kinda glad that the other client just took her dog away without any notice."

"The *other* client? You lost another dog?"

"Yes. The Cavalier King Charles spaniel. That was a surprise. And not of the nice kind . . . He stayed here two days a week. Nice little dog." She'd been stunned when the owners, the Landers, had given notice. But she could not have afforded to offer free day care to him, too. Not on top of Freya and Mack.

"What reason did they give?"

"'Financial difficulties,' according to him. But she said there had been some kind of fraud. Weird, isn't it? You hear about these scam-type things but you don't think it will happen to people you know. Or affect your business."

She pulled a downward twist to her mouth. That made two dogs down; she couldn't face the thought of what would happen if she lost any more clients.

"Yeah," he said, without further comment, and the lack of expression on his face made her feel she was boring him.

"So, how can I help you?" she said, wishing she hadn't confided in him. She knew she shouldn't care what he thought of her, but it smarted that he might think she was dull. "Want to book Bessie in for a pawdicure like Coco's?"

"Paw . . . pawdicure?" His gaze turned to the equipment on the countertop. Beside her was an electric claw filing tool, some clippers, cotton wool, and styptic powder in case of a too-close clip. There was also a caddy holding ten different new-season shades of polish. "That's what you're doing?"

It really was very difficult not to be amused by his daze of disbelief. But dammit, he was a dog owner. A person who owned a pocketbook pooch like Bessie should surely be more aware of these basic tenets of doggy fashion.

She nodded. "Not as frivolous as you so obviously think."

"Did I say it was frivolous? I know some dogs need their claws clipped regularly."

"And some need them polished," she said. She held up Coco's right paw. The little black claws were painted a glossy red. "The red looks very fetching against her dark fur, don't you think?"

Nick made a strangled kind of sound that made Serena suppress a smile.

"So you prefer pink? I like pink, too. But Coco—"

"Why the hell would you put nail polish on a dog?" he growled.

"Claw polish," she corrected him, aware she was provoking him.

But he didn't bite again. Rather, he rolled his eyes to the ceiling in an exaggerated way. That only encouraged her to embellish her story, to see how much doggy nonsense he would take.

"Some dog moms like claw polish on their babies for special occasions. And Coco is going to a family reunion on the weekend. Coco used to be a show dog, and Maddy wants her to look her best." She paused, waiting for his reaction.

"Family reunion? You mean people?" He put up his hand in a halt sign. "Don't tell me you mean dogs?"

"Of course. What else?"

"What else indeed," he said with a hint both of a groan and the grin that tempered the harsh angles of his face in a way she found so devastating.

"Coco and Brutus—"

"Brutus is the millionaire mutt, right?"

She nodded.

"And this poodle's 'husband'?" He made quote marks in the air with his fingers.

She nodded again. "They had five puppies. Maddy and Tom kept Tinkerbelle, but Maddy found it very hard to let Coco's other babies go. In the end Tom laid down the law and found homes for them himself. Three of the partners in his law firm adopted a puppy each and his mom adopted the last one. Every so often they all get together with their dogs in Golden Gate Park."

"So they can all sniff each other's butts?"

"You mean, of course, the dogs?"

"Hold that thought. It's not an image I care to take away with me."

"The *humans* have a civilized picnic. The dogs run around and—"

He put up his hand in the halt sign again. "We all know what dogs do."

"Tom doesn't think it's a great idea, either."

"Tom sounds like my kind of guy."

For an insane split second of a split second, Serena thought of inviting Nick along to the descendants-of-Brutus picnic on Sunday. But he was a client. And hadn't she resolved to keep him just that? Then there was still that niggling sense that he wasn't all he said he was and that he could do damage to Paws-A-While.

Coco started wriggling and she knew the little dog had just about reached her keep-still limit. "Can you help me with the other paw, please?" she said to Nick, as she slid off her stool.

"With the . . . the pawdicure?"

"You interrupted me. I have to catch up on my time."

"You're seriously asking me to help you? I can't guarantee my skills with, uh, claw polish."

"Just keep Coco still while I paint the rest of her claws."

"Okay," he said in that sexy, gravelly voice. "But on one condition."

"Condition?"

"Don't ever tell anyone outside this place that I did it. Because I will deny it with every breath in my body."

"Deal," she said, her lips twitching.

But, as soon as she thought through the logistics of it, Serena realized that asking Nick to help her finish the pawdicure was a bad, bad idea.

The treatment cubicle was designed for one dog and one groomer. At a pinch one dog and two female groomers. Not one dog, one taller-than-average female and one tall, powerfully built male whose body mass dominated the space and whose proximity sent her heart into a series of hiccups.

If she had Kylie helping her, she wouldn't care if their shoulders collided. Or their hands accidentally grazed while they were handling the dog. And she certainly would not have felt self-conscious if their faces moved kissing-distance close.

"You hold her left leg still while I take her paw," she said, only too aware of the tremor in her voice. "I don't want to get polish on her fur."

It was a routine job yet her fingers felt clumsy as she pressed gently down on Coco's little black toe so the filed claw extended far enough for her to paint with the red polish. She did one claw, then the next, rushing through the job with little of her usual finesse. No double coats of polish today. She was too conscious of Nick's nearness. Half giddy from holding her breath every time she felt they were going to inadvertently touch.

"Done," she said, after what seemed an age but could only have been minutes. She looked up as she spoke and just for a microsecond caught his gaze unguarded. In the instant before the shutters went down she swore she saw mirrored the same intense awareness she fought to mask from hers.

So he feels it, too.

Immediately she dropped her eyes, too confused to make sense of it. If he felt it, too, that made all the difference. Her heart hammered against her rib cage. Serena risked a peek back up, but his eyes were the same inscrutable pale blue. She must have imagined it. She didn't know whether to be disappointed or relieved.

"Thank God that's over," he said, releasing his grip on Coco's leg. She had to clear her throat before she could speak. "Not quite."

"How can you bear the smell of that stuff?"

"The nail polish? It's a girl thing. And a girl-dog thing, too, of course."

Her twice-weekly mani-pedi was one of the few things she missed about her old life. She'd been proud of her long, elegantly manicured nails, even when she was that awkward teenager. Now they were filed short and unpolished. Dealing with dogs every day dictated that. She hoped Nick didn't notice. But was he the kind of guy to care if he did?

Willing both her breathing and her hands to stay steady, she reached into a drawer and pulled out a length of red satin ribbon patterned with tiny white bones. Deftly, she tied it in a bow on the puff of fur on top of Coco's head. "There. All done," she said.

"What do you think?" she asked Nick, as she admired the little poodle.

"Charming," he said in a deadpan voice that left her in no doubt as to his real opinion.

She called over to Heather, one of the groomers, and handed Coco over to her.

"Now for Bessie," she said to Nick.

"Whoa," he said. "No colored claws. No way."

"Chill," she said. "You're out of luck. I've given enough freebies for this week."

She pulled out another ribbon, a cheerful yellow one this time, and dangled it in front of him. "But I'll give you this for a bargain price."

Nick Whalen and the ribbon thing still bothered her.

"I noticed Bessie wasn't wearing her bow yesterday," she said. "This color would be pretty with her fur. Want to tie it on her now?"

Nick shook his head. "I'll pass."

"You're sure, now? Bessie doesn't seem Bessie without that cute bow on her forelock."

"I like her better without it. Dogs look dumb with ribbons in their fur."

"I think they look cute."

And he looked cute with that scowl. Although maybe "cute" was not a term that could reasonably be applied to Nick Whalen.

"No claw polish. No tizzy collars. No bows."

"So," she said, her head tilted to one side, "you're not the one who tied that bow she was wearing her first day here?"

He shifted from foot to foot. "Correct. It was tied by a friend who . . . who thought it was the right look for day care."

A friend.

No wife. No girlfriend. But a *friend*.

She tensed. Maybe she'd read this all wrong.

"An old lady friend," he added. Serena was surprised at the rush of relief that flooded her.

"As you know, we have no dress code here for the dogs," she said, forcing her voice to a cool, even tone. "But anytime you change your mind about that bow, feel free to tell me and I'll tie one on her for you." She put the ribbon back into the drawer. "All part of the service."

He made a noncommittal noise that sounded like he was swallowing a very rude expression.

She turned back to face him. "But you didn't come in to talk about claw polish and fur ribbons, did you?"

Suddenly he looked serious. "No, I did not," he said.

Nick chose his first words carefully. "I came to you to talk about Mack."

Serena's brow furrowed. He'd obviously hit her from left field. Good. If he put her off guard, that was all to the better. "Mack?"

"I want to pay for his knee surgery."

The words were out of his mouth before they'd properly formed in his brain. They surprised him as much as they obviously surprised her. But, as soon as he'd uttered them, he realized it made sense. Truth be told, the thought had been percolating since he'd first encountered the big dog.

It could be a very effective way to ensure time with Serena. Time where she might be off her guard.

"Wow," she said. "Why would you want to do that?"

He shrugged. "I told you, I had the same injury. I know how it feels."

"You can't be serious?"

"I mean it."

"That surgery costs a *lot* of money."

"I know. I've inquired about it."

He'd looked up the surgery—a procedure called canine anterior cruciate ligament repair—on the Internet, fascinated that a dog could have the same kind of surgery that he'd had. And, by the look of it, get the same good result. He would view the expense as an investment in his business. It would be worth every cent if it took him closer to cracking this case. And at the same time he would be doing a good deed for a fellow sufferer.

"So why would you do that?" she asked, eyes narrowed.

"Why do you keep Freya here for free?"

She shook her head. "You don't know me. You don't know Mack. It's not the same thing."

"Sure it is. Look, Serena," he said, fighting the urge to cross his fingers behind his back, "there's no ulterior motive here. I just want to help the poor animal. I like Mack. There's something . . . something special about him."

Her face softened in that way it did for a dog. "He is special. You know I'd pay for the surgery myself if I could. But why would Mack be thousands-of-dollars kind of special to you?"

She was suspicious. Of course she was. Damn. Again he'd gone in too hard, too fast. His offer seemed over-the-top. Outrageously generous and therefore unbelievable. Still, it was a good offer and she cared about that dog.

He shrugged. "Better get me to write a check before I ask myself that question and change my mind."

"There's a point," she said.

"Sooner would be better than later for Mack, wouldn't it?"

"Of course it would be. And I know I should tie you down and get that check from you before I let you leave the building. But things have been kinda weird here these last days, what with the Godfreys and the spaniel people. And . . . and I don't know if this is something else weird coming at me from out of the blue."

He would have to backpedal. Soft pedal even. He had to convince her this was a genuine opportunity to get Mack the treatment he needed.

"Remember I told you about my dog Fella?"

She nodded.

"When I was a teenager I was crazy into sports. I spent half my life training. Hours and hours running in the pine forests near where we lived. Fella always ran with me. Always kept up. Never let me down. When I look at Mack I . . . well, I see something of Fella in him." No need to cross his fingers now. That was 100 percent the truth.

"I see," she said, her eyes warming.

Dogs. That's the surefire way to get to Serena.

He continued. "I imagine how Fella would have felt if he had the same injury as Mack. Not able to run. Not able to keep up." He paused. "I . . . I feel like by helping Mack, I'm somehow repaying a debt to Fella." He paused again. Purposefully put a break in his voice. "I know that sounds kinda dumb, but—"

"Not dumb. I understand completely. That's a wonderful story. You must have loved Fella very much."

Would a sniff be pushing it too far? He decided it was. "I . . . I did," he said, killing the sniff but opting for a mournful semi-whisper.

"That makes me look at your kind offer in quite a different light." She hesitated. "But I'm still not sure—"

"There would be no strings attached, if that's what you mean."

"No strings? You're sure about that?" She took a deep breath, and Nick appreciated the resulting swell of her breasts, the hint of cleavage offered by her open-neck shirt with two top buttons left undone.

She lifted a hand toward him and, for a moment, he thought she might touch him. He tensed. But she obviously thought better of it and dropped her hand to her side again. "That whole chocolate bath thing, it . . . Well, it left me with trust issues."

The shadows were there again, behind her eyes, giving her that troubled look that made him want to come out fighting in her corner. Trouble was, if his suspicions were correct, she might not be beyond taking a dive.

"Trust issues?"

"People often weren't what they seemed. They said one thing and meant the other. Their motives were . . ." She looked up at him and he could see the struggle she was having. "But this isn't about me and my trust issues, is it? It's about Mack."

"Yeah," he said, ignoring a twitch of guilt.

"And I'd be crazy to question your truly generous gesture." This time she did put her hand on his arm. Just long enough to seal the deal. He could feel her warmth, even through the fabric of both jacket and shirt.

She looked up at his face. And that luminous, wonderful light of her smile was now aimed at him. "If you really mean it, of course I say yes. Thank you. Everyone here will be thrilled for Mack."

Relief his ploy had worked struggled with pleasure that he had brought that look to her face. Okay, he didn't deserve it. Not when he was deceiving her just like those nameless others—surely men, maybe even the stalker—who had earned her distrust. But his strategy was for the greater good. To bring down the kind of criminals who hurt innocent people like the two doctors whose work with troubled kids was now in jeopardy.

"Great. Operating room here we come," he said. "Do you have a report about Mack's injury from your vet?"

She gestured toward her office. "It's on my computer if you'd like to see it."

He made a show of looking at his watch. "I've got time right now."

"Sure," she said. "Take as long as you need. I'll set you up on the computer and you can read through it. Anything to help Mack. I can't wait to see that big boy running around again."

Gaining access to the computer was that easy.

"Did I say thank you?" Her face was flushed and her eyes glowed.

"You said 'thank you.'"

"Well, I'm saying it again. And Mack would, too, if he could talk. Where do we go from here?"

"We have to discuss the logistics of this. Meet with the vet. Book the surgery. See about rehab."

"Of course."

"How about tomorrow?"

She frowned. "Tomorrow is Saturday."

"That works for me."

"Oh. I didn't think . . ." Struggle was visible on her face. "Okay. You're right. I can do tomorrow."

"What do you suggest? Should we meet here?"

"Here? No. I'm not working this weekend. You could . . . I guess you could come to my place."

She was offering him an opportunity to check out her home?

Better and better. Again he felt that twinge of guilt but shoved it aside. "Great. Your place it is."

"Mack will be there. And Snowball, too, of course. Oh, and Thelma."

"Thelma?"

"My cat. She walked in to Paws-A-While one day and stayed. You know what they say—a cat chooses you, not the other way around."

She must have a big house to accommodate all those animals. Mack alone would need a room the size of a ballpark. How did she afford that?

"So where do you live?"

She pointed to the ceiling. "The apartment above. The entry is next door, the white gate."

Not a mansion but a walk-up apartment? "Okay. Shall we say around eleven?"

"Sure," she said, looking bemused. He'd snowed her; that was for sure. Good. More than anything, he hated to hang around and wait for things to happen.

He headed for the Paws-A-While computer, barely able to contain his impatience. At last he felt he was getting somewhere in this investigation. The Mack knee surgery was an excellent excuse for spending ongoing time with Serena. It was a clever move, even if he did say so himself. A win-win situation. Even for the dog.

"Thank you," he said after she had signed him in to the computer (with a password that was pitifully easy to note and remember). He watched her leave the office, pausing for a beat too long to admire the way her hips swayed as she walked. That uniform titillated as much as it concealed. Did she know that? Should he tell her?

Stay detached. Remain focused. Maintain suspicion.

Again he repeated the words inside his head as he forced his gaze to the screen. But they were not loud enough or strong enough to drown out the insistent thought that an eleven o'clock meeting could so easily segue into lunch with Serena.

Just him and her. Without so much as a pint-sized puppy to come between them.

· Six ·

"So what are your plans for lunch with Nick Whalen?" Maddy Cartwright's green eyes gleamed with the unholy excitement of the married woman who glommed on to any opportunity to rope her friend into the same state of coupled bliss.

Or so Serena saw it. She was beginning to wish she hadn't mentioned the ten-out-of-ten hottie to her red-haired best buddy.

"Lunch? He didn't say anything about lunch. This is a business meeting, Maddy. Nick has kindly offered to pay for Mack's surgery. We're meeting to discuss how we can get the ball rolling ASAP."

"He didn't mention lunch?"

"No, he did not."

Maddy sighed in exasperation. "Serena, a guy does not suggest an eleven o'clock meeting on Saturday morning with a beautiful woman like you, without there being a possibility of lunch."

"And I'm telling you that this is strictly business."

Serena tugged on Snowball's leash to bring him to a halt. They were twenty minutes into an early-morning walk beside the bay

at Marina Green, Serena's favorite park. The top of the Golden
Gate Bridge was still shrouded in fog, but the promise was for the
kind of brilliant, Indian-summer day that made fall by far the best
season in San Francisco. They'd just reached Snowball's favorite
tree. Marina Green was long on grass and short on trees so she
humored him and let him stop and sniff. Maddy did the same for
Brutus.

Maddy turned to Serena and gave a knowing smile. "Yeah.
Right. So this guy is shelling out all this money on a dog just out
of the kindness of his heart. No ulterior motive whatsoever."

"Yes to the first bit. He seems genuinely taken with Mack. I'm
so hoping it will lead him to adopting that beautiful big boy."

"And the second bit? The ulterior motive, I mean?"

"That's where things get a bit weird."

"Weird?" Maddy's eyes widened in alarm. "Serena—"

"Not that kind of weird. Not scary weird."

She knew that Maddy would always blame herself for the terrifying incident where Serena had been held in a choke hold by a
psycho claimant to the will that had bequeathed millions to
Brutus. Brutus's late owner, Walter Stoddard, had left his fortune in
trust to his dog. Walter's disgruntled nephew Jerome had tried to
murder Brutus, first with a poisoned T-bone steak, later with an
outsized bar of chocolate. Then he'd gotten more vicious and
Serena had been caught in the cross fire.

"Not Jerome-type weird or your stalker-type weird?" asked
Maddy.

"No. Not like that. Just . . . puzzling weird. Like, two long-
term clients bailing in as many days. And Nick comes along with
a dog that doesn't suit him at all. He is so not a Yorki-poo kind of
guy and it just isn't . . . right." She knew Maddy would know exactly what she meant without having to explain further about the
Yorki-poo thing. "And he seems like a cop even though he says
he isn't."

Maddy extricated herself from where Brutus had wrapped his leash around her ankles as he sniffed his way around the intriguing Saturday morning scents left by all the local dogs. This stretch of walkway that skirted the yacht harbor seemed to be a particularly popular place for them to leave their olfactory calling cards.

"Serena, I thought you'd gotten over that whole hang-up–about–cops thing. Because of that you didn't want to report Jerome and—"

With the hand that wasn't holding Snowball's leash, Serena waved away Maddy's comments. "I know. And I ended up a quivering wreck because of unresolved fear and anger and yada yada yada—all that stuff the therapist said. But watching Tom give Jerome an ass-kicking in court kinda helped with all that. Man, he brought that jerk down."

"Didn't he?" said Maddy, her lips curved in obvious remembered relish. "But then you didn't contact the police when your stalker started behaving so strangely—"

"You know why. I thought I could handle it myself. At first."

"And then that cop turned out to be such a sleaze. Sorry. I know you probably don't want to talk about all that. But, Serena, you've got to. Talk, talk, and talk 'til it's all gone out of your head." She patted Serena's arm. "You know I'm always there for you."

Maddy made the offer in all sincerity. But Serena knew that for Maddy, Tom now came first. And that was absolutely the way it should be. She would no sooner call Maddy just any old time to spill her problems as she once had than Mack would share his burger with Snowball. It felt like disloyalty to Tom, whom she loved to pieces, but she was secretly glad he was out of town so she could enjoy this rare catch-up time with his wife.

"Thanks, Maddy," she said. Then, to change the subject, she pointed at Snowball and Brutus madly sniffing around the base of a well-watered signpost. "Hey, look at the dogs—they're checking their pee mail."

It took a moment for Maddy to get it but, when she did, she broke into peals of laughter that had a group of spandex-clad joggers pointedly giving the two girls a wide berth as they ran along the pathway.

But when Maddy got her breath back, and they were back to striding along the grass with the dogs, she came back for the attack. "That was very funny, but please don't think you're changing the subject so easily."

"So you noticed."

"I noticed."

"Tell me again about this Nick guy?"

"I told you. Big. Blond. Built."

"So where's the weird in that?"

"Weird isn't the right word. It's just that . . . Oh, I don't know. I can't put my finger on it. But I feel edgy around him, even when we're just discussing his dog's routine."

"Could 'edgy' have something to do with the fact he's hot and all you can think about is how you want to jump his bones?"

"Well, there's that, too."

Trust Maddy to put it into words. *That* was the really weird thing. That first day the door chime had scarcely finished sounding "Who Let the Dogs Out?" and she'd been overwhelmed by instant lust. It was a feeling she didn't trust.

"And he knows he's in the presence of Serena St. James. Chocolate-coated goddess and fantasy figure to America's larger population of red-blooded males. That's enough to make *him* edgy."

"Add that, too. I guess. Though I'd rather you said 'former' goddess. You know I so want to put all that behind me." She could still hear Dave thundering at her about how he couldn't hold his head up in front of his crew when he knew they'd been Googling, then ogling, his girlfriend.

"Shame. You looked so amazing in that tub. And it was all my idea. I was so proud every time I saw the billboards. You know the chocolate people would have you back in a flash for a new campaign."

"And what would they do to top the first one? No. I'm done with it. And all that came with it. As you know, Joel the photographer got the lion's share of the money for the calendar. The job gave me enough to set up the business and support myself for a year and I'm grateful for it. But that's as far as it goes. Paws-A-While is where I want to be now. It's everything I want."

"Everything?"

"Yes. Working with dogs is a dream come true. Fact is, most other jobs involve sick or injured dogs or dogs that have been abandoned or treated badly."

"Like at a shelter or a vet clinic?"

Serena nodded. "But dogs who come to Paws-A-While are loved dogs whose owners care and can afford to spend an outrageous number of dollars for me to look after them. They're happy, healthy animals, and it's a joy to work with them."

"But dogs can't replace people, Serena—"

She'd heard this before from Maddy. "I know, I know. I enjoy working with my staff, too."

"All female. You can't cut yourself off from men forever."

"That's not the intention," said Serena, unable to stop a note of defensiveness from making her voice rise. Her decision to take a sabbatical from sex was not something she had actually discussed with her friend.

Maddy being Maddy had guessed it.

"So what is there to stop you from having lunch with Mr. Blond Hunk?" said Maddy.

"Uh, the slight fact that he didn't suggest it."

"And the chocolate goddess couldn't steer the conversation that way? For heaven's sake, Serena, you've been on the dating outfield for too long. That bastard Dave really did a number on you, didn't he?"

It was a rhetorical question. Serena knew Maddy did not expect an answer. True, it was difficult to forget some of the things Dave (who Maddy now always referred to as "that bastard Dave") had said to her. Things so personal and wounding she'd shared them with no one. And it was true she'd resolved never again to date a guy who wore a uniform. Or acted like he was the take-command type who should be in uniform.

But Dave was long gone. She'd lost the battle to keep Nick Whalen out of her thoughts and fantasies. And did she want to end up some eccentric old woman who doted on her doggies and had no other life?

"I guess I could suggest lunch," she said. Lunch meant nothing. Not a date. Just a more comfortable meeting.

Maddy beamed. "That's the Serena I know and love. Welcome back."

"After all, it's a great thing Nick's doing for Mack."

"That it is," said Maddy with little murmurs of encouragement.

"I could book that little Italian place on Chestnut."

"Sounds good."

"Or there's the . . ."

"Yes?" Maddy prompted.

"I just remembered Mack. We can't take him out to lunch with us. And that's what this meeting is all about. Mack and his knee."

Maddy had suggested that Brutus loan Mack the money for the surgery, but Brutus had already invested so much in Paws-A-While. While Serena was grateful to Maddy, she didn't want to risk her friendship by clocking up too much debt. But she had started thinking it might be her only option not long before Nick had made his offer.

Maddy rolled her eyes. "If it were anyone else but you, I'd suggest you cook the guy lunch."

Serena swallowed hard against even the thought of such a potential disaster. "You know that's your department—and I'm happy to leave it that way."

"Let me guess at the likely state of your fridge." Maddy closed her eyes. "It's empty but for a few frozen diet entrées, a stack of diet sodas, eggs for you to make those eternal egg-white omelets, blueberries, and maybe a bag of salad greens all withered around the edges and going kinda slimy."

Serena cringed and laughed at the same time. "You know me too well. But you've missed a few things. I'm not modeling now, remember. My days of starving are behind me. No more egg-white omelets. Ever."

"So?"

"So there's fruit. Then frozen pizzas, some leftover Chinese takeout, and a stash of Lindt truffles that I like to nibble with the chocolate coating nice and cold . . ."

Serena thought her friend would catapult backward from horror. The food editor of *Annie* magazine was a superlative cook. Even a Maddy-made sandwich was a gourmet treat.

Maddy glanced at her watch. "We've got time if I'm quick."

"Time for what?" Serena could not keep the alarm from her voice.

"To cut short the doggies' walk and whip around the supermarket to get the fixings for lunch."

Serena put her hand up in a halt sign. "Whoa! Let's not get too excited here. The idea is to thank the guy for looking after Mack. Not to scare him away."

"Don't think for one moment that I'd let you loose in the kitchen for this date with—"

"It's not a date."

"Whatever. No, I'll fix lunch and leave it with you. Then, if the conversation goes that way—voila."

"A Maddy-made lunch. Lucky me. Lucky Nick."

"So what does Nick like to eat?"

Serena shrugged. "Don't have a clue." She knew the color of his eyes warmed a degree or two when he smiled. That he looked cute when he scowled. But not a lot else. "Whatever he likes, I'm guessing he eats lots of it."

"What's likely to be a big, hunky guy's favorite meal?" Maddy thought out loud. "Steak? Pasta? Pie? Maybe I could make pot pies." She thought some more. "No. Take too long. Stir-fry? Too fiddly for you." She paused. "I've got it. Lasagna. I've yet to meet a guy who doesn't like lasagna."

"I've yet to meet *anyone* who doesn't like lasagna. But isn't that kind of difficult to make?"

"Can be. But not the lasagna I've got in mind. No-boil lasagna sheets. Italian sausage. Canned tomato pasta sauce. Eggplant. Ricotta. Mozzarella. Fresh herbs. Easy."

Serena gulped. "Sounds easy to you. Intimidating to me. Are you sure?"

"Absolutely. All you have to do is help me shop."

"Now I'm with you. Shopping is something I'm expert at."

· Seven ·

Nick stood outside the Paws-A-While shop front on Filbert Street. The building was old—Edwardian, he guessed. Around a hundred years ago it must have been purely residential. At a later time, the first floor at street level had been converted to a business premise. This was prime San Francisco real estate with a staggering monthly rental.

There was no doubt it was a classy operation. The building was painted a pale gray, the woodwork picked out in white. The Paws-A-While name and logo was printed in red on an elegant gray-and-white striped awning. Stenciled white silhouettes of dogs ran across the plate-glass windows. A tub of brightly colored flowers sat by the door. Next to that was a wall-mounted stone drinking bowl, adorned with carvings of paw prints and bones and the words "Dog Bar" in a fancy type.

Nick could see through the windows to the empty reception area. Only the grooming side of the business operated on weekends and everyone must be out back. He itched for an opportunity to get in there one day and check out that webcam footage.

He looked up to the next storey, where two bow windows jutted out—the apartment where Serena lived. To the left of the shop front was an arched doorway, with any possible access covered by a white, elaborately wrought security grille and door. He pressed the button for Serena to buzz him through to upstairs.

Walking from where he'd parked his truck, he'd passed a flower shop. He'd had to fight the urge to buy Serena some roses. Not a good move for a private investigator hunting down his prime suspect. Instead, he clutched a folder of information about cruciate ligament surgery for dogs. Plus printouts of the vet reports on Mack that he'd emailed to himself from Serena's computer at Paws-A-While.

That computer had given him cause to think. He had way higher than the average IT skills. Still, it had been ridiculously easy to access all the information on both the Paws-A-While staff and the clients—accounts, payroll, everything. That meant anyone there who could crack Serena's lower-than-low-security-level password had the same access. It meant one of two things: she kept any dealings of a dubious nature elsewhere, or she had nothing to hide and trusted her staff.

He heard the sound of footsteps running down some stairs. He quickly disguised his shock and also, he hoped, his disappointment when the door was opened not by Serena but by a fresh-faced red-head wearing running gear. On a leash by her side was Brutus, the squat little mutt with the pugnacious face. He knew immediately who the girl must be.

She thrust her free hand at him. "I'm Maddy, Serena's friend. You must be Nick."

Her smile was friendly, her manner polite, but as he shook her hand, Nick got the distinct impression that he was being inspected with as much scrutiny as one of his brother's prizewinning bulls at the state fair. Brutus joined in, sniffing and snuffling around his feet. Not, Nick hoped, drooling.

"It's a good thing that you're doing for Mack," Maddy said. "You won't regret adopting him. He's a darling animal. A man-sized dog, my husband calls him. Giant size, I say."

"He's big, all right, and I hope to get his knee fixed as good as new." Where did she get the idea he was planning to adopt Mack?

The cute redhead nodded. She held the door for him and he kept it open with his free hand. "Mack's up there waiting for you. Serena, too. Nice to meet you, but I can't stay. I'm cooking for a family reunion and everyone has got different tastes."

Did she mean the people or the dogs?

"Nice to meet you, too," he said.

She took a few brisk steps away and then turned back. He was surprised at the determined set of her face. It was as if she had been saving up something to say and only now felt able to spill it. "Serena is the most gorgeous woman I know," she said.

"Agreed," he said.

"But not just in looks. She's good and sweet and . . . and she may not seem it, but she's vulnerable." Her pale redhead's skin flushed.

"I see that," said Nick. And he did.

But as generous and funny and kind that Serena might be, she might also be a crook. She didn't appear to have the computer of a crook but this early in his investigation he could not dismiss for even a second the fact that she still remained his prime suspect.

"Do you? See the woman behind the chocolate goddess? Too many people . . . men, I mean, they . . . they don't see beyond those spectacular looks."

He had to be careful what he said here. Maddy was Serena's best friend and he'd be crazy to get on the wrong side of her. However, he also had to squash any implication that he was involved with Serena. That could look very bad in any resultant prosecution. "I'm just one of her clients. I never saw her in those chocolate ads. I wasn't in the country at the time. But I do see what a nice woman Serena is. That's why I'm helping her out with Mack."

"Of course." Her flush deepened. "Forget I ever said anything."

Wrong move. He'd offended her and he didn't want that. "Hey," he said. "I see how lovely she is—and not just in the way she looks. I get what you're saying."

She smiled. "I'm glad to hear that. But for heaven's sake, don't tell Serena we talked or I'm toast!"

She waved as she walked briskly away, Brutus trotting at her heels.

Bemused, Nick turned back to the door. How would he write that encounter up in his notes? Not that it meant anything— criminals had friends, too—but Serena certainly inspired loyalty. From a personal point of view he liked Maddy Cartwright. From a professional one, it was useful to have met her. She and her husband might come under his investigation, too.

In the meantime, now was his chance to check out his prime suspect at her home.

He took the stairs two at a time to find the door to Serena's apartment closed. He knocked. His knock was answered by a shrill trill of yipping—Snowball—and a deep, baritone woof that could only come from Mack.

Then Serena answered the door.

Every word of what he'd planned to say flew out of his head, leaving him gawking like a dumbstruck sixteen-year-old.

Her hair was only pulled halfway off her face with the rest waving softly around her shoulders. She wore jeans and a plain dark blue T-shirt. Not baggy Paws-A-While jeans but normal jeans. Though how he could think jeans could be described as normal when they hugged such shapely curves and long, long legs. The T-shirt could only be called modest. High neck. Long sleeves pushed up to the elbows. But how could a T-shirt be modest when it drew a man's eyes to a body that was so sensational it had put her on billboards all round the country?

She was the most beautiful woman he had ever seen. Anywhere. Movie screens included.

"You found us," she said, in that lovely, mellow voice.

Yes. I found you. And I can't have you.

"Your friend let me in," he said, his voice hoarse, willing himself not to think of chocolate-coated anything.

She looked around him and down to the floor. "No Bessie?"

"She's staying with a friend."

"The same one who ties her bow?"

"Yes." His aunt ran a small art gallery in Sausalito. Her business partner Hannah doted on Bessie and had taken her for the day.

"Shame. Snowball would like to see her, I'm sure."

He followed Serena into her living room. Snowball rushed at him and pranced around his feet.

Mack lay on a big, squashy dog bed near the fireplace. He thumped his tail in greeting. "Hey, fella," said Nick and the enormous dog thumped his tail again. Nick put down his folder and hunkered down next to him. He offered him his hand to sniff. Then, when Mack gave him the go-ahead, scratched him behind the ears. Again he was struck by the look of resigned suffering in Mack's eyes.

All these years since he'd lost Fella and he hadn't realized how much he'd missed having a dog. *He who travels fastest travels alone.* But maybe a dog like this would move fast enough to keep up. Once his knee was fixed, that was.

"You can see why I can't keep Mack, much as I'd love to," said Serena, indicating the room with a wave of her hand.

Indeed Mack took up a good proportion of the floor space. The high old ceilings gave the room a deceptively spacious look. It looked both comfortable and elegant, the walls a warm neutral, the furnishings simple. Polished wooden floors. White shutters at the windows. At each side of the fireplace was a bookcase, every shelf crammed with books, right up to the ceiling. More books lay on the coffee table. The art on the walls was eclectic, a moody abstract hung next to a traditional landscape of a lake. Propped against the corner behind the sofa, a guitar case and a music stand made a pleasing composition. So she played guitar. He wondered if she sang.

"Nice place," he said.

"It is, isn't it? Though you might not say that when you see the kitchen and bathroom. They desperately need remodeling. But it's a bit of a tight fit for this big boy, isn't it?" Mack knew immediately she was talking about him. Nick swore his eyes lit up, and his tail wagged way more vigorously than it had for him. "But with Nick's help, we'll soon have you up and running about," she said to the dog, fondling his ears.

Then she looked up at Nick. "Thanks to you," she said. Then she smiled.

By helping Mack, he had earned that special luminous smile reserved, he realized, for dogs and for people she thought loved dogs as much as she did. He might as well bask in it now because when she found out the truth about what he was doing in her life, he would not be warmed by it again.

He pointed to his folder where he'd placed it on the coffee table. "I've brought all the notes on the surgery and the X-rays you gave me. Let's see if we can talk to the vet and the surgeon and get him done as soon as we can."

The wall between the two bow-fronted rooms had been knocked through. In the next room a table was set for a meal. Nick was aware of a delicious aroma wafting through from where the kitchen must be. His mouth watered. This morning he'd run, cycled, and put in a session pumping free weights. Breakfast seemed a long time ago. Was she expecting a visitor for lunch? Damn, there went his plans for suggesting a meal together somewhere without the dogs.

But that was probably just as well.

Stay detached. Remain focused. Maintain suspicion.

He nodded his head over to the table. "Are you expecting someone? If so, we had better get straight to business."

"There's no one else coming. I . . . I thought you might like to join me for lunch." Color flamed high on her cheekbones and she didn't quite meet his gaze.

He caught his breath on a sharp intake of air. For the first time, Nick got an inkling that the attraction he felt for Serena might not run one way.

The knowledge flooded him with conflicting emotions. First, a fierce, exultant triumph that was quickly overtaken by the sobering realization that this would only make his job a hundred times more difficult.

He should pass on that invitation to lunch. Maybe even consider handing this case to Adam, asking his partner to take over. He was at risk of getting in way too deep here. Because he could no longer deny to himself that it wasn't just Mack he was beginning to feel a tug toward.

He took a deep breath. Filled his lungs with the scent of that rich, delicious aroma wafting from the kitchen, then, closer, a tantalizing hint of vanilla and warm, tousled-haired woman.

"Lunch would be great," he said.

· Eight ·

Nick grit his teeth. *Damn.* Whatever had possessed him to agree to Serena's invitation? By saying yes to lunch with a suspect in her own home he risked compromising his professionalism. A public restaurant he could get away with. An intimate table set for two behind closed doors was a different matter altogether.

He could not let her get the wrong idea.

However much he might wish this could be a date, he had to force himself to stay professional. He schooled his face to show polite interest. Nothing more.

"Whatever's cooking smells good," he said with an appreciative sniff.

He'd been cooking for himself ever since he'd been house-sitting for Aunt Alice and was getting tired of his own repertoire. No wonder this aroma had enticed him into a wrong decision. It was almost as enticing as the sight of Serena in tight-fitting jeans.

Almost.

"It's lasagna," she said. "Homemade. But I didn't—"

"Homemade lasagna." He closed his eyes to better savor the aroma. If he wasn't careful, he'd be slavering. He opened his eyes to meet hers, was surprised to realize she was on edge about whether or not he would like her choice of meal. "Bring it on. And don't hold back on the cheese."

Her shoulders sagged in relief, a reaction he found unexpectedly endearing. "Thank heaven. I wondered if you would like lasagna . . ."

"Who doesn't like lasagna?"

"That's what I said to . . . uh, I mean, absolutely." She flushed. "As soon as we've sorted out the stuff about Mack, we can eat."

Said to whom? Maddy Cartwright? Had she and her red-haired friend plotted the meal, discussed him in the girly way his sister and her friends sometimes did when a new guy was on the horizon? That was kind of cute. Not for the first time, he wished he had met Serena under different circumstances.

Because he could not be that guy.

"Sure," he said. "We can eat then."

Nick was a big man, and he had big appetites. His stomach gave a rumble in protest at having to postpone the lasagna promised by that tantalizing aroma. Mack, in the dog bed nearby, just happened to shift at the same moment. Serena immediately assumed he was the source of the embarrassing noise.

"Mack!" She glared at him, reprimand in her voice. Blissfully unaware, Mack thumped his tail, his tongue lolling in a doggy grin.

She frowned, and Nick realized it wasn't annoyance at the dog but rather anxiety that the dog was not on his best behavior. In front of a potential adoptive owner?

There was a note of ill-disguised pleading in her voice when she turned to Nick. "I'm sorry, he does have a few problems with, uh, flatulence. But the vet says that will get better once he can be more active again."

"The poor animal can't help it," said Nick, not feeling the

slightest bit guilty. "The sooner he gets that surgery, the better." He'd forgotten how useful it could be to blame dogs for all sorts of human misdemeanors.

"Amen to that," she said, again her relief visible. "In the meantime, let me get you a drink. Beer?"

"Coke's good for me," he said. He needed his senses on full alert.

He knew he only had minutes while she was out of the room to survey it for clues to her contacts and lifestyle. A lead, no matter how small. Names. Numbers. Anything. He had to make it quick and make it subtle. She'd caught him once before looking too interested in her possessions. If she caught him again, he'd blow the case for sure.

He rapidly scanned the multitude of framed photos that were propped on the mantelpiece. A posed studio portrait of Snowball. Maddy and Tom O'Brien on their wedding day with Serena standing next to Maddy. It was difficult not to stop and examine more closely how she looked in that figure-hugging bridesmaid dress.

Same, too, with the faded print of Serena at around ten years old, hugging tight a nondescript mutt, her eyes glowing. Next was a smiling older couple, their arms slung loosely around each other's shoulders, the man bald and spare, the woman tall and slender with a look of Serena but falling short of her beauty. Then Serena with Kylie and some of the other Paws-A-While staff around a restaurant table. Then Snowball as a puppy. Snowball wet and indignant in a bath. Snowball. Snowball. Snowball. Dog. Dog. Dog.

Quickly, he checked out the small telephone table. It was scattered with fliers and used envelopes with shopping items scribbled all over them. On one was written "J & T—new" and an Oakland phone number that he memorized. Written underneath that was "Call Lydia Sat." Lydia, he knew, was the vet. She had referred

Mack to a surgeon who had not yet seen the dog. An appointment with the surgeon was one of the things he and Serena needed to sort out today.

On the coffee table was a newsprint magazine that on first glance he thought was from the *San Francisco Chronicle* but on second, astounded look proved to be a doggy newspaper entitled *Bay Woof: News with Bite for Bay Area Dog Lovers.* Next to it sat a well-thumbed paperback, *Dogs Never Lie About Love,* and a glossy picture book *Winery Dogs of Napa Valley.*

Nothing there.

He moved on to the bookshelves. Pulled out some titles. Looked for hidden files. By the time Serena came back into the room carrying a Coke for him and a Diet Coke for herself, he was nonchalantly perusing a row of books at eye level.

"There are a lot of titles here by Valerie St. James," he said. "And more by Leonard Oakley. Any connection?"

He'd discovered these names in his investigation of Serena Oakley—also known as Serena St. James—but wanted confirmation from her that they were connected.

She nodded. "Valerie is my mom and Leonard my dad."

"They're authors?"

She put the drinks down on the coffee table.

"Yes. Mom writes about organic gardening and sustainable living. Dad's books are on eco design. They were hippies way back in the seventies and never stopped believing. Much to their surprise, they're right back in fashion."

And selling well, too, he knew from his investigations.

"I recall you said you moved around a lot when you were a kid."

"Yep. All over the country. I remember more than one commune. For a while we even lived in Scotland."

"That must have been fun. An adventure." He thought of his

own existence in the valley. From preschool to high school, never farther than a yellow school bus ride away. He'd itched for the opportunity to see more.

"Not so much for me." She shrugged her elegant shoulders. "All that moving from place to place is kinda disruptive when you're at school. Not great for your grades, not great for your friendships."

"I guess," he said.

And if you're a certain kind of person, you learn to be a loner. To not get too attached to people. To develop the ability to put on a face—be what people want you to be. In short, to breed the kind of personality that could gravitate to fraud.

"You learn to be independent, that's for sure," she said.

That, too.

He fought the urge to crack his knuckles. He was finding it frustratingly difficult to pin her down and categorize her.

"Where are your parents now?" he asked.

"At this exact moment? In DC marching against capital punishment. Placards outside the White House and all."

He couldn't tell if she was embarrassed or proud. Maybe a bit of both.

"And home is?"

"Berkeley. A beautiful old Victorian I wish they'd had when I was a kid."

"Nice for you to have them close."

Serena laughed. "Yeah. But I am so glad I don't share the house with them. It would be such hard work. Their aim is to leave a negative carbon footprint. They live off the grid. Only eat what they grow themselves in their yard or what comes from within a one-hundred-mile radius of San Francisco. No car. No TV. And of course no dogs."

"Sounds admirable."

"And uncomfortable. But we're not here to talk about my parents."

"No," he said. Despite his initial misgivings, he had not been able to find anything subversive in her parents' activities. He picked up his folder. "Let's get things sorted for Mack."

At the sound of his name, Mack thumped his tail and looked up at Nick with those sad, dark eyes. Nick felt he did not have to be a doting doggy daddy to read his plea for human help.

Serena sat across her table from Nick as they ate lunch. Or rather, he ate with gusto; she played around with her salad with her fork. Maddy's lasagna had turned out superlatively well. The cheese bubbled golden on the top and the rich, spicy filling spilled out from the layers of pasta. But Serena was way too nervous to eat.

No matter how hard she tried to concentrate on sensible conversation about surgeon's fees, the possibility of Mack needing to wear a cast, time span of rehab, and so on, other thoughts kept intruding.

Of what it would be like to trace her finger along Nick's sexy mouth. Of what it might be like to kiss that mouth. Or to skip past the kissing stage to get to her and Nick in her bedroom hot and naked and— Her nipples pebbled at the thought.

She pulled her thoughts up short. This was insane.

When she'd answered the door to him she'd taken one look and had to hold on to the doorframe for support. Nick Whalen in a business suit was hot. Nick Whalen wearing well-worn denim jeans, a black T-shirt, and a black leather biker jacket was a step up from hot. Right up to a stratosphere where the air became so thin she felt breathless and her heart pounded so hard and so fast she swore she could feel it knocking against her ribs.

He pushed his plate away, empty now of his third helping. "You're an amazing cook," he said.

"Thank you, but I'm not really. I—"

"Don't be modest. That's the best lasagna I've had for a long time. Maybe ever."

"I'm not being modest. Truly. I didn't—"

"You used Italian sausage instead of ground beef?"

"Yes. Well, I didn't. It was—"

"And eggplant? I liked the way you did the eggplant."

He seemed determined to credit her for Maddy's wonderful, inventive cooking.

So why not let him?

The thought danced insistently around her conscience. What harm would it do to let Nick Whalen think she could cook?

"It was made with garlic and fresh oregano," she said.

That wasn't a lie. She didn't say *who* had cooked the eggplant.

"I like to cook," he said. "Though nothing as impressive as this."

Serena knew, in truth, she was the world's worst cook. Maddy had learned to cook from her grandma, then gone on to train as a professional chef. Fried tofu was about as creative as Serena's mom had ever gotten in the culinary skills department. Never in a million years could Serena make anything that came anywhere near this lasagna.

But Nick didn't need to know that.

"Thank you," she said, accepting the compliment for herself. Cloaking herself in the borrowed garb of cook. And being surprised at how good it felt.

She smiled and met his gaze from across the table. The glacial blue of his eyes had warmed a degree or two, the sharp angles of his face relaxed. He leaned back in his chair with the contented sigh of a well-fed man.

It pleased her.

And it surprised her that it pleased her.

She'd never seen the need to learn to cook. The years she'd been a model she'd had to put hunger on hold and forget about the delights of food. Staying thin hadn't come easily and she'd had to work at it. She'd gotten out of the habit of cooking much besides the basics, and that only when she couldn't avoid it. Living single in San Francisco didn't require expertise in the kitchen. She was surrounded by cafes and food markets where a good meal was merely a matter of the creative loading of a shopping cart.

But this was unexpectedly ... nice. Seeing the pleasure Nick got from the meal Maddy had whipped up in minutes. Enjoying the admiration it earned her. Wanting to impress him further. And all the time, pushing aside the guilt that she had not earned that admiration.

Maybe she would learn to cook if she had a guy like Nick in her life.

"What do you like to make?" she asked.

"The usual guy things. Steak. Ribs. Chili. But I'd like to try this lasagna. Can I have your recipe?"

This Rottweiler type of guy was asking her for a recipe? This could not be happening. Panic threatened to gag her. "Sorry. No recipe. It's ... uh, in my head."

That wasn't too tortuous a stretch of the truth. After all, she had watched Maddy do it. The lasagna hadn't actually seemed that difficult to put together.

"So you're an instinctual cook," he said.

"Uh, something like that." World's worst cook and world's worst liar. "I, uh, never use recipes." What if he asked to look at her cookbooks? How would she explain she didn't have any? Nuking Lean Cuisines was more her area of expertise.

"That's clever," he said. "I have to follow a recipe. And even then I can get it wrong."

Frantically she sought to divert the conversation away from her culinary skills. If he wanted to swap cooking disaster stories, she'd be right in there with the best of them. And exposed for the food fraud she was.

"Uh ... do you make homemade recipes for Bessie?"

He stared at her. "Recipes? For the dog? Hell no. She gets scraps, cans, and kibble."

"I just wondered. Plenty of dog parents . . . I, uh, mean dog—"

"Owners?" he prompted.

"I was going to say guardians," she replied. "That's the most acceptable term."

"Guardians. Right."

"They prefer to cook for their dogs. Maddy has a TV show on home cooking for dogs. And my other friend Jenna sells organic treats through Paws-A-While. They go as fast as I can stock them."

"Is that so?" he said. "I'll . . . uh . . . have to try some for Bessie."

She got the impression he was clamping down on some other, less polite comment about gourmet treats for dogs.

But then he turned to look at Mack. The big dog thumped his tail in recognition of the look and grinned his doggy grin. Nick seemed flattered by the recognition.

Both Mack and Snowball had made it clear they were very interested in the lasagna. She had trained them not to beg at the table, but from where they sat in the living room, she was aware of two pairs of eyes on full alert to the movement of food from plate to human mouth. The way her stomach was tied up in knots, they were guaranteed her share in their dog bowls later on. There was only a trace of garlic for flavor, not enough to make it dog-unfriendly.

"What about Mack?" said Nick. "What does he eat when he's not chowing down on junk?"

The hint of hope that had sparked when Nick offered to pay for Mack's surgery ignited and flamed. "Just regular dog food. You know, just like Bessie."

His laugh was more of a snort of disbelief.

"Okay," she conceded. "Maybe he does eat a little more than Bessie does."

Nick quirked an eyebrow in response.

"Maybe a lot more than Bessie," she added.

"My bet is a whole lot more than Bessie. Mack's a big guy."

"Yeah. Big guys do eat a lot." She looked pointedly at Nick's empty plate. Empty after three helpings of lasagna, that was. "I guess if a big guy was thinking of adopting a dog, he would probably understand that."

"Have you got a particular big guy in mind?"

He's sitting right across from me, she wanted to say. But she had to let him come around to the idea himself.

"You know I want him for myself but, costs aside, it just can't happen," she said. "He needs a yard and lots of exercise. Snowball's an apartment kind of dog. Mack could never be happy in such a small space."

She looked over to Mack, his head on his enormous paws, his brow wrinkled in perpetual worry, but his eyes ever watchful. She could never, ever surrender him to the shelter, though with his knee fixed he would stand a better chance of adoption.

She looked back to Nick. "I was hoping—"

"I was thinking—"

They spoke at the same time.

She flushed. "How could you bear to spend all that money on him and then see him go to someone else?"

"I don't have room for a dog."

"Room in your house or room in your life?"

He shrugged. "Both."

Odd. He already had a dog. "But you have Bessie."

"I . . . I meant a big dog."

"When his knee is fixed you can run with him like you told me you did with Fella. Bet you don't do that with Bessie."

That hit home. She could tell by the tightening of his jaw. The thought of him running through pine forests, those long, powerful legs striding out with tiny Bessie scampering alongside, yellow bow and all, made her want to laugh. The thought of Nick in running shorts, an athletic T-shirt molded to his muscles, gave her an altogether different reaction.

"Of course I don't run with Bessie," he growled. "And I told you, I like big dogs."

She shrugged. "Big dogs, small dogs, they're all amazing to me. The important thing with a big dog like Mack is discipline. You can't risk dominant behavior in an animal that size. People can be scared of them. He has to know you are the leader of his pack. The alpha male."

The alpha male.

Her heart kicked in to that disconcerting rapid beat again. Nick Whalen could not be anything other than an alpha male. A strong, powerful, take-command type of guy. The leader of the pack. The dominant animal.

Just, in fact, the type of man she had learned to avoid.

Her brain kept jumping up and down to remind her of that. But her hormones had an altogether different take on the matter.

"Like you are the alpha female?" His eyes narrowed as he surveyed her from across the table. "On top. In charge." She almost gasped at the charge of sexual energy that shot through her at his words.

She felt about as in charge of the situation as a three-week-old pup separated from its mom. But she couldn't let him know that.

"That's right. Mack knows I'm the boss. I crack the whip."

"Really," he drawled, his eyes narrowed. "I'd like to see that."

"Uh, figuratively of course."

"But I'd have to be the one giving the orders."

"There's room for both an alpha male and an alpha female in a pack. I—"

She choked on her next words when she realized what she had

said. Heat burned her cheeks. Why did these dumb things spill out of her when Nick was around?

A grin played around his sexy, sexy mouth.

"Really?" he said.

"Really," she said, getting up from the table, using the excuse of clearing the dishes to think of something to say.

"That gives me an agenda to work with," he said.

"Good," she said. "Taming a big dog isn't so hard when you know what you're doing."

And taming a big man?

She pushed that thought right to the back of her mind.

"I'm sure I'm up to the job," he said. "But an animal is a serious responsibility. If I commit to something, I stick with it. I need to be sure I can take Mack on."

"Fair enough." She had to clamp down on her urge to get him over the line and sign the adoption papers then and there. He was right. A dog was a commitment. Mack was with her right now because someone else had let him down. That couldn't happen again.

She gathered the rest of the dishes and refused Nick's offer of help. "Would you like cookies for dessert?" she asked.

"Cookies? You bake cookies, too?"

To pretend she had any kind of skill in the baking department would push credulity to the limits. But his eyes gleamed at the very mention of them.

She should tell him the cookies were a test batch of a new recipe Maddy had asked her to taste and evaluate. But she liked seeing that gleam of appreciation leveled at her.

Anyway, cookies were easy peasy, Maddy always said.

"Sure," she said. "Hope you like white chocolate and walnut. Because they're fresh out of the oven this morning. Maybe sandwiched with some ice cream?"

★   ★   ★

Replete with cookies and ice cream, Nick lay back on her comfy sofa while Serena bustled about in the kitchen fixing coffee.

She truly was a dream woman come true. He remembered how his business partner Adam's eyes had glazed over at the mention of her name. But her legions of fans couldn't possible know just how exalted a fantasy woman she was. Because not only was Serena beautiful, sexy and smart; she was also a damn fine cook.

Nowhere in his extensive online research on Serena St. James had it been revealed she was a culinary goddess. He'd found that out all by himself. The taste of that superb lasagna still lingered. And what she'd done to his taste buds with that avocado salad dressing bordered on the obscene.

After the morning's strenuous exercise and the hearty lunch, he felt relaxed to the point of drowsiness. As his mind started to drift, he couldn't help wondering what it might be like to come home to a woman like her. His body reacted instantly at the thought of having her in his bed. Her beautiful long limbs entwined with his. That lovely face flushed with pleasure.

And imagine being welcomed after a long day in a surveillance van with a Serena-cooked dinner. As many helpings as he wanted of the best lasagna a man had ever tasted. Dog snoring at his feet. Kids asleep in their rooms.

He sat bolt upright in his chair. His heart racing, his hands suddenly clammy. Where the hell did that come from?

He who travels fastest travels alone.

The thought that a dog might fit into his life had nudged its way with wet nose and sad eyes into his consciousness. But a woman. This woman. And *kids*.

He swallowed hard. That might take some getting used to.

Getting used to.

Not dismissed immediately out of hand?

He wiped the beads of perspiration from his forehead. Groaned a low, almost inaudible groan that was immediately picked up by two sets of sharp canine ears. Mack gave a gruff reply—somewhere between a bark and a growl—that Nick could only interpret as sympathy from one alpha male to another.

It wasn't that he had anything against settling down with a woman. He'd always thought he'd end up married someday. But this was the first time a woman had made him even contemplate the thought that "someday" might actually be looming nearer.

And she was his prime suspect in a major fraud case.

Permitting himself these thoughts broke every rule in the private investigator's handbook—both written and the other kind.

But the more he got to know Serena, the more he was beginning to think it was a possibility she might have nothing to do with the identity fraud. That it really was coincidence the clients of Paws-A-While were in disproportionate numbers among the victims.

She did not show any overt signs of being a professional fraudster. In fact she gave every impression of having nothing to hide.

On his way to the bathroom he'd managed to quickly divert into her bedroom. Had fought with every fiber of his being to keep a clear head and banish thoughts of a naked Serena in that bedroom with him.

A tabby-and-white cat was curled up asleep on the bed. She had opened a lazy green eye, dismissed him, and went back to sleep. Nearby on the silk comforter Serena's purse spilled open: wallet, cell phone, notebook. He'd itched to pick up the cell phone, but it was too risky. Then told himself that she wouldn't have left it there for him to see if it contained anything incriminating. Especially as she suspected he was a cop.

But then again could she be clever enough to leave the contents of her purse artfully strewn to give an appearance of innocence?

That time he did crack his knuckles. Much to the disdain of the cat.

He had left the bedroom wishing he'd had the opportunity to systematically check through her closet, behind the pictures on the wall, under the rug. But his first impression remained that there was nothing devious there.

Of course she could be a real dumb kind of amateur criminal who just didn't think to hide her cell phone. Again he doubted that. Serena was a smart, successful businesswoman. Paws-A-While appeared to be thriving. And before her days as a doggy day-care director she'd been a model. She'd made a success of that in a hard world where he suspected you had to do more than shove with your elbows to get ahead. If Serena had decided on a life of crime, he had no doubt she'd be professional at that, too.

He thought, too, of her friends' fierce loyalty to her. And of her generosity to the stricken Godfrey family.

No. There were no real signals coming from Serena to suggest she was anything other than what she said she was. Conjecture, suspicion, and the feeling that all was not right at Paws-A-While were all he had to link her to the crimes. And gut feeling was not enough to lay charges.

Which led him to think that after this was over, after the crime was solved and the perpetrator brought to justice and Serena cleared of any suspicion, he could consider a personal relationship with her.

He liked that feeling.

Serena came back into the living room bearing coffee, and he got up to help her with the tray. From the rich aroma that wafted to his nostrils, it appeared she was as good at making coffee as she was at creating delicious meals. As he anticipated she would be at meeting his other needs. Seeing to her needs would be more than a pleasure. He'd make it into an art form.

This was getting better and better.

But first he had to make a decision about Mack.

What had Maddy Cartwright called him? A man-sized dog.

Just the kind of dog he would like for himself. Aunt Alice's house had a decent-sized yard that would give Mack room to stretch his legs. And when Mack's knee was healed he could run with him just like he had with Fella. He hadn't realized how much he'd missed having a dog.

He put the tray on the coffee table. "I've been thinking about Mack," he said.

"Yes?" she said. He could hear the hope in her voice.

"I want to adopt him," he said.

She stopped still. "But you said you didn't have room."

"I can make room."

He was rewarded by one of her megawatt smiles that made him feel like he'd been showered in light. She took a step forward. For a moment he thought she would hug him, but she paused, her smile dimmed by a return of that anxious furrowing of her brow. There was still something unexplained there. But he doubted it was directed to him or connected to a life of crime. The stalker, perhaps.

"Thank you," she said. "And thank you from Mack, too."

"You're welcome. And so is Mack. He's a great dog."

Nick hunkered down beside Mack. Yes. He could see this animal as his. They fit. And Mack would be an ongoing link to Serena. No matter what happened with the Paws-A-While investigation, he would still have an excuse to see her.

Mack thump-thump-thumped his white-tipped tail. Hauled himself up from his dog bed. Then stumbled on his sore knee and fell heavily back onto the bed. Nick winced. Serena had booked a preliminary meeting for Mack with the surgeon for three o'clock Monday afternoon. He would demand the procedure be done ASAP. Tuesday morning if possible.

"He's not having a good day," said Serena. "Some days he can get around fine but others . . ."

"We'll get him as good as new again," said Nick. He patted Mack on the top of his massive head. "Won't we, fella?" The big dog looked up at him with grateful eyes. Then laid his head on Nick's knee. Nick stayed very still. It was a sign of trust that turned him instantly to mush. And from Mack's benefactor to Mack's owner. Or guardian. Or . . . No. Definitely not the other.

"I think you two are going to get on just fine," said Serena, her voice betraying the slightest of tremors.

Nick patted down the dog's solid flanks and scratched him behind the ears. Fella had always liked that. Mack's expression of bliss indicated he did, too. So Nick moved his hand to do the same under the black collar with its multitude of mutt-with-attitude studs.

Then froze.

Every muscle tensed. He felt the color drain from his face and sweat prickle up his spine.

Concealed in among the rows of silver studs on the collar was the tiny, almost imperceptible lens of a micro surveillance camera. The covert, wireless kind that relayed images and sound to a remote receiver. To Nick's trained eye there could be no doubt that was what it was.

He was aware of Serena chatting away about Mack and the brand of burger he favored, but it sounded like it was coming through a thick layer of San Francisco fog.

So this was how she did it.

Correctly angled, the camera had the capacity to zoom in on a credit card and record every detail. Or scan a room and detect every security device. It could record the most private of conversations. What a devious idea. Who guarded their words in front of their family dog?

Nausea threatened to gag him. Every word of his conversation with Serena had been recorded. Right now someone could be examining in close-up the details of his face.

He put his finger over the lens as if it were accidental.

He couldn't say anything. Do anything. If he removed the

collar from the dog, he would alert whoever was at the receiving end.

He attempted to cover the lens with Mack's fur but the dog's short, thick coat didn't allow it. Reluctantly Nick removed his finger from the collar and stood up.

He called upon all his training to mask his expression. To hide the shock, anger, and contempt that rocked him. Had she intended to use Mack today to get access to his personal details so she could fleece him, too? Or did Mack spy on her staff and other clients? Was Snowball equipped in the same manner? He would have to check the little white dog's collar as soon as he got the chance.

He forced his voice to an even, neutral tone. "As I'm going to be Mack's new, uh, dad, I want to take some photos of him."

Delight—or was it triumph that she was getting away with her scam?—gleamed in those remarkable eyes. He could hardly bear to look at her. "Sure. I have a camera. Do you want—?"

"I can use my cell phone," he said, as he pulled it out of his pocket.

It looked like a regular cell but was, in fact, a sophisticated multi-lens piece of industrial spy equipment.

"C'mon, Mack, smile for the camera," urged Serena. Mack tilted his head to the side. "Is that a 'yes' or a 'no'?" she said and laughed.

Ten minutes ago Nick would have thought it funny, too. Right now it was all he could do to stretch his mouth into the semblance of a smile.

Quickly he snapped some images of Mack. Zoomed right in on the almost-hidden camera winking quietly among the shiny studs. Took the opportunity to sneak a close-up of Snowball, too.

He had been played by a master.

Forgotten every rule of his game.

How could he have gotten her so wrong?

· Nine ·

"I can't believe you told him you'd made the lasagna!" Maddy's laughter came through the telephone receiver so loud Serena had to hold it away from her ear. Lucky she had her office door shut to catch up on paperwork, a routine she followed every Monday after the morning dog walks.

Serena waited for her friend's laughter to dwindle to a series of choked giggles before she spoke. "I'm sorry, Maddy. I didn't mean to claim credit where credit was definitely not due. But he was so sure I was this wonderful cook I just kind of got caught up in the moment."

"You mean the scam."

"Would you call it a scam? I didn't mean—"

"Serena, I don't mind. Really I don't. I just think it's so funny. What about the cookies?"

"Wee-ell. The cookies, too."

Maddy laughed again. "It's a good recipe. Tell me, did he like them? You were meant to be taste-testing those cookies for me, remember."

"He really liked them. In fact I parceled up a doggy bag for him to take home. But he left in a hurry and—"

"He left in a hurry? Oh. That doesn't sound so good."

"I admit it was ... a surprise. One minute we were talking about Mack; the next thing he's suddenly remembered he had to be somewhere."

She had spent way too much time puzzling over Nick's abrupt departure in the time since. This was the first time she'd had a chance to talk to Maddy about it. Maddy had been too busy with puppies and picnic food at the descendants-of-Brutus gathering on Sunday.

"Maybe he didn't want to hang around and be hassled into adopting Mack," Maddy teased.

"As if I'd hassle him! That's the funny thing—he'd already agreed to adopt Mack. Seemed really happy about it in fact."

"You must be thrilled about that."

"Yes, I am. I think Nick and Mack make a really good match."

"And Nick and you?"

Serena paused. "Nothing doing. I told you it wasn't a date."

"'Big, blond, and built,' remember."

"I remember. Maddy, the guy is hot. And yeah, I like him. But he could hardly wait to get out of there on Saturday."

Not even to her best friend would she admit how offended she'd been at Nick's hasty departure. Or that she'd brought the cookies into work with a plan to give them to Nick when he dropped off Bessie. Only to find his visit had been so brief it could be counted in seconds rather than minutes. There had been no time for anything except his terse "thank you" for the lunch and her confirmation of the appointment with the surgeon for Mack. "He's just a client."

"Bad luck. What a waste of a good lasagna. But it's great news about Mack."

Serena knew Maddy was trying to cheer her up, but she didn't need her friend's well-intentioned effort. The disappointment she'd felt over Nick's abrupt change of mood on Saturday had only served to reinforce her resolve to take time out from dating. The emotional disruption when something went wrong wasn't worth it. Nick was taking Mack to the surgeon this afternoon—she would not go with him.

She smiled as she replied to Maddy. "The lunch achieved its purpose—Mack is going to have his knee fixed and go to a good home. Who knows, maybe your lasagna was the tipping point for Nick in his decision to adopt. And it doesn't matter that I fibbed about my skills as a cook because—" The other phone rang. "Maddy, gotta dash. The bank is on the other line."

Still smiling, she answered the phone.

On Monday afternoon, Nick drove with his business partner, Adam Shore, to Paws-A-While. Their mission: to retrieve that dog collar.

Nick did not have much to say to Adam. Rather, deep in a morose slump, he churned with the grab bag of emotions that had erupted after his discovery of that tiny, hidden camera.

Anger wrestled with disgust for having let himself get steamrollered by his suspect. He groaned inwardly when he remembered his lasagna-fired moments of never-going-to-happen domestic fantasy. Man, was he lucky to have found that camera. If he hadn't, she would have completely suckered him.

Had his gut instinct deserted him? He had to hold on to the hope that it hadn't. Because if it had, he knew he was finished in this business.

Training could only take an investigator so far. Instinct was as important. He had sensed something suspicious about Paws-A-While and decided to follow his nose. The police were pursuing more obvious leads—career con men, the Russian mafia, and so on. Instinct told him that the identity fraud was a local job.

But an unerring ability to read people—a skill he prided himself on—was what really counted. That was what ultimately solved the crimes and brought in the big jobs.

His career was doomed if he'd lost it.

He'd gone out on his own with Adam both for the freedom to make his own decisions and the flexibility of lifestyle. Not to mention the impulse to help people that had made him join the FBI in the first place. Nothing was going to stop him from making S&W Investigations a success. He could not let Serena's beautiful face and air of vulnerability bring him down.

She appeared to be so genuine. But he had to remember she was a model. From his understanding, the good ones were as much actresses as clotheshorses. They pretended to be someone else for as long as it took to earn them the bucks.

Serena St. James was one of the best.

And yet . . .

Somewhere in that tormented turmoil of his thoughts was a sliver of instinct-fuelled hope that still refused to believe Serena could be involved with the identity fraud. That there was another, more innocent explanation for the high incidence of fraud victims who kept their dogs at Paws-A-While.

But the evidence of a highly sophisticated piece of surveillance equipment was damning. Certainly in Adam's eyes. That pinhole spy camera planted on a dog would give a scammer on the receiving end a good deal of information about its owner's home and lifestyle.

Discovering who had planted it could be a real step forward in the investigation of the crime. And there was no escaping the fact the dog lived after-hours in Serena's own home.

Up until now Adam had not shared Nick's certainty about a link between the fraud and Paws-A-While. This was the first real clue, and Adam had pounced on it. His business partner was an electronics genius and he wanted his hands on Mack's collar ASAP.

But could someone who operated her computer on such a low level of security as Serena have the IT smarts to employ such advanced technology? It didn't compute.

And why did she have the collar on Mack when he wasn't even her dog? Or his, yet, for that matter. Was it an opportunistic thing so she could pick up on anything of interest that might arise in Mack's vicinity? Had she implanted one of those cameras in every single dog at Paws-A-While? If so, why hadn't one of the owners noticed?

The conflicting thoughts continued to churn around in his brain until he could think of little else. The damn collar posed more questions than it answered.

A car horn blared. Damn. He slammed on the brakes to meet a red light.

Beside him in the passenger's seat, Adam cursed. "Get your mind off Serena St. James and on the road before you kill us both."

Nick didn't even bother to deny that Serena and his misjudgment of her was all he could think about. "Yeah," he mumbled.

"Concentrate, man. Just get us there in one piece. We have to get the dog on the pretext of taking him to the vet and then grab that collar."

Nick paused. "It isn't a pretext. We really are taking him to the vet."

"What!" Adam cursed again. "Tell me I didn't hear that."

Nick risked taking his eyes off the road for long enough to scowl at his business partner. "I said I'd pay for Mack's operation. I intend to hold to my promise."

If he wasn't feeling so grim, he'd have laughed at Adam's splutter. "Are you crazy?"

"No. I'm not going to let the dog down."

"And then?"

"I intend to adopt him."

Adam cursed again. "Nick, you've let yourself get too involved with Serena St. James. I warned you—"

Nick grit his teeth. "This is about the dog, Adam. He's in pain and I want to help him."

"You're going to shell out big bucks for a suspected criminal's dog? A dog that might be, quite literally, an accessory to crime?"

"The dog is blameless."

"No matter what the woman has done."

"She might be blameless, too. Whatever happened to the concept of innocent until proven guilty?"

Bad move, Whalen.

He should keep his private thoughts about Serena to himself. Despite his bean-counter appearance, Adam was a tough, astute guy. He was his business partner, not his boss. However, Nick still needed to prove to him he had what it took to make the cut in a highly competitive business.

But he also felt he had to be fair. To Serena. To Mack. And ultimately to his business. Because although lying, duplicity, and misrepresentation were all part of the information-gathering process, ultimately S&W Investigations would succeed on its integrity. He couldn't have it otherwise.

He swung his black GMC truck into a parking space only a few doors from Paws-A-While. The veterinary hospital was a couple of blocks away, and he'd arranged with Serena to pick Mack up to take him to a three o'clock appointment with the surgeon. He hadn't told her he was bringing Adam. But he was easily explained as help to handle the heavyweight canine.

As he opened the car door to get out, Adam asked him to wait. Nick stopped, arrested by his partner's expression, which must surely mirror his for degree of grimness.

Adam didn't hold back. "Nick, you're thinking with your john-son. And you know better than that. So, buddy, get shot of your feelings for the girl and concentrate on the business. You've got to be one hundred percent on your game."

Nick felt like he'd been kicked in the gut. He realized the implication of the "or else" that Adam had not vocalized.

"I've done nothing to jeopardize this case. I know how important it is."

"And I know how sexy Serena St. James is. Man, it would take a statue not to be moved by her. I can't wait to see her in the flesh. Uh . . . so to speak."

Nick clenched his hands into fists so tight they hurt. A fierce jealousy seared through him. And an instant response to spring to Serena's defense.

Adam was a decent guy and meant nothing offensive by his words. Serena tried so hard to disguise herself as dowdy doggy day-care director Serena Oakley. But sexy Serena St. James in that alluring bath of chocolate would always be top of mind to anyone who had seen the campaign. That realization must surely contribute to the anxiety that shadowed her beautiful eyes.

But it was not his place to guard her.

Slowly he unclenched his fists.

Adam was right.

Nick had fought to keep her at arm's length but, despite his best efforts, Serena had crept under his skin. He had to back right off. Images of her played through his mind, like a video in reverse. Serena teasing him about fur babies and pawdicures. Laughing as an enormous, goofy black dog struggled to clamber onto her lap. Serving him the world's best lasagna with a worried frown in case he didn't like it. And finally turning that radiant smile on him.

Why should he be so affected by a woman he had known for less than a week, beautiful as she undoubtedly was? As he fumbled with his seat belt, the answer hit him with a sudden, illuminating clarity.

Adam had crudely accused him of thinking with his johnson.

But Adam was wrong. Nick was thinking with a different part of his anatomy. His heart.

That was the real danger. A danger he had to face head-on and deal with—pronto. Too shaken by the realization to speak any further, he swung himself out of the car and waited for Adam to join him.

He braced his shoulders as if going into battle. If they'd put an emotional Kevlar vest on the market, he'd be the first taker. He needed that caliber of protection to face Serena again.

He strode with Adam toward Paws-A-While. He must not think about Serena as anything other than a possible perp. Lose his objectivity and he could lose everything he had worked for. In short, career calamity.

On the way to the vet hospital he would ask Adam to take over from him in the Paws-A-While investigation. He would still honor his obligation to Mack but he could do that without any further contact with Serena.

It was the only way.

He pushed his way through the Paws-A-While door, grinning in spite of the blackness of his mood at Adam's reaction to the "Who Let the Dogs Out?" door alert. Funny how quickly he himself had gotten used to it.

The check-in desk was deserted. Mornings and evenings were rush hour for day care. There was a bell to ring for arriving day-spa clients.

He scanned the room. The beagle clock, the paw prints on the floor, the smart black-and-white photo posters of dogs on the wall. He recognized some of them now: the two Weimaraners, Brutus, Coco, the tiny Chihuahua in a black, studded leather harness, and, of course, the inevitable Snowball.

What had seemed quirky and cute now seemed . . . sinister. This business was only six months old. Had she set it up with the express purpose of fleecing her clients? To get the opportunity to plant cameras in the collars of well-to-do clients so she could gain access to their confidential information?

That could be so. But he found it impossible to believe that Serena would do anything to purposefully hurt a dog. What grudges she might hold against people remained to be discovered.

Adam followed him through the door to the playroom. Immediately as Nick got to the gate he sensed something was different. There was the usual cacophony of dog noises and that by-now-familiar doggy smell. Serena's pack of favorites ran up to the fence to check out the new people. Bessie tagged along, too; he was pleased to note how well she fit in now. He bent down to scratch her head in the gap between two railings. Too bad this would be her last day here. He stilled. Bessie. Had Serena put a camera in Bessie's collar? A quick inspection didn't find one. Later he would get Adam to run scanning equipment over it to be sure.

He looked up. No one was playing with the dogs. Three girls huddled together near the gate opposite, keeping an eye on the dogs without actively facilitating their games.

He opened the gate and headed to where the women stood. On the way he paused to pet Mack and surreptitiously check on the camera. He was pleased when his dog—*his* dog!—seemed to recognize him. The tiny lens was still there, lurking among the profusion of metal studs on the collar. He looked around at all the other dogs, all of them wearing collars. How many other cameras could be hidden on unwitting Trojan mutts? How the hell would Adam be able to check them all without arousing Serena's suspicion?

Kylie stood with Adele, the young dancer, and a third girl he hadn't met before who wasn't wearing the Paws-A-While uniform. She was taller than Kylie but shorter than Serena and had straight brown hair cut into bangs. He was disconcerted by the way she stared at him with undisguised curiosity. He'd faced that reaction from the get-go at Paws-A-While. Was a single guy such a rarity in this place?

Adam gazed around him. No one observing him would know how shell-shocked he was by the whole Paws-A-While experience, but Nick could tell. To his knowledge, Adam was not a dog lover. It was a credit to his business partner's training he didn't blurt out his opinion on the spoiled, gussied-up pooches he saw around him. Had Adam noticed that Tinkerbelle's pink sweatshirt was printed with a wedge of cherry pie and the words Cutie Pie? Or that the fur of one of the little white dogs had been dyed pale purple?

Kylie's dimples were not in evidence, and she looked uncharacteristically strained. "Who's your friend?" she asked, after she'd greeted Nick. Nick made the introductions.

"Adam's come with me to take Mack to the vet for an appointment with the surgeon," he explained.

Kylie's face went goo-goo as it did when Mack was mentioned. "Serena told me what you're doing for Mack. You won't regret adopting him; he's a wonderful dog."

Does she know about the camera?

And what about the others? Was someone from Paws-A-While right at this moment beaming in on him and Adam via a strategically focused dog collar? He looked back at the dogs in the playroom. The bulldog's collar was the same type as Mack's. The Doberman's had studs, too. There were a heck of lot of dogs and collars in that playroom.

"Thanks. I'm a lucky guy to find him. I can't wait to get him better and take him home."

"What about Bessie?" asked Kylie.

Damn. It was so easy to slip from that essential doting-doggy-daddy persona. "Bessie? She and Mack seem to get on fine."

Kylie nodded. "Here they do. It might be different when they have to share the same territory and form their own pack behavior."

"I'm sure they'll sort it out." Truth be told, he hadn't given it much thought. He only had Bessie in his care until Aunt Alice got back from her travels. But Mack was very big and Bessie was pint-sized. He'd have to keep an eye on them.

"If you need any help with getting the two dogs settled, I could give you a hand," said Kylie.

"Uh. Thank you but—"

"Or Serena could . . ."

Nick could not be sure, but he thought he intercepted a sly wink between Kylie and the other women. Damn but he hated the way females carried on like this—just like those matchmaking women in the valley. He chose to ignore the innuendo. Was annoyed at the narrowed-eye glance from Adam that clearly warned him not to get involved.

"I need to speak to Serena first before I take Mack to the surgeon," he said to Kylie. "Is she around?"

Kylie nodded in the direction of Serena's office. "Locked in her office. She won't come out and won't let any of us in. She does this sometimes when she wants a break to do paperwork but not usually for this long."

Serena had seemed fine when he'd snatched a word with her about Mack this morning. "Is something wrong?" he asked.

"She wouldn't say. Not even to her friend Jenna, here." Kylie indicated the brown-haired woman.

"Organic-dog-treats friend Jenna?" Nick said.

The woman looked startled. "Yes," she said. "How did you know that?"

She glanced surreptitiously at Kylie. But Nick did not miss how both women's eyes narrowed in that devious female way he as a thirty-two-year-old bachelor had come to recognize and dread.

He especially didn't want them playing that game about him and Serena in front of Adam.

"Serena told me," he said, knowing immediately that had given them fuel for their speculation.

This time Kylie gave a swift knowing nod. "Yeah, I heard you guys had lunch on Saturday."

"We had a strategy meeting regarding Mack, yes," he said. "When we were discussing his care she suggested I might buy some of Jenna's products for Mack."

"As if," said Jenna. She laughed, showing perfect teeth. Serena's friend was not unattractive in a stolid kind of way, though nowhere near Serena's level of looks.

But then, who could touch Serena? He felt sick to the depths of his belly that today was the last time he would see her.

"Mack wouldn't do organic food the favor of even a sniff," said Kylie. "He must think Jenna's doughnuts are the real thing. It's junk food all the way for him. I suppose Serena has told you that?"

"Of course," said Nick. "I intend to train him out of that bad habit." He did not appreciate the looks of suppressed mirth his words elicited on the faces of the two women.

Kylie's dimples were back in full force. "Have fun trying."

Under Adam's FBI-trained poker face, he looked bewildered. Nick would have to fill him on the vagaries of his new dog's diet.

Kylie turned to Adam with a calculating look in her eyes. How long would it take before she found out his business partner was single? He was divorced and more than a bit bitter about the opposite sex.

Kylie dimpled up at Adam. "Nick's new dog is a junk-food fiend," she explained.

"Really?" said Adam with a tell-me-more expression.

Nick grit his teeth. It took all his own training to contain his impatience. He did not have time to waste on chitchat. He'd cultivated Kylie, but as he was about to cut his ties to Paws-A-While, he saw no need to continue.

He just wanted to see Serena. His gut nagged that there was something wrong. Then again, she might just want peace and quiet away from these women. And who could blame her? Maybe they'd been baiting *her* about *him*?

Finally, he made a decisive move in the direction of Serena's office. "I'm going in."

"I'll wait here for you with the ladies," said Adam.

Good. With the no-touch-dogs-other-than-your-own policy it would be difficult to check out the collars on the other animals without making a big deal of it. Maybe Adam could take up where Nick had left off working on Kylie. His partner could flirt with the best of them when it came to extracting information from suspects. He'd soon find a way to suss out those collars.

He knocked on the door of Serena's office, right next to the black metal sign where the outline of a Scottish terrier sat astride letters that spelled out The Boss.

"I told you, I don't want to be disturbed." Even muffled through the door her voice had a ragged edge to it.

"It's Nick. I've come for Mack," he said.

There was a pause. When her voice came again it was as chilly as the winds that swept the valley just before the first snowfall. "Kylie will help you with him."

Nick frowned. Was she on to him? Had he given himself away on Saturday? "I need to talk to you about Mack."

No way would he stand outside this door, calling out to her while a too-interested audience monitored his every move. He tried the handle. It wasn't locked. He shouldered the door open and went in, shutting it behind him.

Serena sat behind her desk. Alarm stabbed him when he saw how pale and distraught she looked as she raised her head to meet his stunned gaze. It seemed to cost her a tremendous effort. Her hair was disheveled, and he got the distinct impression that she'd been resting her head on her arms in a pose of despair when he'd knocked on the door. It seemed as if all the vibrancy and life had been drained from her.

"I asked you not to come in." No doubt she intended her words to sound authoritative but they came out a forced croak.

"For God's sake, what's wrong?" Every protective instinct he had surged to the fore and he had to stop himself from striding to her desk so he could put his arm around her and comfort her.

But he was here to end it with her. Not to complicate matters further.

Serena put her right hand up in a halt sign. He noticed it wasn't steady. "Don't come any further." Her eyes were dull, flat pools, her pupils so black and huge they virtually eclipsed the honey-colored iris.

"Serena—what the hell has happened?"

She took a deep, shuddering breath. Now those eyes were narrowed in accusation. Not just accusation but also hurt and betrayal. And all aimed at him.

She choked out the words. "You mean you don't know?"

The last person Serena wanted to see was Nick Whalen. But now that he'd pushed his way into her office, she wasn't going to back away from confrontation.

His reply to her question was a terse "no."

But who knew what thoughts were cogitating behind that implacable façade?

She realized how very little she knew about this man who had taken up so much of her thoughts since the day—was it less than a week ago?—he first strode through the doors of Paws-A-While clutching his cute little dog. Was it a coincidence that so much had gone wrong since he became a client?

She hadn't trusted him from the get-go. Had let her guard down on Saturday, lulled by the warmth in his eyes and the good feelings generated by his kind deed for Mack. That had been a bad mistake.

"You spent a lot of time on my computer on Friday." She did not attempt to keep the accusation out of her voice. How dumb was she to have given him access to her files.

At last a reaction. His jaw tightened. She swore it did. Though those cold blue eyes gave nothing away.

"I read your veterinary reports on Mack," he said. "You know that. In fact you invited me to. I spent some time discovering the difference between the traditional ligament repair that the vet recommends and the newer tibial plateau leveling osteotomy. I think the vet is right, by the way." His voice remained level and calm.

"You didn't look at anything else? Access any accounts? Ferret out my social security number?"

There wasn't a flicker of hesitation before he answered, just the movement of his shoulders as he rolled them and put his hands behind his back. "No."

She sighed heavily. What was the point? Every time she voiced her suspicions about Nick he dispelled them with a glib answer. She had reason to believe he had trawled through her business folders on the computer. No doubt if she was more cyber savvy, she could find a way to prove it. But in the scheme of things right now, how important was it?

Nick moved closer to her desk. For a man with such a broad-shouldered athletic build he was light on his feet. She pushed herself back in her chair until her spine pressed into the chair back and the chair dug against the wall behind her. Standing over her he seemed so big, so intimidating. So overwhelmingly male. But she was too weary to rise from her chair so they were on a more equal footing.

"What is it? A problem with your computer? Or is something wrong with your parents? Maddy? Snowball?"

How quickly he'd learned what was important to her. Under other circumstances that would have pleased her.

She shook her head slowly from side to side. She'd barricaded herself in her office so she wouldn't have to face the staff and their inevitable questions. *Go!* she wanted to scream at Nick. But she didn't have the energy. She just wanted to be left alone to take in the shocking, shuddering impact of what had happened.

"Serena! Tell me." His voice was abrupt with the same edge of interrogation that had put her on edge from the first time she'd heard it. But she felt too numb to care. What was the point of holding back?

Her head felt like it was too heavy for her neck and it was an effort to raise it so she could meet his gaze. "Remember what happened to the Godfreys? The identity fraud thing? Now it's happened to me."

She heard the breath expel in a whoosh from his lungs. Fancied she felt its warmth on her skin. Heard his knuckles crack but did not have the energy to comment.

"What do you mean it's happened to you?"

Now his hands were fisted by his sides. She found herself focusing on his right fist. It was so big. She bet he could do some damage with that fist.

She took a deep breath, but she didn't seem to be able to fill her lungs sufficiently to control her voice. "The bank called me. My accounts cleared out from four different branches. My credit cards to the max. Stuff bought that I wouldn't buy in a million years. Especially when I'm putting every cent I have into my business. Huh! Now I don't have a cent. Might not . . . might not have a business." Her voice rose to a tremulous wobble at the end of her sentence, but she could not seem to be able to bring it down.

He swore. A creative string of words that might have amused

her at any other time. His face was grim. That narrow top lip she'd found so sexy was nearly subsumed in the tight set of his mouth. "You're sure the bank got it right?"

"Oh yes. Insufficient funds to pay Jenna's September invoice. That's what the bank guy started off with. And she's not a big account, believe me."

"What about your other creditors?"

"Insufficient funds to pay the rent. Insufficient funds to pay the feed bill. Insufficient funds for the payments on the puppy potty. Insufficient funds, insufficient funds ..."

The words pounded into her brain so her head throbbed.

She closed her eyes, fisted her hands, and rubbed them so hard over her eyelids she thought she could obliterate what had happened and wake up to find the nightmare was over.

But when she opened her eyes Nick was still there, his face contorted by concern and a goodly dose of anger. Maybe he could use those big fists to smash to pieces the crook who had done this to her.

That was, if the crook wasn't him. He'd been at her computer on Friday. But the biggest withdrawal of her cash had happened at the time he was at lunch with her on Saturday. And if he'd cleared her out, why was he here? Wouldn't he have headed for the hills?

"Did the bank say how it happened?"

"Someone stole my identity. Just like with the Godfreys. Got my details. Pretended to be me. At first the bank said I'd done it. Overspent. Misused my line of credit. I soon set them straight. But ... but they say I have to prove it wasn't me who made the transactions. I don't know how I can do that."

"Did you call the police?"

She shuddered. "No way." And risk getting the cop whose hard mouth said one thing but leering eyes another? "I don't trust police."

She didn't know why she was spilling this to Nick Whalen.

Not when she still had such suspicions about him—nothing concrete, just a feeling he had never brought her in on the full story.

But it felt so blessedly good to get it out of her where it had been bottled up and festering since the bank had called three hours ago. After she'd hung up from the bank she'd made call after call only to come up with the same disastrous result. And then two different clients called to withdraw their dogs from Paws-A-While. With Freya and the Cavalier, that made four fee-paying dogs gone.

Nick was the only person she had confided in about the Godfreys and Freya. Now she was in the same boat as they were—capsized and drowning.

It was cold in that place she had so suddenly been tipped into. She shivered. *So cold.* The shivers ran through her until her entire body was trembling. Her teeth started to chatter. She wrapped her arms around herself, but it didn't help. She tried to talk but her lips were stiff and she couldn't form the words.

"Serena!"

His voice seemed to come from a long way away. Then he was by her side. Leaning toward her. Close. So close his face filled her vision. So close she could smell his leathery, peppery scent. Too close. His brow creased with concern. She didn't want his pity. She could handle this. Had to handle this. She pressed back farther in her seat but she had gone as far as she could go.

She braced her hands on the edge of the desk and pushed. Stood too quickly. Felt dizzy, light-headed, nauseous. She gagged, and her breath came in sharp, shallow gasps. She couldn't seem to fill her lungs. She let go of the desk and staggered instead of stepped. For a heart-stopping second she thought she would fall.

Then Nick caught her. Strong, strong arms wrapped around her and pulled her to his chest. Her breath caught in her throat. She resisted. Struggled. Tried to push him away. But he was so warm, so solid, so reassuring. And she was so darn cold. She stilled. Then released her breath on a long sigh and let herself relax against the solid strength of his body.

She still shivered, her whole body shaking uncontrollably. But heat radiated from him, and she was greedy for his warmth. Nick tightened his hug so her body pressed hard against the steel of his muscles, her head burrowed against his shoulder. In a slow, soothing rhythm he patted her on her back, stroked her hair, uttered a wordless murmur that resonated in his chest.

She didn't know for how long she stood there. But as his heat pulsed through her, her teeth stopped chattering and the shivers started to subside. He ceased the patting of her back and the soothing litany of words and just held her close within the circle of his arms until all she was aware of was her own breathing as it calmed, the steady rise and fall of his chest, the solid thud-thud-thud of his heartbeat, the soft cotton of his shirt against her cheek. With one final tremor that shuddered right through her, she took a deep, steadying breath and knew he had pulled her out of that cold place.

Reluctantly, she pulled away from him. Leaned back against the circle of his arms. Looked up to his face. Wanted to thank him. But what she saw in his eyes stilled the words. Her heart tripped into double time and the color rushed back to her face.

She should shrug off his arms and step back. Open the door and run right back into the playroom with Kylie and Heather and Adele and the dogs she loved and felt so safe with.

But she stayed right where she was. Didn't even marvel that at a time when everything she'd worked for was at risk and her world about to collapse, all she could think of was that Nick Whalen was about to kiss her and she wanted to kiss him back.

· Ten ·

No way could Serena fake this level of distress. She was a victim, not a crook. As much a victim as the Godfreys with Freya or the Landers with the Cavalier spaniel or any of the other people on the insurance company's report.

Nick was as certain of that as he had ever been of anything. As he held her close and felt the violent trembling of her body gradually subside, a tempest of emotion raged through him. Foremost was fury at the criminal scum who had stolen her identity. Closely followed by the overwhelming urge to protect her and avenge her.

But to fight on her side meant switching sides mid-battle, crossing the line and acknowledging her as victim, not perpetrator. That meant a significant turnaround. Both for him personally and for S&W Investigations.

Serena gave a final little sob that reverberated through her slender body and willowy limbs and stood still, leaning against him. Instinctively, he tightened the protective circle of his arms. But she pulled back, then gazed up at him for a long, wordless moment.

Her face seemed crumpled with the aftermath of shock, her eyes unfocused and bewildered, her mouth trembling and uncertain. Her mouth. Her lush, generous mouth. She wore no makeup, but her lips were warm and flushed a delectable pink. How could he look so closely at that beautiful mouth and not ache to kiss her?

But kissing Serena Oakley—alias Serena St. James—would be so much worse than a miscalculation. It could spell disaster.

Then, as her eyes connected with his, they widened, and warm color flushed the skin on her high, elegant cheekbones. Her lips parted. Just a fraction, just the tiniest space between top and bottom, but it was enough.

He was undone.

No matter what it cost him in terms of future or career or what the hell else, he had to kiss her. And kiss her now.

He groaned her name as he bent his head and she tilted hers back to meet him. He claimed that lovely mouth and kissed her. Her warmth and softness enveloped him. This was not Serena St. James, chocolate-coated fantasy woman, but Serena Oakley, warm, funny, generous doggy day-care director with her snarky sense of humor and the secrets that still shadowed her eyes.

Her mouth fulfilled every promise—moist and soft and luscious as it yielded beneath his. He felt intoxicated by the scent of her—a heady blend of sweet floral, vanilla, and warm, beautiful woman. His hands slid down her back to pull her closer so he could feel her warm, supple curves molded to the length of his body. A slight tremor rippled through her body and reminded him that it wasn't so long since she had cringed from his nearness.

He remembered her issues with trust and stalkers and heaven knew what other demons she had hinted at but not shared with him. He held back, reined in his hunger for her, made it an undemanding kiss of comfort and reassurance and respect. Somehow he wanted his body to transmit without words what he was feeling.

Then she made a throaty little moan, wound her arms around his neck, and pulled his head tighter as her mouth demanded more. What had started as a tender kiss flamed into something altogether more urgent, taking him by surprise. For a fraction of a second he hesitated. Cross that line or retreat. Commit to her side or stay neutral. What the hell. He just wanted to kiss Serena. Lips demanded, tongues responded, bodies strained to get closer as pent-up passion erupted. Her hands fisted in his hair; his slid down her back to pull her closer.

Nick could feel the pounding of their heartbeats, hear their ragged breathing in the otherwise silent room. He eyed Serena's desk. How easy would it be to sweep her papers off onto the floor, to lower her back onto its surface, to—

A loud knocking on the door intruded. Kylie's voice called through. "Nick. Serena. You've got twenty minutes to get Mack to his appointment."

Nick groaned against Serena's mouth. Tightened his grip on her.

Damn Kylie. Damn the world outside this door. Damn everything that came between him and this woman.

He did not want to let Serena go.

Serena stood stock-still for a long second. Then broke away from the kiss and wrenched herself from Nick's arms. Her heart was pounding, her nipples hard and aroused; her breath came in short, painful gasps. She felt like a guilty teenager caught making out in her bedroom while her mom stood outside the closed door.

Panting, she smoothed her hair, tugged at her shirt. Thank heaven Kylie had not pushed open the door and caught them. At least this way she and Nick could pretend they had been talking about Mack. Or Bessie. Or how to paint a poodle's claws bright pink in three easy steps.

Anything other than kissing.

She gave herself a mental shake. Oh, what the heck, so they were kissing! Was there anything wrong with that? She was twenty-eight years old and single, for heaven's sake. She could kiss whomever she wanted, wherever she wanted.

Except she liked to keep her private life to herself. And walking in on her boss making out with the sexy new client would be a doozy of a story for Kylie to relay to the other staff.

Serena looked up at Nick to see the same deer-in-the-headlights expression she imagined she had on her own face. His breathing was none too easy, either. He raised his eyebrows, looked at the closed door, and quirked that sexy mouth. Perhaps he, too, was feeling the adolescent-like awkwardness of the moment.

She smiled at him in shared camaraderie, then fought an irrational urge to giggle.

Which was insane. Someone had stolen her identity and all her money. Everything she'd worked toward was gurgling down the puppy potty. And yet she felt like giggling at the thought of being caught by her staff member kissing a client. The same client who, if truth be told, she had been fantasizing about kissing from the moment she'd met him.

The same client who had not told her the complete truth about himself and his dog.

She found it impossible to believe that Nick had anything to do with the identity fraud that had stripped her of everything. For one thing, would he be here, kissing her in her office, if he'd taken off with all her funds? But still, there was still something about him and his Yorki-poo that did not seem right.

Suddenly she didn't feel like giggling anymore. She forced air into her lungs in a deep, steadying breath. Took a step right back from him and wrapped her arms tightly around herself.

"Maybe . . . maybe that wasn't such a good idea." Her mind

was trying to make sense of it. But her body was just clamoring for more. More kisses. More caresses. More Nick.

She didn't dare look at him in case she threw herself back in his arms. Rather she concentrated on her vet tech diploma that was framed and hanging on the wall behind him.

He put one finger under her chin and tilted her face up so she had no choice but to look up into his face. "But it happened, and it was amazing," he said in that deep, husky voice that sent shivers of desire up her spine.

How could she ever have thought his eyes cold? And his mouth. His sexy, sexy mouth. She loved the way the top lip was narrower than the lower one and the way it curled up so sensuously at the corners. It made her want to run the tip of her tongue along it, to taste it again, to—

"Amazing . . ." she repeated, still stunned by the kiss, dazed by the feelings it had aroused. It was amazing all right. Quite possibly the most amazing kiss she'd ever had. After all those months in the self-exiled celibacy zone those unleashed hormones had gone crazy.

"But . . . it . . . it still sh-shouldn't have happened," she stuttered. Heavens above, she couldn't even speak properly!

This kiss had made her already-complicated life that much more complicated. Because it wasn't just about hormones. It wasn't just about awakened sexual hunger. It was about him. Nick. She liked him. Really liked him. Heck, she had even thought she might learn how to cook to impress him. That was a first.

But what was it about him that still didn't quite strike the right note? Why had he left so abruptly that day after lunch? She remembered how upset she'd felt. She hadn't liked that feeling one little bit. Wasn't sure she could cope with being plunged right back into the maelstrom of emotion that being with a man in-volved, the angsting if he didn't call, the constant wondering was it something she'd said, something she'd done. After it ended, the devastation of squeezing a squeak toy just to hear the words "I love you."

"I don't know that this is . . . is the time for kissing," she said. "Not with everything else that's happening." She looked up to him, wordlessly imploring him to understand.

Compassion. There it was in his eyes again. Somewhere behind the heat that was banked down now but still glowing.

"Serena, let me help you," he said. "Tell me what you need me to do, and I'll do it."

Now she gripped her hands together to control the trembling. "I . . . I don't know what you can do to help me. I don't know what anyone could do. I'm only just getting my head around what's happened."

Her voice threatened to tip into hysteria, but with a great effort of will she forced it to stay level. She forced herself not to throw herself into his arms and take every bit of help this gorgeous hunk of man could offer. It was really important to her that she stood on her own two feet and fought her own battles. Not take the easy route as she had done so many times before. Paws-A-While had to be *her* success.

Kylie rapped on the door again. "Hey, guys, hurry up in there!"

Nick placed his hands on her shoulders to anchor her. "Trust me. I *can* help, if you'll let me. We have to talk."

Trust me.

Why was it when people said that, she always felt like running a mile? Why should she trust him? She scarcely knew him.

But oh, how those hungry hormones want to get to know him better.

Serena stepped back so he was forced to lift his hands from her shoulders. Freed from his touch she felt more clearheaded, more able to think. She could not let herself be distracted by the feel of his hands on her body. Even their light touch on her shoulders sent her senses zinging.

She kept her voice low, wary of Kylie on the other side of the door. "Nick, tell me straight out—have you ever lied to me?"

He hesitated for just a microsecond. But she noticed it. Pounced on it like a puppy on a chew toy. "No. But there are things I need to explain—" he said.

Another knock on the door. Now Kylie's voice was edged with impatience. "Shall I ring the vet hospital? Tell them you're not coming?"

Serena cleared her throat, called back to Kylie. "No. Wait. Nick is on his way. And I—"

He put his hand over her mouth. Just long enough for her to be shocked into silence. "Don't say anything about the identity fraud. It's vital you keep it to yourself." His voice came in a harsh, urgent whisper.

She felt suddenly very unsure. Even a bit frightened. "You're losing me, Nick. I don't get it. What does what's happened to me have to do with you?"

"You have to trust me."

"I really don't—"

"Just until I get back. I'll tell you everything then."

Everything? What hadn't he been telling her? How much was there to tell?

Kylie called through the door again. "If Nick can't make it, I'll go with Adam to the vet," Kylie called.

"Adam?" said Serena.

"No need for that. I'm coming out," Nick called through the door. Then to Serena: "Adam is my business partner. Here to give me a hand with Mack."

"But I—"

He had his hand on the door handle. "Remember. Don't tell anyone—and I mean anyone—what happened with the bank."

She shook her head from side to side. "I don't know why I'm agreeing to this, but okay."

Nick opened the door and pushed it wide. She followed him out. Then fought the impulse to snatch her hand to her mouth.

There seemed to be a cast of thousands outside the door. But closer focus showed it to be just an indignant Kylie, a tall, dark-haired man wearing frameless glasses immediately behind her, and beyond that the rest of the staff, who quickly dispersed and pretended to be working.

"About time," Kylie huffed. "If you miss the appointment, Mack might have to wait for days."

"It's all right, Kylie," she said. "Mack will get to the vet on time." She was surprised how normal her voice sounded to her own ears.

On the bookshelf in her office was a snow globe—a gift from Maddy—that contained a figurine of a Maltese terrier dressed in a striped red scarf and a Santa hat. When she'd gone into that office before the call from the bank, all had been right in her dog-centered little world—just like that tiny plastic Maltese. Now, leaving the room, she felt like she was in a snow globe that had been shaken and shaken and shaken and the snowflakes had settled on a completely different world with the ground uneven and treacherous beneath her unsteady feet.

"Everything okay?" said Kylie, looking from Serena to Nick and back again.

It was killing Serena to smile and act as if everything was okay when it was so not okay.

Insufficient funds to pay the wages.

All her hard-earned modeling money—her safety net for the first year of business—gone. If Paws-A-While had to close, Kylie would be out of a job. So would the others. "I had a problem with the darn accounting software. You know how frustrated I get with it. Nick was able to help me. That's all."

Kylie's eyes narrowed suspiciously. "You're sure about that?" She was as protective as a barnyard cat with its kittens. Serena appreciated that. Kylie had started out as an employee but was becoming a friend. She dreaded having to tell her what had happened.

Serena made a point of looking at her watch. "Kylie's right. You've got to get Mack to the vet, pronto."

"You're not going with him?" asked Kylie.

Serena shook her head. Lydia, her regular vet, who was also a friend, had sung the surgeon's praises, and she would like to meet him herself. But she didn't think she could stand having to go out and act normal in front of strangers. And she needed time to think about what had happened with Nick.

Truth was, she felt barely able to stay upright. Nausea rose in her throat at the thought of telling Maddy what had happened— Brutus was a major investor; his funds were at risk. In a way, she was grateful to Nick for his demand not to talk to anyone about the disaster just yet. She wasn't good at sharing her pain with humans. She just wanted to spend time with the dogs and their simple, uncomplicated attitude to life. Maybe then she could come up with some kind of plan.

She turned to Kylie. "I'd go to the vet if I didn't have so much to sort here. But Mack is Nick's dog now. It will help them bond."

"True," said Kylie. "A bit of doggy-daddy together time never did any harm."

Serena did not dare look at Nick to catch his reaction to Kylie's comments.

"Did I hear someone say that Jenna was here?" Serena said.

"She dropped in an order but couldn't wait. She asked could you please give her a call."

Outside she was smiling; inside Serena was churning with anxiety. What if Jenna asked why her invoice hadn't been paid? Jenna was a doctoral student working on her thesis in some highly complex area of mathematics that Serena didn't even pretend to understand. Jenna needed her income from Paws-A-While as much as Kylie did.

This just got worse and worse.

Serena turned her gaze to the tall, dark-haired man wearing glasses who hovered behind Kylie. Leaner than Nick, he gave the same impression of coiled strength in a Clark Kentish type of way. Somehow she'd never thought of insurance assessors as being as built as both Nick and this guy.

"This is my colleague, Adam Shore," said Nick. "He's here to lend some muscle if we need help with Mack."

Adam was impeccably polite but the way he kept his gaze forcedly above her neck made it obvious he was not oblivious to her past as Serena St. James. Could he tell she'd been kissing his friend? If he made some innuendo-laden remark, it might just send her over the top.

How long until she was able to put the girl-in-a-bath-of-chocolate thing behind her? It had made her enough money to start Paws-A-While and to live comfortably in the apartment upstairs. Sometimes she wondered if the notoriety it had brought with it had been worth the money.

One thing was for certain: never, ever again would she pose half nude in a tub of chocolate. Nothing could make her do that again. No matter how much money she was offered—the amount of dollars went up with every call from her agent. Not even if she'd lost everything to identity fraud.

But if Adam was wondering about the chocolate thing, he certainly gave no evidence of it. In fact, the way he was covertly checking out Kylie made her wonder if short, curvy blonds were more to his taste. Maybe that was why Kylie had sounded so eager to go with him to the vet?

Kylie was practically hopping from foot to foot with impatience. "Time, people. You guys have gotta get that big mutt into your car and around to the vet hospital."

"Right," said Serena. Curious about Adam, she walked alongside him to the playroom. "The vet hospital is only a walk away," she explained, "but poor Mack's knee is too bad for him to take weight on it for any distance."

"Nick told me," said Adam. "I'm just here to help."

"Do you have a dog of your own?"

"No," he said. "I live in an apartment with a very dog-unfriendly landlord."

Mack lurched to his feet to greet them, but his knee was obviously bothering him. He suddenly whipped his head around and furiously licked his knee joint. But Nick was immediately there to help him, and Serena noted how the big dog was already comfortable with Nick. "I'll lift him," said Nick to Adam, "then you help me get him into the car."

"Wait," said Serena. "Kylie, can you get another collar for Mack from stock? That really nice embossed leather red one will do the trick."

"Sure," said Kylie and turned on her heel.

Nick stopped what he was doing with Mack. "Another collar?"

She intercepted a quick glance between Nick and Adam that she didn't understand.

"Uh, can I ask why?" said Nick.

Serena pulled a face. "I can't stand this studded number he's wearing. It's way too butch for Mack, don't you agree?"

"I, uh, guess so."

"People are nervous enough around a black dog his size without making him look so intimidating with that brutish collar. He's a gentle giant with a sweet nature and needs a collar to match his personality." She knelt down and unfastened the ugly collar she had disliked from the get-go. "Something smart and cheerful. He'll look very handsome with a red collar."

"You mean you didn't choose that collar he's wearing?" Nick asked.

"Heck no, I hate it. He was wearing it when his owner brought him in. But now that he has a new owner I think he should have a new collar."

She smiled at Nick. It made her feel warm every time she thought of Mack going to a good home. Amidst all the bad things happening, Nick paying for Mack's knee operation and adopting him was a good thing. "Let me give it to you as a gift."

That nerve in Nick's jawline twitched. He seemed mesmerized by Mack's old collar as it swung from her hand. "What will you do with the old collar?" he asked.

"Throw it out. Recycle it."

"Can I have it?" asked Nick, his eyes watching it swing back and forth.

"Oh. Of course. He's your dog now. You might like the studded collar. I'm sorry; it's not my place—"

"No. No. The red collar sounds great. I agree with you entirely. It's just I know someone else who would really like to have that collar."

"It's me," said Adam. "I want the collar." He held out his hand.

Puzzled, Serena frowned. "But you don't have a dog," she said, hanging on to the leather band.

"No. But I will one day and that is just the collar I would like for my dog. When I get him, that is. The collar would look great on a . . . on a pit bull."

Serena shrugged. Adam seemed more a Dalmatian type of guy to her. A Dalmatian with an altogether more elegant style of collar than this. Though black would look okay on a Dalmatian, just not the ugly studs . . .

Obviously her matching-dog-to-owner intuition was failing. First Nick with a Yorki-poo and now his partner with dreams of a macho pit bull terrier. How off target could she get?

She handed the collar over to Adam. "It's yours, Adam. I hope your future dog will be very happy with it."

"Thanks," said Adam, holding the darn collar as if it were studded with diamonds. There was definitely no accounting for tastes when it came to dogs and dog accessories.

Nick spoke to her in an urgent undertone that she had to lean close to hear. "We have to talk. When I bring Mack back."

"I'll be here," she said.

"No. Not here. A coffee shop maybe."

"Okay," she said, not sure why she was acquiescing and hoping like hell that he would make things clearer when they next met.

Kylie came out to help load Mack into Nick's truck. As soon as she had gone back inside and Nick was back in the driver's seat, he turned to Adam. His business partner was gloating over the collar, turning it over and over in his hands.

"Definitely a micro surveillance camera in there. An expensive one. Relaying to a cell phone most likely. Although I think—"

Nick shot him a warning glance.

"Don't worry," said Adam. "I've disabled it. They can't hear us or see us. Whoever 'they' might be."

"Now they'll know we've found it."

"That's a risk we have to take. It might even flush him out."

"We know it's not Serena. You heard her. She didn't put that collar on the dog."

"So she says."

"She was going to put it in the trash."

"And you believe her?"

"Yes, I do. She's got nothing to do with the fraud. Except for being its latest victim."

As he drove away from Paws-A-While, Nick relayed to Adam what Serena had told him.

By the time he'd finished they were parked in the veterinary hospital's designated parking area. For all that rush against the clock, they were five minutes early.

Adam swore. "You better be right about Serena. It's easy enough to check if she's telling the truth. And I will."

For the first time Nick felt angry with his partner. "You do that. But I'm certain she's telling the truth."

"She could be setting herself up as victim to deflect attention from herself. It's been done before."

"Not by Serena. She's innocent." He'd felt his instincts had gotten out of whack. Now that gut feel he'd learned to trust was back. "I'd stake everything on it."

"Everything?" His partner looked at him with cool, level eyes. "You're sure you want to take that gamble?"

"Yes."

"If you're that sure, then we pull out of Paws-A-While. Concentrate on our other leads."

Other leads that so far had not yielded anything of worth, either.

Nick shook his head. "No. Not yet. I still think we're on to something at that place. Now that Serena is a victim, too, I'm thinking—"

"You're thinking with your—"

Now Nick swore. "No. Yes. Dammit. I—"

Adam's tone was somber. "You can't get involved with a suspect."

"What if she's not a suspect?"

"No matter what, she's still a person of interest and that means hands off. You know that as well as I do, Nick."

"Yes, but—"

"No 'buts.' I'm going to verify if she really is the victim she claims to be." Adam paused. "But I see where you're coming from. She's not what I thought she'd be."

"How's that?"

"I didn't think she'd be so . . . sweet."

"Sweet?"

"I knew she'd be hot and she is. That disguise does nothing to hide what a gorgeous woman she is."

Nick growled his protest. From the backseat Mack did his growl-bark thing. Nick smiled. Mack was acting as his wingman already. He leaned over to the backseat and gave him a reassuring pat.

"Settle down, buddy." Adam glared at the dog. "Uh, both of you, I mean. That was just observation. The hot thing I mean. I know you've got dibs on Serena."

"I do not have dibs on her."

Adam gave him a "yeah, right" look before he continued. "Serena St. James. I expected this haughty, stuck-up kind of princess. You know, too good for the rest of us. But she's not that. She's nice. Smart, too. And she's sweet . . . The eyes, I think. There's pain in those eyes. And fear."

Adam's acute insights into people never ceased to amaze Nick. It was one of the reasons he had jumped at the opportunity to work with him in their own business. He *had* to make this partnership work.

"Which leads me back to what I was saying," said Nick. "What if this scam is personal? Aimed at hurting Serena, hurting her business?"

"It's a possibility."

"She's had a stalker after her. Could be something there. A revenge thing."

"Or a sex thing."

Nick gritted his teeth. That thought was too awful to contemplate. But it might explain a lot about Serena. "Maybe. She hasn't confided in me. Yet. But this new development might make her more willing to talk."

"Get the name of the stalker. Pronto. And see if he's on any of that webcam footage from the center."

"There's this millionaire mutt there, too. He and his owners could be at risk."

"Yeah, I've read about him. The guy who tried to kill the dog is locked away in a British jail right now."

"That doesn't mean there's not another psycho out there coveting the fortune that was bequeathed to a dog."

"But for all that, there's still nothing concrete linking Paws-A-While to this identity fraud, and the clock is ticking, man. We can't waste weeks on this case unless we're sure of where we're going."

"Except for the collar. That's concrete."

"Correct. It's a serious little camera in that collar. You said the owner disappeared?"

"Serena couldn't get in touch with him again."

"She didn't have the resources we have to track people down. Get everything you can from Serena about that dog's owner. We still have to check all the other dog's collars. But if Serena is genuine, he's now our prime suspect."

"Mack's old owner," Nick corrected him. "I'm his owner now."

"You mean his 'daddy,' don't you?" Adam rolled his eyes. "That place. Did you see that poster of the damn poodle dyed pink and yellow and clipped like topiary? How can you bear to hang out there?"

"It's okay. At least the owners—sorry, they like to be called guardians—are responsible and care about their pets."

Adam snorted. "Waste of money."

"Maybe. Maybe the beauty parlor stuff. Maybe the Pawlates."

Adam gave a strangled sound at the mention of Pawlates. Nick ignored it and continued. "But if you love an animal, you want to look after it. Don't want it home by itself all day while you're at work. And that can't be a bad thing." He laughed, a short self-conscious laugh, as he realized he'd just sounded like an ad touting the benefits of Paws-A-While.

From where he sat, he could see people trooping into the vet hospital with cats in carry cages and dogs on leashes. A young woman clutched a terrified-looking rabbit tight to her chest. He thought of the exorbitant amount of dollars he was about to spend on Mack. And of how much he was looking forward to taking Mack back with him to Sausalito.

A man should have a dog.

There were other things a man might want, too. A home. A family. All things he'd thought were far in the hazy, nebulous future for him until Serena had brought them into sharp focus.

Home. Family. Woman.

He shook his head to clear his thoughts.

Stay detached. Remain focused. Maintain suspicion.

Too late.

He was already involved.

· Eleven ·

Who had done this terrible thing to her? After the initial shock of finding that the identity theft really had happened and wasn't some horrible prank, all Serena could angst over again and again was *who*? And *why*? Followed closely by *what had she done to deserve this*?

Fussing around with Mack's new collar had distracted her, but as soon as she'd waved good-bye to the big dog the anxiety surged back. She was back in that snow globe struggling to stay upright, hanging on desperately to those slippery sides while it was turned upside down and shaken and shaken and shaken.

She paced the paw-print trail in the playroom, to and fro and around the dog beds, and then realized that was a flag to her staff that something was wrong. No way could she keep this terrible worry bottled up inside for much longer. She had to talk to someone about what had happened or she would snap.

She glanced down at her watch. Nick had been away with Mack for nearly an hour. If he wasn't back in the next thirty minutes, she would call Maddy. Her friend was testing recipes at home today with Brutus, Coco, and Tinkerbelle for company. Tom was a top attorney; he might be able to help with any legal implications of the fraud.

Who? Why?

She had not lost her purse, wallet, or cards. So it was not an opportunistic crime. Someone must have targeted her. Used a skimming device to record the details off of her cards. She shivered with revulsion at the idea. Her stalker? Her first thought went to him. But he was locked away. Dave? No matter how they had parted, he was no criminal. His career in the navy was everything to him.

But she'd attracted a number of weirdos through the girl-in-the-bathtub-of-chocolate campaign. Could it be someone out for revenge because she had slighted him in some way? Or was it somehow connected to the Godfreys? What about the Paws-A-While dog parents who had pulled out their pets citing financial difficulties. Had the same thing happened to them?

Was the thief a he or a she? The numerous websites she had trawled after the shock phone call from the bank said that the gender of the thief did not necessarily have to match the victim. Anyone with a forged card and a stolen PIN could take out money at a cash point.

Her mind was churning so much she could not find distraction even in the company of the dogs she adored. Could not summon the concentration required to get Barry, the chubby little pug, up and moving in a simple game. He just wanted to nap. By contrast Lily, the beautiful border collie who visited Mondays while her owner attended a college course, would play endless commando tunnel for as long as Serena would take part.

But Serena's mind was not on anything but the identity theft. Who was walking around town spending her money, destroying her future? And could Nick Whalen really help her?

There was also the fact that the longer she stayed in the play-

room, the longer she was exposed to Kylie's avid curiosity about
Nick. She could not, would not discuss that with her. Not even
with Maddy.

Heck, she hadn't even allowed herself to think about the implications of that kiss. To take out that memory and play it again
in her mind. She had been way too concerned about the implications of the identity theft on Paws-A-While and the future of her
staff.

But ohmigod, the man could kiss. There was no point ignoring
it. The harder she tried to forget how it had felt, the more the
memory pushed itself to the forefront of her mind. She traced the
outline of her mouth with her finger, remembering the surprise of
the first gentle touch of his lips and the passionate give-and-take
that had flamed so quickly.

What if the staff saw her doing that? She jammed both hands
into the pockets of her jeans. This was crazy. He'd offered comfort. She'd taken it. That was what it had been about.

Snap out of it, Serena! How old was she? Twenty-eight or fourteen? For heaven's sake, she'd been kissed before.

But not like that. Not by him.

She looked at her watch again, tapped it with her finger to
make sure it was still working, as the hands seemed to be crawling
forward so slowly. Five more minutes and she'd call Maddy.

Then, when she next looked up to the doorway, Nick was there
with Mack. The big, hunky man walked slowly and patiently beside
the big black dog as Mack lurched his way through the doorway
and to the gate, just toe-touching with his injured leg.

A surge of both affection for the dog and of gratitude to the
man for the generosity he was showing the animal flowed through
her. But the sudden racing of her heart had nothing to do with
gratitude and everything to do with the increasing attraction she
felt to Nick every time she encountered him. She hurried to open
the gate to the playroom.

Suddenly she felt shy around Nick, unable to meet his gaze, take part in the usual banter about the foibles of the dog-care business. The kiss had changed everything.

She covered her confusion by making a big fuss over Mack. When she bent down to pet him, he reacted as overenthusiastically as usual, making whimpering sounds of pleasure, nearly knocking her over in his efforts to lick her face. How she loved this dog! She would have given anything to keep him. But the next-best thing was that he went to a good home. And, for all the reservations she had about Nick Whalen, that he would be good to Mack was never in doubt.

Finally feeling able to face him, she looked up at Nick. "How did it go with the surgeon?"

Just for a second she saw a flicker of something in his eyes that proved he had been as affected by their encounter in her office as she was. A recognition that it wasn't something she could just shut the door on. Even if she wanted to.

"Good. Really good," he said. "He says it's a routine surgery, Mack will only need a cast on for a week, and he can be the first patient tomorrow morning, which means Mack won't have to stay there overnight."

Serena hugged Mack around the neck. "That's excellent news, isn't it, you big, sweet, gorgeous boy?" She laughed as she bent back to avoid the dog's wet, overenthusiastic tongue.

But that was delay enough. She wanted that "we have to talk" moment. And she wanted it ASAP. There were a lot of answers she needed from Nick. She stood up to face him. "No coffee shop. I need to get outside. How about we take Snowball and Bessie for a walk?"

Suddenly her beloved Paws-A-While seemed oppressive, as if everything around her brought to mind the devastation that would be her lot if she were to lose her business. In her mind's eye she could see her creditors marching in and stripping her of everything she held dear. This place wasn't just her job. Rightly or wrongly, she'd made it her life.

"Sounds good to me," he said, not giving away anything by his expression.

As soon as it took to put harnesses and leashes on Snowball and Bessie, Serena was out on the sidewalk with Nick. The two little dogs were ecstatic at the prospect of an extra walk.

"We usually walk the dogs at Fort Mason," she said. "Okay with you?"

"Fort Mason it is."

She took a deep breath to take in the fresh air and looked around to appreciate another beautiful fall day. The tight knot in her chest seemed to ease. Or was that because she was with Nick, who said he could help her. Nick, who . . .

She had to stop thinking about that kiss!

"Tell me more about what happened at the vet hospital," she said, paranoid about mentioning the identity theft while they were still anywhere near Paws-A-While. She was careful to keep a no-nudging distance away from him.

They made a left onto Franklin but it wasn't until they were waiting to cross at Lombard, several blocks away, that they spoke of anything other than Mack's knee.

Serena was first to broach the subject. "You said there are things you need to explain."

The lights changed. She had to yank Snowball away from the interesting scents on the nearby hydrant, before maneuvering the little dogs safely across the busy road.

They were headed through the gates into the park before Nick replied. "Serena, you've asked me several times if I'm a cop."

"Yes," she said, looking straight ahead, her heart suddenly thudding and her mouth dry.

He spoke bluntly. "I've never been a uniformed policeman as such, but I was an FBI special agent for most of my career."

Serena realized she had been holding her breath and she let it out on a whoosh. Then pulled Snowball to a halt and looked up at Nick. "I knew it," she said. "I just knew it."

She felt like she was in an elevator that had suddenly plunged twenty floors.

Now all her doubts and suspicions added up. Her instincts had not let her down. She had sensed *cop* and she had not been wrong. In her book an FBI agent was definitely a kind of a cop—maybe more of a cop than your regular-type SFPD police officer. She felt a tumultuous mix of righteousness, anger, and disappointment.

Rottweiler. Rottweiler. Rottweiler.

"I was right all along," she choked out.

"In a way, yes."

"In a way? What's 'in a way' about being an FBI agent? That says über-cop to me."

"I said I was with the FBI—past tense."

"Hey, you're confusing me now." She found it difficult to keep the edge of anger from her voice. This man had made a fool of her. "So now you're not a cop?"

"I'm a private investigator in partnership with Adam, the guy you met today." That clear blue gaze was steady without a trace of trepidation or apology.

Her heart thudded so hard it felt like it could bruise her ribs. "So you lied to me?"

"Withheld information is more how I put it. In the interests of the investigation."

"I'll stick with lie."

The word stuck in her throat. She turned away from him and walked onward; she had to concentrate on putting one foot in front of the other. Nick fell into step with Bessie trotting behind him. To the other people heading into Fort Mason, they must seem like an ordinary couple taking their dogs for a walk on a crisp, fall day. Not a man who was not what he'd said he was and a woman who was reeling at his revelation.

Keeping the dogs in line, they walked by the old military buildings of the Battery. The irony was not lost on her. There had been a military stronghold at Fort Mason since before the Civil War. Hadn't she sensed from the get-go that Nick was law enforcement of some kind?

"You guys lie for a living, don't you? How do I know you're not lying now?"

Without a word, he reached into the inside of his jacket pocket and pulled out not a badge but a credit-card style photo ID stating that Nicolas James Whalen was licensed to practice as a PI in the state of California.

She stopped and stared at it. So his full name was Nicolas; she'd wondered about that. Even in the tiny ID photo he looked hot. Curse her darn libido for noticing.

"You told me you were an insurance assessor," she said, handing the card back to him and resuming the walk.

"I told you I worked for an insurance company."

"Another lie."

He shook his head. "Adam and I were retained by an insurance company to investigate a spate of identity theft frauds in the Bay Area and Marin County."

"A *spate* of frauds?"

"Yes. Enough for the insurance company to be concerned by the amount they were having to pay out on claims. I noticed that quite a few of the victims kept their dogs at Paws-A-While." He listed the names of her clients, starting with the Godfreys. "Now there's you . . . the newest victim."

Hot color flushed to her cheeks and then drained away again. There was a flurry of flakes in that snow globe and once again the ground beneath her feet was shifting and changing so she could not keep her balance. "You . . . you mean you think there's a connection?"

"Could be. Yes." The harsh angles of his face and the rigid set of his shoulders made him look every inch the cop.

Nausea rose in her throat. "You think someone at Paws-A-While is responsible?" She struggled to comprehend his words as they hammered into her consciousness.

"It's possible. Among the staff or the clients. The police are convinced these particular crimes are linked to a bigger fraud connected to the Russian mafia. My hunch is it's a local job on a smaller scale."

She stopped, too shaken to go on, too shaken to even notice they had reached the grassy hill with one of the best views in San Francisco of the Golden Gate Bridge and Alcatraz.

"One of my staff. One of my friends. It can't be. I don't believe it."

He didn't say anything further.

Then the full implication of his words hit her. She remembered the suspicion she'd seen in his pale blue gaze that first day when he stood with Bessie in his arms at the front desk of Paws-A-While.

"You . . . you think it could be me. From the time you first booked in to Paws-A-While you thought I was a crook."

He did not deny it.

She had invited this man into her home. Kissed him. Fantasized about making love with him. All the time he thought her capable of stealing from innocent dog lovers, the people who entrusted her with their beloved pets.

The snowflakes whirled round and round and round in that snow globe, disorienting her, and she felt so dizzy she thought she might fall. She blinked her eyes rapidly to keep her world in focus, gripped tight to Snowball's leash.

Nick went to take her arm to steady her. She shook it off.

"Don't touch me," she spat. He cracked his knuckles. She was too distraught to even flinch.

"Serena, if there's a crime, I investigate it. That's my job."

She swallowed against the hurt and anger that slashed through her. "You honestly thought I would . . . would steal from my clients? From good people like Joe and Rosemary Godfrey?"

"It's people like the Godfreys I work to get justice for. As you say, good people." He was tight-lipped, his jaw taut with tension. "I didn't know you. You were . . . suspicious. Working under an alias. Evasive about your past. In disguise."

She gasped. "I wasn't in disguise. Or under an alias."

But when he put it like that . . .

Maybe her escape from Serena St. James to the anonymity of Serena Oakley would appear suspicious to someone who didn't know her. Someone who saw only the facts. "Perhaps it seemed that way, but I—"

"I saw a link between the crimes and your center; Adam saw only a coincidence. I chose to check out Paws-A-While. You were the director. You had to be investigated."

"Investigated!" She recoiled from the sound of the word. "So you pretended to be a dog lover to . . . to . . . infiltrate my business."

"I didn't have to pretend to be a dog lover."

"Why couldn't you have just asked me? Wait. Of course you couldn't. Because you thought I was a crook."

So much fell into place now. Even today Nick had taken twice as long to fasten Bessie's harness as she had to fasten Snowball's. No way was he a legitimate dog person, not in the San Francisco way of it, anyway. It was time for her to do a little "investigating" of her own.

The dogs were anxious to be let off their leashes. When Fort Mason was owned by the military, dogs were allowed to play without leashes. Since Fort Mason had become a federal park, it was strictly an on-leash area. Local dog people exercised their right to disagree and dogs went off leash unless in the actual presence of the police. Freed from their leashes, happily sniffing around the area they came most days for exercise, Snowball and Bessie were totally oblivious to the tension between their humans.

She turned to face him. "So, Nick, you say you're a genuine dog lover. How long have you had Bessie? Or is she a fraud, too?"

"Only two weeks. I am her official guardian—"

"Why is she named Bessie?"

"I don't know. That was her name when I got her. She—"

"Who really tied that bow in her fur?"

"A seventy-year-old woman named Hannah, but—"

"Why did she—?"

Nick put his hand up to stop her. His voice was as much a growl as any Rottweiler under threat. "Serena. Let me finish. Bessie belongs to my great-aunt Alice."

"I knew that dog wasn't yours. I knew—"

"You don't know. And you won't know until you let me finish." He made a zipping motion across his mouth.

He looked so grim and determined that Serena zipped.

Nick continued. "I'm new to San Francisco. Adam is a friend from my bureau days and I came here to join him as a partner in his investigation business. I'd been living in DC. Before that I had a stint in Australia."

"For the FBI?" She didn't know that the FBI actually sent people out of the country.

He nodded. "Yes. They send agents to every country that we want to exchange intelligence with. I was undercover in our embassy."

"Now you're back." The James Bondish truth about him was almost too much to take in.

"My aunt lives in Sausalito. She's on her own. If anyone from our family comes to San Francisco, we always visit with her. I asked could I stay until I found my own place. She was just about to take off on a road trip with some ladies from Seattle she met on a cruise boat. It worked out well for us both. She got a house-sitter and someone to look after Bessie. I got a place to stay and a ready-made cover dog."

So Nick Whalen really was not, and never had been, a Yorki-poo type of guy. No wonder he didn't know how to tie that bow in Bessie's forelock. Or was so clueless about claw polish.

"So that's how you ended up with a purse-sized pooch. It was a total sham from the word go. Bessie. Your job. You."

Us. She stopped herself from saying the word aloud just in time.

Perhaps that was the most hurtful thing of all. That she'd allowed herself to think there might be an "us." The kindness. The kiss. All just part of his ploy. She burned with humiliation at how easily she'd been taken in.

Boy, did she know how to pick 'em. Was there something wrong with her when it came to men?

Her breath caught in her throat when she realized what else she had to add to the list. "Mack. The thing with Mack, that was just another ploy, wasn't it? Just to ingratiate yourself with me."

"No, Serena, don't think—"

She didn't know what to think.

"Did you really take him to the surgeon or just drive around the block and pretend?" She fought it, God, did she fight it, but the thought of Mack being involved in this man's deception made her eyes sting with tears. "What were you planning to do with him after his use to you was over? Dump him at a shelter?" She couldn't keep the break from her voice, but, what the heck, what was one more humiliation?

He stared at her, tight-lipped. "How could you even think that? Nothing changes with Mack. He's booked in for his operation tomorrow. Whatever happens, I want to adopt him."

Serena swallowed hard against the lump in her throat. "Why should I believe you? I don't know what's lie or fact. I don't know why I would trust Mack with you now."

A small group of tourists on a guided walking tour showed rather too much interest, and Serena realized her voice had risen too loud. There was nothing she hated more these days than drawing attention to herself. She willed herself to calm down.

Nick shifted from foot to foot. For the first time since she'd known him he looked awkward and uncomfortable. Somehow it was endearing to see such a big, tough-looking guy seem so unsure of himself. When he cracked his knuckles she held back from saying anything. Though it took an effort.

"Serena, I swear to you I would do nothing to harm Mack. He's a great dog. I want him. I . . . I care about him."

He looked less grim-Rottweiler type, more the kind of guy she could be friends with. Could be—wanted to be—more than friends. Much more than friends.

"I wish I could believe you."

"Trust me. Even though Mack could be a crook himself, I still want him."

Her heart thudded into overdrive. "Mack. A criminal?" Was she hearing things?

"More of an accessory to crime," he amended.

"An accessory to crime? Mack? I don't get this."

"While strictly speaking he's innocent until proven guilty, the evidence is pretty damning."

Serena started to back away from Nick. This was seriously weird. She kept waiting for him to laugh and say he was joking.

But he didn't.

She still doubted Nick's honesty. Now she was beginning to wonder about his sanity.

· Twelve ·

If it weren't so damn serious, Nick would have laughed out loud at the expression on Serena's face.

"You think I'm crazy," he said.

She continued to creep cautiously backward from him. "Of course not. I knew all along Mack should be behind bars. I just . . ."

Now Nick did laugh. "You're clueless about the collar, aren't you?"

He had stopped suspecting her, but her reaction proved to him beyond a doubt that she was in no way involved.

"Mack's collar?" She stopped, bewildered. "You mean the new one I gave him today? How does that make Mack a crook?"

"Not the red one. The black studded one we took off of him. The one with the surveillance camera."

"The *what*?"

He filled her in on the details. What kind of camera it was.

How it worked. Where he'd found it. "It's a sophisticated device but generic. Readily available on the Internet or in a spy shop. You don't need a license to buy one."

Serena's eyes were wide with horror. "And you thought I put that hideous collar on Mack? With a camera in it? Believe me, it was already fastened around his neck when Mack's owner left him at Paws-A-While."

"His old owner, you mean," he reminded her. "I'm Mack's owner now."

"Of course you are," she said. "But a camera. How could I have missed it? I've groomed Mack, taken the collar off to flea shampoo him."

"It's very advanced technology. The lens is disguised in one of the metallic studs. So tiny I nearly missed it."

She shook her head slowly from side to side. "I can't believe this." She looked up at him. "Does this mean someone has been watching me, recording me, the whole time I've had Mack?"

"Yes. The camera was active. Adam has disabled it. Somewhere, someone might be getting worried. Might make a move into the open to see what happened to it."

Serena cursed, the first time he had heard her do so. "That bastard abandoned his dog. I thought that was as low as he could go. Now I find he's stolen from me and my clients."

"Maybe. He's a suspect, that's for sure. But the range of that camera, sophisticated as it seems, might be limited. We won't know how limited until we track down a receiver for it or Adam can get a fix on it with another receiver. Can it actually record credit card details? We don't know that. It's a good bet the fraudster—whether it's this guy or someone else—has had other access to your credit and banking details, too."

Serena looked like she'd been hit by a stun grenade. "He seemed like a nice enough guy. Although obviously he wasn't nice to abandon Mack. You know, I thought he might have died or been in an accident and that's why he didn't come back for Mack."

"That's a possibility. We won't know until we investigate. Serena, this could be important. Tell me everything you remember about Mack's old owner."

"His name is Eric Kessler. A guy in his thirties. Lived in Larkspur. Worked in an IT job in the Financial District."

"That figures. It would help to be tech savvy to get the most from that camera."

He enjoyed the look of concentration on her face as she sifted through her memories. "As I said, he paid up front. Seemed fond of Mack. I remember I got the impression he hadn't tried too hard to wean him from the fast food. That's all. I don't think there's anything else to remember."

She was so pale, except for the flush high on her cheekbones. Her eyes were huge and shadowed with anxiety. This was tough on her. But it would get tougher. He had questions he had to ask her that she would not want to answer. About her stalker. About the boyfriend she'd split from. And there was another fear she had to face.

"Serena, you have to report what's happened to you to the police. You have no choice. Unless you file a crime report the bank and the credit card companies won't treat this as fraud; you will get no recompense."

She shuddered. "I know. The bank guy told me that. But I don't like the police."

He put his arm around her; she didn't shake it off. He brushed a kiss on her dark hair; she did not recoil. Then with a little sigh, she leaned in toward him and relaxed her head against his shoulder.

For a long moment, he stood very still. He breathed in her heady scent, felt the in and out of her breathing, still too rapid and too shallow.

He wanted to protect her; he wanted to look after her. Dammit, he just *wanted* her. Not just for the pleasant, no-strings kind of interlude he had enjoyed with his former girlfriends. Serena was everything he didn't know he'd wanted until he found her.

Now he got that forever-after stuff. Stuff that had always seemed for other people, not for him, not yet. Until now. But he had to win her trust, prove her innocence, get her life back on track before he could consider getting it in step with his.

The sun warmed his back and his thoughts warmed his heart as he stood there with Serena by his side, knowing this calm interlude in a traumatic day must end, not wanting to be the one who ended it. He watched the two little dogs as they explored the endlessly intriguing scents of a park frequented by a lot of other dogs. Snowball started to cavort around Bessie, frisking in an invitation to play.

"I'll go with you to the police. Let me help you, Serena."

Serena twisted away from him.

"I don't get it," she said. "You lie to me. You think I'm a crook. But you want to help me."

He put his hands on her shoulders so she was forced to face him. "Get this straight. I know you're not a crook. I think I knew that on day one."

He was gratified by the twist of her mouth, the nod of her head that acknowledged her relief.

"However, I do think there is a link between the identity thefts and Paws-A-While."

"I get that," she said slowly. "It does seem too much of a coincidence. Though there could be some other link they have in common."

"Can you think of one?"

She shook her head. "The only thing I have in common with those people is the dogs."

How to say this without freaking her? He slid his hands down the length of her slender arms and held both of her hands in his.

"Serena, I don't have any evidence, just a really strong hunch. I think this could be something personal against you. The perpetrator might be after the money, sure, but they might also be aiming to put you out of business."

She gasped. He thought she would protest. But she slowly nodded. "Someone with a grudge against me."

"Or a business rival?"

She shook her head. "No way. I can't believe that. As an industry we support each other. Give each other referrals all the time."

"Okay, you can rule that out." But he wouldn't. "We need to work together on this, Serena."

"I guess," she said, not sounding totally convinced.

"Adam is not as certain as I am that Paws-A-While is the link. He'll pull the plug if we don't get some proof. I have to move quickly. I need names and contacts from you. Your staff. Your suppliers. Anyone with any possible connection that could lead you to think they might want to harm you or discredit you. I need to check the collars on all the dogs in your care."

"Of course," she said.

He gentled his voice. "And I need to know about your stalker, Serena."

She took a deep, shuddering breath. Wouldn't meet his gaze, went inward somewhere where he couldn't follow her. "I can't say his name. I . . . I won't say his name. It's the only way I can protect myself from him."

"Serena, I have to know your stalker's name. How about you write it down for me? That way you don't have to speak it."

She nodded. "Okay."

"Write it for me now, Serena; we don't have time to waste."

Dammit. Reaching into his inside jacket pocket meant he had to let go of her hands.

He gave her the small notebook and pen he carried with him at all times. He noticed her hand wasn't steady when she wrote the name and the letters were a bit wobbly on the page. He didn't recognize the name. But he'd soon find out everything there was to know about him.

"It couldn't be him," she said. "He's locked away."

He didn't want to add to her fears but he couldn't water down the facts, either. "We can't discount his involvement. He might have made contacts in prison."

He put the notebook back in his pocket. Reached out for her hands again. She linked her fingers through his, looked up to meet his gaze. Now he saw the glimmerings of trust in those remarkable eyes. Trust and something else that gave him hope that her discovery of the truth about him had not killed his chances with her.

He who travels fastest travels alone.

This had been the unshakeable maxim for his life. It had served him well.

But maybe the time had come when he didn't want to go so fast or so alone. Maybe his journey might be as successful, and a whole lot more pleasurable, if it were shared.

Two hearts are better than one.

It takes two to tango.

Some of those other old proverbs suddenly made a whole lot of sense as well.

He bent his head and kissed her.

Serena sighed into the pleasure of the kiss. She didn't care she was in a public park and heaven knew who could see her. It was delicious. Her heart started thudding.

She should stop this. Should pull away. She didn't want any more complication in her life right now. But oh, it felt so good. The pressure of his mouth on hers. The taste of him. His strength.

This man was a professional liar.

Trust me, he had said.

She had to overcome her fears, her trust issues, the barriers she had put up against being hurt again. She had to believe in his honesty, the sincerity she saw in his eyes.

Lucky they were in a public space. Because she wanted more than kisses. She wanted the sensual thrills promised by his skilful tongue and hard, strong body.

A sabbatical from sex?

All sabbaticals had to end some time.

She was lost in the sound of his breathing, the thud of his heartbeat.

Then sharp yapping and Snowball's growl, surprisingly threatening for a tiny white furball, intruded. Damn! She pulled away from Nick.

A curious chow had come sniffing around. Snowball, with Bessie as his shrill, yapping cheer squad, was letting the big dog know that a fluffy little Maltese was boss of the park.

"Snowball!"

She was fast but Nick was faster. He got to the two little dogs a stride before she did and shooed the big dog away. All in a few, masterful moments.

"You've got a knack with dogs," she said when he came back to her. As aftermath of the kiss her heart was still racing and her breath coming too fast, so it was an effort to make her voice sound normal. "They like you."

"I like them," he said. "As dogs, not—"

"Dog-kids, I know."

He was a heck of a lot more competent than some of the people she'd interviewed for positions at Paws-A-While. The dogs sensed the strength in him, the alpha confidence.

They trusted him.

She had to trust him, too.

Accept that he had misrepresented the truth in the interests of his job. Believe the evidence of his ID card and the sincerity in his voice. It might be the only way she could keep Paws-A-While in business.

She had to help him in any way she could. "Nick . . . I . . . I want to tell you what happened with the stalker. If there's a chance he's involved and it will help me save Paws-A-While."

Nick's brow creased in concern. "Are you sure you're ready for that?"

"Just hear me out without too many questions." She swallowed hard. "It started with an email through my Serena St. James website. It seemed harmless enough. I emailed the standard 'thank you for your interest' type of email. He emailed some more. I ignored them. After about twenty I asked him not to email again."

"Bad mistake."

She nodded. "He saw that as a sign of interest. He was in love with me, therefore I had to be in love with him. I blocked his emails."

"That didn't stop him?"

"The letters started then. Every day there was a letter."

"Did you go to the police?"

"He didn't make any threats. I thought I could handle it myself."

"But he knew where you lived."

"Not then, he didn't. They were sent to my post office box."

"Did you ever see him?"

"Would you believe he sent me photos of himself? The thing was, he was okay-looking. He could have got a girlfriend of his own."

"But not Serena St. James."

"No. He was totally into the fantasy of me in the tub of chocolate." She shuddered. "Then he sent me chocolate bars. Hundreds of them. I threw them out. But more would come every day."

Thank heaven Nick didn't laugh. She couldn't stand it if he

laughed. "Tell me you went to the police then," he said. "There are stalking laws."

She remembered how unhelpful the police had been—that one officer in particular. "People thought the chocolate bar thing was funny. They asked me to give him their address so he could send them some."

Nick made a sound of disgust. "You should have hired someone like me."

"I . . . I didn't know you then. Anyway, I honestly thought he was more of a nuisance than a danger. Then it stopped. I heard nothing. The police said he had moved on to someone else."

"But of course he hadn't," said Nick, his face a study in grim.

"I lived in the Mission then, a cute remodeled Victorian. It was a good part of the Mission; I always felt safe there. I had a roommate, Kim, a chef friend of Maddy's."

She stopped. Cleared her throat. This was the part she found difficult.

"Just take it as it comes." How could that deep, deep voice sound so soothing?

"I was studying part time. One night I got home from college late and . . . and found him in my bathroom. I thought I was going to die of shock and fear. He . . . he had somehow got buckets of chocolate sauce in there and was tipping them into the tub."

"Wanting to re-create the fantasy for himself."

"He . . . told me loved me. I was gagging on fear and the smell of the sauce. I told him he couldn't love me, he didn't know me."

"Not what he wanted to hear."

"I soon realized that. I tried to keep him talking while my mind raced to figure out what to do. I placated him, pretended to be friends. But he didn't buy it." Her voice rose as she remembered her fear. "He got nasty. If . . . if he couldn't have me, nobody could."

Nick growled a wordless protest.

The faster she spoke, the faster the recounting of this ordeal would be over. She felt she was babbling now. "He ordered me to strip. I refused. He pulled a knife. Then Kim came home, Maddy with her. I heard the door open, but he was too busy describing what was going to happen to me after I was in the tub of chocolate to hear. Thank God they realized something was wrong and crept up the stairs. Maddy had a huge fry pan in her hand, Kim a marble rolling pin.

"He heard something and looked away from me. I grabbed the hair dryer and whacked his hand with it. He dropped the knife. I kicked it out of his reach. The girls threatened him with their weapons." She took a huge, steadying breath.

"What happened then?"

"He started to cry. Like a thwarted little boy." She felt the familiar contempt. "We locked the door and called the police. He was convicted of stalking and committed to a high-security psychiatric hospital. I try never to think of him."

"But we have to consider him as a suspect who might wish you harm."

Serena appreciated that while she was recounting her ordeal, Nick had the sensitivity not to touch her. Now she was through it, she felt able to touch. She placed her hand on his arm. "You investigate him. I want nothing to do with it. It will only feed his fantasy if he thinks I have any interest in him whatsoever."

"Right," he said.

She thought about what he had said about hiring someone like him to protect her. Words formed before she'd really thought out her strategy. But immediately they made sense. "I want you to work for me," she said.

He shook his head. "No can do. The insurance company has retained us for this investigation. That would be a conflict of interest."

"That's not what I meant. I can't afford to pay you, anyway. Not

now. You should come on staff as a dog carer. Go undercover—
that's the right term, isn't it? That way you can see exactly what
might be going on at Paws-A-While."

And she would get to see him every day.

· Thirteen ·

Nick grumbled to himself under his breath as he unwrapped packs of conical, dog-sized party hats. The hats were red with a pattern of paw prints, trimmed at the base with blue feathers and topped with a blue pompon. In its own separate pack was a single black hat, with gold trim and pompons, and the words "Birthday Boy" picked out in gold.

Wouldn't you know it, his first shift on staff at Paws-A-While just had to be the day of Brutus's birthday?

Two days after Serena had proposed the idea, and after Adam had proved Serena was a genuine victim of identity theft, he was on board as a dog carer. The satisfaction of actually being under-cover and getting access to all areas—including those collars—was marred by the prospect of having to feign excitement at the prospect of a full-on canine birthday party.

Worse, he was expected to act as a waiter at the feast. Doggy day care was one thing. Dog parties another. His years of special agent training had prepared him to expect the unexpected—but nothing like this had come up in any training session at Quantico.

Party hats unpacked, his first job was to fence off an area at the far end of the playroom. There the millionaire mutt, his "wife," "daughter," and a select group of Brutus's puppy pals would be served a gourmet dog food lunch and be given party favors to take home afterward.

Putting up the fence was easier said than done with curious dogs intent on monitoring his every move. He was constantly interrupted by butting heads and wet noses and little whimpers of excitement. Thankfully once inside the security of the fence, free from canine companionship, it got easier. He helped Kylie lay a large, heavy, plastic picnic cloth on the floor. It was embellished with cartoon drawings of frolicking dogs.

He made an effort to sound enthusiastic about the just-so placing of the doggy hats but Kylie had overheard his grumbling.

"You're just not into it, are you?" she asked, as he knelt near her on the floor to help her lay the party table. His job was to put food and water bowls and a conical hat at each place. Kylie had to arrange a stack of rubber chew balls as a centerpiece and scatter some dog-safe streamers and novelties around for decoration.

As if the dogs could give a damn.

Kylie's friendly attitude toward him had done a complete turn-around when Serena had informed her that Nick was joining the staff. When he'd turned up this morning dressed in jeans and an official Paws-A-While shirt (made originally for Tom O'Brien and a tad tight across the shoulders) Kylie had been more hostile than hospitable.

Nick decided it was best not to answer with a lie. Kylie would sniff the rat of a sudden change in attitude. "You're right. Party hats and birthday cake for a pack of pooches. It's a sad reflection on our priorities," he said.

Under his guardianship there would be no birthday parties for

Mack. Ever. Mack, who right now would be undergoing his surgery. He hoped—no, he prayed—that all would go well for the big black dog.

"Our priorities at Paws-A-While are to care for every dog here as if it were our own." There was a note of reprimand to Kylie's voice that he didn't miss.

"I get that," he said.

"Well, I don't get why you're here. What's your game, Nick?" asked Kylie, with a noticeable lack of dimples.

"I told you. The company I worked for downsized. As I was last in, I was first to go. Serena offered me this role and I grabbed it."

"Yeah. Right. As if a big, strong guy like you couldn't have got work somewhere other than a doggy day-care center." She narrowed her eyes. "You don't fool me for a minute. I know why you're really here."

Inwardly, Nick cursed. Had Adam said something to her in the time he'd spent alone with Kylie? Had Serena accidentally alerted her to his undercover investigator status? Or was his game slipping?

"You do?" he said, forcing his voice into neutral.

"Yeah. I know you've got the hots for Serena. Wouldn't it be easier to just ask her out? Who do you think you're fooling with this charade of yours?"

He couldn't let his relief let him miss a beat. "Obviously not you."

"I know you've only taken this job to get close to her."

"A man wouldn't be human if he didn't admire Serena. But . . . I don't think dating in the workplace is a great idea. Especially when I have a dog as a guest here."

"Huh! You should be so lucky! I haven't seen Serena date any guys since I've been on staff and I've been here since day one."

"Is that so?" he said, studiously neutral, in spite of his very real interest.

"Yeah. She had a boyfriend in the navy who turned out to be a real jerk."

He'd got Dave's details from Serena and checked on him. He might be a jerk, but he had an exemplary record with the navy. "Maybe she might be ready for someone who's not such a jerk."

"Meaning you?"

He shrugged.

"Don't play that game with me," she said, sitting back on her haunches. "I know what guys like you are like. First you take the backseat and you're 'yes, ma'am, no, ma'am, what can I do to help, ma'am.' Then when you start boinking the boss suddenly you're throwing your weight around and lording it over people like me."

Nick forgave her the crudity because of the flash of fear he saw in her eyes. "I'm not after your job, Kylie," he said.

"Then what are you after? Serena?"

There was no use denying his attraction to Serena. Kylie seemed to pick up the signals of man-woman chemistry with radar-like precision. "I like her. Yeah. I'd like to get to know her better."

"Well, do something about it—like ask her on a date. Leave the jobs here to professional dog people."

He didn't want Kylie to feel her job was under threat. Unless, of course, she turned out to be a fraudster.

"Look, Kylie, Serena told me you needed some muscle around the place. Said she'd been thinking of putting on a guy to help with the heavy work, walk the bigger, more boisterous dogs. I'm your guy. Use me. I won't be here forever and Serena knows that. Obviously this isn't a career move for me."

"Hmph," said Kylie, but she did appear placated. "It didn't start that way for me, either. I used to work at a bank before I got into dog care. When I started here I thought it would be something temporary. But the job grew on me. Now I love it and I intend to stay for as long as Serena needs me."

"I get that, too."

Kylie had worked at a bank? That had not showed up on the job application he'd glimpsed on Serena's computer last week.

Kylie paused, a bunch of cheerful streamers in her hand. "You know the newbie always gets put on potty cleanup?"

Nick blanched. "But that fancy latrine outside flushes. Serena showed me."

Kylie laughed. "Yeah, when the dogs make it to the outside. With this many of 'em there are sometimes accidents. When the call goes out for mop and bucket you'll be the one answering it."

"Right," he said.

"Still keen to work here?" Now Kylie was enjoying herself.

There were worse undercover assignments. He was just having trouble thinking what they were right now. "Absolutely," he replied.

He got up from the floor as Kylie gave the table setting a final once-over. In the end it looked as good as it would for a table load of toddlers. His sister back home would kill for a table setting as cute as this for his nephew's birthdays.

Kylie stood up and stretched out her back. "Talking of muscles, how's that friend of yours, Adam?"

"Adam's good."

"He's a nice guy," said Kylie.

Nick had to suppress a grin. "He asked after you, too."

That was no lie. With Nick full time now at Paws-A-While, Adam had taken over the background checking of the Paws-A-While staff—starting with Kylie. He'd thrown himself into the assignment rather more enthusiastically than the job called for, Nick thought. But then, the entire staff of Paws-A-While was young and female.

"Did he, now?" said Kylie, dimpling. "Well, the next time he asks after me, you just remind him he's got my number."

"He does?" Nick couldn't keep the surprise from his voice. Adam was taking his information-pumping activities with Kylie very seriously.

"And I just might be free on Friday night when Finn has a sleepover at his buddy's house," she said.

"I'll be sure to tell him."

What the hell was going on here? Nick felt a twinge of unease. Serena had told him Kylie was an inveterate matchmaker and loved fixing people up. But she didn't date much herself as her priority was her son. For all her smart mouth she was vulnerable. Nick knew misrepresenting oneself was part of this job. But he would warn Adam to take it easy with Kylie.

Kylie stretched her back out again. "We're running on time; the other guests should arrive soon."

"Other guests?"

"Apparently Brutus's mom, Maddy, is remodeling her Pacific Heights mansion, so they can't have a party at home. They had a picnic last weekend for his doggy family. This is his celebration with the pals in his day-care pack. Tinkerbelle, his daughter, is already here, as you know. His son Tyson is coming to join the party, too. Coco will be thrilled to have another of her babies here."

"You think Coco recognizes the puppies as her babies?"

Nick tried to keep the skepticism from his voice. He knew what happened with farm animals; their offspring became just another animal no different to any other of their species.

Kylie shrugged. "Coco licks them and grooms them as if they're her puppies. She doesn't do that to any of the other dogs. That says mommy to me."

"And Brutus? Wouldn't Tyson be a rival?"

"Maybe. They get on. As Serena says, the dogs soon find their place in their pack. Besides they've all been fixed, so that solves a few problems with male aggression."

"Who are the other guests? The, uh, humans, I mean?"

"Maddy and Tom, of course, Brutus's parents."

"Of course," Nick echoed. He had to force himself from

cringing every time Kylie used the term "parent" to refer to dog owners.

"Maddy and Tom are good friends of Serena's. Tom's mom is coming, too; she's a nice lady. Tyson is her dog."

All this fuss for a dog. "How old is Brutus?"

"No one knows. He came from a shelter. But his first guardian—the old man who died and left him all the money—celebrated on the anniversary of the day he was adopted. He always had a party for him. Maddy told me she continues the celebration in the old man's honor."

"So that's it for visitors?" His initial research had virtually ruled out Maddy Cartwright and Tom O'Brien as suspects. But Tom's mom was an unknown quantity.

"Oh and Jenna, too. You know, Serena's other good friend."

"Organic-dog-treats Jenna?"

Kylie nodded. "That's right. She's made organic dog biscuits in the shape of a B for Brutus for party favors. Every dog at Paws-A-While will get one to take home."

"But they're not all invited to the party?"

"Ohmigod, no! Can you imagine the logistics of it? All the dogs here get a special treat on their birthdays. If their parents want to host a special party, that's up to them. Brutus is our top VIP client; not all the parties are as lavish as this."

"Right," said Nick.

Jenna was on the list of regular suppliers Serena had given him. Initial checks found Jenna to be everything Serena had told him. Grew up in the Bay Area and stayed there. Now doing her postgraduate degree at Berkeley. One clever lady by the looks of it. And with not so much as a parking ticket on record.

The woman who supplied the organic dog shampoos and conditioners had also checked clear. There were a surprising number of suppliers still to go. He found it amazing how many people supplied products of one kind or another to a doggy day-care center.

He had already determined that Mack's collar was the only one with a hidden camera. Now Adam's priority was the hunt for Eric Kessler, while also checking out Kylie and the other girls who worked at Paws-A-While. The clients who weren't victims of the fraud were also under investigation. But Nick could continue that in the time Serena had allocated for him to work "helping" her with her bookwork on the computer.

That was, when he was done with setting up for the pooch party.

As he set up a table out of reach of noses and paws, he sensed Serena come through the door from the reception. Even over the sounds and smells of the playroom he recognized her footfall and her warm, vanilla scent. He turned and there she was, carrying a big tray held out in front of her. He strode over to open the gate before she could even attempt to do it for herself.

No ogling the boss lady.

That was an impossible task. Man, she was beautiful.

She looked different today—he'd noticed that first thing this morning when he'd reported for duty. Her shapeless Paws-A-While shirt was unbuttoned. Underneath she wore a tank top that made no secret of her curves. And her jeans fit like a glove on her long, slender legs. He liked the difference and he didn't mask the admiration in his eyes.

But she was obviously determined not to respond. To treat him as just one of the staff.

"That looks great, guys; you've done a wonderful job," she said, smiling. He'd hardly seen her since Monday. She'd spent that evening with Maddy and Tom, the next with her parents. He was impatient to get her alone.

"Mr. Muscles here has been a great help," said Kylie.

"Thanks, Kylie, I appreciate you showing Nick the ropes," said Serena.

The tray was laden with some of the best-looking cakes Nick had ever seen. Frosted cupcakes topped with fans of fresh strawberries. Chocolate brownies. Crisp pastries with creamy fillings.

Within seconds Serena was immediately surrounded by dogs. And Nick.

His mouth watered. He'd gotten up at the crack of dawn to get through his usual grueling workout before he started on the early shift at Paws-A-While.

"Food for the human party animals, and it looks good," he said. "Did you make these?"

She shook her head. "Maddy did."

"Can I taste?" he asked. Without waiting for permission he reached out his hand to sample a particularly toothsome-looking brownie.

"Paws off," said Serena. "They're for the dogs."

Reluctantly, he withdrew his hand. But Nick had a highly developed sense of right and wrong—that was what had led him to working in law enforcement. It wasn't right for canines to be fed cake when hardworking humans were denied.

"It's obscene to give stuff like that to dogs. First Mack and the junk food. Now cakes and pastries? Sugar, fat, and heaven knows what else. Surely they shouldn't be eating those?"

"And you should?" she asked with a teasing challenge in those gorgeous eyes. This was one difficult assignment. How could he work for Serena, act like her subservient staff, when it was all he could do to stop himself from pulling her into his arms and kissing her senseless?

"I've been working all morning, not like those pampered pooches," he said.

She smiled a sexy little smile. "Of course you have," she said. "Which cake do you like the look of best?"

His hand hovered above the tray. They all looked wonderful. "The brownie I think." He picked up the biggest slice of the chocolate treat.

"Good choice," said Serena. "It's made with ground liver and carob."

Nick snatched his hand back. "You're kidding me." Nausea rose in his throat at the thought of how close he'd come to chowing down on a liver brownie.

"You're sure, now?" she teased. "It's very good for your fur and immune system."

Nick knew he'd gag if he tried to answer her. He glared at Kylie, who was nearly bent over in a paroxysm of giggles.

"I told you they were for the dogs," said Serena, her eyes dancing.

"These are dog cakes?" His words were underscored with disbelief.

"Every one. They're Maddy's specialty. She and Tom are bringing more in now. There's one for every dog at Paws-A-While."

Nick was not often lost for words. Now he was, to use an expression he had picked up in Australia, gobsmacked, so astounded he could only stare at the platter of cakes in Serena's hand.

"You're not the first one to be fooled," Serena said with her delightful laugh.

"They look like they're from a fancy cake shop."

"But they taste very different, I can assure you."

She came very close and handed the tray to him. This close he detected a distinct dog food smell that made him suddenly lose his appetite.

"Could you please take these over to the party area and put them on the high table out of reach of the dogs," she said in a very officious voice. Then in a husky whisper, "I can't be seen to treat you differently to any of the other staff."

"You can crack the whip on me anytime," he whispered back. She flushed, looked as though she wanted to say something in response, then glanced at Kylie.

"C'mon, get moving," she said instead. "We've got guests arriving at any minute."

"Yes, Boss," he replied. Then in a lower voice: "Just tell me what you want me to do most and I'm at your command. Anything."

She flushed a deeper shade of pink. "Ah," she said, looking up—avoiding his gaze—"Brutus's family is here."

Nick looked over to see Maddy, with another tray of those deceptive-looking cakes; a tall, well-built brown-haired guy whom he recognized from his photos as Tom O'Brien; and an elegant gray-haired woman who must be Tom's mother. She held in her arms another ugly, squashed-faced little dog who could only be the progeny of Brutus.

"Gotta go greet the guests," said Serena.

"Yes, Boss," said Nick with a mock salute. "Anything you say, Boss."

"Suck-up," whispered Kylie.

· Fourteen ·

The puppy party was well under way. Serena stood just inside the temporary fencing and surveyed the festivities with a poignant mix of pleasure and sadness. Paws-A-While meant everything to her, and she couldn't bear to believe it was under threat. She and her wonderful team did this kind of thing so well. It would be Halloween in a few days and that should prove to be fun, too.

She smiled as she watched Brutus bolting down a cupcake. He had refused to wear his Birthday Boy hat. He had, in fact, squashed it flat in his effort to rid himself of it. Same with his "I'm the Birthday Boy" tank top. The only thing that remained of the star of the day's party finery was the jaunty blue Birthday Boy bandanna. Brutus didn't seem to mind bandannas. He often arrived in day care with one tied around his neck. He looked very cute. Well, as cute as such an ugly little mutt could look.

The rest of his pack were in various stages of disarray. Only Cleo the basset hound and Pixie the teacup Pomeranian had kept on their hats, though the basset's had fallen to the back of her neck. Coco was fastidiously licking the carob coating from a kibble cookie. The rest of Brutus's pack buddies—and his puppies—were snuffling down pupcakes with no finesse or manners but, hey, what else did you expect from dogs?

Snowball was practically breathing in an oat-and-alfalfa cupcake and had pink cream-cheese-and-strawberry frosting smeared all through the white fur of his muzzle. As soon as he'd gulped down the last bite, he pushed aside the Pomeranian and snatched her brownie. The tiny dog let him take it without putting up any defense, then looked up appealingly to the nearest human—who just happened to be Nick—for help.

"Snowball—drop it!" Serena ordered, but Nick was already troubleshooting.

Within seconds both dogs were chewing on liver brownies.

She signaled her thanks with a wave. Nick was really good with the dogs. And he looked good in the Paws-A-While shirt she'd had made for Tom for the center's launch. It was tight on him, the fabric taut across every bulge and ripple of his magnificent chest and shoulders. Her breath caught and her nipples pebbled and tingled as she imagined tracing her fingers across the bare skin of that chest. Of kissing a path down and along his six-pack . . .

She shivered. Not with cold; it was warm in here with all the furry bodies and frantic activity. No. She might have tried to send desire packing, but it sure didn't want to stay on vacation. It was back home in full, fierce force. And focused entirely on this man.

She wrenched her gaze away from Nick's biceps and back to the doggy party. She couldn't stand here by herself enjoying the view for much longer. With this number of dogs, there was always work to be done.

There was the odd growl and yip as a tasty tidbit was defended and a few water bowls were tipped over but, between herself, Kylie, Nick, and the human guests, everything at Brutus's birthday party was going great.

She caught Nick's eye and smiled. His carefully controlled expression told her what he thought of the extravagance of it all. Maybe he had a point. But the party and the dog treats and the indulgences were all about the pleasure they brought to people rather than pups. Serena didn't kid herself for a second that the dogs could care less about their party.

Nick might deride the term "dog-kid." However, to many of her clients who didn't have kids in their lives, for one reason or another, their dogs were child substitutes. Serena counted herself among their numbers.

She lavished love on Snowball. But she considered she got the better deal of the bargain. Snowball gave her unconditional love in return for very little. He had even risked his life for her that horrible time when Brutus's would-be murderer, Jerome, had her helpless in a choke hold. Her little white dog had latched onto the villain's thigh with a ferocity that had surprised everyone. Jerome probably bore Snowball-bite scars to this day.

Even on that dark day in February, when she had been reduced to a squeak toy to hear the words "I love you" on Valentine's Day, Snowball had quietly licked her arm as she sobbed. A dog was a wonderful confidant at times when you didn't want the world to know you were hurting.

"Snowy is having fun," Maddy called over, as if she could read her mind.

"I'll make him send you a thank-you note," she said in reply, "you know, signed with his paw print."

Nick rolled his eyes heavenward, which made her smile.

She was proud of how well Paws-A-While balanced the line between practical care and indulgence, proud of how she'd built the business to be what it was in six months. And she'd fight with everything she had to save it.

Late Monday afternoon she'd reported the crime to the police. Not with Nick by her side; it was something she wanted to do by herself. To her surprise it hadn't been as bad as she'd thought. The cop who had made her so uncomfortable was nowhere in sight. In fact the officer taking the report had treated her with interest and respect.

Maddy's laughter rang out again over the doggy pandemonium as she took photos of Brutus's big day. She was such a good friend. After the walk with Nick at Fort Mason, Serena had gone straight to Maddy's house. When she'd told her friend about the identity fraud, Maddy had hugged her and told her not to worry about Brutus's investment just now. And Tom was there for her with help and advice and an offer of free legal representation. Tom was definitely one of the good guys.

She noticed Nick had moved around the table and was talking to Tom. Good. With a private investigator and an attorney on her side, she might just have a chance to beat this thing.

She looked at her watch. Dammit. Where was Jenna with the party favors? Serena wanted the B biscuits arranged in a basket out of the way of the dogs as a party centerpiece. For the benefit of the humans, of course. If Jenna didn't get here soon, it would be too late.

A sudden thought chilled her. Please don't say Jenna wasn't supplying them because her last invoice hadn't been paid?

"Serena!" Maddy called over. "Come over for a photo."

"Oh no, I—"

"I won't take no for an answer." Maddy put down the camera and stood, hand on hips, waiting for her. "Don't stand over there being the boss. Join in the fun."

"Okay," she said. Posing for a photo was once second nature to her. Now she did not like to give any of herself away to the lens.

She headed to where Maddy stood between Tom and Nick behind the picnic cloth where the dogs were munching up a storm. Maddy made a space for her and pulled her in so Serena stood with Maddy on her left and Nick on her right. For a moment she stood there, paralyzed by his nearness, rendered shaky-kneed by the rush of desire that hit her. He smelt so good it was intoxicating. *Sexy beast.*

"I'm proud of that brave face you've put on," he murmured in an undertone. "No one here would know how worried you are about everything. Well-done."

He was proud of her? It was a nice feeling.

Maddy handed the camera over to Helen O'Brien.

"Can you please take a nice one of the four of us?" Maddy asked her mother-in-law.

The four of us?

Since when was there a "four of us"?

She could tell both Maddy and Tom liked Nick. He was so quickly at ease with her friends, even with Tom, who was not the most outgoing of men.

Maddy winked and slung her arm around Serena's shoulders. Serena stood in an agony of discomfort. Every instinct urged her to snuggle against Nick's side, embrace his strength and warmth. But although they'd kissed, she wasn't sure when she stood with him. Then there was the fact that in the staff's eyes he was meant to be her employee, not her date. She didn't want to risk Nick's undercover status. Or her authority.

"Move a bit closer, kids," ordered Helen. "I can't fit you all in the frame."

Nick put his arm around Serena and pulled her close. She stiffened for just a second before she relaxed against him. Then looked up at his face just at the precise instant he looked down at her. He smiled as their gazes met and she smiled back. The look he gave her made her feel as though she was the only person in his world. Again she had that feeling that everything else faded away, the noise of the dogs, the laughter of the human guests, to just him and her.

Flash!

Helen's camera went off.

Serena edged away from Nick but his arm was firmly clamped around her and he would not release her. She loved the feeling of security and safety it gave her.

"I think I blinked," Maddy complained.

"Another one, please," said Helen. "Say 'sex.' "

Serena couldn't. She just couldn't say that. Not standing so close to this man who made her think of nothing but sex. Not when she was being watched by the staff, Kylie's eyes bright with curiosity. Not when she thought of how much she wanted everything to be perfect with Nick if things between them ever got that far.

"Sex!" hollered both Maddy and Nick, while she and Tom just laughed.

Helen snapped again. "That's a lovely one of all of you," said Helen.

"Great," said Maddy. "I'll email it to everyone."

"You haven't got my email address," said Nick.

"We'll get it from Serena," said Helen with a big smile for Nick.

Tom turned to Nick. "Better you than me caught forever on film in that god-awful shirt. You're very welcome to it."

The little group fell apart as arms dropped and they stepped aside from one another. Serena felt suddenly self-conscious, flooded again by doubt. The photo had grouped her with Nick as a couple. She'd liked the feeling. Maybe liked it too much.

Nick chatted easily with her friends. He fit in. Was that from genuine liking for them? Or was it all part of his game, to get people to warm to him so he could extract from them the information he needed? What happened afterward? When the job was done, did the instant intimacy evaporate?

What did that mean for her? When he—or the police, whoever moved fastest—tracked down the criminal who was stealing her clients' identities and put him behind bars, would that be the last she ever saw of Nick Whalen? It was tempting to lean on him,

let him help solve her problems. But what if he pulled that support away and she went under?

The thought sent a stab of pain through her, the intensity of
which surprised her.

She looked up to see Jenna bustling toward her with a big
cane basket. At last.

"So sorry I'm late," Jenna said, "but they're all done up and ready
to go."

Sure enough, the B-shaped dog biscuits were each wrapped in
cellophane and beautifully tied with paw-print-patterned blue
ribbon. "I . . . uh . . . got held up," said Jenna, flushing and smiling
up at the man behind her. The sexual innuendo was obvious and
it made Serena's skin crawl.

What was *he* doing here?

Serena tensed.

"What's up?" said Nick in a low tone that only she could hear.

"My boyfriend, Tony," said Jenna, by way of a general introduction.

"I don't like the guy," Serena whispered back to Nick. "I never
like any of her boyfriends, but this one really gives me the creeps."

For such a smart woman, Jenna had appalling taste in men. She
always ended up with bullies. Men who appeared charming at
first but then ended up intimidating her, even to the point of violence. Serena had no idea why—maybe some childhood abuse or
violence her friend had never chosen to confide in her about.
Who knew?

Whatever the reason, her track record with men was one of
the reasons someone as brilliant as Jenna was reduced to baking
dog biscuits to help get her through her studies. Almost without
exception, she dated guys who thought nothing of accepting expensive gifts from her. Gifts Jenna foolishly thought would make
them love her. She'd had a good job in IT before she decided to

study for her PhD. But she didn't appear to have a cent in the
bank.

Jenna had managed to hang on to this guy for nearly a year.
They'd just moved in together in a nice apartment in Oakland.
The kitchen was so tiny Serena couldn't understand how Jenna
could bake in there—but then, what the heck did she know about
baking? Jenna had moved there because Tony liked it and that was
that.

Three of the dogs scampered away from the table to mill around
Jenna's ankles. The dogs loved her treats so much they must be able
to scent them through the cellophane. Jenna nudged them aside
with her foot.

"Thank God Mack isn't here," she said to Serena. "He would
have bowled me over to get at this." Jenna was always nervous of
the enormous animal who, with his unerring instinct for treats,
could sniff her sample goodies out from wherever she hid them.
He was particularly partial to the carob-frosted doughnuts.

She put the basket of dog goodies on top of the table. "Happy
birthday, Brutus," she said, with a wave to Maddy and her family.

"Thanks so much, Jenna," said Serena. "You're just in time to
sing 'Happy Birthday.'" She indicated the large, chocolate-frosted
cake Maddy had placed on the high table. A six-inch-high red candle in the shape of a bone sat in the middle. Nick would be pleased
to note that this cake was for human consumption.

Maddy lit the candle. She paused for a moment and Serena
knew she was remembering Walter Stoddard, her eighty-two-year-
old landlord and friend, who had left a will appointing Maddy
guardian of both Brutus and his millions. She started to sing.

Jenna raised her eyebrows at Tony, a gesture that Serena didn't
miss. Jenna was a dog lover who made an income selling organic
dog treats. But if Tony thought singing "Happy Birthday" to
Brutus was uncool, then Jenna would agree. This please-her-man-

at-any-cost thing was something that bugged Serena about her friend.

Still, Serena noticed that Jenna mouthed the words as everyone sang. Nick joined in, too, in a deep pitch-perfect baritone voice that sent shivers racing along her spine.

"Happy birthday, dear Brutus, happy birthday to you . . ."

As the birthday song trailed to an end, Serena moved closer to Jenna. She lowered her voice. "I'm having some cash-flow problems and am a bit late paying your invoice. But I'll get it to you as soon as I can."

"No problem, hon. Whenever," Jenna said, also in a discreetly quiet voice.

Serena put her hand on her friend's arm. "Thanks," she whispered. She might not have a vast number of friends, but she felt truly blessed with the ones she had.

Jenna spoke at normal volume. "Tony has a new job so we're flush at the moment."

"Congratulations," said Serena to Tony, trying to summon up a sincere smile for Jenna's sake. She wasn't too sure of what Tony actually did for a job, sales of some kind she thought.

He nodded his acknowledgment of her congratulations. "It's all good."

In new chinos and jacket that looked more Gucci than Gap, he certainly appeared more prosperous than she'd seen him. To Jenna, Tony was the handsomest thing on earth, as she had repeatedly told Serena. Serena conceded the guy was good-looking; he worked out and kept fit. But she just didn't like him, for no other reason than instinct. Oh, and the fact he didn't like dogs. He made no bones about that.

"Nick, let me introduce you to Jenna and Tony," she said.

"We met on Monday," said Jenna. "But I didn't know you worked here now, Nick. I thought you were a client."

"Circumstances change," said Serena.

"I only started today," he said. "So far so good."

Jenna grinned. "Serena is a tough taskmistress. I hope she's treating you well."

"I jump to her every command," Nick said in that sexy, sexy voice, his eyes focused on her.

If that was the case, Serena could think of a few commands she'd like to give him. But not at Paws-A-While. She'd need to be alone with him. Alone and in total privacy.

"I'm keeping him in line," she said with mock severity.

Serena noticed that Jenna, too, was wearing new clothes. Her attitude toward Tony softened a little. At least he was sharing his good fortune with Jenna, unlike his predecessors, who'd done nothing but sponge off of her.

But she wished Jenna had asked her to go shopping with her to choose clothes that better suited her looks. Serena, with all her model expertise, itched to give her academic friend a makeover, but Jenna had always resisted.

"People can like me for the way I am or not at all," she would say. Usually with a barbed comment about the efforts Serena made to keep herself in shape.

Of course she was right. Serena had gotten way too hung up on her looks when she'd been modeling. Especially her weight. It was ironic really, how with all that emphasis on appearance, she'd ended up here in a dowdy uniform and Birkenstocks and happier than she'd ever been.

That was, until the phone call from the bank.

After the birthday cake for humans had been sampled, Maddy came up to say good-bye. She gave Serena a big hug. "Everything will be okay," she said. "I promise."

"Oh. Is there a problem?" asked Jenna.

"Of course not," said Maddy. "But Mack's gone in for his operation today."

"That's right," said Jenna. "I forgot. Fingers crossed he'll be okay."

"The vet hospital phoned not long ago," said Serena. "Apparently all went well. Mack is now sleeping off the effects of the anesthetic."

Nick moved closer again. "When can we pick him up?"

"Around three," she said. "After the vet gives him another once-over."

"I want to take him home to my house in Sausalito. That's home for him now."

Serena was taken aback. Somehow she'd thought she might ask Nick to help her upstairs with Mack and she'd look after him. She was a trained vet technician after all. But Mack was Nick's dog now. "Okay."

"I want you to come with me."

"To your house?"

"Yes. You can help me with Mack and we can talk."

"Talk . . . talk about his rehab program," she said for the benefit of anyone overhearing. She still didn't want her staff thinking there was anything personal between her and Nick except when it came to dealing with Mack. "Good idea. Can I bring Snowball?"

"Sure."

She lowered her voice again. "Tony. I don't know why I didn't think of him. He could be the one. Jenna is in and out of here all the time. He sometimes comes, too. I don't know why because all he does is sneer at our setup."

"Just because he's a creep doesn't make him a criminal," said Nick. "But you give me his details and we'll check him out."

Serena turned away. "Right, everyone, cleanup time. The dogs need attention, too. They've all eaten so will need to go out back." She turned to Nick and made a very stern, manager-type face. "That means you, newbie."

She laughed at the expression on his face.

She was looking forward to seeing Mack. She'd saved him a

nice liver brownie and put it in the fridge for when he was able to eat. But she wasn't so sure if what she was about to do was the right thing—being alone with Nick at his house with only the dogs to chaperone them.

· Fifteen ·

Nick spent the entire drive home from Paws-A-While to his home in Sausalito wishing he was Mack. Not that he was an oversized, dopey black dog with an injured knee all stitched up and encased in a purple cast. No. He wished he was sitting in the back of his truck with his head cradled on Serena's lap, her long, elegant fingers stroking his head, scratching behind his ears, and caressing his body. All to the sound of her voice crooning sweet words about what a big, beautiful boy he was.

His plan to get her alone with him had backfired badly. Now he had to share her with Snowball, Bessie, and that convalescing center of attention, Mack. Instead of Serena sitting in front next to him, her lovely long legs right where he could see them— touch them even—he had Bessie. Serena sat in back with Snowball and a semicomatose Mack.

It was all a guy could do not to get jealous of his own dog.

"He's belted in, but I want to hold him to keep him secure," she'd explained when he'd protested her choice of seat. "We can't risk his leg being jarred or knocked. You heard what the vet said."

"I heard," he said.

He cared about Mack. Of course he did. He could hardly wait until his dog's injury was healed and he could run with him and play Frisbee with him and do all those guy-and-his-dog kinds of things he'd missed out on for years.

But he could hardly wait to be with Serena, too. And do all those guy-and-his-gal kinds of things this special woman inspired. He wanted her sitting up front with him. Why in hell would she rather be in back with his dog?

Just ask her on a date, Kylie had urged. Well, yeah, easier said than done. That might have worked if they'd met under more normal circumstances. They'd gone past that now. In her book, he'd gotten off on the wrong foot with her by investigating her as a prime suspect in a criminal fraud. That was way past asking-her-out-to-dinner-and-a-movie type protocol. He knew he had some catching up to do in the trust department.

Dogs were undisputedly the best way to get Serena on his side. Corralling her into helping him with Mack tonight was a no-brainer way to ensure he had time alone with her. Time to win her over to the idea of having him in her life on a more ongoing basis.

By the time they were heading over the Golden Gate Bridge, the three dogs were all settled and snoozing. Mack was zonked from the aftereffects of the anesthetic, painkillers, and anti-inflammatory medication. Snowball and Bessie were just plain pooped from running around at Brutus's birthday party.

When Nick had the chance to turn around, he saw that even though Mack was asleep Serena still kept her hand anchored to the big dog, her fingers curled into his fur. It was to secure him but also, Nick thought, to let Mack know he was with people who cared about him now.

Not for the first time, Nick wondered about what kind of person Eric Kessler could be to abandon such a nice dog. It certainly seemed to demonstrate the callousness needed to defraud and steal from innocent people. Kessler could be their guy.

"You are such a good boy," crooned Serena from the backseat.

"Well, it's nice of you to say so," said Nick, "but I think you've thanked me enough for looking after Mack."

"Oh, but I . . . I wasn't . . . I mean . . ."

Nick grinned. He didn't need to turn around to guess her flush of confusion. "Sweet," Adam called her. His friend was right. For all her gorgeous looks and semi-celebrity status, she really was sweet. But the sweet was seasoned with sass and he liked that.

"You mean you're calling Mack a good boy and not me?" he said with mock affront.

There was silence from the backseat for about a second. "I think you're a very good boy . . . uh . . . I mean man . . . uh . . . person. Heck. You know what I mean." He could hear the smile in her voice.

"Yeah, I guess I do," he said, letting her off the hook.

"I feel guilty about leaving early from Paws-A-While," she said, after a moment.

"Don't be. Kylie was glad to lock up for you and earn some overtime."

"That was lucky, because I really did want to come with you."

He gripped tighter on the steering wheel. "Good," he said. He was falling for this woman—but so far she'd given little indication of what she felt about him. This was an excellent sign.

"Yes," she said. "With everything else that's happened, we haven't had a real chance to talk about—"

Us, to talk about us, Nick thought.

"Mack," she said.

Nick was tempted to bang his head against the steering wheel. Not a good idea when he was negotiating the turn off 101.

"You mean his rehab? Physical therapy? That kind of stuff. I'm prepared to do whatever the vet prescribes. At my cost. He's my dog now and I'm responsible for him."

"That's exactly what I meant. You see, I . . . I got kind of a shock when you told me you were taking him home so soon. I've gotten used to having him with me. I . . . I'll miss him."

This was better. His strategy was working out just how he'd planned.

"You can visit Mack anytime," he said.

"I can? At your house?"

"Sure. He'll be with you at day care, too, remember. At least while the investigation is under way."

"About that. Mack's day care, I mean. I want it understood he stays at Paws-A-While for free."

He shook his head. "No way. I'll pay for him the same as I pay for Bessie."

"Please, Nick. Let me do this for you. It's only fair after all you're doing for Mack."

He would find a way to ensure she wouldn't be out of pocket. She was generous to a fault. Mack was his responsibility now and he took that seriously. In the meantime he didn't want to argue. "You can take his fees out of my wages."

She paused half a beat. "As I've got you working for free, that works out just how I want it." She laughed, but the laugh then turned into an anguished sound that tore at his heart. "Why am I so blithely talking about whether you pay a fee or not when Paws-A-While might not exist for much longer?"

The anguish in her voice made him want to pull the car over and take her in his arms to comfort her. But, dammit, he couldn't, not on this stretch of road.

"Serena, I promise you, with me and Adam on the case, we will find who has done this. Adam is tracking down the status of both your stalker and Eric Kessler to find out what Kessler knows about that collar. As you know, your friend Tom O'Brien is looking into the legal implications."

"Yes." Nick got the impression she was swallowing a sob. "Tom said he'll do everything he can to make sure the banks and credit companies don't drag their heels when it comes to claiming fraud insurance."

"Good. He's a nice guy, Tom. Maddy's cool, too. I liked the mom, Helen, as well." That was no lie. He had enjoyed their company. He didn't know many people in San Francisco and looked forward to seeing the O'Briens again. Tom and he had talked about going horseback riding one weekend. Did Serena ride? He realized there were so many things he wanted to know about her. This afternoon was a good place to start.

Serena sniffed. "I've got good friends. I'm lucky."

He cleared his throat. "You can count on me as a friend. You know that." He wanted to be way more than friends, but friend was a start.

She hesitated, making it clear he still had some way to go to win her trust.

"Yes. Thank you," she said.

The change in engine noise as Nick drew up outside the driveway to Aunt Alice's house in the Sausalito hills caused Mack to stir. He gave a little whimper deep in his doggy throat. Nick winced in sympathy. He knew full well what it felt like to have this knee repair done. Still, the vet had said the ligament was only partially torn, which would make healing quicker and the resulting repair stronger.

He intended to carry Mack in by himself, but Serena would not hear of it.

"Let me help," she said.

"He's a deadweight—too heavy for you."

"I'm very strong."

It would be easy for him to simply carry Mack over his shoulders in a fireman's lift. However, if Serena insisted on helping him and that involved brushing shoulders and getting close, who was he to refuse her offer? He liked the idea of working with her, period.

Still, he was surprised how much strength there was in Serena's slender frame as she helped him slide Mack out of the truck. The big dog was awake but too out of it to fuss or struggle. With him holding Mack's shoulders and Serena holding the dog's hips and injured leg, it was a cinch to slide him out of the truck. Snowball scarcely stirred, just opened one round dark eye from under his fluffy white bangs and went back to sleep.

"Where to?" said Serena when they'd carried the big dog through the front door. She was flushed with exertion and breathing just a little quicker than usual, the rise and fall of her breasts emphasized by the snug tank top she wore under the open shirt.

"Everything is ready for him," he said, indicating the outsized new dog bed he'd bought and set up in front of the fireplace. As per the vet's instructions, he'd lined the bed with plastic sheeting and newspaper in case of accidents.

"Hey, you got Mack the same bed I have for him," she said, sounding pleased.

"I learn from the best," he said. She didn't need to know how carefully he'd scrutinized the fittings of her apartment the day he'd visited for lunch.

Together they lowered Mack into the bed. The outsized dog settled as best he could, while favoring his back right leg with the purple cast. With a heavy sigh, he settled his head on his front paws and looked up at them with his big, expressive eyes and sad frown. The one-ear-up-and-one-ear-flopped thing just added to the poignancy of it.

"He must be wondering what the hell happened," said Nick.

Serena crooned and stroked Mack around his head. "Poor baby," she said. "It feels bad now, but it will be worth it when you can run around with the other dogs."

Even doped up and drowsy, Mack attempted to wag his tail at the tone of her voice, but it was a feeble effort. "You've got a beautiful new home and a great new dad—"

"Stop there," said Nick and put his hand up in a halt sign. "Serena, let's get this straight. I will not be this dog's daddy. I'd prefer master or owner but I'll go with guardian to please you."

"To please me?" Her eyes widened.

He could deny it. He could say it was to please Mack. But why lie? There'd been enough lies.

"Yes, to please you. Frankly I don't think the dog gives a damn what I'm called so long as I feed him and care for him. But it seems to be important to you."

"Oh," she said. Confusion and pleasure warred on her face but a half smile won out. Mack stirred and she lifted his hindquarters to make him more comfortable. Her shirtsleeves were rolled up and Nick noticed how toned and strong her arms were.

Serena would be a great help on a farm.

It wasn't the most obvious observation to make about Serena St. James. But he wasn't thinking of the sexy siren with the seductive eyes, her perfect body just asking to be licked free of its silken coating of chocolate. It was a valid observation to make about the Serena he knew—strong, savvy, and confident with animals. As well she had—in his book—the most important attribute of all for a farmer's wife: she could cook.

He could see her in the valley fitting right in on his farm. One day.

Right now the valley was the last place he wanted to be. As soon as he was able, he'd escaped from what he'd seen as the straitjacket of a predetermined life. His father and his father's father and his father's father before that had farmed in the valley. His brother

Sam had accepted his destiny without question. Sam willingly farmed the parcel of land his grandfather had left him. He also farmed the adjoining land his grandfather had left Nick. The resulting income was what allowed Nick to do things like adopt an injured dog with a big vet hospital bill.

The land was prime real estate, on the fertile flat with good water and views of the river and the eternally snow-capped mountain that stood guard over the valley. Nick had been offered good money for that land many times but had never been tempted. The land was his backstop, his security, a place he knew was always there for him. One day, maybe years from now, he might want to return and make a home there. He would never, ever sell.

Would Serena like it in the valley? The slow pace of life, the social life centered on family and school and church might be too slow for Serena St. James. But Serena Oakley? He would have to take her there so she could see for herself.

Serena got up from Mack's side. "He's settled, though we need to put a big bowl of water within easy reach. If you sort that out, I'll go get Snowball and Bessie from your truck. The windows are down but I don't want to leave the dogs any longer."

Nick got the water for Mack, then followed Serena out the front door. He found her standing on the porch, drinking in the view of the bay, gloriously blue in the late-afternoon sun, white sailboats scudding across the water to San Francisco. The burnished roof of the Palace of Fine Arts glinted in the distance.

It seemed very right she should be there at his home, albeit his temporary home. He hadn't known her long, but he had the feeling that wherever she was would seem like home to him.

He came up behind her and put his hands on her shoulders. She stiffened for a moment at his touch, and he remembered how recently it was that she'd cringed from him. Then she relaxed on a deep, outward breath. He slid his arms under hers and pulled her back against his body, her back to his chest, the curves of her bottom against his thighs. He rested his chin against the side of her head.

"Some view, huh?" he said.

"If I had superhero vision, I could see Paws-A-While from here," she murmured. "It's beautiful. The house. The view. I love it."

You're beautiful and I love you, he thought, breathing in the intoxicating scent of her. He nuzzled into the satiny smooth skin of her neck and was encouraged when she tilted her head back with an almost imperceptible sigh of pleasure.

Love?

So soon?

Oh yes. This was it. She was The One. He knew that with absolute, unshakeable certainty.

He pulled her closer and she rested her hands on top of his. His body reacted instantly to her closeness.

His woman.

Every male instinct urged him to pick her up, carry her into the bedroom, and make her his. But Serena needed gentler handling than that. There were her trust issues. The stalker. He didn't want to scare her off. Then there was the work scenario. They needed to talk about how they would handle this. It would be best if they kept their relationship private at this stage. He turned her around to face him. Her face was flushed, her eyes luminous, her mouth ripe for kissing. "Serena, I—"

In the distance a neighbor's dog barked. Serena's eyes widened and she dropped his hands. "Ohmigod, the dogs."

The truck was just yards away from them, the windows down, the two animals clearly visible asleep. Nick saw no need to panic. But maybe Serena was panicking over something altogether different. He'd noticed how effectively she could use the dogs to put a distance between them when it suited her.

"What am I doing up here admiring the view when the dogs are still in the car?"

"The dogs are just fine," he said.

She dropped his hands and headed toward the steps. "Can't risk leaving dogs too long in cars," she said.

Nick had to laugh. If he didn't laugh, he'd grind his teeth in frustration. Dogs. Did they always come first for Serena?

He stomped inside to check on Mack.

· Sixteen ·

With Bessie still drowsy in her arms and Snowball by her feet straining at his leash to sniff every new interesting scent he could find in the front garden, Serena paused to step back and admire the house Nick was looking after for his aunt.

Built on the hillside that rose steeply from the main street of Sausalito, the small, Victorian-style house was one of the most beautiful she'd seen. It was not at all the place she'd imagined Nick would live in. She saw him in a ranch-style house, cedar maybe, very masculine with lots of space. But boy, was this the kind of house she would give her eyeteeth to own.

It nestled in the hillside behind a low stone fence, white-painted clapboard with the decorative railings on the porch and the upstairs balcony picked out in gray. The front door was a surprise splash of bright red. A fat palm tree was the focal point of the front garden. Roses rioted over the fence, lush with fall's final flush of generous yellow blooms. Hydrangeas with big heads of faded, dried flowers flanked either side of the steps up to the porch. A tub of impatiens, the same cheerful flowers she had in pots in front of Paws-A-While, sat by the front door in welcome. She breathed in the scent of roses that suffused the air.

A wave of longing swept over her. She liked old houses, not just for their charm and character, but also for what they represented— permanence and stability, two things lacking in her early life. This house was perfect. Lucky Nick. Lucky Nick's aunt.

A child with a different personality might have thrived on her parents' peripatetic lifestyle. Not her. She'd longed for suburban security and an established circle of friends. While living in a succession of rented houses and communes with her parents, in shared apartments with her friends, in the little remodeled Victorian in the Mission, she'd dreamed of exactly this kind of house. With a garden just like this, too; she wanted more than a window box and some tubs one day.

For those few minutes on the porch she'd reveled in the bliss of feeling safe, secure, and cherished in the circle of Nick's arms. As soon as she'd heard his footfall behind her she'd stopped registering the view. Not with him holding her so warm and so tight.

Him. Her. Home.

It felt so right.

She sighed. *Wake up, Serena.* This wasn't her home, and with the price of Sausalito real estate she'd never live in a place like this— even without the prospect of losing her business and her bank account because of the fraud.

But there was no price on daydreams. For that brief time on the porch she'd let herself lean back against him and imagine what it would be like to live here—or somewhere like here—with Nick. Nick and three dogs. Nick and maybe three kids.

Kids? How did the image of a towheaded little boy with pale blue eyes suddenly push its way into her fantasy? A little girl with Nick's coloring would look adorable, too. Two girls and a boy? Or two boys and a girl?

She'd never before let herself dream of kids; she hadn't felt settled enough for that. Or gotten the guy right. Deep down, she
wondered if she had what it took to make a good mom. Kids
meant commitment; kids meant not giving up and walking away
when things got tough. Did she have that sticking power?

She cuddled Bessie so close the little Yorki-poo whimpered.
"Sorry, sweetie," she said, and kissed her on the head. Fur babies
were all she could cope with right now. But if things worked out
with Nick . . .

Still reeling at the right-from-nowhere thought of those three
blond kids, she went back inside through that cute red door. As
soon as she got inside she was struck all over again by what an utterly perfect home it was. She hadn't had a chance to appreciate it
when she'd been helping Nick with Mack.

The house was every bit as appealing inside as it was from the
outside. Painted in airy shades of white it had been modernized
without losing any of its quaint charm. The rooms had been
opened up so she could see right though to a wall of French doors
at the back. Framed paintings and interesting pieces of pottery and
sculpture had been artfully arranged to lift the simplicity of rooms.
She wanted a good look at those when she got a chance.

Bessie struggled to be put down. When Serena did so, the little
Yorki-poo scampered toward the back door. Snowball strained to
follow.

"The yard is safe for him if you want to let him out," said Nick,
who stood leaning on the mantel of the fireplace near Mack.

She couldn't meet that penetrating blue gaze. He'd run scream-
ing for the hills if he could read she'd been fantasizing about having
his kids.

"I'd like to keep an eye on the little ones," she replied. "Snowball and Bessie are good friends. But this is Bessie's territory and
I'm not sure how she'll react to him being here on her turf."

She followed Nick through the living room, a dining nook,

and a kitchen that opened to the backyard. Bessie was already scratching at the door to be let out.

The backyard was pretty, too. And great for dogs. Leafy trees for shade. Lots of grass. Fenced for security. There was a water bowl attached to the tap that automatically filled so dogs would never run out of water. Two doghouses sat side by side in a sheltered spot. The big one was shiny with newness. Serena smiled to see it was modeled along the lines of a cedar ranch house just like the one she'd imagined for Nick. On closer inspection she saw the smaller one was a scale model of his aunt's actual house. The words "Bessie's House" were hand painted across the eaves.

Bessie took off, running around and around in circles and yapping in invitation for Snowball to join in. Territorial disputes? Forget it.

"Dog heaven," she said to Nick, who stood next to her. She would have liked to slip her hand into his, but she still felt ridiculously shy around him.

"Yeah. Between here and your place Bessie has a great life."

"Mack will, too. This will be wonderful for him."

He shrugged. "Until Aunt Alice comes back and I have to move. I was planning on a condo but that's out of the question now."

"Did you think of that when you decided to adopt Mack?"

"Sure. A dog means a big change of plan. I'm ready for that now."

He looked intently at her as he spoke. Did she read some message for her there? Her heart started doing that tripping-over thing.

"It would be great if you could get a place like this. It's so beautiful." She couldn't keep the wistfulness from her voice.

"I thought you'd prefer contemporary to cozy."

She indicated the garden and the house with a sweep of her arm. "I guess I'm an old-fashioned girl at heart because I think this place is just perfect. It doesn't seem like an old lady's house at all."

Nick laughed. "Wait until you meet Aunt Alice. She's no stereotypical old lady. She moved here years ago for what she calls its 'bohemian vibe.' She hates how touristy Sausalito has become, but tourists are the lifeblood of the gallery she runs here."

"I noticed there were a lot of paintings inside."

"Some are hers, some by artists she couldn't bear to part with. She's quite a character."

"You sound fond of her."

"She says we're kindred spirits because we both wanted to get out of the valley where we were born. Difference is she'll never go back there whereas I'm keeping my options open. All the rest of my family is still there, parents, brother, sisters, and a whole parcel of cousins."

Lucky, lucky Nick.

"I envy you that, your family, your roots," she said. "I've got some cousins in England on my mom's side I met once and don't even remember and no one on my father's side."

"My family's okay. But there are times I would happily swap with you. C'mon, let's go inside and get a beer. Or coffee. Or Diet Coke. Whatever you like."

"Diet Coke sounds good," she said. "We'd better check on Mack, too."

"He's as out of it as a bear in hibernation," Nick said.

She laughed. "No wonder, with all the meds they've given him."

The big dog looked comfortable, though his leg with its bright purple cast now stuck out at an angle. She knelt down beside him and gently repositioned the injured leg. "My special boy," she murmured. Then she started to stroke around his ears the way Mack loved.

She felt Nick's hands on her shoulders.

"Serena," he said in that gravel-rough voice that sent shivers down her spine. "You've stroked that dog's ears so much there soon won't be any fur left on them."

He pulled her to her feet and turned her to face him. "There's a boy here who wants your attention, too."

He was joking but there was a watchfulness in his eyes that made her aware of how serious he was. She knew she was guilty of hiding behind the dogs rather than facing situations she found difficult. But she didn't want to hide anymore.

"You want your ears stroked?" she asked with a teasing edge to her voice that she hoped disguised the fact she was suddenly paralyzed with nervousness. "Like Mack?"

She was twenty-eight years old, her image emblazoned on billboards across the country in nothing but bikini undies and a cloak of chocolate, but she was nervous before this big, tough guy who had made her dream way beyond the boundaries she'd set to keep her life comfortable and safe.

"Well, if you're offering . . ." He bent his head closer to hers.

In his black T-shirt and jeans that molded to the strong muscles of his thighs and butt, Nick Whalen was the hottest guy in the universe and she felt dizzy at his nearness. But it wasn't just his looks. For all her initial worries about him being the same type of man as those who had hurt and disappointed her, he had proved himself to be a rock.

She could stroke his ears; she could stroke . . . Well, she could stroke him all over. Then lie back and let him stroke her. Her life had been peaceful with no sexual interest in it, but she was beginning to remember how passion was way better than peace.

She cupped his face in her hands, enjoyed the graze of his beard under her fingers, met his gaze full-on as his eyes narrowed with interest. Slowly, she slid her hands up toward his ears. He had nice ears, well formed and flat to his head. She reached out and traced the edges with the tips of her fingers, caressed the lobes and gently tugged on them. She felt a shudder run through his body. "You like that, big boy?" she said.

"Ruff-ruff," he replied, his voice hoarse. Serena laughed a low, husky laugh—she was enjoying this. Pleasing him was a pleasure in itself. Her laughter seemed to echo through the house.

Nick's breathing was loud and ragged. There was an old-fashioned clock somewhere and she could hear it tick-tick-tick. Mack shifted in his basket. She was aware of the rapid thudding of her own heart.

"Scratching, too? You like scratching?" she murmured as, with the edges of her nails, she scratched the short stubble of his hair behind his ears, making it a slow, tantalizing caress.

He growled a deep sound in his throat that was pure aroused human male and nothing to do with pretend dog noises. The sound seemed to connect with every nerve ending in her body. Her nipples tightened to painful peaks and her thighs clenched in a spasm of desire. She found the look of pure bliss on his face very sexy. Heck, she found everything about him very sexy.

Still with teasing lightness, she feathered her fingers down and along the strong, hard line of his jaw. Then she reached his mouth, that wonderful mouth that felt so good on her own. Her breath quickened. She traced the fuller lower lip along the edges, then the top lip she found so incredibly sensual.

He took the fleshy pad of her finger between his teeth and nipped it. She gasped. It was more pleasure than pain, a sensation that shimmered through her. He took hold of her wrists and pulled her hands away from his face, holding them by her sides. She leaned forward to press her mouth against his.

"Boss lady in charge," he murmured against her mouth.

"Mmm," was all she could manage in reply. This felt too good to interrupt with talk.

She traced the seam of his lips with her tongue until the tip of his tongue met hers. Kissing Nick was heaven. She pressed her body close to his. His muscles felt like a rock wall. The man was built like a fortress.

His strength attracted her. In the past she had feared being taken over, having her life taken out of her hands, but the only feelings she got from Nick were of security and safety. He was man enough to let her be a boss lady without feeling threatened. But was she woman enough to let go and trust him to look after her?

This full-frontal kiss had a lot going for it. Breast to chest. Thigh to thigh. Every part of her body aware of the contact, his heart pounding against hers. She didn't resist when Nick released her hands to slide his up the outsides of her thighs, warm and strong and confident. She trembled with pleasure and arched her back to get closer.

The sound didn't register at first, the loud shrill of a cell phone. Not hers. She broke away from Nick's kiss, looked questioningly at him. He shook his head. "Ignore it," he said and claimed her mouth again.

The cell phone fell silent, only for the landline in the room to start. Nick cursed, pulled her close to him again, kissed her so she scarcely heard the phone. The second it stopped his cell started again.

The mood was broken. She couldn't help the anxiety invoked by an incessant ringing of a phone. "They . . . they're not giving up," she said, too breathless to speak coherently. "It might . . . might be urgent."

"It had better be urgent." He stepped back but took hold of her hand and led her to where his leather jacket was flung over the sofa. "I'm not letting go of you." With his right hand he pulled out his cell from a pocket and checked the caller ID, all the while holding on to her with his left hand. "It's Adam."

"Better take the call, then," she said, pulling regretfully away from him, forcing her breath to return to normal.

Nick cursed. Of all the damn times for Adam to call. He was sorely tempted not to pick up. But Adam might be trying to reach him with information about the case. Information that could help him help Serena. He had no choice. He flipped open his cell.

Adam had news, all right. Nick spoke briefly to his business partner, then disconnected.

Then he turned to Serena. Her cheeks were flushed, her mouth swollen; strands of hair had come loose and fallen across her face. He groaned his frustration and closed his eyes. The sight of her made him unable to concentrate on the investigation that, with a phone call, had intruded so rudely.

When he opened them, he was better able to control himself. Although Serena didn't look any less alluring, any less kissable. It would be so easy to put this news on hold and start again with Serena where they'd left off. But that wasn't how it worked for him.

"Adam reports that your stalker is still safely locked away."

She closed her eyes briefly, her relief palpable.

"Adam says that"—he nearly said the stalker's name but stopped himself in time—"he is unlikely to be plotting trouble for you from his cell. He's terminally ill. Cancer."

She paused. "I don't care one way or the other what happens to him so long as he never comes near me again." She took a deep breath. "And Eric Kessler?"

"Adam has tracked down Eric Kessler and is on his trail."

"That's good news, isn't it?" She gave a wry smile. "Though the timing of its delivery could have been better."

"Agreed," he said, taking her hand again.

She squeezed his hand in response. "Is it a breakthrough?"

"Could be. Kessler is high on the suspect list. Adam has also been working on Tony Cross. What he's found out about him is not such good news for your friend Jenna. The guy has got a record as long as my arm. You name it, he's done it. Criminal trespass, assault, trafficking stolen property are just some of the things Adam dug up on him."

The color drained from Serena's face. "That's not totally unexpected. I'm not surprised at all. I don't like Tony one little bit." She looked up at him, fear and worry for her friend etched clearly in her expression. "Poor Jenna. I've got to warn her about him."

He shook his head. "Not a good idea to show our hand. He's a suspect now."

"But what if he hurts her?"

"Come here," he said, leading her to the sofa. He could, at least, have the pleasure of snuggling with her as they spoke. "Your friend's a big girl, Serena. She lives with the guy. She might not welcome your interference. But we'll have him under surveillance. Either by Adam or another guy who works for us on this type of job."

"So you think Tony might be involved?" She shuddered. "He's always given me the creeps."

"He could be our guy. But so could Eric Kessler. It all hinges on that collar and whether or not he planted the camera."

"If Adam finds him, what does that mean for you?" The expression in her eyes told him she already guessed the answer.

"I'd planned to cook you dinner. But now I've got to go meet with Adam at the office." He didn't try to hide the regret he felt.

"Shame," she said with a sigh. "What about Mack? He can't be left alone. Do you want me to stay here with him?"

"There's nothing I'd like better than to come home after a night in a surveillance van to find you here waiting for me." He kissed her. "But I don't know when I'll be back. I'll take you and Snowball home. I'll ask my aunt's friend Hannah to come and keep an eye on the dogs for me while I'm out. She loves Bessie and is looking forward to meeting Mack."

Serena didn't do a good job of hiding her disappointment at the way the evening was ending. "I wish . . . I wish it had turned out different here."

"Me, too," he said. "But we've started something we're going to go on with, Serena."

She turned to face him directly. He pushed clear the lock of hair that always fell across her cheek. "That is, if you want that."

She leaned closer and kissed him on the mouth. "Yes. I want that," she said. "I want that very much."

· Seventeen ·

Next morning, Serena sat in her office with the Maltese terrier snow globe in her hand. Idly she shook it so the snow danced all around the little plastic dog in the striped scarf. The flakes settled in drifts around his tiny toy feet. No matter what was happening in that toy's world it kept on smiling its static doggy grin.

That was just how she felt today, a smile hovering around her lips, no matter how gloomy the outlook from the bank. No matter how worried she was about Jenna. Or puzzled over Mack's collar. Little shivers of anticipation and pleasure ran through her body when she thought about Nick, and that smile turned into a grin.

When Kylie popped her head around the door she didn't miss that grin, though Serena hastily tried to subdue it.

"You're looking very happy," said Kylie. "Any particular reason?"

Serena shrugged, knowing that smile was still lifting the corners of her mouth. "Do I need a reason?"

Kylie took a few steps farther into the room. "No. I just wondered if it had anything to do with your newest employee, you know, the big blond hunk who's just come in to work late."

"Nick? Is he here?" Darn! Why did she have to sound so eager and jump halfway up from her chair?

"Yeah, that's the one," said Kylie with a big, knowing smirk.

Serena settled back into her chair and tried to look nonchalant. "Yes, well, he called to say he would be delayed, and of course I'm anxious to hear how Mack is doing."

"Of course you are." Kylie's dimples were in full evidence.

Serena sighed. "Am I that obvious?"

"It's been obvious since the day Nick first got here with that honey bunny of a dog of his." Kylie laughed. "Of course, I'm talking about obvious on both sides," she amended, much to Serena's relief.

"Really?"

"Sure. That guy was smitten from the get-go. And I'm pleased for you. I've got to say I didn't like the idea when you told me you'd hired him. But he's okay. Pulled his weight yesterday and the dogs like him. That's the most important thing."

"Of course it is." Two nice girls Serena had employed over the first weeks of Paws-A-While hadn't lasted. They'd needed jobs but it had soon been obvious that they weren't dog people. The dogs had soon let her know that. She'd learned to trust their judgment.

"And you like him?"

Kylie was inquisitive. Over-inquisitive sometimes. But there was genuine concern in her eyes.

"Yes, I do like him," Serena said. "A lot."

Kylie's eyebrows lifted questioningly. "So?"

"It's early days. Who knows?"

Kylie's smile was wide and heartfelt. "Fingers crossed. You deserve a good guy after what you've been through. Nick . . . he seems all right."

"He's more than all right; he's . . . Kylie, I'd appreciate it if you didn't say anything to the others. It's all been a bit sudden and I . . . I don't trust sudden."

During the girl-in-the-bath-of-chocolate campaign she'd been burned by people who thought they knew her because she'd been in the public eye.

Kylie put a finger to her mouth. "Lips are sealed. I won't say a word. Though don't be surprised if other people notice there's something going on between you two. The chemistry is kind of obvious."

"Is it? Really?" She was twenty-eight, but she was right back there in her gawky, uncertain teens. *Does he like me? Do you really think he likes me? What makes you think he likes me?*

"Sizzling," said Kylie, with relish.

If the desk hadn't been between them, Serena would have given Kylie a hug. "Thanks," she said. There was something very trustworthy about Kylie. For all her matchmaking and gossip, Serena knew she would honor a confidence if asked.

"Talking of said handsome newbie, Nick wants to come see you. Shall I tell him you're busy?" Kylie teased.

"I think I could spare him a few minutes," said Serena, grin back in full force. "He probably wants to fill me in on Mack's progress."

"Sure he does," said Kylie, laughing, as she left the office.

Serena was still smiling when Nick rapped briefly on the door. She prepared to race around her desk and into his arms. The grim expression on his face extinguished her smile and held her in place.

"Morning, boss lady," he said in a voice that, while not a monotone, was not sparking with happy-to-see-you vibes, either.

He closed the door behind him.

"Nick," she said, unable to keep the tremor from her voice, "is everything okay?" It was a redundant question because it so obviously wasn't. She felt at a disadvantage behind her desk and took the few steps around it so she faced him.

"Serena, I have to tell you something." Serena felt again that sensation of being in an out-of-control elevator plunging twenty floors.

She swallowed hard. Here it came. Yesterday was a mistake. He'd had time to think. He couldn't handle being with a woman who other men fantasized over. They should cool it . . .

"It's okay, Nick," she forced herself to say. "If you've changed your mind about us, I—" It stuck in her throat to say she "understood" because she darn well didn't.

"Changed my mind? Hell no," he said, reaching for her, pulling her into his arms for a Nick-sized hug. Serena sighed with such heartfelt relief she felt her whole body relax as she leaned gratefully close to him. "Don't even think about changing your mind because I won't let you," he added.

"I'm not changing anything," she said, her voice muffled from where her head was buried in his shoulder against the crisp cotton of his Paws-A-While shirt. She breathed in the delicious Nick smell of him.

"Good," he said.

He pulled away but captured both hands in his so she had to look up into his face, then planted a swift kiss on her mouth that went a long way to reassuring her of his interest.

"First thing I have to tell you is that Adam has got an address for Eric Kessler. The guy has gone to ground in San Diego."

"San Diego? So the jerk never had any intention of coming back for Mack."

"Guess not. He's tried to cover his tracks."

"But not too deep for you and Adam to unearth, I hope."

"We'll find him and get an answer about Mack's collar. Be sure of that. We're booked on a flight to San Diego at lunchtime. We'll stay overnight."

"That's great," she said, not understanding why he had looked so grim when he came into the office. The sooner they could confront Mack's former owner, the sooner they could question him about that hidden camera. She realized how much she was counting on Eric Kessler being the culprit. It would be very hard to take if someone she knew had been robbing her and her clients of so much. "But I don't like that you're away overnight when we're only just—"

"I know," he said. "But the sooner we get past all this, the sooner we spend more time together. I don't like leaving Mack, either."

"Mack." She felt plunged into guilt that she'd been so glad to see Nick she hadn't thought to ask about Mack. "How is he?"

"He's great. Ask me about how I am instead. I hardly slept last night because of that big mutt." He was grumbling, but she was relieved to hear genuine affection in his voice. She so wanted this adoption to work.

"What was the problem?" she said.

"Dunno. I kept up the meds to the schedule the vet prescribed. Mack seemed okay, but every time I left the room he kept giving these enormous sighs and whimpering and looking at me accusingly with those big, sad eyes."

"He must be in pain. Ohmigod, poor Mack, we need to get him to the vet. I'll call and make an appointment." She twisted to move past Nick, but he held her still.

"I don't think so. I felt around his leg and he didn't even wince. He's eating okay, too."

"That's good. Did you try him on that healthy kibble from . . . ?"

Nick released her hands. He shifted from one foot to another. He avoided her eyes. In fact the former federal agent looked guilty as hell. "It was late when I left Adam. I grabbed a burger on the way home and—"

"You got one for Mack."

"Yeah. I know I said I was going to only give him healthy food, but I remember how much that knee surgery hurt." He squared his shoulders and met her gaze. "I decided it was not a good time to force change on him."

He was so serious it took a good deal of effort for Serena to stop her mouth from twitching into a smile. "He's your dog."

"I didn't give him fries, and he had some of the kibble, too. I'm going to break him of that fast-food habit, believe me."

She couldn't stop the smile. "Just not right now."

"Correct. And you can forget the fancy-schmanzy treats. This dog will get big, meaty bones and table scraps and the kind of kibble farm dogs eat—"

"I'll watch your progress with interest," she said.

"You don't think I can do it."

"Weell . . . it might have been an idea to start as you mean to continue. Already he sees you as a source of the good stuff . . . Uh, not that I think it's the good stuff, it's Mack who thinks that."

Nick groaned. "Maybe you're right."

"So did the burger fix the whimpering?"

"No. The only way I got any sleep was when I shifted him and his dog bed into the bedroom with me. Only then would he settle."

Lucky, lucky Mack.

Not that she wanted to be curled up in a dog bed on Nick's bedroom floor. No. Nick's bed with Nick in it was her preferred place in his bedroom. She wondered if Nick wore pajamas to bed or slept naked. Naked. She'd bet naked.

She blinked to clear her focus; her eyes were in serious danger of glazing over. "So you both got some sleep."

"Yeah, well, when Mack wasn't snoring. You didn't tell me he snored like a grizzly."

"I shouldn't laugh, should I?"

He pulled her to him, held her in the loose circle of his arms. "Don't you dare." His words sounded severe but his eyes were warm.

"No laughing, then," she said, trying so hard not to laugh she started to choke. Silently, Nick patted her on the back with his big, capable, soothing hands until she breathed more easily.

"So how's that big Mack now?" she asked when she could speak normally.

"Hannah offered to babysit him while she caught up on paperwork—"

"Don't you mean dog-sit?"

"Yeah, well, whatever you call it. When I got up to go to work he started the noise again and wouldn't stop until I sat with him. So I couldn't leave him with her."

"You brought him here? Is he in the playroom? I can't wait to see him." Serena went to move toward the door, but Nick held her arm to stop her. His voice went very serious, his face back into grim mode. "Worry about Mack later. First you have to hear the second thing I need to tell you."

Serena's heart started hammering. Whatever he had to say couldn't be good. Not with that tone of voice.

"It's about Kylie," he said.

Nick didn't want to subject Serena to another emotional hammering. He hated having to give her more bad news after all she had already been through. In fact, he'd considered shielding her from this. But he didn't want any kind of evasion between them. Serena had to hear what Adam had found out about her employee.

Serena's brow furrowed. "Kylie? Please don't tell me you're not getting on with her. Because she just told me she liked you and enjoyed working with you. Don't forget she's my number one employee; you have to do as she says."

Great. That made what he was about to say sound even worse. "It's not that. I like Kylie, like working with her. But Adam—who also likes her, by the way—has discovered something about Kylie that you should know. That could be relevant to what's happening to you and the other victims."

"I can't imagine what that could be, but go ahead and spill," she said.

"Kylie has a criminal record."

"What!" The color drained from Serena's face.

"She was also fired from a bank where she worked as a teller. I didn't see anything about this in the résumé you have in her personal file."

Serena put her hand to her forehead. "Whoa. Wait. Get back to the criminal record. Kylie? I don't believe it."

There was no sugarcoating the facts. "She was caught for shoplifting from a department store. Expensive makeup."

"Ohmigod. Wait. How old was she?"

"Sixteen."

"A teenager. That explains it. It was probably a dare."

"The police took it seriously. She was fined, had to pay court costs, and do sixty days' community service."

Serena frowned. "That was harsh. Aren't juvy records confidential?"

"They can be sealed when the juvenile reaches eighteen. But only if they petition the juvenile court. Kylie and her family might not have known that."

Serena shook her head. "Poor Kylie. It was fourteen years ago. She was a kid. Plenty of kids shoplift. It's . . . it's like a rite of passage."

"Some say that. But it doesn't make it right," said Nick. "Did you shoplift?"

"There was the odd candy bar, yes. Thank God I was never caught. You?"

"Never." He was no Goody Two-shoes when he was a kid, but shoplift? He'd never even been tempted.

"And the bank?"

"That was three years ago."

"You think this means Kylie could be the one behind all this?" She gestured with her hands to indicate her bewilderment. "I find that impossible to believe."

"To tell you the truth, so do I. But you can't let it go unchallenged, Serena. We have to confront her about it."

"We?"

"Yes. I have to be there."

"I'm sure Kylie has a reasonable explanation."

"We need to hear it."

Looking like she wanted to throw up, Serena walked around to her desk, picked up the phone, and called through to the playroom.

Just minutes later, Kylie came bustling through the door, Tinkerbelle snuggled in her arms. Tinkerbelle wore a tiny pink hoodie printed with the words "Glamour Grrr-l."

Nick suddenly realized that if this dog's father, Brutus, was a millionaire mutt, that made Tinkerbelle an heiress. If things got ugly, there was the possibility of Kylie holding Tinkerbelle hostage. He scoped the room, rapidly preparing an action plan and escape route in case of that eventuality. Then told himself to stop being so stupid and overreacting. No way—no matter whatever else she might have done—did he believe Kylie would harm a dog.

When Nick closed the door behind her, Kylie stilled. Her smile faded. "Is there a problem?"

Serena sat down at her desk. She indicated the chair opposite her. "Better sit down, Kylie."

Kylie looked from Serena to Nick to Serena again. Nick clenched his fists by his sides. He genuinely liked Kylie and hated to see how she struggled to conceal her anxiety over this summons.

"Kylie, this is really hard for me," said Serena. "But it's come to my attention that you have not disclosed everything about your past employment record."

Kylie's lips thinned. "You mean the bank." She cast a hostile look toward Nick. "Three guesses who brought that to your attention."

Nick didn't say anything. He was trained not to show reaction, more observer than participant in these proceedings. Watching Serena, he admired how composed she was; he could only guess at how this felt for her. Her relationship with Kylie went beyond employee status.

"Then I guess you know about the police record, too?" said Kylie.

Serena nodded.

"All for a couple of lipsticks," said Kylie. "How dumb was I?" She gave a nervous laugh, completely lacking in mirth. "I've nearly told you about that incident so many times, Serena."

Serena's lovely mouth was downturned. He guessed her hands were tightly clenched together on her lap beneath her desk. "Why didn't you? I couldn't care less about it, Kylie—though I don't condone stealing. As I said to Nick, so many teenagers shoplift. Most of them don't get caught."

"Yeah, I was the lucky one," said Kylie with a snort of that mirthless laughter that was so at odds with her pretty, usually cheerful face.

"The bank is a different matter," Nick interjected.

Kylie cast him a look of loathing. Nick was surprised at how it affected him. He genuinely liked her. But she'd become a suspect and this had to be done. No matter the outcome, it would always be seen to be his fault. There'd be no more shared confidences over setting up a dog party.

"Does *he* have to be here?" Kylie asked, indicating Nick with a toss of her head.

Serena looked questioningly to him. He nodded.

"Yes," said Serena.

"That figures," she said. Nick remembered her fears that he was out to steal her job from her.

Kylie stroked the brindle fur of the so-ugly-she-was-cute little dog without seeming to realize she was doing it. Tinkerbelle gave little grunts of pleasure, lapping up the attention.

"C'mon, Kylie, what was it all about?" said Serena.

"I didn't tell the bank about the shoplifting charge when they employed me. I knew that wouldn't look good and I really needed the job. Finn was only five, and I'd been left with debts when his dad and I split."

Serena nodded.

"I had a real asshole of a manager. He started coming on to me straight away, you know, flirting, innuendo."

"You mean sexual harassment," said Serena.

"Yeah. Though it took me a while to realize that's what it was."

"Why didn't you report it?" asked Serena.

"He was my manager. I really needed that job. It had security, good health insurance. I thought he'd stop when he didn't get anywhere."

"But he didn't . . ."

Nick felt anger rise in his throat on Kylie's behalf.

"Believe me, I tried to stay out of his way," she continued. "But he wouldn't take no for an answer. To cut a long story short, he found out about the shoplifting charge. When I didn't give in to blackmail he sacked me before I had a chance to resign. How good does that look? Sacked from a bank without references, even though I'd only been there two months."

Nick felt sorry for Kylie. But even working at a bank three years ago she could have picked up enough knowledge to use in an identity fraud. Kylie was in a position of trust at Paws-A-While. She had access to Serena's computer.

Serena looked up to him with imploring eyes, then back to

Kylie. This was a difficult situation. Neither he nor Serena could tell Kylie why she was being grilled. Not when there was a chance—no matter how remote—that she could be involved with the fraud.

"Kylie, I wish you'd trusted me enough to tell me this before," Serena began. "You've been so great and—"

Kylie's face flushed deeper and her eyes glittered. She got up, so abruptly Tinkerbelle yelped her surprise. Kylie handed the little dog over the desk to a startled Serena. "I'm not hanging around to get sacked. This is just what Mr. Muscles here was angling for." She glared again at Nick. "Well, my job's vacant now, and you're welcome to it."

Serena's eyes were huge with alarm. She stood up and quickly cleared the few steps to get to Kylie's side. "No. I wasn't going to fire you. I understand what happened. I don't want to lose you." She was hindered from reaching out to Kylie because she was holding Tinkerbelle in her arms.

Kylie's mouth twisted. "Yeah. Sure. Then anytime the books don't balance or there's something missing from stock, you'll think it was me, and *he* will be here to remind you of what I did when I was sixteen."

Nick took a step forward. "No, Kylie. You're wrong about that."

"No. I was wrong about you," Kylie hissed. "I told Serena you were a good guy."

"Kylie, it doesn't have to be like this," said Serena. "Please."

Serena thrust Tinkerbelle at Nick. "Take this wiggle butt, will you," she said. Tinkerbelle, fed up with being passed around like a parcel, yipped and scrabbled with her claws to get down but Nick held her secure.

Kylie stripped off her Paws-A-While shirt and flung it on the chair, leaving her in a T-shirt. "I'll miss you, Serena, and I'll miss the dogs. God, how I'll miss the dogs. But I can see things are going to change around here and there'll be no place for me."

"Kylie. No. Please." Serena's voice rose.

Kylie shook her head. "Watch out, Serena, while he takes over here. He'll be lording it over you as well as everyone else before you know it."

Serena, distraught, looked up at him. "Can I tell her—?"

"No." His gut feel said Kylie was innocent of any wrongdoing, but the investigation could not be compromised at this stage.

He had to admire Serena's professionalism. She let Kylie know she was valued, but she didn't implore her to change her mind. "Kylie, you're upset. Go home and have the rest of the day off. Come in tomorrow and we can talk about it."

"There's nothing to talk about. I'm outta here, Serena, and I won't be coming back." Kylie turned and stomped toward the door. She turned to give Nick a final glare, then slammed the door hard behind her.

Serena was so shocked by the confrontation with Kylie, she shook all over. She gripped the edge of the desk so tight her knuckles went white. No way had she expected anything like that to happen.

"Should I go after her?" she asked Nick. "I really don't want to lose her. I don't give a damn about the shoplifting thing, and I believe her about the bank."

He shook his head. "Let her cool down. She loves this place. She got a shock. Though she must have known her past would come out sooner or later."

"You don't think she's a crook, do you?"

"My gut says no. I believe her. Her story about the bank is easily checked."

"What about Adam?"

"He was . . . surprised." He'd been amazed at how shaken Adam had been at the discovery. "But we have to be professional.

Not let personal feelings affect our work. She could be a clever
con woman."

"Like you thought I was?"

"I happen to know that all you have is a few parking tickets to
your discredit."

"Paws-A-While won't be the same without her." Everything
had gone so wrong since she'd got that call from the bank. Well,
not quite everything. One part of her life had gone very right.
Nick.

"What was that Kylie said about you being after her job?" she
asked.

"Just that. In her words, she thought once I started boinking the
boss—as she put it; I'd rather a less crude term—I'd lord it over the
staff."

Serena flushed. "Ohmigod, did she say that? About, uh, boinking the boss? Is that what everyone here thinks?"

"Do you care if they do?" Nick said, pulling her to him.

"Of course not." She looked up into his face. "But the . . .
uh . . . about the boinking . . ."

"You're wanting to know when?" His voice deepened to an
even huskier tone of sexy rasp.

"Oh yeah," she said.

He claimed her mouth in a swift, hard kiss that sent her heart
racing. Effortlessly, he picked her up and sat her on the edge of her
desk. He bent his head to kiss her again. She kissed him back with
passion, her lips parting, her tongue darting in to meet his. She slid
her arms up around his back. Frantically she tried to remember
what was behind her on her desk. Folders. Her snow globe. Scissors? Were there scissors?

For the first time, she wished she had a sofa in her office.

He broke away from her mouth to plant kisses along her jaw,
down the column of her neck, to nudge aside the fabric of her
shirt and nuzzle against the sensitive hollow of her shoulder. His

hands slid over her shoulders and skimmed the side swell of her breasts. His hands felt so good on her body, so right.

The nagging worries were still there—remorse for Kylie, fear for Jenna, anxiety over the future of her business. But the magic of Nick's kisses somehow pushed them to the back of her mind.

Nick groaned. "Dammit! I have to go to San Diego." He straightened up so that he looked down into her face, his hands on her shoulders while hers rested at his waist. His eyes were a shade darker with passion and regret, expressions she thought were probably mirrored in her own eyes.

He was right. This was not their time. She knew she should slide off of the desk and agree that he should go. But the temptation to keep him with her for just a few more minutes was too strong.

"Did I give you permission to go to San Diego?" she said, in her best boss-lady voice, trailing a finger down his face, from his cheekbone to the angle of his jaw.

"You want me to beg?" he said, his eyes narrowed. He captured her finger, kissed it before releasing it.

"I kinda like the idea of you begging."

"Depends on what I'm begging for," he said in that deep, gravel voice.

"I'll think of something interesting," she said, with a little shiver of excitement.

"In the meantime I do have to go to San Diego to track down Eric Kessler."

"I know," she said.

"Now," he said, without making any attempt to let her go.

Serena sighed and slid off the desk. "You go get him. Don't forget to take the collar with you."

He hugged her tight, then let her go. "Can you take Mack home with you tonight?" he asked.

"Sure, I'll get Kylie to help me . . ." She stopped. "Darn. I'll miss Kylie in more ways than one. Please be right about her coming back."

"She has a child to support; that's a powerful incentive." Nick tilted her chin up so she had to meet his gaze full-on. "I know you feel bad about Kylie. But Kylie should have told you about that bank job."

"She would have been worried I wouldn't have employed her."

"Yeah. I understand that. But she would have saved herself a lot of grief if she had told you about it once you'd gotten to know and trust her. Don't blame yourself."

"I feel terrible about it. She must be so upset. I'll call her tonight."

"No. Wait until after I've spoken to that bank."

"But, Nick, I—"

"No buts. We're talking fraud worth a hell of a lot of money here, Serena. Your money, your business. Until we know she's innocent as opposed to suspecting she's innocent, Kylie is still a suspect."

"You're tough, Nick," she said, unable to keep the hiccup from her voice.

"In my world you have to be tough."

"I guess," she said. She was glad he was on her side. "What you said last night about Jenna. I've thought about it and I don't agree. I have to warn Jenna about Tony."

"Serena, I—"

"Nick, I'm not going to just sit back and do nothing while you and Adam go chase the bad guys. This is my business, my future. I'll be careful. I have to talk to Jenna about Tony. She's my friend; I would never forgive myself if something happened that I could have prevented. But I might also be able to find out more about Tony."

"I'll never forgive myself if Tony takes revenge on you. Be careful, Serena."

"You be careful, too. You're doing something far more danger-ous than I am. Take care, okay?" She leaned up and kissed him on that sexy, sexy mouth. "I . . . I'll miss you."

He enfolded her in a big hug that made her feel warm and secure and excited all at the same time. But bereft when he re-leased her.

"I'll miss you, too, Serena," he said. "But I'll be coming home to you as soon as I can."

"To me and Mack."

He groaned and laughed at the same time. "To you and Mack."

"And Bessie."

This time it was more groan than laugh. "Anything else in the menagerie?"

"Of course I have Snowball and Thelma, my kitty."

"Okay. I'll be coming home to you and Mack and Bessie and Snowball and Thelma." He gave her another swift hug. "Good-bye, Serena. I'll keep you posted."

He was laughing as he went out the door.

· Eighteen ·

Serena stifled a yawn as she hurried to her breakfast date with Jenna. When she'd arranged to catch up early at a favorite cafe on Union Street, she hadn't counted on Mack keeping her awake for so much of the night with his whining and snoring.

Jenna was already sitting at a table with an open newspaper in front of her and two coffees. She looked up and smiled. "Your granola and yogurt with a side of sliced strawberries is on its way," she said, folding the newspaper away. "I'm waiting on cinnamon bagels."

This wasn't the first time Serena had met with Jenna for breakfast. With her schedule at Paws-A-While and Jenna's study commitments and doggy treat business, early was often their best meeting option. It was a joke between them that they each always ordered the same thing.

"Thanks," said Serena as she slid into her chair opposite Jenna. The cafe was popular and the tables packed close together. "I so need that coffee. I hardly got a wink of sleep last night."

"Oh," said Jenna with a lascivious lift of one eyebrow. "So things are heating up with the new employee."

"No! Not that . . . uh . . . not yet." Serena paused, puzzled. "Hey, I was going to tell you about Nick this morning. How come you already know that we . . . well, that we're together?"

Jenna rolled her eyes. "Hello? Brutus's party? It was pretty obvious. Even Tony noticed something was going on between you two."

Tony. Now was her chance. But the words choked in her throat. She needed to build up to telling her friend that the man she loved was a convicted criminal. She'd crunch through the granola first. Maybe by her second coffee she'd muster enough courage.

"Kylie said the same thing," she said. "About Brutus's party. Funny, as I wasn't sure myself then about Nick."

There had been no word from Kylie. Serena had half expected she would just show up at Paws-A-While as if nothing had happened. No such luck. She'd told the other staff that Kylie had taken a personal day and their reactions made her believe that Kylie had not told them what had happened. Heaven knew what she'd tell them if Kylie didn't return to work soon.

She missed Kylie and wanted her back, had spent the time since their meeting yesterday wondering how she could have handled the confrontation better. This morning she was going to be darn careful she didn't offend Jenna. While at the same time warning her that her live-in boyfriend had a serious criminal record.

"Nick's not even here. He's in San Diego—"

Great PI she made. Already she'd spilled Nick's whereabouts when it was meant to be kept hush-hush.

Jenna quirked the eyebrow again, only this time it looked disapproving. "He's taking time off work?"

Now she would have to lie. "Some urgent family thing. He . . . uh . . . didn't say . . ." Dammit. This was not going the way she planned it. She'd have to recover some ground.

"Secrets between you already?"

Secrets? The only secrets she wanted to discuss were Tony's.

"No! I didn't want to hear the details of his ... his father's health issues. I'm tired because Mack is keeping me up at night."

"A problem with the surgery?"

Serena knew Jenna was feigning interest. Her friend found Mack intimidating and scary. Jenna was much happier with the smaller dogs. Trouble was, Mack liked her. Or rather he liked the dog treats she kept in her pockets as samples for clients. Serena had told Jenna over and over that Mack's interest in her was motivated purely by greed, not any desire to knock her over with his enormous paws and big, strong head. Jenna remained unconvinced.

Serena couldn't really blame her friend. It was a fact that shelters found it difficult to get black dogs and black cats adopted. Mack was huge and mainly black and some people would never like him because of that. Which made Serena all the more grateful to Nick for giving Mack a home.

"No, the surgery seems fine," she said. "No infection. No swelling. Not that I can see anyway. He's keeping his meds down. It's odd."

"Yeah, well, I don't know if I should feel offended or not that you haven't stopped yawning since you said good morning."

"Ohmigod, I'm so sorry. I'm just so tired. Mack moaned and whimpered every time I left his sight. That set Snowball off then, all edgy and yappy. I had Bessie with me as well. Thankfully, she's so sweet she's no trouble at all." Serena yawned again just at the thought of it and quickly covered her mouth with her hand.

"Maybe you'd better get Mack to the vet in case there's something wrong."

"Lydia is going to do a house call this afternoon; thank heaven she was available."

"Better protect your boyfriend's investment." Jenna munched her bagel.

"Investment?" Serena frowned. "That's a funny way to put it. And by the way he's not my boyfriend."

Serena didn't want to jinx anything by referring to Nick as her boyfriend when they hadn't even gone on a date. Then there was the fact that she tended to feel trapped when people started putting labels on her relationships.

Jenna shrugged. "Kylie reckons he virtually admitted to her he offered to pay for Mack's surgery as an excuse to see you."

"Oh. Well." Serena couldn't help flushing. "If that's true, it's kind of sweet, isn't it?"

"Come on, Serena. It's obvious he's head over heels for you. Just like a long line of guys before him."

Serena looked around at the other tables to make sure no one had heard her friend's thoughtless remark. "Jenna, that makes me sound like some kind of . . . of . . . well, you know," she said in a hushed voice.

"Sorry. I didn't mean to imply that. It's just this guy's interest is so obvious to everyone but you."

Serena pulled a face. "Remember high school? I couldn't even get a date for prom."

"Until you grew boobs and ditched the braces. Then the boys came running. That was even before your nose job."

Serena's hand went automatically to her neat, straight nose. "Hey, it was a deviated septum, remember. That they got rid of that bump at the same time was just a bonus."

Jenna snorted. "Yeah. Right. That you'd had your nose fixed was the first thing I noticed about you when we met up again after all those years."

Serena took a deep breath. "I know you think we should all be as nature intended, but I hated my nose and I'm glad I had it done. It photographed badly, too. I would never have got any modeling work with my old nose."

Serena wasn't sure she was that comfortable about where this conversation was going. It wasn't the first time they'd had it. Sometimes she wondered why she persevered with Jenna. Maddy often asked her the same thing. But she always came back to the same point. Jenna had known her before the whole girl-in-a-bath-of-chocolate thing. Knew her as just plain Serena Oakley long before she'd made her name as Serena St. James. It was a link she valued.

Luckily, Jenna seemed determined to defuse things. "Would you believe I'm coming around to the idea of giving nature a helping hand sometimes? What's the difference between fixing your nose and dyeing your hair?" She leaned over the table. "I've had some streaks done. Notice? A hair-coloring virgin no more."

Serena looked closely. Sure enough, her friend's hair that had been the same soft, pretty brown since high school was now artfully streaked with expensive, wheat-toned highlights. If she hadn't been in such a funk about the identity fraud and worrying about how she was going to tell Jenna about Tony, she would have noticed straight away.

"It looks amazing," she said. "Wow! After all this time you've taken the plunge. I can't believe it." Serena herself had started experimenting with her hair color as soon as she'd been able to afford to buy a home coloring kit. She'd done streaks, gone red, gone blond, even a purple streak at one stage. Now she'd settled on her own color as the one that best suited her.

"You like it? Tony paid for it. He wants me to go blond, but I thought I'd take it a step at a time."

Serena's heart sank somewhere below the level of the cafe's floorboards. If Jenna thought she'd be impressed by Tony's generosity, she was way off the mark. She noticed Jenna was wearing another new outfit, rather flashier than she usually chose. Tony's taste again?

"That was nice of him," she said in as neutral a voice as she could muster. "Uh, how are things going?"

Jenna's eyes shone. "With Tony? Perfect. He is so great, I can't believe it."

"I'm so glad for you." It was difficult for Serena to force enthusiasm.

"He's the one, Serena. This time I think I've finally got it right."

Serena swallowed a retort. How could she burst her friend's bubble?

"Are you enjoying the new apartment?"

Jenna shrugged. "It's okay. A touch on the small side. But it's a start. Tony is very happy there."

"I wondered about the kitchen."

Jenna frowned. "What's wrong with the kitchen?"

"Nothing. I just thought it seemed small to be doing all your baking."

Jenna's frown lifted. "It's fine. You just have to be organized."

"That's good to hear. I'm glad it's worked out."

"The apartment's fine for now. Who knows? We might need something bigger before too long."

Serena froze with a spoonful of granola halfway to her mouth. "Jenna. You're not—"

Jenna smiled. "Not yet. As you know, I've never been that excited about the whole baby thing. But Tony wants a son . . ."

And if Tony wanted a son, Jenna would darn well give him one if it meant hanging on to him.

"That . . . that's a surprise."

Jenna's face tightened. "That a man wants to have a child with me?"

When would she learn how easily Jenna took offense? "That's

not what I meant. Of course it isn't. I was just . . . surprised. You haven't known Tony that long and—"

Jenna pushed her empty coffee cup away from her across the table. "You don't like Tony, do you?"

"No. I mean yes. Of course I like him. He's very handsome and—"

"Don't lie, Serena. You've never liked my boyfriends. And I don't care for yours. I never thought much of Dave and I made no bones about it at the time."

"No. You didn't. And you were proved right, of course."

How could she let her know about Tony without revealing just how she had discovered his criminal record?

"I don't know Nick yet so I'm keeping an open mind about him," said Jenna. "He seems okay. Maybe we can double date or something sometime."

"Uh, yeah, that would be fun."

Not.

Jenna looked down at her watch. "Look, hon. It's been great to catch up but time's up. The doggy cafe down the road has run right out of carob cookies and they're waiting on a delivery."

Serena's heart thudded. It would be easy to say good-bye without saying anything, but she could not let her friend go without warning her that she might be in danger. Nick had said Tony's record included convictions for assault.

She put her hand on Jenna's arm. "Jenna, before you go. I have to ask you something. How . . . how well do you know Tony? I mean, if you're planning on having a child with him. I'm just wondering . . ."

How else could she say this without revealing Nick's part in an investigation that was totally secret?

Jenna's eyes narrowed. "Have you been Googling Tony or something?"

"No. I just, well, you haven't known him for that long and . . ."

"You've never been a good liar, Serena. Even when we were kids." She lowered her voice so Serena had to lean closer over the table to hear her. "Tony told me all about his time in jail not long after I met him."

Serena nearly spluttered into her coffee. "You . . . you know?"

"Yes, I know all about it. I love and admire him all the more for him wanting to overcome his past."

Criminal trespass. Assault. Trafficking stolen property.

Had Tony confessed to all of that?

"Th-that's very . . . admirable of you," Serena stuttered.

"There's nothing admirable about it. He's done some bad things, I grant you, but he's paid his debt to society. I love him and I accept him the way he is. I met him on campus, you know. He's gone back to school, doing everything he can to make a new start."

Jenna was always like this at the start of a relationship. Infatuated and totally blind to any flaws in her lover. But she'd been with Tony for nearly a year. Perhaps this was the real thing for her.

Maybe Serena was wrong about Tony. Maybe she should share in her friend's joy. Make happy noises for her. But the fact remained: nothing Jenna said could make Serena like Tony. Even before she'd learned about his past, Tony gave her the creeps.

"What about his new job?" she asked. "Uh, what exactly is his new job?"

"Sales. He can fit his studies around it."

"Does his employer know about . . . about . . . ?"

"His new employer knows everything about his past and is prepared to trust him and give him a break."

"Okay . . ." Serena honestly did not know what more to say.

Jenna took some bills out of her purse and laid them down on the table. "Serena, I know you're concerned about me and I appreciate it. But I love Tony, and you'd better get used to him being in my life."

The "or else" hung unspoken in the air between them.

Fond as she was of Jenna, Serena doubted that their friendship would survive if Jenna stayed with Tony. But that could very well be a moot point. The more she heard about Tony, the more convinced she was that he could be the Paws-A-While link to the identity frauds. If she was proved correct, then when it all blew up she would be around for Jenna to help pick up the pieces.

"Are you still coming around for the inaugural Paws-A-While Halloween party?" Serena asked.

"You betcha." Jenna grinned. "Tony has picked me out a really good costume. And he looks hunky as hell in his."

Serena bit back a retort. "I'm sure he does. I'm looking forward to seeing you in yours."

They both stood up from the table, and Serena hugged Jenna. She pulled back from her friend so she could look her directly in the face. "I know you don't want to hear this, Jenna, but be careful."

A look flashed across her friend's eyes that Serena could not interpret. But her first thought was that Jenna wasn't as free of doubt about Tony as she said. Serena hugged her friend again.

She had never been able to understand how a woman as smart as Jenna could stay with a man who hurt her. She hoped against hope that her friend hadn't got herself in above her head with Tony Cross. But she'd done her best to try to protect her.

As she walked back to Paws-A-While she found herself longing for Nick's return. *Her boyfriend.*

Maybe that was a label she could get used to.

· Nineteen ·

It was nearly lunchtime and Serena was grooming one of her favorite Paws-A-While dogs, the darling old golden Labrador Freya, when her cell phone rang.

Her heart did that skip-a-beat thing when caller ID showed Nick's name. She realized that she hadn't heard his voice on the phone since the day he first called to book Bessie into day care. Those gravelly tones seemed to hum testosterone down the phone lines.

"Hey, I was getting worried I hadn't heard from you," she said. "How's it going in San Diego?"

"I'm not in San Diego anymore. Now I'm in Carmel. Adam and I got an early flight and drove straight here from the airport."

Serena was so shocked she nearly dropped the phone. "Carmel? What the heck—?" She completely forgot that she wanted to tell him about her breakfast with Jenna.

"Eric Kessler is not our guy," Nick said bluntly.

Serena felt a plummeting pang of disappointment. She hadn't realized just how much she was counting on Nick coming back with the identity fraud solved. "But Eric Kessler put that black collar on Mack. He was spying on us." She kept her voice very low, aware that it could carry to the next cubicle where Heather was grooming another dog.

"He claims his ex-wife put the collar on Mack and he knows nothing whatsoever about any camera."

"And you believed him?" Freya made a whimper of protest that Serena had stopped brushing her so Serena switched the cell phone to her left hand and used her right hand to brush the Lab with a special, soft-bristled brush. Freya was so frail that Serena had to be extra gentle over the bumps and ridges of her bones.

"Yeah. I did. He's not a nice guy but he wasn't lying. He seemed to think it was hilarious his wife had put a spy cam on his dog."

"*If* she did. Did he say why he never came back for Mack?"

Nick was silent. Serena could hear him take a short, deep breath.

"He told me Mack was his wife's dog. They'd adopted him together, but as far as he was concerned, Mack belonged to Claire Kessler."

"That makes sense," said Serena. "Remember I told you how I thought he must have been owned by a woman the way he acts like such a baby with me?"

"Yeah, the big galoot," said Nick. His voice was underscored with a real affection for the dog that warmed Serena's heart.

"But it doesn't make sense that a woman Mack loved that much doesn't have her dog with her. She must be heartbroken."

"Kessler paints the ex-wife in a pretty bad light. Says she took off to live in Carmel, abandoning both him and Mack."

Once more Serena strained to remember her impressions of Eric Kessler. He'd seemed a pleasant enough kind of guy but so ordinary he'd scarcely registered. "Okay, so they split. That doesn't explain why he didn't come back for his dog."

"Kessler told me he put Mack in Paws-A-While and then told his ex where to go to get her dog. He said he paid a week up front."

"True. He did. But I'll swear he never said anything about going to live in San Diego. Or that he had a wife."

"According to him, he told his wife he couldn't take Mack to San Diego and she had to come get him and take him to wherever she was living."

"But she never showed . . ."

"And he never checked to see if she did?"

"I definitely never heard from him again." Serena paused. "Mack was loved by a woman. Maybe that woman. I find it hard to comprehend she could do that to him."

"It looks that way. According to Kessler."

Serena could not help the catch in her voice. "So if he's to be believed, Mack was abandoned by both of them, the poor baby."

She was so overcome with sadness on Mack's behalf, she brushed Freya around her face and behind her ears with extra special attention. The elderly Lab stayed very still, and the expression in her milky old eyes was one of bliss.

"You are the best, best girl," Serena crooned.

"Did you just call me the best *girl*?" Nick's gravelly voice, warm with amusement, came through her cell.

"Of course not. You know you're the best *boy*," she murmured back. My God, could there ever be a more masculine guy? Little shivers of awareness ran through her, fired just by the sound of his voice. "I'm grooming Freya."

As she held the phone with one hand and brushed Freya with the other, Serena thought about how loved Freya was by her guardians, Joe and Rosemary. Though it obviously went against the grain for them to accept charity from her, they'd swallowed their pride so their beloved dog got the best care. Whereas poor darling Mack had been abandoned by both his awful owners. And before that by some other unknown jerk, which was why he'd ended up at the shelter where the Kesslers found him.

Mack would never, ever be abandoned again. Not while she

had breath in her body—and she felt sure Nick felt the same. She wished she had the resources to help all abandoned dogs. When Paws-A-While was in the black, she vowed to give a good percentage of her profits to animal rescue.

"How is the poor old girl?" asked Nick.

"She's not a poor old girl; she's a lucky old girl," said Serena, giving the Lab a final brushing. The last stage of Freya's grooming was a wipe-down with a slightly damp cloth and she couldn't easily do that with one hand.

"Can you please hold for a moment, Nick?" she said. She quickly found Heather and asked her to take over Freya for her.

She scratched behind Freya's ears, then took her cell to her office and closed the door. Now she felt she could talk to Nick more freely without worrying about being overheard.

"So if Eric Kessler denies knowing anything about the spy camera and says his wife must have put it there, where does that put us? If she didn't know Eric had booked Mack into Paws-A-While, then the camera might have nothing whatsoever to do with the identity fraud."

"Unless they're working together on a scam. That's a real possibility. I believed him when he said he didn't put the collar on Mack; that doesn't mean he didn't know his ex did. That's what I'm in Carmel to find out."

Serena knuckled her hand and brought it to her mouth. "Nick, be careful."

Nick laughed. "I can look after myself. But I appreciate your concern."

His voice had that just-about-to-end-the-conversation tone about it.

"Nick, don't let her take Mack back; he's"—she was about to say "ours" but stopped herself just in time—"yours now. I hope there's a very hot place in hell reserved for people like the Kesslers who abandon their pets."

"No way will she have ever anything to do with Mack," said Nick, grim determination in his voice. "She'll have to fight me for him."

Serena loved that protectiveness in his voice. She realized how wrong she had been to judge him on her past experiences with cops. He was strong, but he was not a bully. He would fight for his dog. He would fight for his woman. More than anything, she wanted to be that woman.

In his career as an FBI special agent and now as a PI, Nick had one weakness he had to struggle to overcome.

He'd been brought up—by his strong, feisty mom and his father, who adored her—to respect women and be a gentleman. That made it difficult to interrogate and come down tough on a female suspected perp. Especially one like Claire Kessler, who on paper gave every appearance of being a decent, respectable person. What in this case would make his job easier was that—according to her ex-husband—she had so cruelly abandoned her dog.

Though he strove to be impartial until he had ascertained the facts for himself, his personal connection to Mack brought him to the quaint town of Carmel-by-the-Sea already prejudiced against her.

Carmel had an idiosyncrasy in that the houses were not numbered. However, he and Adam, following advice from Eric Kessler, had tracked her down to the small restaurant where she worked.

It was tucked away down a laneway between an art gallery and a gift store. The laneway was punctuated with tubs of cheerful flowers. A flowering vine scrambled over an archway that led to a sunny courtyard filled with round tables and wrought-iron chairs. To the left of the archway was a wall-mounted dog water fountain, very like the one Serena had, and a bowl of dog biscuits obviously meant for customers' dogs.

The sweet scent of the vine's flowers mingled with something delicious. Beef? Onions? Garlic? Whatever, Nick's mouth watered. He'd grabbed a coffee and a muffin at the San Francisco airport before picking up his car and driving the two hours to Carmel. To his stomach that seemed a long time ago now.

There were just a few people sitting around the inner bunch of tables enjoying coffee and late-morning snacks. He was suddenly so hungry he felt like grabbing the piece of cheesecake from the plate of the woman sitting at the table nearest to him.

A young, casually dressed waiter approached and asked could he show him and Adam to a table.

"We're not here to eat," said Adam, his abrupt tone fuelled, Nick felt sure, by the same hunger he was feeling. Whatever was cooking in that kitchen sure smelled good—nearly as good as Serena's lasagna, the taste of which had haunted him since that Saturday at her apartment.

He had to force his mind back on the job. This time there was no dog around to blame for any embarrassing tummy grumbles.

"We need to see Claire Kessler," he said to the waiter.

"She's in the kitchen," said the waiter, eyeing them with undisguised curiosity. "Can I take her a message?"

"Tell her we're here to talk to her about her dog, Mack," said Nick. He couldn't keep the edge of disgust from his voice. If her husband was to be believed, this was the woman who had abandoned Mack at Paws-A-While, leaving her dog to a fate that, if it were not for Serena's generosity, could have been grim.

Mrs. Kessler must have left the kitchen as soon as the waiter gave her the message, for within minutes a woman was heading toward him. She was younger than he had expected and attractive, around Serena's age probably, slim, medium height with light brown hair pulled off of her face. Her face was flushed and she wiped her hands on the front of a white chef's apron.

She didn't give him and Adam a chance to introduce themselves. "Are you cops? You're here about Mack? You've found the bastard who did it?"

Nick was disconcerted to see her brown eyes glinted with anger and pain and accusation. He exchanged a quick glance with Adam, who looked as bemused as he felt.

"Did what, ma'am?" Nick asked.

Her expression became wary. "Don't you know?" Her hands went to her hips as she looked from Nick to Adam and back to Nick. "Just who are you guys?"

Nick took a step toward her. "Nick Whalen from S&W Investigations." He indicated Adam. "Adam Shore, my business partner. We're working on behalf of the Paws-A-While doggy day-care center in San Francisco."

Her eyes went very wide, without even a blink of recognition at the name of Serena's business. "Huh?" she said. Then she frowned. "Did a certain ex-husband by the name of Eric Kessler send you?"

"No, ma'am," said Adam.

"Then what the heck is going on? You're talking to me about some place I've never heard of when I thought you were cops come to tell me you'd found out who . . . who killed my dog, Mack." Her bottom lip began to tremble and tears glistened in her eyes.

"What?" Nick and Adam exploded with the word at precisely the same moment.

Claire Kessler sniffed back her tears. "You mean you didn't know? I don't get this."

"Neither do we," said Nick. "Please, I'm so sorry to hear about your dog. Can you tell me what happened? It may have some bearing on our investigation."

Again she looked from one to the other, frowned, but seemed to decide to hear him out. She took a few steps away from the occupied tables. Nick, followed by Adam, stepped back so the three of them moved out of earshot of the customers.

"I . . . I . . . don't really know. My ex told me Mack was hit by a car and left . . . and left dead at the side of the road." Her eyes teared up again, and it was obvious she had to make a real effort to speak. "He told me he was trying to find who'd done it. When you said you wanted to talk to me about . . . about Mack, I thought . . ."

Nick didn't handle female tears very well. Claire Kessler looked so upset it was all he could do not to rush into comforting words. If she was telling the truth, her ex was the worst kind of cruel bastard. But his training told him he needed the facts before he could make a decision on which member of this estranged couple was lying about Mack. Or their connection to the identity fraud.

He gentled his voice. "I know this is upsetting for you, but I need to establish we're talking about the same dog here."

"Mack?" She wrung her hands together. "He was . . . the dearest animal. Big and dopey but as sweet as sugar. When we got him he wasn't six months old, this huge, galumphing creature with the most enormous paws who thought he could snuggle onto my lap like a tiny puppy."

Nick cleared his throat. "What color is . . . was he?"

The answer came without hesitation. "Black, with a white tip to his tail and one white paw. I used to say that . . . that it looked like he'd dipped his paw in the cream jug."

There was no doubt as to the emotion that shone through her tear-brightened eyes. *Love.*

Nick swallowed hard. Face-to-face with Claire Kessler, Eric Kessler's story did not make sense. A part of him hoped that she was talking about a different animal. Because his gut told him this woman would not have abandoned her dog.

Nick asked the clincher question. "Why did you call your dog Mack?"

"We got him from a shelter. The people there called him that when they discovered he was addicted to—"

"Fast food," said Nick heavily.

"Why, yes," she said. "He was such a quirky dog like that. Even his ears were a bit off. He had one ear that stood up and the other flopped down. It looked so cute on a dog his size."

Nick checked to make sure there was a chair nearby. In a moment, Claire Kessler might need to sit down.

He looked to Adam, who almost imperceptibly raised one eyebrow. "Mrs. Kessler," Nick started.

"Claire," she interrupted. "I don't ever again want to be called by his name."

"Claire," he said. There was no easy way to say this. "Your dog, Mack, isn't dead."

She snatched her hand to her throat, her eyes blazed. "How could you say that? My ex *did* send you, didn't he? Only he would play such a cruel trick."

Pity for the woman surged through Nick. "This isn't a trick. There couldn't be two dogs that match your description. Mack is alive. Trust me."

The color drained from her face and she went deathly pale. She clutched onto the back of the nearby chair for support. "Mack? Not dead? I . . . I don't believe you," she whispered. "Though I . . . I want to believe you."

"Five weeks ago, Eric Kessler booked Mack into Paws-A-While, paid a week in advance, and then never came back."

Claire Kessler took a quick intake of breath but seemed incapable of saying anything.

Nick continued. "After some time, our client retained us to track your ex-husband down."

For a cover story, it had holes in it. As if Serena would hire two expensive PIs like him and Adam to hunt down a dog's owner in search of a few weeks' fees. But he figured Claire Kessler was too shocked to even think about the plausibility of his story.

"You found Eric in San Diego?"

"Yes," said Adam.

"And what lie did he come up with to explain why he didn't come back?" Her mouth twisted with bitterness.

"We don't know that it was a lie—" Adam began.

Nick broke in. "He told us that he told you he wasn't able to care for Mack anymore and that you were meant to pick Mack up from Paws-A-While."

The color flooded back into Claire Kessler's face. "The bastard, bastard, bastard . . ." Her voice broke on a suppressed sob.

"You say he told you Mack was dead," said Adam.

"Hit by a car in front of our old house in Larkspur," said Claire. "Oh God, he must really, really hate me. And Mack. How could he abandon our dog like that? I thought he loved him or I wouldn't have trusted Mack with him until I got settled in a place where I could have a dog."

"Obviously not," said Nick, thinking with revulsion of Eric Kessler. No wonder there had been an undertone of gloating when he spoke about his ex-wife.

Claire Kessler was silent for a moment. Then a radiant smile stole across her face. "Mack's alive? He's really, truly alive? Ohmigod, this is like a miracle."

Nick felt sick to his stomach. Mack belonged to this woman. She had been parted from him through no fault of her own. She would want her dog back. Where did that put him?

"Where is Mack now? Is he okay?" she asked, her voice thick with emotion.

"Serena Oakley, the proprietor of Paws-A-While, kept him on, even though your husband—uh, ex-husband—didn't pay for more than the first week."

"That is so kind of her. I'll pay her back. Every cent he owed." Then she sobered. Her eyes narrowed. "I'm still finding this hard to believe. How do I know this isn't some other cruel trick?"

Nick pulled out his cell phone. "I've got a picture I just took a day ago."

He called up a photo of a drowsy Mack reclining in his dog bed in front of the fireplace at the house in Sausalito.

Claire greedily scanned it. "It's him . . . my darling boy. Oh, Mack." Her voice broke. "But what am I going to do with you?" For a moment Nick thought she would kiss the screen. Then she looked back at him. "What's that purple cast on his leg?"

"He's had a cruciate ligament repair operation on his knee."

"Ohmigod, poor Mack," she said. "Well, Eric's not one hundred percent bad if he paid for Mack's surgery."

"He did not," said Adam.

"Then who—?"

"I paid," said Nick, fighting to keep the disappointment from his voice. This woman had every right to have her dog back. "I adopted Mack."

"You adopted Mack?"

His voice was a growl in an effort not to let her see how he was hurting at the thought of losing Mack. "Mack was a very lucky dog. Someone else might have taken him to a shelter when his payment ran out. Not Serena Oakley. Even though she lives in an apartment, she took him home with her every night while she found him a good home."

"She found you."

"Yes."

"Mack . . . You've fallen for him, haven't you?" Her voice quivered and Nick realized how hard it must be for her to find her dog resurrected.

"Mack? Yeah. I've gotten pretty fond of him." *Fond* didn't come anywhere near to explaining how he felt about Mack.

"And Serena Oakley? She sounds like a wonderful woman."

"She is. Yes, she is."

"Oh," she said with an upward intonation to her voice.

Oh. How did this woman imply so much with that one little word? *You've fallen for her, too, haven't you?*

Nick heard a sound from Adam next to him that sounded suspiciously like a stifled laugh.

Then Adam cleared his throat. "Ms. . . . . Claire. When he was left at Paws-A-While, Mack was wearing a black studded collar. Eric Kessler told us that you put it on the dog."

Nick was grateful to Adam for jumping in with the tough question.

Bright patches of color flared high on Claire Kessler's cheeks. She looked down at the ground, unable to face him or Adam.

Guilty.

"Did you or did you not put that collar on Mack?" Nick asked.

She looked up to face him. "He found the camera, did he? Eric, I mean."

Nick shot a glance to Adam, who shrugged one shoulder.

"As far as I know Kessler did not find the camera," said Nick. "I did."

She chewed on her lower lip. "I'm not proud of myself. But our marriage was going nowhere. I suspected he was having an affair. Maybe more than one affair. I worked late nights and weekends as a chef. Someone I knew had a nanny cam hidden in a teddy bear. So I bought a cheating-husband cam off the Internet."

"And?"

She shook her head ruefully. "Mack is not an ideal vehicle for a spy camera. The angles it captured weren't that great. But it recorded sound very well." Pain contorted her features. "I found out enough to confirm my suspicions."

"I'm sorry," said Nick. And damn sorry her story rang so true. He cursed under his breath. *Another suspect wiped.*

"That's why I left San Francisco. I came down here to help

out my cousin who owns this restaurant. She had a difficult birth with twins so I'm subbing for her until she can go back to work."

"What information did you get from the collar after you left Mack behind?"

"Nothing." She looked shamefaced. "A cheating husband can drive you to terrible depths. Once I was out of the marriage I was disgusted with myself for having used that camera. I didn't want to know what he was up to any longer. The receiver broke, and I never had it fixed."

Nick believed her. He trusted his gut instinct that told him she had nothing to do with the identity scam. From Adam's lack of questions he deduced his partner felt the same. They were not just back to square one but to square zero.

The trips to San Diego and Carmel had done nothing but eliminate another two suspects.

And lose him his dog.

He cleared his throat. "You'll be wanting Mack back as soon as possible. He's still convalescing, but as soon as his knee is healed I can drive him down here."

Claire wrung her hands together. "Oh God, this is so difficult. Carmel is the most dog-friendly town in the country, but everything is so unsettled for me. I . . . I want Mack back desperately, but . . . I have to think what's right for him. Not . . . not for me." She drew in a deep breath. "Maybe it's for the best if you keep Mack with you."

"I can't do that," said Nick.

"But you said you adopted him? I got the impression you really care for him?"

"I do," he said gruffly. "Which is why I don't want to get attached to him only for you to come back for him when your circumstances change."

She slowly shook her head in one of the saddest gestures Nick had ever seen. "You misunderstand me. My situation is no better than it was when I left Mack with Eric," she said, her voice filled with pain. "I'm staying in my cousin's spare bedroom. No way could that household accommodate Mack. Eric, of course, is dragging the chain on the property settlement so I can't afford a place on my own. It . . . it wouldn't be fair to Mack to shift him from person to person. I mean for you . . . for you to keep him permanently."

Nick fought conflicting reactions of sadness for her and elation that he got to keep Mack.

"I . . . I just want to ask you some questions first," she said.

"Questions?" said Nick, too shaken to know what else to say.

"Yes. Like, do you have a big yard?"

"Yes. There's plenty of room for him."

"He needs a lot of exercise."

"I plan to run with him daily once his knee is fixed."

"Good. And about the fast food. Do you intend to feed him burgers and fries?"

Was that a trick question? He had to answer honestly. "No. Maybe the occasional burger as a treat. But I don't think that kind of diet is good for him."

The relief in her eyes showed him he'd made the right answer. "That's great. Eric thought Mack's addiction was a joke and constantly undermined my efforts to wean Mack right off of the fast food."

She nodded. "Okay. I know you care enough for him to pay for that surgery, and now I feel happy he's in good hands. Mack is . . . is yours." Her voice fell away on the last words.

Nick was so damned grateful to her that all he could do was mumble his thanks.

She took a deep, shuddering breath. "Do you want me to sign something to make the . . . the adoption official?"

"That won't be necessary."

"I only ask one thing. Could I visit Mack sometimes? Not just yet. I don't want him to get confused while he's bonding with you. But when you judge the time is right."

"Of course," Nick said. "And Serena will want to meet with you." Serena and Claire seemed to speak the same language. He had a feeling they would get on very well.

"I've got another question," said Adam. "The spy cam receiver. Do you still have it?"

"Yes. I've got it in my purse. I haven't gotten around to taking it to the electronic recycling place."

"Can I have it?" asked Adam.

"Sure. I'll go get it." She turned and headed back into the restaurant.

"She's nice," said Adam in a low voice once Claire was out of earshot.

"She sure is," said Nick.

"And a babe," added Adam.

"Is she? Of course she is," said Nick. Truth was, he had registered that Claire was cute. But that was as far as it went. Only Serena held any interest for him in a man-woman way. And he suspected he would feel that way for the rest of his life.

"But not as hot as Kylie," added Adam, much to Nick's surprise.

"What do you mean by that?" he said. "Don't tell me you're thinking with your johnson about a possible suspect." He could not resist quoting Adam's words right back at him.

"Hey, man, don't get me wrong. I just said Kylie was hot."

Nick thought there was more to it than that, but Adam was saved from further interrogation by Claire's return with the broken receiver. Nick and Claire exchanged contact details and then he and Adam were on their way.

Once out of the laneway, Nick stepped up his pace with a sudden urgency. He had felt utterly gutted at the thought of losing Mack, even though he had only been his dog for a few days.

It was unbearable to think what he'd feel if he lost Serena.

He had to get back to San Francisco as soon as he could and tell her how he felt about her.

He cracked his knuckles.

Would that be before or after he had to tell her S&W Investigations was no closer to cracking the case than it had been the day he had followed the paw-print trail to Paws-A-While?

He'd have to do some fast talking with Adam, too, to convince him to keep pouring their time and resources into sniffing out the doggy day-care connection. All his strong leads had fizzled to nothing. Yet deep in his gut he remained convinced that the scam somehow originated from Paws-A-While.

He knew the drive back would seem interminable.

· Twenty ·

Why did she have so many darn clocks around Paws-A-While? Serena thought as she caught herself yet again checking the beagle clock in the reception area.

Where was Nick? She'd heard nothing but a brief phone call to report on his meeting with Claire Kessler. All she knew was that Mrs. Kessler was off the suspect list and that Mack now officially belonged to Nick. She ached to hear more details. And she ached to see Nick. She wondered if her sleepless night last night was as much to do with missing Nick as Mack's disruptive behavior.

I will not look up at that clock again; I will not look up at that clock again.

She looked down at her watch instead.

Would he ever get here?

The staff were asking her that question, too. They were short staffed without Kylie—Kylie, who did the work of two people and who Serena missed desperately. She felt ill every time she thought of the scene in her office, of Kylie's shock and hurt and anger. Even though Kylie had done the wrong thing by with-holding those details from her past, Serena was haunted by a sense that she had betrayed a friend who had been nothing but good to her. She'd left message after message for Kylie but with no reply.

Willing herself to keep her eyes away from her watch, she re-arranged the display of doggy beauty goodies to disguise the gaps where products had been bought but not reordered. Until her credit was re-established, she did not dare commit to even a cent that wasn't essential.

She was fussing with the bottles of Sexy Beast fragrance when "Who Let the Dogs Out?" chimed and suddenly Nick was there.

Her heart didn't just do the skip-a-beat thing. It actually seemed to stall as she drank in the tall, powerful handsomeness of him. It only started to beat again when she realized the look in his eyes told her he was as glad to see her as she was to see him.

Her first impulse was to run to him and fling herself into his arms. But the fact he wore his Paws-A-While shirt restrained her. In front of the team, she had to keep up the pretense that Nick was just another employee. Though from the sly glances she had intercepted from the staff from the day Nick came on board, she was beginning to wonder if they were fooling anyone.

But if the speculation about her relationship with Nick kept the Paws-A-While team from wondering why clients were leaving and products not being reordered, and from discovering the fact they were all under investigation, she guessed that had to be okay.

Even though there was no one in the reception area with her, she thought she had better keep up the role-play just in case some-one came in.

"Nick, glad to see you back. We're short staffed with Kylie not in again today so—"

She didn't get the chance to finish. Nick took two great strides toward her and swept her into a big, exuberant hug. "I've missed you, too, boss lady."

He squeezed her so tight she found it hard to breathe. Or was that shortness of breath because of her proximity to his big, hard body, the Nick-scent filling her senses and—oh yes!—the pressure of his mouth on hers, hard and possessive.

She melted against him, twined her arms around his neck, kissed him back. "I missed you every minute you were away," she murmured against his mouth.

Then jumped quickly back when she heard the door to the playroom open. Adele popped her head around the door, looked, and took in the situation with a knowing smirk. "Great. Nick's here," she said. "We've been waiting for him."

Serena felt herself color as she fought for composure. "Is it urgent, Adele?" she asked.

"We could do with some help with the puppy potty. Heather thinks it could be a blocked pipe."

"Great," Nick groaned.

Serena took a deep breath to steady herself. "Nick will be with you in a moment," she said in her best boss-lady voice.

"Sure, I guess you two have got business going on here," said Adele, not even attempting to suppress a cheeky grin as she turned to go.

Serena waited until the door closed behind her youngest employee before turning back to Nick. "Do you think she saw us?"

"Who gives a damn if she did?" said Nick, pulling her to him again.

She looked up at him. "Aren't we meant to be undercover?"

"With the investigation, yes. But us? I want things out in the open. We've got nothing to hide."

"Except I'm meant to be your boss."

"So you set the rules. Do you have a rule that says you can't date the staff?"

"No."

"Especially when we both know I'm not really your employee, that my role here is just for the purpose of the investigation."

He was right. Of course he was right. There was nothing to stop her going public about her relationship with Nick.

Except her own fears.

Fear of looking foolish if things backfired as badly as they had with Dave.

Fear that once the investigation was over and they weren't forced together the fire between them would fizzle out.

Fear that she would lose control of the safe life she had established around her business and her dog.

But most of all, fear that she was incapable of making a commitment. She didn't seem to have what it took to have a successful relationship with a man.

She nodded. But Nick quickly picked up on how tentative she seemed. "Don't bowl me over with enthusiasm," he said with a wry twist to his mouth.

"It's not that. It's . . . I guess I'm a private kind of person. I lost all claim to that privacy when I did the chocolate campaign, and I've had to claw it back. I suppose right now I'd like things . . . things between us to develop without everyone knowing about it."

"That's a point," he said. "Though I'd be proud to have people know about us."

"Please." She reached out to lay her hand on his arm. "It's not that. I'm very proud to be seen with you. But I told you the first day I knew you that . . . that I wasn't very good at commitment. That I didn't stick at things. I was lucky to graduate high school. I dropped out of college and then flitted from one job to another, never sticking at anything. I'm . . . I'm not great at relationships."

Nick shook his head. "The Serena I see and the Serena you see yourself as are two different people."

She frowned. "I don't understand."

"You say you don't commit to anything. What about all this?"

He swept his arm around to encompass the room. "What's this but commitment? You're obviously a businesswoman with vision and the acumen to see it through. You've certainly won the respect of the other businesspeople in this area. I discovered that in my initial investigations."

"Yes, but—"

"No buts. I haven't finished. So you dropped out of college? So what? Don't I see a veterinary technician certificate framed on your office wall?"

"It took me years to study for that."

"But you stuck at it and finished it, right?"

"Eventually." It hadn't been easy fitting the necessary study and work experience around her modeling and waitressing commitments.

"You've got good friends, too—Maddy, Jenna. That says something about commitment."

Why was it that she'd carried around these negative thoughts about herself for so long? For years she'd blamed her parents' undisciplined lifestyle and relaxed style of parenting for her lack of direction. But she was twenty-eight years old now; she couldn't blame her parents forever. And when she looked back on it, her parents had always loved and cared for her in their own way.

"As for your relationships," he said. "Hell, you met the wrong guys. Until now. I'm the guy for you, Serena. You were just waiting for me."

He grinned as he spoke, but his eyes told her his words were not a joke.

She smiled. "Maybe."

"No maybe about it."

She tried to be serious, but her mouth kept quirking upward into a smile. "You're very sure about that."

"I'm sure all right."

"It's early days yet."

"I've had enough time to make up my mind."

"Does this mean we're officially dating?"

"Damn right it does," he said as he planted a possessive, determined kiss on her mouth.

Serena laughed, as sudden joy bubbled through her at the idea of Nick becoming a more permanent part of her life.

Adele chose that moment to pop her head around the door again. "Nick, we're starting to have overflow problems."

"Right on it," said Nick. "Just another minute."

Adele left and Nick turned to Serena. "Before I'm back on potty duty, I have to bring you up to speed on exactly what happened in Carmel."

Quickly he filled in the gaps of what he'd told her in their brief phone call after he'd left his meeting with Claire Kessler.

"You'll like her, Serena," he concluded.

"You obviously do," Serena said.

"Yeah, I did."

"What . . . what does she look like?" Serena asked.

Nick gestured at about his chest height. "Medium height. Slim. Brown hair. Nice smile."

"Pretty?"

"In a wholesome kind of way."

"Oh," she said, unable to keep the edge from her voice.

Jealousy.

It was a character trait she was not proud of. Didn't admire it in others. But it seared right through her nonetheless.

Nick paused. There it was again. *Oh.* That one word that women seemed to invest with such a range of meaning. But this time he was left in no doubt as to what Serena meant by it and he puzzled why.

She looked up at him, those beautiful honey-colored eyes wide with uncertainty.

Then it hit him. Gorgeous, sexy Serena St. James had posed half naked in a bathtub of chocolate, to the ongoing delight of the red-blooded male population of the U.S. That woman on the billboards gleamed with the confidence of her own seductive powers.

But underneath that perfect body, that lush mouth, those eyes full of promise, beat the far more uncertain heart of Serena Oakley, who, for some reason unfathomable to him, doubted her own attractiveness.

He would do everything in his power to make sure she always knew how beautiful she was. Beautiful in every way.

"You're jealous," he said.

Her denial was too quick. "Jealous?" she echoed. "Of course I'm not. Don't be ridiculous." Her gaze dropped to the level of the stenciled paw prints on the floor.

He put a finger under her chin and tilted her face up so she was forced to meet his eyes. "Listen," he said. "And listen good. Claire Kessler is a nice woman. But I am not in any way attracted to her."

"I didn't say you were." Serena pressed her lips right together. Her shadowed eyes denied her words.

Nick continued. "There is not a woman on this planet who could hold a candle to you. Not in my eyes anyway."

She was silent for a moment, then smiled a tremulous smile. "I guess yours are the only eyes that count."

"You'd better believe it," he said. "And I'm not just talking looks, either. You're gorgeous. That's undisputed. But it's all those other things about you that have got me hanging around."

"You'll have to tell me all about them sometime," she said.

"Tonight," he said. "You. Me. The dogs. At my house."

"Oh," she said. This time the way she said the word had such a sensuous edge to it that the blood rushed southward from Nick's head. "What shall—?"

There was a loud knocking on the playroom door. This time Adele looked agitated when she appeared. "Nick. Now. Please."

"Yes, ma'am," he said with a mock salute and a regretful glance to Serena. He would like to get her back to his house right this second.

But puppy potty duty called. He was hoping to be around Serena and Paws-A-While for a long time. He'd better get familiar with the plumbing.

TWO hours later, Serena stood opposite Nick in the playroom. Her veterinarian friend Lydia Stevens stood between them. On the floor nearby, Mack lay on the doggy day bed. Half the dogs were out on their afternoon walks so the room was relatively quiet. As the humans spoke, Mack's head turned from her to Nick and back again. His forehead was creased, his "up" ear on alert. She swore he understood every word that was being said.

Serena's heart warmed as she looked down at the big dog. Thank heaven he did not have to go back to his former owner. Not when she and Nick had invested so much in him. Not just in financial terms but in care and affection. He wouldn't be confined to the bed for long. Already he could hobble around the room, putting weight on the leg in the purple cast, seemingly without any pain.

"A remarkable recovery," said Lydia. "But there are other problems, you say?"

Lydia was a tiny, fine-boned blond with a pixie-pointed face and a swing of fine pale hair cut in a sleek bob. Even when she wore a white lab coat she was always quite the fashion plate.

No one ever guessed she was a vet. In fact, she was phasing out of her general practice as a physician to concentrate on pets with behavioral problems. She had a popular "Pets on the Couch" segment on the radio that was gaining her more and more publicity and a growing number of patients whose problems were not always physical. Maddy had made friends with her when she'd gone to her for help with Brutus. After his old master, Walter Stoddard, had died, it had appeared the little dog might die of a broken heart.

Lydia had diagnosed Brutus as in need of a new alpha male in his life, a role Tom O'Brien had stepped into, though unwillingly at first. She and Maddy and Serena had then become friends as well as clients.

The pet shrink got straight down to business. "When did the whimpering and crying start?" she asked Nick.

"When I took him home after his surgery," he said. "I thought he must have been in pain."

Lydia shook her head. "Not pain of the physical kind. More pain of his psyche."

Serena stifled a laugh at the what-the-hell-am-I-doing-here look on Nick's face.

"His psyche?" he repeated.

Lydia nodded again. "Mental anguish manifesting itself in his behavior."

"I thought it might have been an aftereffect of the anesthetic," said Serena, thinking to her vet tech studies.

Lydia shook her head. "That would have long worn off. Remember, he had his surgery early morning. No. I think the behavior is more linked with the change of residence than the surgery. Dogs still have deep links to their wolf heritage, you know. Separation anxiety and behavioral disorders can often be traced back to primal pack behavior."

That made sense. But it wasn't an explanation. Serena stifled a yawn. She noticed the shadows beneath Nick's eyes. She wanted a diagnosis and a treatment program. Pronto. She couldn't go through another sleep-deprived night like she had last night. And she suspected Nick felt the same.

I could think of better ways to deprive Nick of sleep.

Now Lydia addressed her. "So what happened the next night?"

"Nick was out of town so he left Mack with me in my apartment." Serena leaned toward Lydia to emphasize her point. "Where he had slept without any problem or disruption for the previous five weeks."

"The same symptoms? The moaning, the whimpering?"

"The second I was out of his sight. Then the other dogs got agitated. Even the cat was affected."

"And the next night?"

"That would be tonight," said Nick.

"At which residence will Mack sleep tonight?" asked Lydia.

"My house. Which is now Mack's house," said Nick.

Mack thumped his tail and tried to get up at the mention of his name.

"Down, Mack," Serena said at the very same time as Nick did. They met each other's smiles.

"Hmm," said Lydia.

"Will you be at Nick's house tonight?" she asked Serena.

Serena nodded. "For dinner, yes."

"Well, I suggest you pack your pajamas," said Lydia.

"What?" Serena and Nick had another simultaneous exclamation moment.

Lydia steepled her index fingers together. Serena wasn't sure if her friend was parodying the manner of a TV shrink or being dead serious.

Lydia smiled. "This is an easy one to solve. In a wild dog pack there is always an alpha male to which all other dogs defer."

"I get that," said Nick.

"There is also the alpha female who bears his puppies and is the top-ranking female in the pack," said Lydia.

Serena nodded. "I get that, too." What she wasn't sure of was which way Lydia was heading.

Lydia looked from Serena to Nick, to Mack, and then back to

Serena. Her intelligent blue eyes danced with amusement. "Mack has chosen you, Nick, as his alpha male."

Nick looked pleased; his broad shoulders set even straighter, and he seemed to grow even taller in height.

"And you, Serena, as his alpha female."

"Ookay," Serena said, not totally surprised at Lydia's summation but still not sure what point her friend was making.

Lydia clapped her hands together. "So he wants you together. With him."

Mutual exclamation number three emanated from Nick and Serena.

Lydia continued. "Mack doesn't see it as the natural order of things to have his alpha male and alpha female living apart in different packs. When they sleep apart, that's when his separation anxiety kicks in."

Nick snorted. "That's the biggest load of—"

"Animal instinct," said Lydia. "So, Serena, that's why I told you to pack your pajamas."

Serena felt herself flush. She looked at Nick. An enormous grin spread across his face as he took in the implication of Lydia's prognosis.

Feeling totally disconcerted, she looked back at Lydia. "But I . . . but we . . . we haven't . . ."

Yet.

"Or I could prescribe a calmative medication for Mack, see if that works," said Lydia.

"No," said Nick. "Mack's had enough meds."

Lydia smiled, and Serena got the distinct impression her friend was thoroughly enjoying herself. "Well, you both know what to do then, if you want a good night's sleep. Problem solved."

Nick was obviously having a great deal of difficulty not erupting into laughter.

He was still grinning when Serena returned from escorting Lydia to the door.

"So are you packing your pajamas for your visit to my house?" he asked.

Serena smiled a slow, deliberate smile. With unhurried steps she walked up to him, put both her hands flat on his chest, and looked up into his eyes. She curved her mouth into a teasing smile. "I don't wear pajamas. Ever. I sleep naked," she said. "Do you?"

· Twenty-one ·

Nick had more than one appetite on his brain when, after the last dog had been picked up from Paws-A-While, he went next door to collect Serena from her apartment.

The second appetite was for food—and lots of it. The muffin at the airport and the hastily grabbed burger on the way back from Carmel had left him with a gnawing hunger. But thoughts of food fled his mind when Serena answered the door.

"I just have to leave some kibble for Thelma, my kitty, and I'm ready to go," she said.

Was that the sound of his jaw dropping to the floor? He was too gobsmacked to utter a word in reply.

Serena looked different. Gone was the shapeless Paws-A-While uniform. Instead she wore a black dress, short and tight, that hugged every incredible curve and showed off her long, slender legs. The Birkenstocks were nowhere to be seen. High-heeled shoes that strapped around her ankles brought her practically to his eye level.

She wore makeup, too, her beautiful, lush mouth slicked with scarlet, her eyes all dark and smoky.

It was the first time he had seen Serena with her hair down. The dark waves tumbled wildly around her face and over her shoulders. She looked hot. A million dollars' worth of hot. A woman who appeared on TV with Oprah and on the covers of magazines.

A woman he didn't know.

"Nick?" she asked. "Are you okay?"

He cleared his throat. "I'm fine."

"I'll only be a second," she said. "Come on in."

"I'll, uh . . . wait here," he said. Then stood mesmerized by the sight of her back view as she headed toward the kitchen to tend to her cat. The high-heeled shoes gave her ass an incredibly seductive sway.

But this sensational-looking woman didn't look like Serena. Not his Serena, anyway.

Nick had never been short on confidence, but he was suddenly thrown back to that first day in the patch of park outside the S&W Investigations headquarters. He'd sat cracking his knuckles and wondering what in hell Serena St. James would see in a small-town guy like him. Not that it had even been a possibility then—not when he'd suspected her of being a criminal.

Now, with her out of earshot, he slowly cracked his knuckles, one after another.

Within moments she was back. "Let's go," she said.

"You look . . . great," he said, unable to find any better word.

"Thank you." She paused, smoothed her hands down her thighs as if she wanted to stretch the dress out longer to cover more of her legs. "It's . . . it's been a long time since I dressed like this." She looked at him with an expression that tore through his heart.

Trust.

He felt humbled he had in some way helped her to come out of hiding and regain the confidence to wear a sexy dress.

"You look beautiful," he said. Then he made a big show of looking behind him and down at the large purse she carried. "But where are those pajamas?"

She laughed and reached over to kiss his cheek. To his heartfelt relief she laughed like his Serena and she smelled like his Serena, that heady scent that was just her own.

With her help, he secured the dogs in his truck. Serena climbed into the passenger seat beside him. Those legs! How could he concentrate on driving with those slender, go-on-forever legs folded so elegantly beside him?

I sleep naked. Do you? Ever since the minx had uttered those provocative words the thought of Serena naked in his bed had been top of mind. This was his first sight of her legs. Up until now they had always been covered by a thick layer of denim. He was going crazy imagining how the rest of her looked stripped of her clothing.

He forced his eyes to stay on the road as he pulled away from the curb outside Paws-A-While.

"Have you thought about dinner?" she asked. "Can we pick up some takeout?"

"I'd like to take you out to a restaurant, but we have the dogs to think about. Mack's still slow and Bessie isn't that used to having him on her territory."

"Takeout is fine. Really it is."

He ran the list of food options through his mind. Suddenly he knew exactly what he wanted to eat. He realized he'd been craving it all day. "Your lasagna," he said. "I could think of nothing I'd like more."

"My lasagna?" she said in a strangled voice. "Uh, isn't there something else you'd rather have?"

"Nothing," he said.

"But I—"

"You don't have to cook it yourself. Just tell me how it's done and I'll prepare it. You can just sit in the kitchen, sip on a glass of wine, and supervise."

"Not . . . not a good idea," she said.

"You think I can't cook?"

"Uh. No. No. It's not that."

He nodded. "I get it. You don't want to share your secret recipe with me."

She looked straight ahead, her face screened by a tumble of that gorgeous hair. "Yes. That's it. I . . . uh . . . I never reveal my culinary secrets."

"In that case, it will be me who sits in the kitchen with a glass of wine while I watch your every move. I'm sure I'll pick up some tips, even if I can't decipher your secret recipe."

"No!" The word seemed to explode out of her as she turned to face him. He was surprised she took the cooking thing so seriously. "No," she repeated more calmly. "You've had a long day. You can just relax while I cook. I . . . uh . . . I can't concentrate with someone else in the kitchen."

Nick was disappointed. He'd liked the idea of him cooking for her. He didn't like the idea of him out in the living room and her away from him in the kitchen.

He knew he could easily rustle up something else. A spaghetti sauce. Steak. A quick chili.

But he had his heart set on Serena's lasagna. If getting it had to be on her terms, so be it.

"The salad with the avocado dressing. Can we have that, too?" he said, trying not to sound as if he were pleading.

"Avocado dressing? Sure thing," she said.

"We'll stop off and shop on the way home," he said.

"The supermarket near Marina Green. That's the one I want to go visit."

"Not a problem," he said. Serena—without pajamas—and Serena's lasagna. It sounded like the recipe for the perfect evening.

★   ★   ★

Serena stood in Nick's kitchen, enfolded in his "Licensed to Grill" barbecue apron, totally and utterly freaking out.

This lasagna had seemed so darn easy when Maddy had made it. Maddy herself had said it was idiotproof.

Not to this darn idiot.

To let Nick believe she had cooked lunch that day in her apartment had seemed such a good idea at the time. She had slipped into her assumed role as "good cook" so easily. But sitting there in his truck outside Paws-A-While, she just hadn't had the chops to confess the truth about who had actually cooked that wonderful lasagna. To admit she couldn't show him how to cook her "special lasagna" because she didn't have a clue how to make it herself.

Trouble had started at the supermarket. She'd done her best to remember which aisles she'd shopped with Maddy. But panic set in when she'd been faced with all those different brands of pasta, of sausage, of tomato sauce. She hadn't been able to dither, not with Nick so interested in what she was choosing. At another time she would have found his interest cute but not when she was so desperately afraid of being caught out.

After confidently purchasing eggplant and onion, she'd dispatched Nick to buy some wine. Then cowered behind a display of about a million different brands of pasta sauces and called Maddy. But her call went through to voice mail. What the heck. Closing her eyes and choosing the item her finger landed on was as good a method as any. In the end she thought she'd made a reasonable approximation of the products Maddy had loaded into the cart the day they'd shopped together.

Now she faced the stove. *Deep breath, deep breath.* This really couldn't be that difficult.

"How's it going in there?" called Nick. "Sure you don't want some help?"

"Quite sure, thank you," she trilled back, injecting a confidence in her voice she was impossibly far from feeling.

She looked at the ingredients she had strewn out on the countertop before her.

Onion. Yes. She could do onion. Even if she wasn't quite sure if Maddy had used them.

Dammit! She'd forgotten why she didn't like chopping onions. Her eyes smarted, and she squeezed them tightly together. Rubbing them only made the discomfort worse. Still, she managed to chop the onion finely. Okay, not with quite the speed and finesse Maddy had demonstrated when slicing vegetables. But it would do.

Success! Not only were the onions browning nicely in the fry pan but they smelled good, too. Delicious in fact. Then she added the chopped-up Italian sausage.

"Something smells great," Nick called from the living room.

It did, too. Serena sniffed appreciatively. For heaven's sake, throw all this yummy stuff together and cover it with grated cheese and it couldn't fail to taste good. She didn't know why she'd been so worried. This was going to be a cinch.

Nick's stomach was ominously close to growling when he sat down at his aunt's wooden dining table. He sniffed the taste-bud-tantalizing aromas that wafted from the kitchen. His mouth watered so hard in anticipation he was in danger of drooling like the Paws-A-While bulldog.

Then Serena, divested of his apron and looking sensational, marched triumphantly from the kitchen. She bore the rectangular baking pan in front of her like a trophy, then slid it reverentially onto the table. Fresh from the oven, the golden cheese bubbled enticingly across the surface of the dish.

"Wow!" he said. "This looks awesome."

"It was nothing," she said with a modest smirk. "Enjoy!"

Scarcely able to control his greed, Nick used the knife Serena handed him to plunge into the layer of bubbling cheese. Only to meet an unexpected resistance.

He pressed harder with the knife. The top layer of pasta, instead of being soft, was as hard and unyielding as a fine layer of cement board. He used more force with the knife, only for the lasagna to tip inward. Hard, curling edges of uncooked lasagna sheet revealed themselves as the coating of cheese slid away.

"Is everything okay?" asked Serena from where she hovered over the edge of the table.

"Fine," he said. To penetrate the top layer enough to cut himself a slice was more a job for a hacksaw than a knife.

"It isn't fine, is it?" Her voice rose with anxiety. "That looks burned on the edge. I . . . I must have left it in the oven too long."

He made reassuring noises as he hacked though the layers enough to free a rough-edged square. "Let me serve you first," he said, as he levered it onto Serena's plate.

She eyed the portion of lasagna without touching it. "I . . . uh . . . I'm not used to your oven."

"Of course," he said. "Probably the thermostat is set different to yours."

He managed to release a square to put on his plate, then used his fork to transfer a generous portion to his mouth. It crunched when he chewed it.

The lasagna *crunched*.

Manfully, forcing a look of enthusiasm on his face, he bit into a chunk of something tasteless and rubberlike. He kept it on his tongue, in an effort to identify it.

Eggplant. Bitter, under-cooked eggplant.

It took all his self-control not to spit it out.

He picked over those gray, unappetizing bits before he tasted his next mouthful, aware of Serena's watchful eyes. The sausage tasted good. So did the cheese. But nothing else about this dish resembled in any way the superlative lunch he'd been served at Serena's apartment.

That time, the eggplant had been a triumph—redolent of garlic and fresh herbs, soft and sweet and melt-in-the-mouth. The layers of pasta had absorbed the varied yet perfectly balanced flavors of the sausage and the sauce to make a memorable impact on the palate.

He gulped down a mouthful of wine to help him swallow this poor imitation of Serena's previous triumph. "Delicious," he lied.

Across from him at the table, Serena pushed her portion of dud lasagna around her plate with her fork. There was an expression of profound misery in her eyes as she watched him manfully transfer forkfuls of her prized recipe to his mouth.

"I'm glad you think so," she said.

The dogs. Where were the damn dogs when he needed them? During his childhood, Fella had often been the recipient of unwanted food from the family table. He thought back to that Saturday lunch at Serena's apartment and remembered how the dogs in the next room had been slavering for their share.

Now Snowball lay nearby but didn't even stir. Surreptitiously, Nick nudged him with his foot. The Maltese looked up at him with round, dark eyes and seemed to sniff his disdain. Mack stayed steadfastly in his dog bed, even though he'd been successfully hobbling around Paws-A-While all afternoon. No, Mack seemed to say, *that* is not worth getting out of bed for. Nick didn't even bother with Bessie. He knew she would turn her dainty little Yorki-poo nose up at such an unfortunate offering.

Then he realized the lasagna had onions in it. Onions weren't good for dogs. There was no way he could slip a portion or two of this truly awful meal to the dogs even if they wanted it. With no rescue in sight he knew he could not endure another bite. He pushed his plate away with a sigh of what he hoped sounded like repletion, not relief.

"Think I'll try some salad now," he said.

"Sure," said Serena in a quiet little voice that tore at him. "Let me serve you."

To his relief the salad was every bit as delicious as last time. In fact the dressing was one of the best he'd ever tasted. He ate two servings.

Serena just nibbled on a few leaves of lettuce and pushed the rest to the side of her plate.

Nick chased the last leaf of radicchio from the plate. Tasty as it was, salad was no meal for a man of his build. He had woken very early in San Diego and been flat out all day. He was still hungry. But he didn't let on for fear Serena would offer him more lasagna.

"That was . . . wonderful," he said.

Her mouth twisted downward. "No, it wasn't."

"The oven . . ." he began, not really believing the disastrous dish was the fault of the oven. That eggplant should have been fried in olive oil and garlic long before it ever hit the oven. And there was something radically wrong with the pasta sheets.

Serena compressed her lips in the way she tended to do when agitated. "It wasn't the oven. It was me."

To Nick's alarm, tears welled in those beautiful, luminous eyes. "I'm a hopeless cook. Always have been. Probably always will be." Now her lovely lush mouth began to tremble.

"But the lasagna you made at your house was wonderful."

She shook her head. "Maddy cooked it."

"Huh?"

Her mouth wobbled some more. "I never . . . I never actually said I cooked it. In fact I tried to tell you, but you were so sure I'd made it. Seemed so pleased I'd made it. In the end it was easier not to keep denying it."

"Oh, Serena." Now he recalled she had kept trying to interrupt his lavish exclamations of praise.

"I . . . I wanted to impress you." Her voice trailed away.

She looked so woebegone, her makeup smudged beneath her eyes, her hair dampened into waves that fell over her forehead.

He got up from the table and took the few steps needed to take her in his arms. "You impress me just by the fact you wanted to impress me," he said. "If you get my meaning."

Wordlessly, she nodded.

"What about the cookies?" he asked.

"Maddy," she mumbled into his shoulder.

Scratch that thought of Serena making a farmer's wife. Not in the cooking department anyway. With her empathy with animals and her physical strength she might prefer to work outdoors with him.

"I hope you told Maddy how much I liked the cookies," he said.

"She was delighted with the feedback; she was testing the recipe for her magazine."

"What about that amazing salad?"

Serena pulled back to face him. A watery smile struggled to life. "All my own work. The avocado dressing is my mom's recipe. You'd expect good salad in a vegan household, wouldn't you?"

"You can make that salad for me anytime."

"But not the lasagna." Even she seemed to gag at the very mention of it. "I wonder what went wrong? It seemed so easy when Maddy did it."

He shrugged. "I've never cooked lasagna myself. But the pasta sheets tasted kind of uncooked." He decided to gloss over the inedible eggplant.

"But Maddy didn't cook them; she put them straight in the pan." She paused, frowning. Then he saw the lightbulb moment illuminate her face. "I don't think I bought the 'no boiling required' kind. That was it. I'll go to the kitchen and check the pack."

She went to pull away from him, but Nick stopped her. "Serena, who cares? You tried. You impressed me."

"And next time you'll cook."

"That's right."

He used his index finger to tenderly wipe away the smears of black makeup from under her eyes. She sniffed. "I'm not great with onions," she said.

"Buy the frozen kind all chopped up," he said. He was all for shortcuts when it came to cooking.

"I guess," she said, her eyes still vulnerable.

He bent his head and kissed her. She kissed him right back, her mouth eager and responsive.

And suddenly that other kind of hunger was the only thing on Nick's mind.

· Twenty-two ·

Nick was strong, he was tough, he was smart. He was, without a doubt, the most physically attractive man she had ever met. Tonight, in black jeans and a gray shirt, he was the hottest of the hot.

But the tipping point for Serena was that Nick was kind.

He could have reacted very differently to the lasagna debacle. On more than one occasion she had called him a liar. "Liar" was a fitting label for her tonight. But he had not chosen to use it.

"The dinner was a disaster," she murmured against his mouth, "not the kind of impression I wanted to make."

He kissed the side of her mouth in a way that sent shivers of longing through her body. "I can think of other ways to impress me," he said.

"Let me guess," she murmured. "Should I start like this?"

She slid her hands through his hair and angled his head down to meet hers. She pressed teasing little kisses along the line of his jaw, then stopped at the corner of his mouth. Then planted another line of kisses ending at the other corner of his mouth. She kissed his nose. Then the line of his cheekbone. Gently, she swept tiny, featherlight kisses over his eyelids. Only then did she kiss his mouth.

What started as fun quickly turned urgent as her lips parted under his, her tongue darted in to mate with his. She pulled away. "I think I could impress you more if we were somewhere more comfortable," she murmured.

"The living room," he said. He walked her backward until they reached the sofa and he gently pushed her down onto the seat.

Soon kissing didn't seem enough.

As Nick kissed Serena, her throaty little murmurs of delight sent his senses into overdrive. He ached so much to make her his that it hurt. The part of his brain that wasn't fogged with want began to think logistics. *Stairs. Bedroom. Bed.*

She started to unbutton his shirt, first one button and then another. Slid her warm, sure hands onto the bare skin of his chest. He reacted with a shudder that reverberated through his body in shock waves of excitement. Serena laughed against his mouth, a low sensual sound full of pleasure and promise.

He pulled her tighter. Felt her heart pounding against his chest. Found the zipper on the back of her dress and tugged. Pushed her dress off the smooth skin of her shoulders and down to her waist. She wiggled to make it easy for him, kissed him more fervently as he brushed his fingers over the swell of her breasts. She gave a little moan of appreciation. Her hands slid down to rest at his waist. Then she hooked her thumbs into his belt.

Sofa.

Here. Right now.

He broke from the kiss, eased her back against the sofa, feasted on the sight of her, that glorious hair tumbling wildly around her shoulders, her mouth pink and swollen from his kisses, her breasts . . .

Her breasts. Wrapped in a black, lacy bra, they were beyond perfect, her tight, aroused nipples pushing against the lace. Her body was even more perfect than the chocolate-coated images the ad campaign and calendar had hinted at. He cupped her breasts in his hands, thumbed the hard peaks, and she pushed herself closer with another of those insanely arousing murmurs.

Serena.

He kissed the delicate curve of her ear, bent his head to kiss the beautiful hollow of her throat, intoxicated by her scent. Pushed aside the lace of her bra—

Only to feel her tense.

With great effort he stopped, pulled back, struggled to get his breath under control.

"You okay?" he managed to get out.

Even the floor would be fine.

She was looking over his shoulder. "We're being watched," she whispered.

In an instant Nick was on full alert. Off the sofa. Crouched on the balls of his feet, tensed, his hands held flat in front of him ready to fend off danger. Fight if necessary.

To meet the intense gaze of his dog.

"Mack!" Nick growled.

Pleased at the sudden attention, Mack made his ponderous way closer toward the sofa. His mouth was creased in his doggy smile, his tail wagging.

"Stay!" Nick commanded.

At the sound of stifled laughter, Nick turned back to Serena. She leaned toward him, her black dress rumpled around her waist, her breasts heaving with the effort of suppressing her mirth.

"I meant we were being watched by a dog," she said, her eyes bright with humor. "Not a stalker. But I so appreciate your readiness to fight for me."

That Serena could joke about a stalker was something Nick's brain only scarcely registered.

He turned back to glare at Mack. Already he loved the animal. But right now he did not appreciate the interruption.

"Bed," he commanded, pointing at the fireplace. "Now."

"Bed? Okay," said Serena, her voice rich with laughter. "I'm good with that."

As Nick watched, stupefied, she stood up from the sofa. Her dress slid down the length of her hips and legs to pool at her feet. She wore only her bra, a triangle of black panties, and those follow-me-home shoes strapped around her ankles. Nick had never seen anything so seductive.

Serena enjoyed the conflicting looks that played across Nick's face. Impatience. Humor. Lust. And something else. Something warm and wonderful in those pale blue eyes that made her quickly step out of her dress and take the next few steps to reach him. She twined her arms around his neck.

"I don't want an audience; do you?" she murmured.

He swallowed. "You mean the dogs?"

She nodded. "Much as I love them, I'd be happier if they were on the other side of a closed door."

He picked her up. All five-ten of her. As if she weighed nothing.

"Bed it is," he growled as he headed toward the stairs.

Serena squealed. She protested. She laughed. But Nick did not put her down until they reached the top of the stairs. And she loved every second of it. He made her feel cherished, protected, and on fire with desire for him.

He kicked open the door of his bedroom and pulled her in after him. She got an impression of white-painted walls with a big iron bed in the center, the linen in crisp, blue-and-white stripes.

But her senses were too taken up with Nick to register anything else. His taste. His scent. His hard, muscle-packed body. The sound of his ragged breathing.

They kissed, urgently, hungrily. With impatient fingers she fumbled open the remaining buttons on his shirt, tugged it off him. She let him deal with his belt but helped him push down his jeans. They broke the kiss as he kicked off his shoes, followed by his jeans. Then he stood in just his boxers.

She caught her breath. His body was magnificent. Broad shoulders, the muscles of his chest and arms pumped and defined. Just the right amount of hair on his chest. No wonder he had the strength to carry her up the stairs as if she were a featherweight. His legs, too, were muscled, long, and firm. She noticed a white scar on his right knee that stood out against his tan—no doubt the aftermath of his knee surgery. That was the only flaw in his masculine perfection.

But Nick did not give her time to stop and admire him. He pulled her to him again. Skin against skin. Her breasts pressed against his bare chest, her hips against his. She thrilled to the evidence of his arousal. She was ready for him, too. Knew that from the very first day she'd seen him at Paws-A-While she'd wanted this, wanted him. Wanted him so much she trembled.

He pulled her down to sit next to him on the bed, then untied her shoes, one after the other, making the act an erotic caress. Who knew her instep was an erogenous zone?

Then he cradled her face between his large hands, tilting her to meet his gaze, warm now with passion and tenderness. His voice was deep and husky. "This is special. Us. You know that."

She turned to kiss the palm of his hand. "Yes," she murmured. "I know that."

Her heart swelled with emotion so strong it thumped-thumped-thumped against her chest. But she felt incapable of articulating just how special this was to her. She would have to show him.

Then he had her bra unhooked and there was nothing between them but their underwear. And then not even that.

He lowered her to the bed. She gave herself up to bliss as he stroked and explored, discovered her most sensitive places, just what pleased her. His breath in the hollow behind her ears, his tongue teasing her nipples, his fingers trailing across the backs of her knees, her thighs, the curve of her hip before moving to more intimate caresses. He groaned his appreciation as she did the same for him, glorying in his body, exulting in his response. His rapid breathing, his tension, made her sense he was on the edge, straining to hold back. To wait until she was ready.

No need. She arched against him, loving the feeling of his body against hers, the tickle of his chest hair against her breasts, urging him. "Now, Nick. Please."

He took care of protection. "Now," he murmured as he entered her.

She welcomed him to her body. She wanted him, oh, how she wanted him. She knew she was falling in love with him.

So why did she freeze as soon as he started to move inside her?

He was so strong, so heavy, and suddenly she felt like she couldn't breathe. Her heart started to beat wildly, not with passion but with panic. Her old fears of being dominated. Of losing control. Of losing herself.

Nick seemed to know straight away. He stilled. Raised himself on his elbows. Stroked the damp hair away from her forehead. "It's okay," he said in a deep, soothing voice.

Then slowly, without breaking their intimate connection, he rolled her over so she lay on top of him. She pushed herself up so she straddled him. Immediately, the feeling of suffocation lifted. She took in a deep gulp of air. Then another.

This was embarrassing. Not what this amazing man would expect from Serena St. James. But then, hadn't Dave told her that her admirers would be disappointed at how the reality of her didn't match up to her posters?

She couldn't even cook Nick a lasagna.

And now this.

Tears smarted her eyes. She bit down on her lip to stop its wobbling. Then turned her head away so Nick wouldn't see. So she couldn't see his disappointment. His anger, maybe.

But he cupped his hand under her chin and gently turned her to face him. She made herself meet his gaze, dreading his reaction. All she saw was concern and compassion. Those qualities that so surprised her in this tough PI.

"I ... I ..." she stammered. But he placed his finger on her mouth to hush her.

"Hey, boss lady," he said. "You set the pace. You be in charge." He flung his arms behind his head in a gesture of surrender, his biceps rippling as he did so.

"Really?" she said, amazed at the instant rush of arousal that dispelled the last of her anxiety.

"Just think of me as your own personal sex slave."

This big, muscular, wonderful man her *sex slave*?

Serena laughed, a throaty, joyous laugh. Felt an exhilarating freedom. And an immense gratitude that he understood her so well.

She narrowed her eyes in mock command. "Okay, sex slave. Lie back and listen. You are there for my pleasure. You only move when I let you move. You only touch when I say you can touch. Do you get that?"

"Yes, boss lady," he growled.

The gleam in his eyes showed he was as turned on as she was. Hey, this could be fun. She started to move rhythmically against him. It felt so good. *He* felt so good.

He let her find her own pace, her own rhythm, as she rode him.

"Now you touch ..." she started, but suddenly she couldn't find her breath. *"Oh!"*

Pleasure started to ripple through her in ever-tightening waves. "Nick," she gasped. He took that as an order. And when he thrust up to meet her, his power and strength sent her soaring into climax, crying out his name and urging him to come with her.

Nick woke hours later, hungry. Not for Serena. He would always be hungry for Serena. That was a given.

No. He was replete with sexual satisfaction. Making love with Serena had been everything he'd dreamed of and more. The second time had been even better than the first. By the third they'd gotten to know each other's rhythms as if they'd been together for years. But he needed food. The day had started so early at the airport. Dinner had been a no-show.

Serena slept with her head on his shoulder, her dark hair spilling across his chest and one long, smooth leg resting over his. He slid out of bed so as not to disturb her. She gave a little murmur of protest deep in her throat but then nestled into the pillow to sleep again.

He went downstairs to the kitchen. Thawed a frozen pizza in the microwave and then slid it into the oven, turned to the highest setting. He watched it through the glass door of the oven, willing the cheese on top to bubble and cook quicker.

Then was surprised by warm arms sliding around his waist from behind.

"Do I smell pizza?" Serena murmured.

He turned around. She wore a towel wrapped around her. It just covered her breasts and barely covered her bottom. Replete? Who said he was replete?

"Want to share?" he asked.

"I'm starved," she said.

Tempted as he was to divest her of the towel then and there, he decided he needed fuel to keep up his stamina. Being her sex slave was demanding work.

They sat on barstools in the kitchen. She must have been as hungry as he was for she ate in silence interrupted only by appreciative little murmurs that were maddeningly like the noises she made when she was aroused.

"Enough," she said finally, leaving her last slice only half eaten. "Thank you." She licked her lips and sucked on her fingers. Nick felt his eyes glaze as he watched her. He put down his own slice half eaten, too.

She looked him in the eye and smiled. She knew exactly what he was thinking, the minx.

"Just what I needed," she said.

She got off her stool and turned away. The towel started to slip from her body. She looked back over her shoulder at him. The expression on her face was just like in the posters that had made her famous.

"Are you coming back upstairs?" she asked. "I hope so. Because it's my turn to be your sex slave now."

· Twenty-three ·

Of all the jobs Nick had dreamed about during the long years at college and his training at the FBI, tying Halloween bandannas around the necks of a posse of pampered pooches wasn't one of them.

The bandannas were black, printed with orange, glow-in-the-dark pumpkin jack-o'-lanterns and the Paws-A-While logo in one corner. As bandannas went, they were quite stylish. He didn't even object to wearing one himself as the Paws-A-While staff had been instructed to do on October 31.

The bad news was that he wasn't great at tying bandannas on dogs, especially ones that protested. The good news was that Serena noted the trouble he was in and came over to help him.

He looked up from where he was tying a bandanna around the neck of the sad-eyed basset hound. Even though the dog was placid enough, she still moved around enough to make it difficult for Nick to tie the square of fabric the way the boss lady had directed.

Serena smiled as she knelt down next to him on the playroom floor. The smile she reserved for dogs was nothing compared to the smile she gave to him, her lover. If he hadn't already been in love with her, he would have fallen head over heels just because of that smile.

"Need some help?" she asked in her soft, husky voice.

Her shoulders touched his and he stilled, breathing in her nearness, enjoying the intimacy and the subtle joy of just being beside her.

For the past two nights Serena had stayed over at Sausalito. Mack had slept through the night. He and Serena had not. They had been the most wonderful two nights of Nick's life.

He wished that the world of dogs and Halloween and identity thieves did not have to intrude on precious time getting to know this woman.

"I can't tie this damn thing so your logo shows," he grumbled.

"Tsk-tsk," she pretended to admonish him. It brought back sizzling memories of what it was like when she took charge in bed. Now *that* was a boss lady . . .

He had to force his mind back up north to the Halloween bandanna. Serena took it out of his hand, then deftly tied it around Cleo the basset hound's neck. Serena tweaked it and fluffed it until it sat all perky and crisp with the Paws-A-While logo prominently displayed.

"Let me watch while you do the rest of them," he said. Tweaking and fluffing were not in his skill repertoire.

She sighed. "They have to look good, I spent so much on them before . . . well, before. At the time it seemed like a good marketing idea to give each dog its own Halloween bandanna."

"Of course it is," he said. "When they all go out for their walks today they'll look so cute people will ask where they came from and want to send their . . . their . . . dogs here."

Nick couldn't believe he'd come so close to saying "dog-kid." He thought back to the day when he'd made a conscious decision to cross the line and fight on Serena's side. He was now so firmly entrenched he would fight any battle for her. But he still balked at schmaltzy doggy talk.

"You think so?" she asked.

"I know so," he said firmly. Though already one of the dogs had managed to pull his bandanna to the front and chew it to shreds. "And your regular clients will be very pleased at such a clever gift."

He wanted to lean over and kiss her, but she still insisted they try to maintain the façade he was just an employee. It was a lost cause. There wasn't a staff member who hadn't guessed their secret. But if that was the way Serena wanted to handle it, then he would play it her way.

Serena gave the basset hound's bandanna a final tweak and scratched her behind the ears before sending the droopy-eared dog on her way.

Ruff-ruff, thought Nick, remembering how Serena managed to turn scratching behind his ears into erotic foreplay. He could hardly wait to get her alone again. Be her sex slave. Or vice versa.

"Cleo is coming to the party as a hot dog," said Serena.

Had he heard right? "Say that again."

"A basset is a great shape for a hot dog costume," she said. "She'll look adorable. Cleo's mom is still in hospital, but her son brought along Cleo's costume."

"You mean . . . the human son?"

"Who else would I mean?" Serena sat back on her bottom and smiled at him. "You still don't get what it means to live in dog world, do you?"

"For your sake I'm trying," he said. "But I don't get this hot dog costume. You mean like a sausage between a bun with mustard on top?"

"That's right. Only Cleo is the sausage. The bun halves go on either side. The costume works really well with a dachshund, of course."

"Of course it would," said Nick. Serena was right. He was still a stranger in a strange land when it came to dog world. "I know the humans are wearing costumes this evening, but the dogs . . . ?"

"Sure, the dogs will be in fancy dress. That's what Halloween is all about."

"So why the bandanna?"

"It's just for the daytime and for those dogs who are too skittish to dress up. Or whose owners don't want to dress them up. Besides, it wouldn't be safe for the dogs to wear their costumes all day. Barry's alligator costume, for example."

"The pug will be wearing an alligator costume?" Nick said faintly.

Serena frowned at his ignorance but her eyes danced. "It's so cute. It's a bit too big for him and it kinda looks like he's been swallowed by the alligator."

"I . . . I guess I have to see it . . ." Nick said. Even then he might not believe it. "But I didn't get a costume for Mack. Or Bessie."

"Done," she said. "Kylie . . ." She paused. He knew Serena was upset that she still hadn't heard from Kylie. "She . . . she organized their costumes. You have to plan well ahead for Halloween in San Francisco."

"And their costumes are?" He dreaded what he might be about to hear.

"A king costume for Mack. You know, a crown and a fake fur-trimmed cloak."

"Appropriate," Nick said. "And for Bessie?"

"What else but a fairy? Kylie chose an adorable little yellow tutu and a matching headband with gold stars. I'm sure your aunt would approve."

Nick groaned. But, oddly enough, he was sure Aunt Alice would love the idea. "We'll have to get some photos for her," he muttered.

"Helen O'Brien is bringing her camera. And we'll all take shots of course."

He was glad the O'Brien family would be coming. He could do with some moral support from Tom.

He had to go pick up his own costume at lunchtime. He wondered again what Serena would be wearing. He'd asked, but she wasn't telling. At one stage, he had thought of suggesting matching costumes. Then sanity had kicked in. That would have really freaked Serena out. Not because the idea was ridiculous but because it would look too much like commitment. For all the intimacy they'd shared, the barriers they had broken down, he still sensed she was holding back from him. If it were up to him, their relationship would be on the fast track.

"I have a thought for Mack's costume," he said. "Adam fixed the receiver for the camera and dropped it off here. I know you don't like the studded collar, but I'd like to put it back on Mack. With all the people coming here this evening we might pick up something useful."

"Good idea," she said, but he noticed she paled. For a few minutes they'd been able to forget the identity fraud and the fact that they were no closer to solving it.

Oh. My. God. Serena thought she might faint with desire at the sight of Nick in his Halloween costume. He strode around Paws-A-While flourishing his sword at the staff and making them laugh.

He'd come as a Roman gladiator. Russell Crowe as Maximus in the movie had nothing on Nick. The dark chest plate molded to the ripped muscles of his powerful chest and arms, and the short tunic and leather skirt showed off his strong legs, with the laced-up leather sandals that went all the way up to his knees. The leather wristguards were hot, hot, hot. He wore a short black cloak that he flipped back as he menaced a giggling Adele—dressed as a sexy Queen of Hearts—with his sword.

And then he was there with her. "Bullets and bracelets," he said, his eyes hot with admiration. "My very own Wonder Woman."

"You like?" she asked, striking a model pose. Her Wonder Woman costume had the traditional tight red top with the eagle emblem, blue, star-spangled high-cut pants, gold headband, and metal cuff bracelets. Best of all were the high-heeled red boots that made her feel like a real superhero.

"You have to ask if I like it?" His voice was gruff.

"I wore this costume for a modeling job. They gave it to me, but I hadn't worn it since." If Nick hadn't come in to her life, she would not have dared to wear Wonder Woman tonight; rather she would be shrouded in a flowing witch's costume.

Nick's eyes narrowed. "Was that job for a big apartment complex downtown?"

"Yes, I narrated a virtual tour of the different apartments. Why do you ask?"

"I was out of the country during the chocolate campaign. I swore I never saw you and yet you seemed somehow familiar. I did a lot of house hunting on the Internet before I came to San Francisco."

"You must have seen me twirling my golden lasso to open the door to the show apartments." She laughed. "That was hardly the highlight of my modeling career."

"I remember thinking if there were women like that in San Francisco, it was the place for me."

"Really?" she said.

"Really," he said, as he pulled her close for a kiss.

She hesitated for only a fraction of a second before kissing him back. She no longer cared if the entire party saw her; she could not resist her gladiator.

She kept on kissing him as he bent her over backward in a theatrical flourish. When he swooped her back upright it was to the collective applause and "woo-hoos" of the Paws-A-While staff and guests.

Flushed and laughing, she linked her arm with his as she pulled him along to chat with the guests. A pleasing number of clients had accepted the invitation to stay after hours with their dogs. She just wished Kylie was here; she'd helped her plan the whole event. After she'd chatted with the Godfreys and admired Freya's cowgirl costume, she headed toward the O'Briens.

Maddy and Tom were into animated movies. They'd come as Mr. Incredible and Elastigirl, and they certainly looked incredible in matching red-and-black superhero outfits.

Their dogs were in costume, too. Brutus had started the party with a lion's mane around his neck, but he had wriggled out of it so many times Maddy had given up. Now he just wore his Paws-A-While bandanna.

"The girl dogs look adorable," said Serena.

Coco was a fairy-tale princess in a pink conical hat and flowing chiffon headdress. Tinkerbelle was dressed as Tinker Bell in a pale green dress and gossamer wings.

"Pity Tinkerbelle keeps turning around to gnaw at her wings," said Maddy with a laugh. "Why do we inflict this on them, Serena? You've got Snowball dressed as a devil."

"Because it doesn't hurt them and it makes us laugh?" Serena suggested. "The dogs are happy if they make us happy."

"No comment," said Nick. "I'm not saying a word."

"Wise man," said Tom.

Jenna came over to join them. "You look sweet," said Serena.

Jenna was dressed as Dorothy from *The Wizard of Oz*. "I love those red shoes."

"I love your red boots," said Jenna in turn. Then blundered into her usual tactlessness. "Even if they are kind of . . . well . . . tacky."

"Tacky?" said Nick. "I think they're the sexiest thing I've ever seen." He pulled Serena even closer. "Because they're worn by the sexiest woman I've ever seen." He glared at Jenna.

"Hey, what about my black boots?" said Maddy, sticking her leg out in front of her.

"They're the sexiest thing I've ever seen," said Tom dutifully. He really was a sweetheart of a husband, Serena thought.

"Where's Tony?" she asked Jenna. She smarted from the boot comment but, as she'd done so many times during the course of their friendship, she didn't say anything. Jenna could be thoughtless and inappropriate sometimes, but Serena was sure she never meant any harm.

"He couldn't make it," said Jenna.

"That's a shame," lied Serena. They'd have a lot more fun without that creep.

"But he'll meet us all at the Castro," said Jenna.

"Great," Serena forced herself to say.

Going on with her friends to a bar in the Castro had seemed a good idea at the time. After all, the Castro, San Francisco's vibrant gay and alternate lifestyle neighborhood, was still the place to be on Halloween, despite the city's attempts to encourage people to celebrate elsewhere. But that was before her run of sleep-disrupted nights. Serena had to stifle a yawn. Heather was sleeping over at Paws-A-While to look after the dogs. Right now Serena could think of nothing better than to pass on partying in the crowded streets of the Castro and go straight home with Nick.

★　★　★

The last thing Nick wanted to do was socialize with a suspect. Nick didn't believe for one moment that Tony Cross was a reformed man. There was something about the way Jenna's boyfriend was too polite, too eager to please. And for someone with his record to choose a police costume for Halloween was more a taunt to authority than an homage.

And he didn't like the way the guy looked at Serena in her Wonder Woman costume. Not that he could blame any man for admiring her. She looked sensational as the TV goddess he remembered from his childhood. With her tall, slender figure and masses of dark hair, the tight, sexy superhero costume was perfect for her. Tom had let out a loud wolf whistle when he'd seen her. But Nick knew Tom's admiration was completely lacking in lechery.

Serena had gone white when she'd first seen Cross in the dark pants and shirt of the local police department. The costume seemed so authentic Nick wondered if it was, in fact, the real thing obtained with the idea of some future impersonation.

But he did his best to calm Serena. "I'm sorry," she said in an undertone so the others couldn't hear. "He's such a creep, and I've got this hang-up about cops. Present company excepted of course."

"Why is that? The anti-cop thing?" he asked. He slowed his pace so he and Serena dropped behind the others as they pushed their way through the crowded sidewalks of the Castro. He practically had to shout to be heard over the noise of the crowd and the music that blared from every bar and restaurant.

"My uncle, my mother's brother, was arrested and beaten in the Berkeley student demonstrations in the 1960s. The family was left with a distrust of police. A distrust they passed on to me. Then I had a bad experience with a cop myself."

"But you're over it now?"

"Not really. But I'm trying. And then to see *him* all dressed up . . ." He felt the shudder run through her body.

She was still so fragile, not physically but emotionally. No

wonder after first that terrifying stalker experience and then the
identity theft. Nick felt an overwhelming urge to shield her from
any further bad experiences. For the rest of her life. He tightened
his grip around her shoulder. "Serena, you know I'm here for you
now."

"I do know," she said. "But it might take me some time to get
used to that." She softened the words with a sweet kiss on his cheek.
"I don't mean that in a bad way. I just need time."

"I intend to give it to you. All the time in the—"

Suddenly she broke free from his arm. "Stop. Look. I see Kylie!
I swear it's her. Dressed in a Minnie Mouse costume. C'mon, let's
go find her. I have to talk to her."

She twisted away from him and pushed her way into the crowd
of revelers. Nick found himself stuck behind three tall vampires,
and by the time he got past them Serena was gone.

Ohmigod, she just had to find Kylie. Serena hadn't realized
how much she'd missed her until she caught that glimpse of her
in a spotted red dress and mouse ears. Kylie. She had to apologize.
Explain. Beg her to come back to Paws-A-While.

"Kylie!" she shouted but realized her voice was swallowed by
the noise of the crowd and the music. That old Halloween favorite "Monster Mash" blared out of a nearby bar in a relentless beat
that throbbed through her head. Pulsing neon lights on the shop
fronts dazzled her.

She stopped. Desperately scanned the crowd. Was that a pair
of black mouse ears and a red bow? She took a step forward. No
Kylie. She tried to move to the side but was blocked by a hideous Voldemort, arms linked with a Grim Reaper. It was hopeless.

She cursed. Felt tears prick her eyes. Her shoulders slumped.

She turned back to Nick. "I can't see her—" And found herself smack-dab up against Tony Cross, his face just inches from hers.

He clamped his hands down hard on her shoulders. "Gotcha," he said.

She yelped.

"I saw you were lost," he said. "I came to find you." Beads of sweat glistened on his forehead.

"I don't want to be found. Not by you." She tried to push him off but his grip on her shoulders was too strong. "Go back to Jenna."

A group of girls dressed in raunchy nurse costumes and shouting out the lyrics of "Monster Mash" shoved her right up against Tony's chest. She gagged at the smell of his sweat, the musty odor of his costume.

"You like me. Good. Because I like you," he said. "I've always liked you." His hands slid down her shoulders, fondled the sides of her breasts over the tight Wonder Woman bodice. "You're so sexy in those chocolate ads."

She shuddered her revulsion. "Get off of me." She tried to knee his groin, but he shifted sideways so all she did was rub her thigh against his. Bad move. His hands slid down to her bottom. Panic rose in her throat. All her fear of cops and remembered terror of her stalker welled up inside her. She gathered all her strength to push against his chest.

He reeled backward.

But it wasn't just her shove that had freed her of him. Suddenly Nick was there. *Gladiator versus cop.* Nick swayed sideward to duck Tony's fist, then grabbed Tony's right arm and pinned it behind him to immobilize him. Tony's other arm flailed wildly but couldn't connect with anything. He grimaced with pain and frustration and screamed a string of profanities. Serena didn't think even Jenna would find Tony handsome at that moment. "Move and I'll snap your elbow," she heard Nick snarl.

Serena felt woozy with relief, but then Maddy was there to hold her when her knees buckled. Tom helped Nick restrain Tony. Then Kylie was there in her Minnie Mouse costume. She was holding hands with Adam, who was dressed as Dracula. Dracula wearing glasses. Kylie caught sight of her, waved, and smiled her familiar, open, friendly smile. Thank heaven.

They weren't far from her but because of the noise and the crush of the crowd she couldn't hear what Adam was saying to Nick. But Nick's face got grimmer as Adam spoke. Then Tom went away and came back with two policemen. Real ones.

"I've got to see what's going on," Serena said to Maddy, as she pushed forward closer to Nick.

Now the policemen were cuffing Tony.

"What the heck—?" she started to ask Nick.

"He assaulted you and he assaulted me. In front of witnesses. That's enough to get him arrested. But there's more. Adam's been going through the surveillance tapes from the cash point where stolen credit cards were used. Cards belonging to the Godfreys and other victims in Marin County whose houses were burgled. Kylie came to Adam's house to meet him for their Halloween date—"

"They're dating? Kylie and Adam?"

"Looks like it." Nick grinned briefly before he continued. "Kylie recognized Tony on the tapes despite the baseball cap and the jacket with the collar upturned. The tattoo on his wrist was the clincher; his sleeve didn't cover it in several of the frames. Adam knew we were out partying in the Castro with Jenna and Tony so he and Kylie came looking."

Serena let out a breath she hadn't realized she'd been holding. "Tony's our guy," she said.

"Looks like it," said Nick.

"It's over," Serena said. She slumped against him. "Thank God."

Serena watched the real cops lead the fake cop away. She desperately wanted to talk to Kylie. Thank her. Beg her forgiveness. Ask her to come back to Paws-A-While. But Kylie was deep in conversation with Adam.

Then Serena remembered Jenna. She swiveled back to see Jenna also watching Tony being led away. Her friend's face was twisted in anguish and then she started to sob, great tearing sobs that wrenched at Serena's heart.

"I have to go to her," Serena said.

Nick held her arm. "No," he said. "She lived with him. She must have known what he was up to."

Serena shook her head. "She never realizes what jerks her boyfriends are until it's over. Or if she does know, she refuses to acknowledge it."

She pulled away from Nick, but his grip on her arm was iron hard. "Serena, she must have known Cross was involved in this," he said. "You told me he'd bought her clothes and presents."

"Because he had a new job. That's what she believed."

His voice hardened. "I'm warning you, Serena, let her be."

She wrenched her arm away, and finally he let her go. She rubbed her wrist. He'd gripped so hard it hurt, and the pain felt worse somehow because he had caused it. Controlling her. Telling her what to do. Just like those other take-command guys in her past who had made her life so unhappy.

Rottweiler.

Her eyes narrowed and she almost spat out the words. "You're warning me? Warning me like you warned me about Kylie? Look what happened when I listened to you. I lost my friend. Lost my best dog person. I'm not going to lose Jenna because of your warnings."

She was tired. She was distraught. She didn't know if she was being completely fair to Nick. But she had to be fair to her friend, too. Her friend who had lost everything tonight. How would Jenna recover from this?

"You're making a big mistake," said Nick, grim-faced.

She looked at Jenna in her Dorothy costume, disheveled now, her face ravaged by tears, her eyes empty. "I have to go to my friend," she said.

Then walked away from Nick.

· Twenty-four ·

The next morning Serena sat at her desk at Paws-A-While. Heather, who did not celebrate Halloween, had gone home, leaving Serena alone with Snowball, Mack, Bessie, and Maddy's three dogs. The dogs had the run of the playroom. There were no Saturday spa appointments until after midday.

Now that Tony had been arrested the identity fraud could be put behind her.

To Serena's joy, Kylie had called first thing this morning to make things right. Adam had filled Kylie in on everything that had gone on at Paws-A-While these past weeks and all was forgiven. Things should get back to normal on Monday.

In the meantime, this was a great opportunity to catch up on administration. She could plan for the future again, confident that her credit would be restored. The reordering of stock alone would take her a good two hours. So why was she sitting there staring at a blank screen?

She picked up the Maltese snow globe and shook it. The snowflakes swirled and whirled around the tiny white dog with his stripy scarf and then settled slowly again around his feet and the miniature shrubs in his toy garden.

She wished she could accept change as readily as that little plastic dog. Why had she blown off Nick last night in favor of Jenna? Jenna, who never seemed to learn a thing from her disastrous relationships but just went barging into the next one to make the same mistakes all over again.

Loyalty. That was what had made her do it. Loyalty to an old friend. A friend who had introduced a criminal to Paws-A-While.

Misplaced loyalty, more like it. Jenna had known all along about Tony's criminal record but had never warned Serena about it. He'd come in and out of Paws-A-While with the same access as her friend. How many times had he been in the reception area helping Jenna unpack her products? Right next to the computer. Was that when he'd skimmed her details? Or had he gone into her office and riffled through her purse?

She must have known what he was up to. Nick's words echoed through Serena's head. Had Jenna been so desperate to keep Tony in her life that she'd overlooked the fact he was robbing her friend?

Last night, for the first time, Serena had felt disgust permeating her pity as she'd comforted the sobbing, distraught Jenna. Serena had taken her home all the way to Oakland, seen her into bed, and left with assurances she'd be in touch. So far she had not lifted the phone.

When she did so, it would be to call Nick.

She missed him. She'd never spent a more miserable night, tossing and turning, drifting into sleep and then awakening to the shock of an empty pillow beside her. And the sound of Mack's moaning misery.

Nick might not have been long in her life, but it was enough to let her know she wanted him around for a whole lot longer. Maybe . . . maybe even for the rest of her life.

She thought back to how she'd felt that day on the porch of his aunt's house in Sausalito when Nick had stood behind her and enfolded her in his arms. How good it had felt. She remembered her dreams about those mini-Nick kids.

Up until now, she'd wondered if that happily-ever-after stuff might not be for her. But why shouldn't it? Nick said she'd had no luck with relationships because she'd met the wrong guys. *I'm the guy for you, Serena. You were just waiting for me.*

He'd had to lie about his job to her, but since he'd come clean about that, had he been anything but honest about his intentions?

The sex was amazing with Nick. But it wasn't just about sex. Security, stability, a family of her own, all that could come with committing herself to Nick. And love. Oh yes. No formal words of love had been exchanged, but there was love.

She realized how wrong she'd been about Nick. He wasn't a Yorki-poo type of guy. But he wasn't a Rottweiler, either. She couldn't—shouldn't—put a label on him. Not that there was any-thing wrong with Rottweilers. She was sure there were some very sweet ones. They just weren't her type of dog. But if she wanted to compare Nick to a dog, surely he was a Mack type of guy. Unique. Different. Special. *A soul mate.*

She leapt up from her chair, then sat down again. She had to call him. Tell him how sorry she was about last night. Tell him how much she missed him. How much she . . . how much she loved him. She looked at her watch. She didn't need an excuse to call him, but surely he'd want to come pick Mack up before too long?

As she put her hand on the telephone, the "Who Let the Dogs Out?" chime rang out. Nick! It had to be him. Maddy wasn't due for another thirty minutes to pick her dogs up.

Serena pulled her hair out of its tie and fluffed it around her face. Thank God she wasn't in her shapeless, sexless uniform. Rather she was wearing skinny jeans and a soft cashmere cardigan in a lovely buttery shade. It was buttoned up to the neck but she undid the top button and then the next two.

She was flushed and buoyant and planning what to say to him when she answered the door. To find Jenna on her doorstep.

Serena struggled to mask her disappointment. Her friend's face was almost hidden by the most enormous bunch of white lilies. But through the flowers she could see Jenna's woebegone expression, her eyes red and puffy and tearstained. "I'm so sorry, Serena."

Serena's mood deflated. She'd had more than enough of Jenna last night. But she couldn't do anything other than open the door wide. Jenna thrust the flowers at her. "Can you ever forgive me?"

Years of history between her and this woman kicked in. Serena suppressed a sigh. "Of course you're forgiven. Come on in. I was just about to make some green tea." She wasn't, but it would give her something to do while she endured Jenna's predictable dirge about how meaningless her life would be without Tony.

She let Jenna follow her to the little kitchen out back near the treatment room. She laid the flowers in the sink and filled it with water. There was no vase here big enough to contain them; she would take them up to the apartment later. The scent from the flowers with their fat, powdery stamens was so sweet it was almost overwhelming. But it was a nice thought.

Jenna followed her around as she'd expected. Unexpectedly, she was quieter and more subdued than she had ever been after one of her breakups.

"I was so stunned by last night, I didn't take in exactly what happened," said Jenna. "One minute we're all having fun; the next minute Tony . . . Tony's being dragged off by the police."

You mean she didn't know about the fraud?

Or, more likely, couldn't face up to the fact that Tony was involved in something so serious.

Serena decided to be very cautious about what she said. "As you know, Tony . . . he assaulted me, and he assaulted Nick."

"I'm so sorry, Serena," Jenna said again.

Serena made a shushing motion with her hand. "That's okay, Jenna. Apology accepted; no need to say sorry again. Come on, let's take our tea into the playroom and sit with the dogs. I'm the only one here."

"Do we have to? Go in with the dogs, I mean?"

Serena paused. She could take Jenna into the TV room or even her office. But she'd suffered enough inconvenience already because of Jenna. "Yes, we do. Mack has made an amazing recovery, but I still want to keep an eye on him."

"Mack's here?"

"Yes, and so are the other family dogs." She'd never used that term before but it fit. Maddy wasn't bonded-by-blood family, but she was family of the heart. And Nick? She yearned for him to be family. And that included their dogs.

"Okay," said Jenna, still sounding reluctant. Serena had sometimes wondered why Jenna didn't have a dog of her own.

Serena held the gate open for Jenna, then followed her into the playroom. It was her favorite room, the heart and soul of Paws-A-While. She thought, as she had so many times before, what a perfect job this was for her. To lavish love on dogs and be paid for it was a dream come true.

Heather had done a great job cleaning up after the party. All that was left was a row of carved pumpkin jack-o'-lanterns set up well out of the reach of hungry dogs, and a couple of tables and chairs the guests had used. She headed for the nearest table and put down her tea.

The dogs immediately rushed toward her; even Mack hobbled along at quite some speed. She greeted them all with pats and strokes and loving words but was surprised when not one dog came near Jenna.

"Mack isn't hassling you today," she said to her friend.

"That's because I haven't got any samples on me," said Jenna with a nervous laugh. "No doughnut specials."

"So it's purely a case of cupboard love as far as you and Mack are concerned?" said Serena with a smile.

At the mention of his name, Mack barked. Jenna cringed. Serena understood her friend's fear of the huge black dog so she told him to come sit on the other side of her.

"Now, Jenna, what next? Have you been to see Tony at the police station?"

Jenna shook her head. "Not until I know what really happened last night." She scrunched up her brow. "What did Tony say to you?"

"To me?"

"You two were looking pretty friendly."

"Friendly? Jenna, you're kidding me. Was that before or after he assaulted me? I told you he . . . he was groping me."

Jenna's mouth was tight. "That's not how it looked to me. You looked . . . close."

"Close? I was trying to get away from him. I was frightened."

"So that's why his hands were on your butt."

Serena stared at her. "Let's get this clear, Jenna. Tony grabbed me and wouldn't let me go. I had nothing to do with it."

"Sure you didn't. You were flaunting yourself in that whorish costume. He couldn't keep his eyes off of you."

Serena could hardly believe what she was hearing. "I was with my . . . my boyfriend. And Tony was with you. I told him to get his hands off of me and go back to you."

"Wh-what did he say?"

"Nothing. He just kept on trying to maul me—" She stopped, arrested by the pain in Jenna's eyes. Tony might repulse her, but Jenna loved him. And Serena was recently familiar with the pain of jealousy. "Jenna, there is no need to be jealous. I don't go after other women's boyfriends."

Jenna got up from her chair and started to pace up and down, up and down the width of the table. "That's bull. What about Tim McHugh?" she said.

"Tim McHugh?" Serena shook her head, puzzled.

"Think back, Serena. Think back to our senior year."

Serena tried to lighten the conversation. "You mean the year I grew boobs."

But Jenna was deadly serious. "The year you grew boobs and stole my boyfriend."

Serena looked up her in alarm. "Jenna, I don't know what you're talking about. I never stole your boyfriend."

Jenna ceased her pacing. "It makes it worse that you don't even remember him." Her mouth twisted. "Tim was the first boy I had sex with. I loved him, but he asked you, not me, to his prom."

"Did I go?"

"Don't mock me, Serena. Of course you went. Then told me all about how boring he was."

Serena frowned. "When I knew you were sleeping with him? That doesn't sound right. If I'd known that, I wouldn't have gone out with him in the first place."

"You didn't know," Jenna muttered. "Nobody did. My father would have killed me if he'd found out."

"Then how can you blame me?" The thought of Jenna festering this resentment for ten years was horrifying. "Don't do this, Jenna. We're friends. And don't link it to Tony. Believe me, I never encouraged him."

"So he came on to you."

"Maybe he was drunk." Though she hadn't smelled alcohol on him.

"He probably didn't know what he was doing."

That was Jenna all over. Making excuses for the deadbeat boy-friend's behavior. The deadbeat boyfriend who had had his ass hauled off to jail last night. Why wasn't Jenna more concerned about that?

"Look, Jenna, you're tired, you've had a shock, and you're not yourself. Why don't you sit down and finish your tea and then go on home."

Jenna slumped back down into her chair. "I'm sorry—"

"Please don't say you're sorry again." This time Serena knew her smile was strained.

This situation with Jenna was getting weird. She wondered if Jenna was on some kind of medication. Or off some kind of medi-cation more likely.

Jenna drained her tea. "Before I go, I want to ask you something. Do you know what they charged Tony with?"

"Assault." Why didn't Jenna go to the police station and find that out for herself?

"Anything else?"

"Should there be anything else, Jenna?" Jenna shrugged and didn't meet Serena's gaze. "Come on, Jenna," said Serena. She re-membered what Nick had said. "You live with the guy."

"Did he . . . did he admit to anything else?" asked Jenna.

Serena felt like shaking her. "I know you want to protect him. But if he's done something wrong and you know about it, you have to go talk to the police."

The irony of the conversation was not lost on Serena. Here she was, with her history, urging her friend to go see the cops.

"Why was Kylie talking to the police last night?" asked Jenna.

How much did Jenna know? How far would she go to protect Tony?

"Jenna, you know something, don't you?"

"Maybe. Was it . . . was it something to do with stolen credit cards?"

"You knew he was involved with credit card fraud?"

There she went again. Serena Oakley. Hopeless PI. Giving out details it might have been wiser to shut up about.

Jenna nodded. "I suspected it," she said.

But she didn't say anything? Just let her boyfriend rob a whole lot of people? Including her? Serena would never have believed Jenna capable of that. No matter how much she wanted to hang on to her man. Nick had been right. Serena felt the last remnant of respect for her friend dwindle away and die.

"You didn't tell me about Kylie," said Jenna.

Serena decided to give Jenna the information she wanted just so she could get her out of Paws-A-While. "Kylie identified Tony."

Jenna paled. "What do you mean?"

"Tony was caught on a surveillance camera tape using a stolen credit card. He had tried to disguise himself, but Kylie identified a prison-inked tattoo on his wrist."

"Wh-what was the tattoo?" Jenna asked.

"A cross. Like his name, Cross."

"So there was no doubt?"

"No."

Jenna leapt from her seat, fists clenched. "The dumb-ass," she screeched. "After everything I did for him."

The fury in her voice echoed around and around the near-empty playroom.

Serena pushed back in her chair, too shocked to do anything but stare. The expression in Jenna's eyes switched from cunning to crazy and back again.

Serena had seen eyes like that before. On her stalker. "Wh-what did you do for him, Jenna?" she managed to choke out from a throat constricted by fear.

From next to her came a low, primeval growl.

Mack.

"Shut the damn mongrel up," snarled Jenna.

Mack growled again.

So did Snowball. It was a menacing sound for a small, fluffy white dog.

Serena got up from her chair. *"You,"* she breathed. "Not Tony. *You."*

Jenna nodded. "You think you're so smart, Serena. But you didn't have a clue, did you? When you apologized to me for my late invoice payment, I almost peed my pants trying not to laugh."

Her cruel words hit Serena like a punch in the belly. But she sensed she needed to be careful with her reaction. Her friend was ready to blow. "You're the smart one, Jenna. We both know that. How . . . how did you do it?"

"I started off by contacting your clients who bought a lot of my products and told them they would save money if they bought from me directly."

"You . . . you undercut my prices?"

"Some of the clients, like those goody-goody Godfreys, only did it once or twice before they realized the implications it had for you and stopped. With the others, the difference between the wholesale price you would have paid me and the price I charged them meant more profit for me, a little pain for you."

A giant-sized shaft of pain shot through her. "Why? What did I do to you to deserve that?"

"You patronized me. Looked down on me. Always trying to give me a makeover. And you stole my boyfriend."

"Jenna, I—" Jenna seriously believed that. There was no point trying to reason with her.

"Tony had quite the little shrine to Serena St. James in his apartment, I discovered."

Serena shuddered at the thought. "What then, Jenna? You were so clever."

"I've always enjoyed a bit of embezzlement on the side. Right back to college days when I ran a gambling scam. But when your clients asked to pay by credit card, my ideas got bigger. I got a portable skimming device to steal all the details off of their cards when they paid me, and I was on my way."

"And . . . and me? Did our friendship mean nothing?"

"I enjoyed bringing you down, Serena. You didn't even remember Tim McHugh's name. You could have had any guy in school. But you had to steal my guy."

All the while Jenna had been talking, her eyes darted around the room. But they kept returning to the spotted tote bag she'd brought with her. Serena had noticed it because it was such a clash with Jenna's outfit. No wonder it clashed. Now she doubted it was a fashion accessory.

Serena swallowed hard against her sudden terror. Sweat beaded on her top lip. There was more than enough room in that bag for a gun. Or a knife.

The sickly scent of the white lilies permeated the room. Funeral flowers. Did Jenna speak so freely because she intended to make sure Serena would not be around to repeat her confession to anyone?

A horrible feeling of déjà vu threatened to freeze Serena to the floor. She was back in the bathroom with her stalker. That time, she had been lucky her friends had come home when they did and given her the chance to lash out with the hair dryer. But this time she was on her own.

Or was she?

The dogs were by her side. Vigilant. Sensing something was wrong. Snowball snarled and Mack growled again, that deep, primeval growl that would have turned her insides to jelly if she hadn't known the dog would never harm her.

But the sound freaked Jenna enough to have her suddenly lunge for her tote bag and pull out a gun.

Serena didn't know whether Jenna intended to shoot Mack or herself. Either way, she wasn't going to let it happen.

Fuelled by a rush of fury, she instantly shouted a command. "Mack! Get her!"

In one bound, Mack launched his massive weight and clamped down on Jenna's right forearm with his huge jaw. At the same time, with her left hand, Serena grabbed Jenna's wrist and twisted it so hard the other woman's fingers released and the gun thudded to the concrete floor.

With her right hand Serena shoved Jenna with such force the other woman grunted, staggered, and crashed backward against the metal pool fence that marked the boundary of the playroom. Without any further command, Mack reared up to his full, terrifying height, put his enormous paws on Jenna's shoulders and pinned her to the fence, his bared teeth just inches from Jenna's face. Then there was a white flash and Snowball went on the attack.

Jenna screamed.

For just a split second, Serena's eyes met Jenna's. She was shocked at the rage she saw there. Rage. Fear. And then a shift to cunning. "Serena, please," Jenna choked out.

But Serena was over any feelings for the so-called friend who had brought deception and danger to Paws-A-While.

Without a word, she yanked down two of the dog leashes that were hanging on the fence. Using Coco's hot pink leather leash, she lashed Jenna's right arm to the metal railing of the fence. When Jenna tried to struggle Mack growled and pushed harder to immobilize her. Serena used the fluorescent yellow of Bessie's leash to tie Jenna's left arm to the fence.

It was all over in what seemed like a flash.

Nick sat outside Paws-A-While in his parked truck, cracking his knuckles like crazy. He desperately wanted to see Serena but wasn't sure what kind of reception he would get after last night. Once again he'd pushed her too hard, too fast. And then he'd gotten between her and her friend.

The lights were on in Paws-A-While. He reckoned she was in

there with the dogs. She wouldn't leave them on their own. He wished he could see what she was doing. Then he remembered the receiver for the micro surveillance camera planted in Mack's collar. It wasn't spying. Not really. He was just going to test how well the camera worked. He slid it out of his pocket and switched it on.

Even before the image came into focus he heard Mack growling, a sound that made the hairs on the back of his neck stand up. Then Jenna's voice: "A portable skimming device to steal all the details off of their cards when they paid me, and I was on my way."

Jenna.

She was the mastermind. Tony merely her lackey.

Her voice sounded unhinged.

And, as far as he knew, Serena was alone with her.

Nick was out of that truck so fast he scarcely registered he'd opened the door. He called the police on his cell while he was unlocking the front door to Paws-A-While. Then ran without pausing through the reception area and into the playroom.

The noise was the first thing to greet him. Mack's fearsome deep growl that sounded like something wrenched from the throat of a wild beast. Two other sets of vicious snarling. All accompanied by a chorus of shrill yapping.

Jenna, her face white with terror, was immobilized by a pack of Paws-A-While dogs and tied up with brightly colored dog leashes. Mack had her pinned back to the playroom fence, his plate-sized paws planted firmly on her shoulders, his muzzle right up next to her face, his lips pulled back from his face in a terrible snarl that revealed his razor-sharp white teeth. His drool dribbled on the fabric of her shirt.

Snowball hurled himself at Jenna's legs, prefacing each attack with a fearsome growl. The drops of blood at thigh level on the fabric of her torn pants indicated he had already met his target at least once. Brutus sat and stared up at Jenna's face, growling fiercely without pause, which must have been disconcerting for Jenna.

Coco and Tinkerbelle ran around and around Jenna's legs, utter-ing a series of high-pitched yaps that evoked a feeling of panic just to hear them. Bessie joined in but with just the occasional yip.

A short-barrel revolver—it looked like a Springfield XD compact—lay on the ground out of reach.

Serena stood on guard, her arms folded against her chest, breath-ing heavily, triumph emanating from every pore. "She went for us. We went for her," she explained.

"Call them off," choked Jenna.

"No," said Serena, in her commanding boss-lady voice.

Two strides took him to Serena's side. "Are you okay?"

She nodded. "But I'm sure glad to see you." She leaned against him when he put his arm around her.

"Wonder Woman in action," he said, his admiration overcom-ing his fear for her.

"You could say that."

"Call off the damn dogs," cried Jenna.

Nick turned to face her. "Not until you tell us every detail of the frauds you committed against Serena Oakley and the clients of Paws-A-While and the whereabouts of the proceeds. I need dates, bank accounts, everything. I particularly want to know where the cash is that you stole from Serena."

A sly look stole across Jenna's stolid features. Even in the unen-viable position in which she found herself she intended to scam him by denying it all afterward.

"You are being recorded—and videoed," he said.

"Sure I am," she sneered. "Where's the camera?"

"On Mack's collar. He's captured a very good angle of your face." Nick held up the receiver to her. "See. Not quite wide-screen TV but more than adequate as evidence for the police and courts."

Jenna's resulting string of curses was among the most colorful he'd heard at any time in his career.

"I want something more coherent than that," he ordered. "C'mon. Start talking. Or I'll tell Mack to get a little closer."

Jenna started talking.

"Down, Mack," commanded Nick. Immediately, Mack pulled away from Jenna and put all four paws on the ground. "Then drop," said Nick. Mack dropped to a comfortable recording position near his quarry. "Good boy."

Nick checked the leashes that Serena had used to secure Jenna. She'd done an excellent job. "Keep talking," he said to Jenna.

Mack looked up and tipped his head to one side, his gaze intent on his master's face. "That brave act of heroism deserves a burger," Nick said to his dog. Mack tipped his head to the other side. "Maybe two," said Nick.

Serena called off the other dogs.

"Oh, Snowball." Serena scooped up her little Maltese and rained kisses on his furry, white head. "That's the second time you've fought for me, you brave little boy."

"What about this big boy?" Nick asked.

Serena must have sensed his uncertainty because she put Snowball down and came to him, walked into his arms, and hugged him as tightly as she could. "After . . . after the way I behaved last night I thought I'd never see you again."

"I'll never forgive myself for not getting here earlier," he said, holding her.

And then the police sirens wailed down Filbert Street.

· Twenty-five ·

Serena sat cross-legged on her living room floor playing her guitar. She hadn't played it for a long time. But she badly needed distraction to stop herself from reliving the devastating scene of Jenna's betrayal just hours before.

Nick was in the kitchen fixing her some lunch. She hadn't had to ask him for some quiet time alone with her music and her dogs. He had seemed to sense she needed it.

She strummed a series of random chords, playing whatever music her fingers found. As she fooled around with different rhythms, different chords, she felt the tension begin to ease. She remembered a tune she used to play as a teenager, a calming melody that had brought her peace during the turmoil of those years.

She played to a doggy audience. The three dogs had placed themselves around her in a protective semicircle. Mack was closest, head on paws, brow creased, his eyes watching her every move. She could still see the wolf in her beloved gentle giant. Whether Jenna would have used the gun or not, Serena would never know because she and Mack hadn't given her so-called friend a chance in hell.

Snowball lay to one side of Mack, Bessie the other. The music seemed to soothe the little dogs, but they also didn't sleep. Serena knew they were still watching out for her.

She kept on playing. Gradually she felt her fears fade away with the music. Nick was here. The dogs were here. She was safe.

Nick stood at the doorway to Serena's living room. He thought he had never seen such a beautiful picture. Serena's head bent over her guitar, her dark hair falling across her face, her elegant fingers creating music that seemed to soothe the soul of everyone in the room. Dogs included.

He'd seen the guitar on his first visit to her apartment but had never had the chance to ask her if she played. There was still so much he looked forward to finding out about her.

Mack thumped his tail in greeting and Serena looked up. She smiled that special smile that Nick knew was only for him. For a long moment their gazes locked. A knot of emotion seemed to tighten around his heart. He would never, ever forgive himself for not having been there when she needed him. Though Wonder Woman had done an amazing job of defending herself and disarming her assailant.

He cleared his throat. "You okay?"

She put down her guitar. "Much better, thank you. It . . . it was such a shock. I still can't believe Jenna had been building up to all that since high school."

Nick settled down in the armchair beside her. "It was traumatic all right. Do you need to see anyone? The police suggested a counselor."

She shook her head. "All I need is you."

He picked up her hand and held it. "I'm here."

Serena squeezed his hand in reply. They sat in silence for a few minutes before Serena spoke again. "You know what was one of the biggest shocks for me?"

There were a lot to choose from. "No," he said.

"That Jenna didn't make those expensive dog treats. She paid a couple of college kids a pittance to cook them for her."

"It was just another scam for her."

"I don't think she even liked dogs. She just saw them as an opportunity to make money."

"I daresay other, worse things she's done will surface."

"And yet . . ." Serena's face was pensive.

"And yet you still feel sorry for her?"

"Yes. And that's just plain dumb, isn't it?"

Nick shook his head. "There was a genuine thread of friendship there before Jenna twisted and distorted it."

"I keep wondering what I could have done differently."

"Nothing. You can't be responsible for Jenna's warped mind. Just remember the fun times you had with her and put the rest behind you."

"Well, I certainly won't be baking cookies to take to her in jail."

Nick laughed. "Uh, if your cookies are like your lasagna . . ."

Serena's eyes danced. "I might surprise you with some home baking some time. It can't be that difficult."

"Remind me to be out of town that day, will you?" He'd decided there was only room in the kitchen for one person in this family, and that would be him.

Serena unfolded her long, willowy limbs and got up from the floor. To his delight she promptly sat down in his lap. Nick smoothed her hair back from where it had fallen across her face. Then he kissed her, long and thoroughly. This was where he wanted her. With him. The sight that had met him at Paws-A-While would be emblazoned forever in his mind. If Mack hadn't been such a hero, it could have been a different story.

"I should have gotten there earlier this morning," he said. "But I had a good reason for being late."

Serena pulled back from his embrace so she could better see his face.

"Aunt Alice came home," he said.

"Wasn't she still on vacation?"

"She decided to come back early."

Serena couldn't keep the disappointment from her voice. "So you have to move out. Oh, Nick, that's such a shame. I love that house."

"I know you do. Which is why I want to buy it."

Serena crinkled her small, straight nose. "Huh? I don't get it."

"After all the years in Sausalito, Aunt Alice has decided to move to Seattle."

"Seattle? How could she leave her beautiful house?"

"Her mind's made up. She wants to sell."

"And you want to buy."

He cradled her face in his hands and looked deep into her eyes. "I want to buy that house for us, Serena."

"For . . . for us? To . . . to live in? Together?"

"Yes." He didn't want to wait any longer to show his hand. "What do you say?"

She smiled her luminous smile. "I say yes!"

His heart sang at her answer. Now would be the time for him to whip out a little velvet box and pull out a diamond ring. But for Serena to agree to living with him was an enormous step forward. He'd give her some more time before he talked marriage.

Serena could not contain her joy. She planted tiny kisses all over Nick's face until he was laughing and protesting and kissing her back all at once. But finally she sobered and pulled back from his kisses, though she had no intention of vacating his lap.

"Nick, you know how much I love your aunt's house and I can't imagine anything more wonderful than living there with you in it. Snowball and Thelma will be moving in, too, of course."

"Of course."

"What about Bessie? Do we get to keep her?"

"She'll be going with Aunt Alice. But she'll visit."

How could she ever have thought that his eyes were cold?

"But I'm wondering about house prices in Sausalito," she said. "Your aunt will want a fair market valuation."

Nick drew a deep breath. "I own a plot of land back in the valley. My grandfather left it to me, and my brother farms it for me. It's valuable land. My neighbor has wanted to buy it for years. I intend to sell to him."

Serena twisted around in his lap. "Nick. No. You can't do that. Do you know how amazing it is, to own land your grandfather farmed? No way can you sell it."

As a kid she had longed to have those deep connections. If you were lucky enough to have it, you did not sell your heritage. Even for a wonderful house in Sausalito.

"I don't want to sell the land, Serena. But my business is new and you're right about house prices in Sausalito. If I want to buy Aunt Alice's house for you, I have to sell my land."

"For *us*. You said you were going to buy it for *us*." She liked that word, "us." Or at least she liked it when Nick said it. "There is another way, Nick."

She saw hope in his eyes. And relief. Nick did not really want to lose that land. But he would sacrifice it for her. That made her all the more determined that he would not have to sell.

"Keep talking," said Nick.

"Every week my agent calls me and asks me to reconsider my decision not to pose for the chocolate people again. Their sales started sliding when the campaign ended. Each time the offer from them gets higher. It's really high now, Nick. Sausalito-house-price high."

He shook his head. "Serena, you said you would never get into that bathtub of chocolate again. You spoke about it as if it were your worst nightmare."

"You're right. I also said I would never wear sexy clothes again. Certainly not a Wonder Woman costume. Before I met you, I'd vowed to never have sex again."

"I'm glad you changed your mind about all those things." He kissed her mouth slowly and tenderly. "But what about your stalker? I thought you weren't going to risk ever encountering someone like him."

Serena still couldn't help shuddering at the memory of her stalker. But she was determined not to let the past damage her hopes for her future. "I realize what happened was his problem. Not mine. I didn't make him a psycho. And there's another thing. I was scared of a total stranger. Then my close friend turned out to be just as much of a psycho. How much worse than that could it get?"

Nick's expression was sober. "Those are brave words, Serena. I'm wondering what's brought about this change."

Now it was her turn to cradle his face in her hands. "I wasn't brave before, believe me. It's all because of you, Nick. Can't you see? You've shown me how strong I am. You cherish me and protect me and make me feel safe. You've given me back my confidence."

He put his hand over hers where it rested on his cheek. "I'm honored you think that way. It's quite a turnaround."

"Turnaround? I'd rather call it transformation. It's love, Nick. I . . . I . . ." She faltered. But she couldn't lose her courage now. Not when their future depended on it. She thought of that love-heart chew toy, crammed in the bottom of a drawer in her office. It had served its purpose, but she didn't need to hear it ever again. Not when she could put voice to the words herself. And maybe . . .

maybe hear them back in the deep, husky voice of the man she adored. "I love you, Nick."

"Serena, I love you." The expression in his eyes gave her no cause to doubt that. "I love you more than you can know."

"It's . . . it's love that's made the difference to me," she said.

She kissed him again. When it ended they were both flushed and short of breath. She was beginning to think bedroom, and all signs indicated that Nick was, too. But she had more to say. She pulled away from the kiss. "So what do you think of my idea?" she said.

"That you slide back into that bathtub for another ad campaign? No. I don't approve, not when you've hated the idea so much."

"Not the bathtub. The agency is talking something less racy. Something I think I can handle. I'll be doing it for us. Oh, and for my grandchildren."

"Grandchildren?"

"Maddy says I should shoot another campaign before I get old and wrinkly and overweight so I can prove to them I was once young and slim."

Nick smiled. "It's a thought. But I'd rather you said 'our' grandchildren."

"*Our* grandchildren," Serena said, loving the sound of it. "And by the way, this time it's a swimming pool."

"A swimming pool of molten chocolate?"

"You got it. In Hawaii. A beautiful pool with palm trees and everything. Don't ask me how they'll do it. Or how they'll clean it up afterward. I just have to swim around in the chocolate."

Nick's eyes narrowed thoughtfully. "I wonder if you would need a private assistant? Someone to lick all that chocolate off of you after the shoot?"

"I think you should apply for the job," she said with a delicious shiver of desire. "We could practice lots before the shoot."

"Sounds great to me."

"There's something else about Hawaii, Nick." Serena wound her arms around his neck so his face was very close.

"Apart from the palm trees and the swimming pool of chocolate?"

Her heart started to pound so hard she felt he must be able to feel it. "Yes. They . . . they say Hawaii is a wonderful place . . . well . . . a wonderful place for a honeymoon."

His eyes darkened fully two shades of blue. But he didn't miss a beat. "Really?" he said. "I hear San Francisco is a great place for a wedding."

"I've heard that, too," she said.

"Perhaps we should try it," he said. "Do you think the boss lady could schedule a wedding in sometime soon? Her own wedding?"

She smiled, her heart making as much music as her guitar ever had. "Yes, please," she said.